MICHAEL SIEMSEN

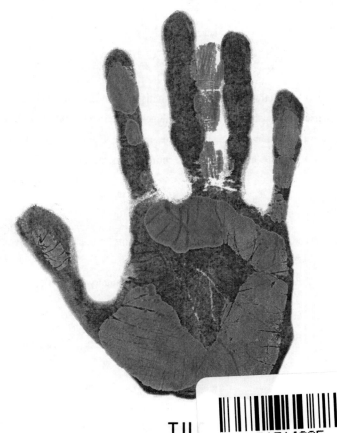

THE

DIG

FANTOME

First Fantome trade paperback edition January 2011
Second edition March 2012

FANTOME and logo are trademarks of Fantome Publishing, LLC, the publisher of this work.

Manufactured in the United States of America

1 3 5 7 9 10 8 6 4 2

ISBN 978-1456347949 (print)
ISBN 978-0983446903 (ebook)

Connect with the author:
facebook.com/mcsiemsen
www.michaelsiemsen.com
mail@michaelsiemsen.com
twitter: @michaelsiemsen

This book is dedicated to Vicky

"The real voyage of discovery consists not in seeking new landscapes but in having new eyes."

-Marcel Proust

ONE

Dr. Garrett Rheese sat in a canvas folding chair and watched his workers toil. How miserable life must be for those born to a race cursed by God. He wondered, did the Kikuyu have the least inkling of the offense their very presence gave to civilized sensibilities? Even shutting one's eyes to the physical unpleasantness—the giblet lips and simian nose, the spring-wire thatch of hair, the revolting eating habits—there was still that incessant, cacophonous jabbering. And to top it all, they stank. He would send every one of them home to their kraals and shantytowns were they not such cheap labor. Oh, yes, the Almighty had been in a spiteful mood the day he created the Kikuyu.

"Enzi!" Rheese shouted. "Tell your boys to get the bloody compressors away from the edge!"

The lanky brown foreman glanced across the clearing and frowned— the big, noisy units were indeed perched dangerously close to the pit's unstable wall. How many times must he tell the boys?

"Too sorry, Professor," he replied. "Too very sorry—I'll push them back, *chapu-chapu!*"

Enzi knew that the men took a certain passive-aggressive satisfaction in forgetting certain rules, but how foolish to risk their own safety merely to irritate the *mkundu*. He chuckled in spite of himself at the epithet, Swahili for "the anus," as the Englishman was known by one and all—though, wisely, uncertain just how much Swahili the professor knew, they refrained from using it within his earshot.

After wrestling the two heavy compressors a prudent distance from the edge, Enzi peered down at the sizable excavation, breathing in the sweat-

and urine-scented air. His laborers knew they were not to piss down below, but with Rheese docking their pay for every minute at the surface, they often preferred to risk it. Enzi scanned the welter of black arms and backs, gleaming with sweat, picking, drilling, and jack-hammering at the fractured rock walls and floor, working ankle deep in muddy water. He had watched this particular dig grow wider and deeper for the past three weeks. They had created countless craters just like it elsewhere in Kenya, and countless more would no doubt follow.

Ever watchful for slackers, Enzi spotted two men standing idle at the far end.

"Chui, Kanu, get you tools out of water!" he barked, glancing back to see if the professor was still watching. Luckily, he must have retired to the air-conditioned shade of his RV. Looking below again, Enzi saw that Chui had hefted his jackhammer to bang away at a seam in the far left corner, but what was Kanu doing? He was simply standing there in the opposite corner, like a child in trouble at school.

"Kanu!" Enzi shouted again. "If you pissing over there, you pumping out the floor tonight!"

Kanu twisted his head around and motioned subtly with his chin for Enzi to come over.

"What . . ." Enzi stopped himself. If Kanu had found something important, there was no need to alert the entire site.

Enzi walked casually to the lift and rode the rusty, rattling box down to the bottom, where the stench, noise, and heat intensified. Sloshing through the mud in his black rubber irrigation boots, he crossed to the far end of the pit, where Kanu appeared to be pulling at something in the craggy rock.

"What you find, Kanu?" Enzi said softly.

Kanu turned with wild eyes, scanning the area beyond Enzi's shoulders before stepping back a little so the foreman could see.

"What you . . ." Enzi shot a look at Kanu, standing slack-jawed beside him in the muddy water amid the din of picks and jackhammers. Moving closer to shield the find from curious eyes, he reached out and touched its seemingly delicate surface. It was fixed tightly in the limestone matrix, its exposed end giving a little as he ran his fingers over it. The texture was rough, but perhaps only from the flaky bits of rock and fossil shell embedded in it. Bewildered, Enzi let his gaze drift upward, scanning the sedimentary strata from the oldest dolomitic limestone vein at ankle height, all the way to the top. How many millions of years below the surface had they dug? The imprints of Cretaceous Period fossils a few meters above him provided a rough answer.

Enzi glanced behind him and wondered how the professor would react. It depended upon the man's mood—he was as likely to bestow a "Great job!" as a snarling "Why are you wasting my time with this rubbish?"

"Zuberi!" he shouted. "Get Professor!"

A tall, hunched fellow in patched blue-gray dungarees raised a shoulder and hand in question.

"*Mkundu!* Get the *mkundu!*"

Garrett Rheese sat at his now-muddied breakfast table and glowered at the source of his newest problem, working out mentally all that he must soon explain.

He dropped it with a clunk onto the wooden tabletop and picked up a piece of the stone matrix that had held it for who-knew-how-long. In one side, Rheese could see the imprint of the artifact; its pattern captured perfectly in the calcite as if it had been molded right there. He could already hear the first question: "Tell us, Professor, do you always use pneumatic hammers in the extraction of rare fossils?"

Wiping the sweat from his bald pate, he considered hiding it. The artifact was obviously too important simply to discard, but without detailed photos, drawings, and samples thoroughly describing its discovery location and provenance, it would be an irrelevant find. He had spent the past hour trying to come up with an alternate explanation. *Half a meter below*

Lower Cretaceous sediment . . . What is that—a hundred million years old? It could be worth its age in cash, but it could also be nothing but an unwelcome spotlight on his true objectives in this godforsaken country. The project's checking account would not be refilled, the University and Museum Group would smear his name for good, and he would never find what he *knew* to be here.

With a sigh, Rheese taped the object between two foam pads and locked it in the safe beneath the bench seat. He needed to take a walk.

Sitting in the shade of the canvas mess fly, Enzi heard the trailer door swing open and glanced behind him. His eyes met with Dr. Rheese's for only a second before he turned back to his cardboard plate. The professor's face had lacked its usual look of simmering irritation. Was it fear he had seen in its place?

Whatever the reason, the professor's order to halt all digging for the past seventy minutes told Enzi all he needed to know for now: the artifact was genuine, and he would be telling many lies for this Englishman in the coming days.

TWO

The UPS courier rang the doorbell at 312 Kaspar Avenue. Her big brown van idled behind her, parked beside a 2000's Jetta—she liked the U-shaped driveways in this neighborhood because there was no street parking and it meant she never had to back out of the driveways.

A pair of eyes appeared in the diamond-shaped window, and the door swung open.

"Hi there!" said the pale twenty-something attached to the eyes. He wore a tight gray T-shirt that read BRAND NEW, which she found ironic because it had that intentionally distressed look, along with several drips of blue and orange paint. The same paint had ruined his baggy jeans and polished his left big toenail. She thought he'd be a good-looking man in five or six years, when his jaw filled out more and his chin gained some definition.

"Three packages for Matthew Turner," She said as she held out her brown scanner for him to sign. The boy looked at it and then at his hands.

"Crap! Hang on a sec," he said, and disappeared to rummage about for something out of sight. She was pretty sure she heard something break before he reappeared wearing latex gloves. "Hah-hah . . . sorry. I usually have some hanging by the door."

She'd seen it before, OCD types who didn't like to touch anything, because they thought they were going to catch the plague. He took the scanner to sign. She wondered if his messy hair had been styled that way, or if it was simply a mess. Its straw-colored streaks could have been highlights or from real sunshine—by the pallor of his skin, she was betting highlights. He handed back the device and she read the name.

"Are *you* Matthew Turner?" she asked with a raised eyebrow.

"Yup, afraid so . . . Do you mind bringing them in? I'm not a serial killer or anything."

Not funny, she thought. "I can put them right inside the door, is that all right?"

He nodded and stepped back. She glanced around the interior and gathered, from the open boxes and bare walls, that they were moving in. Seeing the gaming chair on the floor in front of the TV, the chaos of game consoles, and the style of the furniture, she sensed a bachelor vibe.

"Um . . . not to pry, but is this *your* house? I mean, do you live here alone?"

"Sure do. And yes, it's *my* house. Not renting or anything. Awesome, right?" He grinned.

The courier slid the last and biggest box into the house and stood back up.

"Yeah, *awesome.* So are you some millionaire's lucky kid or what?" She never minded coming across as nosy.

"Nope, just lucky." He flashed a pearly white smile.

"Well, have a good day, sir," she said as she turned back through the open doorway. *Kind of cocky, but intriguing.*

"You, too!"

The new cell phone on Matthew Turner's new desk began to buzz, and then chimed out its default ring tone. He shut the door and jogged to his new office, picked up the phone, and frowned at the unknown number displayed on the screen.

"This is Matt," he answered.

"Hi, Matt, this is Daphne at Nautique Exotics."

"Oh, hi, Daphne, so glad you called . . . Is it in?"

"Yes, it is. Will you be picking it up, or would you like to take advantage of our free delivery service?"

"Um . . . well, if I drive my V-Dub over there and the Porsche back, could someone get my old car back to me?"

"I believe I could arrange that, sir."

Matt spun in his chair and cracked his knuckles with nervous excitement. As the newest multimillionaire in Raleigh, he was making a big splash with the local purveyors of luxury goods.

His new iPad prompted him to accept some license agreement for an app he'd downloaded. With all of the highly useful apps out there, this was going to take most of the day, he thought. And he hadn't even started on the useless apps! He wondered if there was someone he could hire that would just intuitively know what kind of stuff he would like on there and install it all for him. Is that what other rich people did? *Ugh, but then some random dude would be touching my stuff . . .*

His cell buzzed again, and he snatched it up before the ring began.

"This is Matt," he said, making a mental note to change the ring tone before it grew truly annoying.

"Hey, Matt!" It was George from the museum. "You finish yet?"

Matt grimaced and slapped the END button. *Crap!* He was supposed to have gotten back to them a few days ago, but he had hardly glanced at the artifact. He spun his chair around as he put on his thin leather gloves and scanned the messy office for the package that had arrived three days ago. He scuttled the rolling chair over to an open box nearby and picked it up, digging into the foam peanuts. His cell phone began to vibrate again behind him, and he rolled back to silence it.

He frowned as he looked at the piece from the box, turning it over in his hands. It was a three-inch section of smooth, dark-stained wood, decoratively beveled on three sides. A squiggly line of dry, cracked glue marked the only unstained side. Two holes indicated where the piece had previously been screwed into something.

Unable to recall if he had locked the front door, Matt set the wood on the desktop and debated whether to go through the house to make sure everything was secure before proceeding. Caution won and he did his rounds. *Note to self: get security system activated.* He flopped back in his chair and opened his desk drawer, pulled out his armband timer, and slid it up to his forearm. He turned it on and pressed the BATT button to check the charge—plenty of juice. He rolled the chair under the desk and fidgeted until he was comfortable.

He inhaled deeply and said aloud, "Okay . . . ready for you."

With the timer set for one minute, he pressed START. He stretched his hands out before him, flat and steady, approaching the wooden piece as if about to give it a back massage.

Contact.

The usual rushing sound filled his ears as he felt his body roll forward into someone else's. Sometimes it felt as if he were surging forward, sometimes backward—he had never understood what determined the direction. His eyes focused, adjusting to the other person's as he went through his well-practiced routine.

I'm male. I'm forty-seven. My name is Jakob Herz, and I was born in Dortmund, Germany, in 1892. The year is 1939. I live in Kalisz, Poland. I am frightened. They are in the neighbors' house already. I open my grandmother's writing table to remove the jewelry. I will hide it in the chimney.

Goddamn it! He sent me some Nazi crap again and didn't even warn me! That's it, Georgie—you're done.

Through Jakob Herz's eyes, Matt found himself digging through this ornate desk, hearing shouts and gunshots outside and in other homes nearby. He has a pistol upstairs. . . . . Should he retrieve the pistol? Matt says, *Hell yes! Shoot the first son of a bitch that comes through the door!* But he knows he has no control over the experience. Jakob is apparently more interested in hiding these items in hopes that his family will be able to retrieve them when they return from the lake tomorrow. Matt and Jakob both panic because the soldiers will not be gone by the time the family returns, unaware of . . . Five loud wooden taps on the front door, and Matt wondered if the imprint would fade out or if the sixty seconds would elapse in time to save him. He was not in the mood to feel a bullet rip through their body.

Rewind.

I open my grandmother's desk to remove . . .

Again . . . more.

I open my grandmother, Hilde Weiss's, desk to remove . . .

That'll do it, thank you. Wow, new speed record!

Matt's hands drew back reflexively as the timer began buzzing in his head. He struck the STOP button on his arm, glanced around the room, and took down some notes. A quick look at his phone revealed that George had called again while he was reading the piece. *Oh, don't worry, George. We're going to have a nice little chat shortly. Now, let's see if we can't meet granny Hilde.* Resetting his timer for five minutes, he reached for the wooden piece again.

The ear-sucking, familiar disorientation, and he found himself with Jakob in the same panicked state. *Fast-forward . . .* Jakob again—penning a letter. *Must have been an emotional letter. Nope, earlier . . . c'mon, hurry up to the next imprint.* Matt waited through the letter. He had never been able to fast-forward past an unread imprint. Some kind of stupid limitation set by those that handed out psychic powers.

Jakob picked up the letter to review it and a few seconds later, dark space took over the scene. Matt thought about the car awaiting him just ten little miles away. A candlelit room coalesced out of the mist before him.

I am Hilde Weiss. I'm female. I'm thirty-four years old. I was born in Paris, in 1832. The year is 1866. I live in Dortmund, Germany. I am happy that my husband, Samuel, has given me this wonderful gift. "Where did you get it, love?" she asks him as she runs her fingers over its smooth, dark-stained surface.

There's Samuel. She looks at his eyes . . . loves those eyes . . . more so at this moment, apparently, than normally.

"It was Danke Stern's," he says. Hilde looks back at the desk and strokes it again. "It's eighty years old."

Seventeen eighty-six—Yahtzee!

They look back at Samuel. He's ready for his thank-you kiss, and likely a more demonstrative kind of thank-you as well.

Matt waited impatiently for the timer to shock him out of it. He'd been the woman in these situations enough times already. *Come on, let's go. Job done.* "I love you, Samuel! How did you get it from her?" A reasonable question, it seemed. It looked as though these folks weren't exactly living the high life in this one-room hovel.

But before Samuel answered, Matt slapped the STOP button on his timer and wrote more notes on his legal pad. Then, pulling his gloves back on, he shoved the piece deep into the box of popcorn. Where had he put all the tape guns? He quickly pulled a strip off one of his own boxes, sealed the top, and stuck the return label over the old label. He breathed his first sigh of relief as he dropped the package onto his doorstep and walked back inside. The house was clean again.

"New York Metropolitan Mus—" George answered.

"Hi, Georgie," Matt said with a menacingly pleasant tone.

"Oh . . . hey, Matt! I got cut off. Tried to call you back, but—"

"Yeah, right. To answer your question, yes, I did finish with it. I'll admit, I was pretty shocked to discover what it is you sent me."

George's gulp was clearly audible.

"Look, Doctor Meier made me!" George said with quaking voice. "See, this Jewish family with living descendants—"

"That was it, okay?" Matt interrupted. "The last read. I'll e-mail you my notes later."

He hung up the phone with George suspended in mid apology. Leaning back in his chair, he put his feet on the stack of boxes beside his desk. Everyone always had such noble motivations, but none of them ever actually understood Matt's objections—not at nine years old and, apparently, not now at twenty-five.

The soldiers had already entered the house. They probably shot that guy on sight. Matt shook out his face and tried to clear his head.

The Porsche!

Leaping up from the chair, he went to the master bedroom and flipped through the stack of long-sleeved shirts draped over a box labeled "Bathroom" in purple marker. He selected a black turtleneck and swapped it for the paint-stained T-shirt. He ran his fingers over the paint on his jeans and decided to keep them on—it had already dried. Socks on, shoes on, he stopped at the mirrored closet door. He looked at himself up and down and decided he would buy a weight set—his arms were way too thin. People would continue to wonder about him, he decided, until he appeared more like a man and less like a teenager. He raised his chin and rubbed the recalcitrant goatee that had refused to grow in over the past week.

He grabbed a knit cap and a pair of black gloves from the closet shelf and headed out. As the front door to his new house shut behind him, the cell phone on his desk began to buzz, followed by that annoying ring tone.

"Beautiful vehicle you've just bought, Mr. Turner," the sales manager smarmed.

Matt turned the key a single click and checked that the odometer read zero.

"Thank you, sir. I'll be sure to put it to good use." He looked at the manager through his sunglasses, admired the sheen of the silver slacks and jacket. "You mind me asking what kind of suit that is?"

"Uh, sure, it's Zegna. Would you like one? My brother-in-law manages the Saks near RTP."

"Hmmm . . . maybe. It's very nice. I'll give you a call if I ever have occasion to wear one."

Matt took a deep breath and removed his gloves. His bare hands glided over the steering wheel and then felt about him—seats, dash, headliner . . . He breathed in the smell of the leather, reveling in the *newness*. He stepped out and ran his hand over the shining black body. All new.

"Well, if there's nothing else, Mister Turner," the manager said, extending his hand. Matt faked a smile and tilted his head to the side to examine the man's fingers. Nothing on the right hand, wedding ring visible on the left. Was this the kind of guy who did the two-handed "I genuinely like you" clutch? Matt determined he probably was, and quickly slipped his gloves back on. He put out his hand, and the manager gave a single, not-too-tight squeeze—quick shake, just the one hand. Matt slid back into his car, feeling ensconced in the intoxicating cloud of newness. He watched the manager return to the showroom to greet another customer, this time with a double-handed shake. Ah, but he didn't have their money yet.

Driving home, Matt decided to call his sister, Iris, to see if she wanted to stop by to see the new ride. Then he remembered that he'd left the cell phone on his desk. And then he remembered the reading on the piece of stained wood earlier, and his good mood faded for an instant. The 911 GT2 hugged an S-turn, and Matt smiled again. He knew that he couldn't keep spending like this much longer, so he recommitted himself to ending the shopping spree . . . *after* fully furnishing the house, and one nice tropical vacation. Reminding himself how easy it was to make more money, he began listing what he would buy next should he hit the jackpot again.

Merging onto Highway 440, he pushed the turbo to 110 mph. He slowed a bit after the third car honked at him for weaving in and out of lanes. What was he supposed to do? At 95, it felt like the Jetta at 40, and begging to go faster.

In his absence, his cell phone had accumulated six missed calls and four new voice messages, vibrating itself off the desk and onto the floor. He found it and scrolled through the missed calls. 440205553836? Way too many numbers, he mused. Forty-four . . . wasn't that UK? He listened to his first message. A woman with one of those oddly attractive English accents spoke.

"Hello, Mister Turner, this is Danielle Sloo from the Museum of—"

The call-waiting tone interrupted before Matt could finish rolling his eyes. Dr. Meier just wasn't going to leave him alone, was he? He pulled the phone away from his ear to see the caller ID. A New York area code . . . his parents' number. *Gotta get my contacts entered into this thing.*

"Hey, Mom, what's up?"

His mother's ever-concerned voice replied, "Hello, dear, how *are* you doing?"

"I have to say I'm doing well, Mom. How about you?"

"Oh, you know, just work, work, work. I spoke with Iris this morning, you know. I hope you're not just spending all that money, dear."

"Oh, I'm not, Mom, don't worry." He pulled the window blinds to look lovingly out at the gleaming black Porsche in the driveway. "I'm making some pretty good investments."

"Well, I know you'll be responsible, honey. Anyway, so there's someone here who would like to talk to you."

Matt went rigid in his chair.

"Mom, it better not be Dad. You *know*—"

His father's familiar gruff baritone interrupted. "Hey there, son."

Matt covered the mic with his thumb and breathed a shaky sigh. Why the hell would she do this to him?

"Yes?" he replied, his fury evident.

"Now, son, let's not start this off on the wrong tone, you hear me?"

"I could *end* this off with the *right* tone, Dad. How'd that be?"

"Well, that wouldn't be appreciated much, Matthew."

His father got a few more syllables off, but Matt had already hit END.

Standing up, he muttered aloud, "Why is everyone screwing with my head today?"

He decided to play some Xbox to zone out. The last thing he wanted to think about was his "detective" days with Dad. Working in homicide, his father had been unable to stop himself from taking advantage of his son's talent during investigations. At age nine, it had been a flood of attention and approval from a usually absent parent. In the beginning, no one understood exactly what Matt experienced. When he held the evidence—a piece of clothing or a cigarette butt, or sometimes an actual weapon—he simply sat quietly for a few minutes until someone pulled it away from him. Of course, he would be pretty upset afterward, but the information he provided was a gold mine of leads for the department to follow. It wasn't until he turned twelve that he told his father he wanted to stop. And he had been wheedled or coerced into working over a hundred more cases after that, his last at age fourteen.

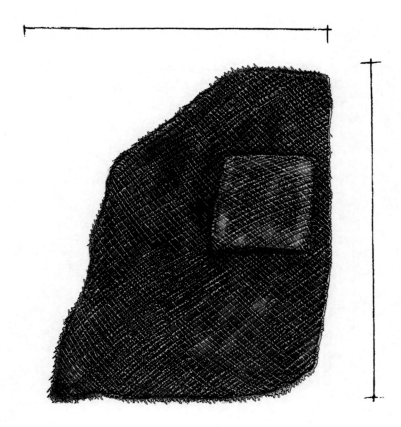

THREE

"Jon, the tour will be coming through here in just a few," Tuni St. James announced through the partly open office door.

"Uh-huh," Dr. Meier grunted as he squinted at the computer monitor.

She took a step into the room. "So I'll just be showing them in then," she persisted, and he glanced up at her over his bifocals.

"Yes, good," he said, and couldn't stop himself from a quick pan up those long legs. She turned and left, and he shook his head. He'd never found himself attracted to tall women in the past, but something about Tuni's smooth, café au lait skin and elegant yet revealing wardrobe compelled his gaze to linger. Also, he had never been much for accents, but hers, a mix of London English with a drop of South African . . . ah, well, a quick twist of his ring and long look at the desktop photo of his wife, and his guilt would be relieved.

What was wrong with a lunchtime visit to Macy's? Granted, the shopping trip had been inspired by Tuni's glance at his red and gray-patterned sweater vest and her comment, "Well, don't you look dashing today, Jon!" He couldn't recall the last time he had felt dashing, and decided he could use a few more sweater vests of varying pattern and color.

He squeezed his eyes and reread the e-mail for the third time, glancing between sentences at the attached photo. Peter Sharma, his former assistant, had sent it late last night. Meier thought the signature on the e-mail was quite impressive. His protégé had earned a promotion to director at the revered Cambridge Museum of Natural History.

THE DIG

Dear Dr. Meier,

Attached hereto you will find a photograph of an artifact excavated from a sub-Jurassic dig in southeastern Kenya three weeks ago. The object itself was recovered from strata estimated to be between 150-200 million years old. As you can imagine from the photo, this discovery has caused quite a stir in the organization.

Potassium-argon dating equipment was shipped to the site (the Kenyan government has prohibited removal of the object from the country), and repeated tests have verified the initial estimate of the artifact's age. Needless to say, the nature of the object has resulted in doubts about the accuracy of these tests.

I am aware that your facility has no staffed metallurgy expert, but I do recall your occasional use of a more precise "dating technology," which I am hoping can be lent to the CMNH. I have not discussed details of your methodology but have only expressed to the board that you have an expert who, with your express approval, might be able to bring himself and his equipment to the site with some urgency. Obviously, the board has approved release of funds for such a trip, as well as compensation to your establishment during said expert's absence from regular duties at home.

I eagerly await your response and can discuss further details of the artifact via telephone, as I am certain you have questions unanswered by this brief note.

Warmest regards,

Peter Sharma
Director, Mesozoic Research
Cambridge Museum of Natural History
Cambridge, UK

Dr. Meier removed his glasses and rubbed his eyes. At first glance, the object appeared to be a simple piece of torn fabric with a wide, sewn-in belt loop in the middle. But Pete's e-mail mentioned metallurgy, which inspired a closer look at the photo.

Someone had laid the piece flat on a white surface beside a metric ruler. It was about sixteen centimeters in width and height, though it was straight on only one side, where the fabric appeared to have been folded over and restitched to itself to create a seam. The belt loop suggested this would be the waistband of a pair of slacks, or perhaps a sort of fine chain mail worn over one's inner clothing. Or maybe it wasn't clothing at all but a piece of a satchel, stitched from metal to increase its weight-bearing capacity. Alternatives flew through his mind.

It would be extraordinary enough to find a piece of woven fabric in so deep a sediment, due to (a) the obvious lack of any species present on Earth at the time with the necessary intelligence to create such an item, and (b) the fact that it hadn't deteriorated out of existence millions of years ago. That it was crafted of metal fibers removed some of the shock over its longevity. But it remained outright inconceivable that an intelligent being possessed not only the weaving skills but all the considerable array of technology that would be required to mine and isolate the raw minerals, create the alloy, and spin or extrude the threads. There were just too many aspects to consider, and none of it made a damned bit of sense.

He tugged at his neat gray beard and sighed.

The object was simply an OOPArt—an out-of-place artifact—he decided, like the zinc-silver alloy vase found in the 1850s near Dorchester, Massachusetts, in 100,000-year-old rock. Or the rusty screw recovered from a piece of 20-million-year-old feldspar. There were long lists of mysterious out-of-place artifacts that no one could explain, though many professionals had invested years of research to no satisfactory end. If this one couldn't be debunked, it would likely be added to the bottom of the lists.

It was an easily dismissible unknown, but Meier could not just shelve it so blithely—especially considering that Pete, a solid scientist with a healthy sense of skepticism, seemed fairly well convinced. He picked up the phone and dialed George Miller's extension.

"Yes, Dr. Meier," George answered between indelicate slurping sounds—obviously, he was eating.

"George, I need to speak with Matthew Turner."

A choking sound replied.

"George . . . ?"

"Yeah—yes sir, um . . . after the, uh . . . I don't know how easy that's going to be."

"I don't care—make it happen."

He hung up the phone.

Dr. Meier's door swung open, and in walked Tuni, followed by a stream of people with notepads in hand and name tags pinned to their shirts.

"What the hell is this!" he spluttered.

Tuni's eyes narrowed as she crossed her arms.

"The tour that was scheduled two weeks ago for this very moment, Doctor," she replied through her teeth, "of which I reminded you but a few short minutes ago. Please, ladies and gentlemen, file in around the director's desk—and feel free to touch anything you like."

FOUR

The monsoon irritated Dr. Rheese to no end. As he sat protected by the canopy jutting from the top of his RV, the back legs of his lawn chair began to sink in the mud.

"Blasted bloody useless piece of . . . !" he muttered, and stood up. He had sent home all but a few of his laborers. Across the trench in front of him, Enzi and the other two men he kept on-site were wrestling with the tarps in the wind. It wasn't as though Rheese really cared what happened to that corner of the excavation now, but in the interest of appearances, he would make his best effort to feign appropriate concern for its preservation.

As Enzi gestured for one of the men to anchor the tarp's corner with a rock, Dr. Rheese surveyed the encircling forest around them. It was thick in this area. They had chopped down quite a few trees to clear this particular patch (with appropriate permission from the government, of course). The pack of thieves had demanded 60 percent of the proceeds from the logging company, leaving Rheese with a piddling eight thousand pounds sterling for himself.

Now he wished he had cut down three times as many trees, if for no other reason than the uneasiness he felt at night. Who knew what could be on the other side of that black wall? He almost didn't mind walking it in the daylight—it would actually serve as a rather nice escape from the flies drawn to the dig site, if it weren't for the snakes. He'd seen two already: a mamba, eight lithe feet of gray-green terror moving along the forest floor faster than he could trot; and—perhaps even scarier—a puff adder, the length and thickness of his leg, lying camouflaged almost to invisibility right where he had been about to sit.

He glanced to the other side of the pit, where the light tower sat on its four-wheeled carriage. He always hated turning off the generator before bed, knowing that the few hours of light from his laptop screen was all that would remain between him and the primal darkness.

The satellite phone in the trailer began to ring, and Rheese skidded, nearly sprawling in the mud, in his haste to reach it.

"Rheese here," he said into the large handset.

"Doctor, this is Peter Sharma. How are you today?"

"Glorious. What do you have to tell me, Mr. Sharma?"

"We're trying to get you some new equipment and an expert to certify the results, but it may be another couple of weeks."

Rheese's biceps tensed as he restrained himself from throwing his one communication link to the civilized world through the window and into the mud and rain.

"Listen to me, Sharma, I'm not staying out in the bloody rain and flies, twiddling my thumbs for two more blasted weeks! At the very least, I'm bringing back the crew to get digging again."

"Very well, Professor," Sharma replied, his voice taking on a soothing diplomatic tone. "As long as you keep the work away from the discovery location. Also, it would be a good idea to get more photographs of that corner, from various angles and distances, in case anything should happen. We only have those few you e-mailed."

"Yes, yes," he replied and hung up. Finally, he could get back to some real work!

Rheese had given up on any chance of the artifact paying off in the near future. Still, he was well aware that if the thing proved authentic, his name would forever be tied to its discovery. That was *something,* anyway. But would it get him out of his "nice" Mayfair house and into a Kensington castle? Not likely. And so, unbeknownst to Peter Sharma, Rheese now had authorization to resume his private plans.

He had no intention of continuing digging in this place. The artifact recovered from the soon-to-be famous northeast corner of dig site 00876-B223KY had actually revealed for him the site's *lack* of value.

Rheese unrolled his satellite maps to the red circle around the current site. He could see why he had identified its potential from the geologic markers in the area, but realized now why it was illogical. He slid his finger to a different circle, also marked in red pencil, several centimeters to the left. After an unsatisfying sip of cold tea, he found a metal ruler and calculated the distance: four kilometers west.

Garrett Rheese had gone through this process enough times in the past that he had the steps down to a routine. A childlike excitement came over him as he prepared for the coming month.

First, identify site: done! Second, identify intermittent "finds" to keep the museum interested and the money rolling in. He moved over to the laptop and opened his personal catalog spreadsheet. In his career, Rheese had worked all aspects of an excavation, and he knew that finding missing bones from nearly complete dinosaurs was a heady thrill for legitimate paleontologists. Over the years he had accrued a healthy sum of "missing bones," for which he kept a well-maintained catalog. The world's only intact #4 left metacarpal from a *Saurophaganax*? Easy—sealed in a box in his basement, on a shelf with hundreds of other rare or unique bones. After a couple of weeks' digging, call up the lab and let them know you've found something they'll like. Have Jimmy ship the package to the site, repack it with some native minerals it was "found with," and send it off to the lab. They're all happy, and better yet, the project checking account gets refreshed.

Scanning his list of known species discovered in Kenya, Rheese decided on an early Cretaceous encephalopod's spinal disc. He smiled at the thought that many of his "finds" threw scientists so far off base that he had already caused permanent damage to humanity's understanding of recorded history. A marine creature discovered in an area known to have been well above sea level for the past billion years? Well, obviously someone made a mistake somewhere. Maybe those paleogeographers would just have to redraw their maps of Pangaea. So what if it was completely off? Of course, his shenanigans were immensely destructive, but how much of his life had he wasted digging up the past for the sake of science? *Meaningless, all.*

There was a light rap on his trailer door.

"Yes," he said cheerily.

Enzi opened the door and popped his head in.

"The tarps are secure, Professor, and it look like rain easing up a little for rest of the night. Okay I send home Chui and Zuzuwi?"

Rheese leaned back and peered outside through the door. The tarps did look well set. The men had strung a few together and weighted the corners along the top to form a blue triangular umbrella that would keep the corner dry.

"Very well, Enzi. You planning on going back to camp as well, then?"

Enzi tried not to appear distracted by the doctor's good spirits.

"Oh, no, sah. I would not leave you here alone. I stay in equipment trailer with sleeping bag. No problem, sah."

"Good man, Enzi. Send them back. Next time, though, you can go yourself, too—just leave me a few men for security. Let *them* squat it in the trailer, eh?"

Enzi responded with the usual nod and quick, practiced smile, then closed the door behind him. Rheese could hear him speaking to the two men outside in Swahili. He didn't speak a lick of it, but he knew they spoke ill of him behind his back. Who wouldn't? And besides, it kept their morale up to have a common antagonist. The thought of letting Enzi sleep in one of the empty beds in his RV flashed through his mind for a second, but he didn't actually consider offering.

He rolled himself back to his laptop and started a new e-mail to send to Jimmy Moon back in London. He copied and pasted the container ID number from his spreadsheet into the message, then suddenly cocked his head to the side.

What was that outside? It sounded like the distant crack of a falling tree. He had heard that distinctive sound just over a month ago, when the trees were being cleared from this site. It was like several snaps, building in volume ahead of one very large crack, followed by several smaller ones at the end. He had thrilled at the power of the earthshaking thud when the bigger ones hit the ground.

There! Another one, closer. Now he could hear Enzi and the other two, talking in hushed voices. He stood up and cracked the door open. All three stood a short distance away, staring into the forest blackness to the north-east. One of them whispered something, and Enzi shushed him. Rheese opened the door some more and peered out in the direction they were staring. Their eyes all remained fixed on the tarped corner where Kanu had found the strange object. Rheese noticed that the usual din of chirping insects had ceased entirely.

"What is it?" He whispered to Enzi, who stood nearest the trailer.

"They good Christians, Professor," Enzi whispered. "They think we disturb the devil. We open gateway to hell."

The earth shook for a few more seconds, sending Zuzuwi running for the Jeep. More cracking, but this time it was clearly from the woods—heavy crashing, so that the ground shook continuously.

Zuzuwi shouted something from the Jeep, and Chui yelled back at him. "Tembo, Che! Tembo!"

Rheese's stomach tightened as he stumbled down the steps. Enzi ran away toward the equipment trailer.

"What is it, Enzi?" Rheese shouted to his back, unsure if he should follow. The headlights from the Jeep swung across his face as Zuzuwi spun it around and paused for Chui to jump in before skidding off in the opposite direction.

"Tembo," Enzi shouted back. "Elephant!"

It knocked over a small tree as it crashed into the clearing, and continued its clumsy stampede into the rain-filled rays of the spotlights. Rheese caught a glimpse of its face and trunk before running to the other side of his RV and sliding into the mud behind the front tire. Enzi was trying to load the double-barrel shotgun from the equipment trailer while the rampaging elephant continued on its path straight to the tarped corner of the pit. He watched it try to stop itself with its enormous hind legs, but the tarp gave way instantly and the trunk disappeared below. The rest followed, bringing with it a ton of loose mud, the tarps, and the rocks used to anchor them.

Enzi ran to the edge of the pit in time to see the debris settle over a good portion of the beast. Its head appeared to be turned too far to the right, the neck likely broken. A free leg writhed as the animal released a few desperate groans from beneath the mud.

Dr. Rheese moved tentatively from behind the RV and saw Enzi standing at the edge of the pit. He walked through the downpour of the clearing and joined Enzi to watch the pitiful scene.

"Is it dying?" he asked quietly.

"Not survive that drop, sah. See his neck." Enzi clicked the shotgun barrels shut and started toward the lift.

"Just look at the bloody mess it's made. . . . Wait, where are you going, Enzi?"

"Going go stop it pain, Professor."

Rheese didn't say anything. He wouldn't have thought to shoot the animal for its own benefit. *Enzi's a good black,* he thought—*probably a better man than I.*

Though the prospect revolted him, Rheese decided to stay and watch. At the very least, it would make a good story for the future, however sickening in the moment.

The lift touched ground, and Enzi slogged cautiously through the mud and puddles until he reached the corner. The stumplike hind leg no longer struggled, and for a moment it appeared that the creature was already dead. Then he saw the brown and black eyeball roll back and lock its gaze on him.

The sheet of mud covering its side heaved subtly, then subsided, as the animal strained to breathe. He saw the last few inches of its trunk emerging, pink-tipped, from the mud a couple of meters away. Enzi looked back at the eyeball. It was large and blood-rimmed beneath long, goopy eyelashes, and seemed to plead with him in a painfully human manner. He raised the shotgun to its head and wondered if that would be the right spot. The pellets might not make it through the thick skull. He'd seen their skeletons before; as children, he and his friends had occasionally come upon them when playing in the forest. The tusks were always gone, though.

Perhaps a shot through the trunk there, straight to the brain . . .

The eye blinked slowly, and Enzi decided to proceed.

Watching from above, Rheese flinched at the flash and blast of the shot. He watched Enzi stand there for a moment, looking at the dead creature, then turned back to his trailer. His fogged watch face reminded him that it was past midnight and the sun would be up in six hours.

Enzi crouched down and pushed open the heavy gray eyelid with his thumb. The massive creature's side no longer heaved. It was dead. He looked back to the professor but only caught the faint click of the trailer door closing in the distance. Walking back to the lift, he examined his bloodied, dirty shirt and dungarees and realized he had no spare clothing at the site. Unfortunately, he would have to get into the sleeping bag naked and hope they would be mostly dry by morning.

He stripped down in the equipment trailer and, after wringing out his sodden pants and shirt outside, hung them on the hydraulic supports that held up the top hatch. He found a packing blanket and used it to dry himself as best he could.

"Ah, uh, here you are, Enzi."

Startled, Enzi turned to see Dr. Rheese averting his eyes while holding out some fresh clothes. Perhaps the man had a heart after all—perhaps he was not entirely *mkundu*.

"Sir, I cannot . . ."

"Quiet, Enzi. I'm not in the habit of thinking of others—I'll be able to pat myself on the back for this for years to come."

"Thank you, sah. I don't know how to . . . I will wash like new for you next week."

Rheese walked away, saying, "Don't worry, man. Keep them." *You couldn't get them clean enough for me ever to wear again.*

"Sir, I . . ."

Enzi realized the magnitude of such a gift. The shirt off one's own back. He had misjudged the strange, irascible Englishman. He felt guilty until finally drifting off to sleep.

FIVE

Matt Turner lay sprawled on his new couch, surfing Tahitian resort Web sites on his iPad. One in particular, the Grand Regency Royale, had exactly what he sought. A golden box on the left side of the ACCOMMODATIONS page elegantly announced in an italicized script that they would be open during their renovation and expansion project. He picked up his phone and dialed the toll-free number.

The woman, in an accent of indeterminate origin, declared that a few of the new rooms would be opening in the coming weeks, and yes, they would contain all new furnishings, and yes, he could make a reservation ensuring that he would be the first guest ever to occupy the room of his choice. He gave his credit card number, asked for her name, and mentioned that he would take care of her when he arrived. She thanked him for the thought but then regretfully mentioned that she worked in the company's Newark, New Jersey, offices. He told her he'd figure something out, to which, of course, she replied that he was most kind but it really wasn't necessary.

Next call, Iris.

"Hey, sis," he said as he clicked again through the photos of the resort.

"How you doing, Buster? You run out of money yet?"

"Not quite. I think I've got around a hundred bucks left in my checking—oh, yeah, and about five mil in the money market account alone. Listen, you need to stop telling Mom I'm blowing all my cash."

"But you are!"

"Didn't say I wasn't, but why do you have to get her all worried? She's probably popping Xanax as we speak. Anyway, what are you doing in three weeks?"

"Um . . . three weeks?" She rustled some papers. "What's that, like, the sixth? Studying for finals."

"When are finals?" His doorbell rang.

"The eleventh and twelfth, why?"

Matt held the cell phone to his ear with his shoulder and looked through the diamond-shaped window in the door. UPS guy. He grabbed the gloves hanging by the door and opened up to sign for his package while continuing to speak into the phone.

"Well, I'm thinking you can study even more effectively on a powdered-sugar white sand beach. Is it just these two?"

"Just these two what?" Iris replied, puzzled.

"UPS guy." The driver took back his scanner-and-pen thing and gave Matt a courteous smile before returning to his truck. Matt gently kicked the boxes through the doorway, removed his gloves, and returned to the couch.

"What are you asking me here, Buster? You wanna go to the beach? What are we talking: New Hanover, Crystal Coast, or what?"

"Tahiti, sister. All expenses paid, of course."

"Dude, you can't get a *real* date to come with you to frickin' Tahiti? I've got finals—no way!"

"Come on! You don't even have to *do* anything! I just don't want to go alone or with someone I don't even know."

He paused on a picture of the sun setting behind a steep, forested mountain that dropped down to a beach lined with gently swaying coco palms.

"Don't be an idiot. A trip like that you gotta plan like months in advance. What about my classes? What about my roommates eating all my stuff? No, you need to find yourself some chick that wants a free ride to Tahiti. Think about it—how hard can that be?" She paused for a minute as Matt sulked quietly. "You spoken to Melissa recently?"

Matt stood up, his face twisting into a scowl.

"Are you kidding me? *Her?* I don't even think about her. She's nothing."

"Easy, okay? I know she hurt you. I was just wondering if you've spoken recently."

"No." His voice cracked a little. "I seriously haven't thought about her in ages."

"You know you're gonna find one better than her. I know she drove you crazy with all her old crap."

Matt had begun pacing in front of his huge new plasma TV. "Exactly. Old records, old books, even old clothes. What was she thinking, coming into my apartment in some thrift shop dress that she *knows* I'm not going to get near? Then complaining that I never want to be next to her! I'm telling you, I *never* felt at ease around her. It was like a panic attack if she was anything but naked."

"Ew!"

"No, you know what I mean!"

"Anyway, it sounds to me like her ditching you was the best thing that ever happened to you. You probably should have done it yourself. . . . you know, since you don't even think about her or anything . . . Welp, I'd love to hear you vent some more about your ex, but I have to get back to my books."

"You started it. Love you."

"Love you, too, Buster."

"Come to Tahiti with me!"

She was already gone.

He slumped down on his couch, popping his iPad up and just snagging it before it toppled onto the hardwood floor. He sat back and imagined that white sand between his bare toes, swimming in the warm ocean, or biking through pristine woods in a T-shirt and shorts. Happy sigh.

What was the resort woman's name? Shisha something—it sounded like "critic," but Eastern European. Crytsik? There was no doubt an "h" and a "z" or two in there somewhere. He bought a nice gift basket online to be shipped to her attention at the company's office in Newark.

Gloves back on—time to see what was in the boxes. He cut open the tape on the first box with a key and reached inside. Ah, yes, very nice! The new dishes. He guessed correctly that the second box would be the silverware. After a lengthy unpackaging session, he had the dishwasher filled and running. Outside went the boxes, bubble wrap, and Styrofoam. Off with the gloves—the house was clean again.

His cell phone buzzed from the TV room, and he caught it on the third ring.

"This is Matt."

"Matthew Turner, Jon at NYMM. How are you today?"

"Very well, Dr. Meier. The therapy sessions since that last chunk of Nazi history have been helping a great deal."

Matt could hear Dr. Meier not quite blocking the mic and whispering to someone. The someone whispered back before the director replied.

"That was a joke, right, Matthew?"

"Yes, Doctor, but it was no joke when I told George I wouldn't be assisting with anything else, so I'm assuming this really is just a friendly call to see how I'm doing today."

"Of course . . . of course, Matthew. Could you do me a favor, though, and check your e-mail?"

"I take it I'm not getting an apology for the desk thing?"

"No, I won't be apologizing. Perhaps if you realized the significance of this desk . . . May I share with you?"

"No, no interest."

"Well . . ." The director was clearly flustered. "The Herz family sends its heartfelt thanks to you."

"What? You told someone about me?"

"No, no, of course not. What I meant was they send their thanks to the 'team' involved. I have not disclosed your ability to anyone."

"So who knows at this point? There was a time I could count on one hand, you know?"

"Matthew," Meier said reassuringly. "I apologize—not for the desk, mind you—but for whatever I may have done to make you question your trust in me as it pertains to your ability. I can assure you that the 'circle', as it were, has not expanded beyond George Miller, Peter Sharma, and myself. I made that promise to your uncle when we first met . . . And *you* were the one that brought George into it after Peter left, if I recall correctly."

Matt thought Dr. Meier was starting to sound too much like his dad.

"Whatever." Matt slid his iPad over and refreshed his in-box. One new message appeared from jmeier@nymm.org. He tapped the message with the subject "FW: Artifact."

Scrolling down, he saw that it originated from Peter Sharma, his original "handler" at NYMM. Seemed he was still working in England.

The attachment opened, and Matt leaned in to look at it. It looked like a tall wall of variegated sediment, excavated by pick and shovel or perhaps a backhoe. Someone had drawn a red circle over the digital photo, but there didn't appear to be anything to see there. He went back to the e-mail and opened the second attachment. Now, here was something interesting.

"Are you still there, Matthew?" asked Dr. Meier.

"Yeah, I'm still here, just looking at the pics. What is it?" It looked like a piece of window screen, but with extra stitching on one side and some kind of flap on the top.

"There are many theories as to *what* it is, but its function is not the focus of interest at the moment. The few who are even aware of its existence are far more keenly focused on the *when*. Your competitors say it is older than one hundred and fifty million years."

"My *competitors*?" Matt replied with incredulity.

"Yes, your competitors: potassium and argon."

"Ah, funny man. I thought I only had to compete with carbon fourteen."

"C fourteen doesn't provide dates past about sixty thousand years. You should really read up a bit more on your peers."

Matt stared at the photo as the questions filled his head. He opened the third attachment. It was another photo of the object, but much larger and shot from a different angle. He could zoom in on this one, and did so until it blew up to pixel level, then pinched out one level.

"So, how long have civilized humans been around?"

Dr. Meier leaned back in his chair and gave a thumbs-up to George, who stood beside his desk, watching eagerly.

"Pertinent question. Well, we could have a long discussion on the dawn of civilized societies, Matthew, but I think a key point right now is when the Bronze and Iron Ages took place. You see, *Homo sapiens* hadn't figured out the whole metal extraction, smelting, and mixing thing until then."

"Okay, so when was that?" Matt answered, annoyed at Meier's smug tone.

"Nine thousand years ago. Simple pottery before that; the oldest fired-clay pots we know of are from fourteen thousand years ago. That would be about the extent of human technology anywhere in the world."

"And the potassium thing said it was more than a hundred and fifty *million* years old?"

"Well, they couldn't actually date the fabric itself. The estimation is based upon the minerals it was embedded in."

Matt's skepticism set in. Anyone could say they found a hammer buried with a Stegosaurus. But, he supposed, these researchers like Pete Sharma wouldn't be pursuing this if it were that easily dismissed.

"Okay, so if I were to believe that it was as old as the stuff it was found in . . . that'd be saying what? That humans were more advanced at a way earlier date than everyone has believed so far?"

"Well, Matthew, there's a rather important fact that you're missing here."

There was that smugness again. This call would be ending soon.

"What's that, Doctor?" Matt said with a yawn.

"That the earliest humans—and we're talking *really* primitive and not that bright—didn't exist on earth until only a couple million years ago. You recall your work with Lucy?"

Matt remembered the tiny lump of bone they had handed him. As usual, he had been able to "experience" only the scientists who had discovered it. He had never been able to pick up emotional imprints from people or their remains. But from what he recalled, they had said it was three million years old. So the fabric in this photo was from, say, a hundred and forty-eight million years—give or take a week or two—before the oldest known human ancestor?

"So this is from aliens then, you're saying."

"We have no idea, Matthew. But it would be pretty interesting to find out, wouldn't it?"

"Yeah, I suppose it would. All right, I'm interested enough. Go ahead and ship it to me, and I'll have a go at it when I've got a chance."

"Obviously, there are some pretty important people for whom this item's security and protection are of great importance. It cannot be moved from its present location."

"Okay, so you're asking me to fly to New York? London? I'm about to go to Tahiti, so maybe I'll stop by on my way back." Matt's call-waiting tone bleeped in his ear. He pulled the phone away to see who was calling—it was blocked. "Look, Doctor, I have another call I need to take."

"Matthew, this might be the most important discovery in the history of mankind."

"Okay . . . well, then have you considered that maybe it's too high-profile? Since *you* brought it up, you remember what happened when you had a seventeen-year-old brought in to examine that Lucy skeleton? We obviously couldn't talk about what I might have to offer in the investigation, so it not only made the museum look stupid, it also put way too much attention on *me*. I'm not interested in being tested, mocked, talked about on the news, or called for interviews. Let everyone's imaginations run wild with this thing. It's probably a piece of some knight from the Crusades' chain mail that fell in a crack. A few earthquakes later, there you go—he was hunting *T. rex*."

Silence on the other end of the phone—obviously, Meier was having a word with the someone again. Then he returned. "This is quite humorous, Matthew. I . . . uh . . . I don't think you could realize just . . . hah! Well, it really just reemphasizes how much we need you on this."

"What exactly is so festive, Dr. Meier?" Matt moved his thumb over to the END button on his phone's screen.

"Well, it's just . . . that there have been some key scientists all over this mystery since its discovery, and, well, you pretty much just stated—actually, *exactly* stated—the best theory they could come up with to date. Right down to the source era of the Crusades. Quite impressive, despite the flippant manner in which it was expressed. And off the top of your head, too—hah!"

Matt had the sneaking feeling his ego was being stroked, but what the hell—it was working; he did feel rather impressed with himself.

"I'll tell you what, Doctor, I need to check this voice mail, but I'll think about it and call you back. But listen, nothing's changed with the rules about me, yeah? No one knows anything unless I approve."

"Yes, of course, Matthew. Now don't wait too long getting back to me . . ."

Matt hung up and took a deep breath. It may have waited 150 million years—what was another few weeks?

He checked his voice mail and listened to the message from FedEx. Apparently, they were trying to deliver a package to him, but the street name they had was Jasper Avenue instead of Kaspar Avenue. He called to sort it out.

By the time he was finished with his deliveries and some cleanup, Matt had stopped thinking about Meier's photos. He was back to his vacation plans and the prickly task of finding a suitable guest to join him.

SIX

Garrett Rheese awoke to an insistent tapping on his trailer door. How long had they been knocking? His workers wouldn't dare—not even Enzi. What time was it? The light outside suggested a little past sunrise.

The tapping grew more insistent, and an unfamiliar voice called his name.

" . . . we need to speak with you."

Kenyan accent, speaking impeccable English.

"Just a moment," he replied as he stood up unsteadily and shucked on a pair of khakis. Sneaking a peak through the blinds, he could see a gray government SUV and three men poking around. One was clearly the driver; another wore a plain black suit but with epaulettes on the shoulders, apparently with bars of rank. Military? The third man, also in a suit, carried a large belly, several chins, and a shiny black walking cane. He must have been the door rapper.

Rheese had had to report the find to the Ministry of the Interior, in accordance with the terms of his license to excavate in-country, but there had been little fanfare in response. They had requested a daunting stack of paperwork, including the standard no-export agreement to ensure that they not lose any treasures from the national patrimony. But what was this visit about? A change of heart on the value of the find, clearly. Perhaps they wanted to seize the artifact and conduct their own incompetent research.

Rheese finished tying his boots and slid his pith helmet over his head. About to turn the door latch, he had a thought and went to his safe. Suddenly, the overwhelming interest of others had changed his perception of the artifact's value. He turned the key, locking the safe, withdrew the key from the lock, and searched for a suitable hiding place. Not on his person—they would check. Indeed, if they really wanted it, they would tear this trailer apart from top to bottom. There was only one place they wouldn't want to look.

The loo.

The key disappeared into the dark blue liquid and clinked onto the metal bowl. After a quiet flush, Rheese pocketed a stack of American hundred-dollar bills from his briefcase, then swung open the door to greet the men with feigned delight.

"Lovely morning, good sirs. How may I be of assistance?"

The fat fellow with the cane spoke first.

"Dr. Rheese, good morning to you. I am Kenneth Odumbe, and this is Ohun Modi from the Ministry of the Interior. We have come to—"

Rheese cut him off. "Yes, yes, of course, gentlemen. We all have our grandchildren and our gray hairs. Let us not have this carry on until they are in college and the hair is all gone." He lifted the pith helmet to reveal his glistening pink pate, and retrieved the sheaf of bills from his pocket. He shook hands with Mr. Odumbe, then with Mr. Modi, leaving a folded stack of bills in each eager palm. He glanced at the driver, who appeared to feel left out, and shook his gloved hand as well, giving him a single hundred. Stepping away, he smiled at them but then noted something off in their expressions. The well-nourished Mr. Odumbe was holding the cash as if it contained something foul-smelling. Rheese then looked at the ministry man, who looked equally confused but was counting the bills nonetheless.

"Very well, then," said Rheese with a chipper smile. "I'll just be returning to my business and you good gentlemen can find your way."

Kenneth Odumbe's face turned serious; his hand still held the apparently revolting cash almost at arm's length. *A bribe wasted?* Rheese wondered.

"Dr. Rheese, I think there has been a misunderstanding. We did not come to collect money from you, though the gift is certainly appreciated."

Into the pocket it went, and Minister Modi followed suit. "We have come to investigate the preservation breach."

"I beg your pardon?" Dr. Rheese replied.

"Bombo over there, Doctor. He was apparently startled from the Masai-Mara Game Reservation, several kilometers from here, and we are to examine the carcass to rule out wrongdoing. After which we will order the cleanup crew to recover the remains."

"The elephant! Of course." *Garrett, you buffoon!* he thought. "It's right over there, gentlemen."

"Yes, sir." Ohun Modi opened a folder and clicked a ballpoint pen to write notes. "We can see that. Did the animal come into contact with you or any of your men prior to the fall?"

"Oh, no, not at all. The bloody thing came crashing through the trees over there and fell straight into the pit. All quite tragic, I thought."

"So no interaction at all, then, Doctor?" Modi clarified.

"None—that is, not until after it was already at the bottom there, thrashing about."

"Oh, and what interaction took place at that time?" The fat one glanced back at the carcass, then took a step toward Rheese.

"Well, the thing was clearly in agony, and so we did the only decent thing! I had my site foreman, Enzi, put it out of its misery." *Don't say that! Garrett, you blithering git, why did you say that?*

Both men stepped toward him now with shocked expressions.

"You did *what*?" asked Modi, incredulous.

"Well, Enzi . . . the site supervisor . . . see, we keep a shotgun for the beasties . . ." He gulped. "Not the *elephantine* beasties, you understand, but the others. And, well, he went over to it and gave it a clean one to the head. It was at peace after that. We had a quiet moment and said a prayer for its soul."

Silence replaced his lies as the two officials communicated with each other using their eyes and then began to walk toward the lift.

Where was bloody Enzi when he needed him? He would have been so easy to throw under the bus, and *he* was the one who pulled the trigger anyway!

"Can you operate this crane device to get us down there?" asked Modi.

"Of course, of course. Just step right on and slide that little gate closed. Safety first on our site here . . . that's the thing, safety at all times."

The driver remained behind Dr. Rheese as he lowered them into the pit. He appeared to be looking over Rheese's shoulder to see how the lift was controlled. No trust. What was he going to do—leave them down there to starve with nothing but a cask of amontillado?

Rheese made his best effort to appear unconcerned as the men examined the dead elephant. He watched from the corner of his eye as the Modi bloke appeared to be estimating the angle of the shotgun blast. The professor wondered if the creature had begun to smell just yet. How long had it lain there? Certainly no more than eight hours. It couldn't be in too bad a shape—other than the broken neck, mashed-up face, and brains blown to aspic. Rheese withheld a chuckle as he paced and puffed at a cheap cigar.

As the lift surfaced again ten minutes later, Modi started right in. "So you say the animal was shot after it had already fallen?"

"That is correct, sir. And my foreman, Enzi, can tell you all about it upon his return."

"And where is this Enzi fellow now?"

"Well, I'm not exactly sure about that. It's likely he is traveling back from our base camp with some men to—"

"To assist with removal of the evidence? If this creature was shot after it fell, tell me, sir, how was it shot from below? The blast appears to travel in an upward angle through the base of the trunk. A shot such as this would come from a man standing in front of an upright elephant."

A vehicle could be heard rattling up the dirt road, and soon the Jeep appeared with Enzi behind the wheel. With him sat four others.

Impeccable timing, Enzi. "Ah, here now, gentlemen. This is my fore-man, Enzi. He'll be able to answer all your applicable questions."

Enzi parked the Jeep, and all the men jumped out, anxious to see the enormous carcass. Enzi, wearing a solemn expression, walked straight to Rheese and the investigators. "You from the Ministry, yes? I call as soon as I reach telephone this morning."

Odumbe raised a thick eyebrow. "*You* placed the call this morning?"

"Oh, yes, sah. Enzi Wata—I am the site foreman." He reached out his hand. After the handshakes, Modi and Odumbe walked Enzi to their SUV and began to question him out of Rheese's earshot.

Rheese walked to the other four men standing at the ledge and attempted to instruct them to clear the loose mud away from the new slope created by the toppling elephant. At first they stood there looking doubtfully at him while he mimed and pointed, but then one of them appeared to grasp his meaning and then explained in Swahili what the *mkundu* had said. They all rushed off to comply, grabbing shovels along the way. Rheese turned back toward the SUV and saw the two government men and Enzi chuckling among themselves while the driver poked around outside the equipment trailer. A few friendly good-byes later, Enzi came strolling over to Rheese with a smile.

"All taken care of, Professor. They send cleanup people soon."

"What exactly did you tell them?" Rheese asked with an unconvincing smile as he watched the departing SUV over Enzi's shoulder.

"I tell them what happen. How it crash through trees, fall into excava-tion, and I shoot with shotgun."

"And they were pleased with that, eh?"

"Pleased, sah? I think not so pleased, but Mister Modi write down notes and they say cleanup people coming soon."

"Right. Good, good, Enzi. So, the laughing at the end there—what was that about?"

"Laughing, Professor?" Enzi's face morphed to frank innocence.

"Never mind. So I told these men to secure that slope, to be sure nothing more falls down on top of the creature." He glanced back at the elephant. "They say anything about clearing the debris for their cleanup gang?"

"No, sah, they say we not touch animal or the mess around. They clean up everything."

Rheese began to walk back to his trailer and then remembered. "Blast it!" he shouted as he stomped the drying mud.

Enzi turned and asked the problem.

"When those men are done over there, I need them to empty my septic tank. But they are *not* to throw away *anything*."

He received a blank stare in return.

"I accidentally dropped a bloody key in the loo!"

Enzi nodded, understanding.

Behind Dr. Rheese's trailer, the two lowest-ranking men, who had drawn the septic tank duty, had placed the end of the hose into a garbage bag and zip-tied the top of the bag around the hose. They had agreed this was the safest way to proceed without "losing anything." Unfortunately, the first trash bag had burst, and the rest of their work had to take place amid a large puddle of lumpy blue liquid.

When the tank was empty, the men stood behind Enzi, who asked on their behalf if they might enter the trailer to search for the key from the inside hatch.

After a glance at their soiled boots and pant legs, Rheese said, "You must be bloody daft. Show me the hatch—I'll check it myself."

Enzi lifted the small panel beside the base of the toilet and moved aside for Dr. Rheese to slip in, gloves and flashlight at the ready. He tried to hold his breath but caught a nasty snort before he could turn his head. He sucked in another breath, through the mouth this time, and tucked his head and the light into the small opening.

And there the bugger was!

It was just within reach, beside the drain plug. Key in hand, he stood up in triumph, then held it under the faucet, washing it well with hand soap.

"Please drop these in the outside bin, if you don't mind," he said.

Enzi accepted the latex gloves and let the trailer door swing shut behind him.

SEVEN

Dr. Jon Meier hung up his desk phone after leaving the fourth message for Matthew Turner in as many days. The man was clearly ignoring him. Peter Sharma, meanwhile, had not been as patient with his calls, which now averaged five a day. Dr. Meier considered telling him it was a lost cause. Turner was a millionaire now and too selfish to consider the big picture around the Kenya discovery. If opening the doors to an entirely unknown past weren't inspiration enough, what did anyone have to offer him?

He knew the exact moment when he had blown any chance of getting Matthew onboard, and now chastised himself for the slip. It was the first voice mail he had left him after their initial conversation. Meier hadn't realized he had thus far omitted the part about actually traveling to the forests of Kenya. It occurred to him later that day that his cheerful close of "Kenya awaits!" may not have been the best idea.

Meier's computer speakers emitted the familiar tone, and he switched back to his in-box. Pete was asking what it would take to have "the expert" on-site in Kenya in two days. Meier typed his honest assessment: "Another $10 million." He deleted that and searched his office for an idea. *Another ten . . .*

"That's it!" He said aloud. He just needed to get Turner another ten million dollars!

He dialed the extension.

"Yes, Doctor Meier?" George answered.

"I need you in my office in five minutes, and bring Hank Felch with you."

"All right, but, um . . . Hank is setting up the exhibition for this afternoon's—"

"Four minutes, fifty seconds, George."

Hank Felch cursed to himself as he tried to wipe the dust off the old animatronic Stegosaurus. Whoever had painted it last had left the original texturizer layer instead of resurfacing the whole thing. Laziness, pure and simple. Now, as he tried to clean it, little bits fell off, leaving obvious unpainted speckles. *Great!* he thought. People would be strolling through here in just a few hours, and they had a dino who appeared to have suffered horrible acne in its adolescence. Not to mention the scale was completely off. Probably someone's bright idea to save space for the installation.

Hank had worked at the museum for seven years and longed to return to "real work," though he did little enough to advance himself toward the goal. As he shined the plastic eyeball, he recalled the days of being lauded "for extraordinary contributions to the study of impact events" and, before that, receiving the Principal's Award for Outstanding Field Recovery for identifying an apparently unrelated pile of bone fragments as being an entire *Brachyceratops* scapula.

"Hey, Hank," George's voice called out with its usual waver of reluctance.

Hank did not turn to answer. "Don't ask me anything, Georgie. If I don't finish fixing this mess in the next coupla hours, Meier's gonna bowl with my head."

"Um . . . actually, Doctor Meier wants to see you. Sorry, I tried to tell him."

"Perfect!" Hank shouted, and threw down his rag.

Three minutes later, Hank and George Miller sat before Dr. Meier's desk. Hank cleaned his glasses on his shirt and brushed some plaster fragments out of his curly brown beard, oblivious of the pieces in his chaotic mop of hair.

"Gentlemen . . . ," Dr. Meier began. "We need to come up with ten million dollars."

George looked over at Hank, his large, watery eyes tinged with desperation. Hank didn't flinch. He simply replaced his round glasses and waited for more information. Meier began flipping a gold doubloon over his fingers, clinking it on his ring with each roll.

"Hank, do you remember Matthew Turner? Used to come around from time to time as an intern . . . "

"Yeah, I think I met him," Hank said. "I heard he's a gazillionaire now. Some sort of treasure hunt near Georgia that paid off."

Dr. Meier smiled and held up the gold coin.

"You are correct, Hank. And as a matter of fact, *this* is the very coin that he traced to that spot in the Atlantic. This Spanish doubloon, which I have kept on my desk for the past couple of decades . . . well, it found its way into young Turner's possession for a brief time. Four months later, a photo of Matthew appears on the cover of the *Times,* standing on the deck of a fishing boat with a chest of gold and silver that had been lost for hundreds of years."

Hank nodded. That was about the extent of what he knew, though he hadn't known that the director's doubloon had anything to do with it.

"Obviously Matthew has a singular gift for tracing items to their source. And you, Hank, among my staff, know the most about other lost treasure out there in the world, do you not?"

"I do," Hank replied, tickling his fingertips with his beard. "Now, separating legend from genuine shipwrecks and the like, well, there're a lot of people out there doing that these days—actual companies, in fact."

George suddenly realized exactly where Meier was going. "I think I can narrow it down for you, Hank," he said. "What 'lost treasure' is out there that there's a well-known sample of? Like Doctor Meier's gold coin, for instance?"

"Ah, right . . . Well, I'd have to look through the database for an accurate number, but I'd say it's in the hundreds just for the NYMM. But all this stuff has been tracked numerous times without success. I seriously doubt that . . ."

As Hank droned on, Dr. Meier and George shared a look.

"Hundreds?"

Dr. Meier knew that Matthew was ignoring his calls. He decided to have Tuni call him from her cell phone to increase the odds of his answering. It worked.

"This is Matt," he answered after two rings.

"Hello, Mr. Turner, this is Tuni St. James."

Where did he know that name from? *Interesting accent.*

"What can I do for you, Tuni?"

The ambient noise told her he was driving. She sat in the leather chair in the corner of the office, with Dr. Meier, George, and Hank hovering over her. Their script, with explicit notes, sat on her lap as she twirled her long hair with a lazy finger.

"I have a proposal for you. I understand you have a talent for tracing lost gold."

Matt let off the gas a little and held the phone tight to his ear. "Okay . . ."

"My employers have access to a piece of silver that washed up on a beach a long time ago." She paused but heard only the soft hum of the moving car. "It's from a well-documented vessel that sank with chests of silver destined for the Confederate army in 1864. Would you be interested in recovering it?"

"Tuni, is Doctor Meier standing near you?"

She looked up at the director and mouthed, "He knows."

Meier shrugged. If Matthew wasn't hooked at this point, there was nothing else they could do. He nodded for her to continue.

"Yes, as a matter of fact, he's standing over me right now, wearing a green and charcoal-patterned sweater vest."

"Please put him on the phone," Matt said evenly.

She handed Meier the phone.

"Matthew?"

"Why are you playing games, Doctor?"

"Well, my friend, I realized that I needed a bit more of an incentive for you to help out with this very important situation. It just so happens that the doubloon to which you helped yourself is not unique in its potential. The silver coin Tuni spoke of is very real, sitting in the safe in my office, and would very likely lead you to an estimated twenty-seven million dollars' worth of its brothers at the bottom of the Atlantic."

A long silence followed. Meier could hear that Matt had stopped driving. At last, he spoke.

Matt finally said, "You told her about me?"

Meier glanced at Tuni, "Your techniques are safe, Matthew. I thought I made that clear."

"I hope so, Doctor. I'll be there tomorrow."

Meier hung up, handed the phone back to Tuni, and smiled.

"He's coming tomorrow."

As George and Hank high-fived, Tuni stood up. "Are you done with me, Jon?" she asked.

"Oh, yes," he beamed. "And well done, Tuni. I'll need you here early tomorrow, though—I'd like you to escort him when he arrives."

"Very well," she replied, and turned on her heel to leave.

"Oh, and I'll need you to accompany him to Kenya."

She turned and looked at him coolly. "You're out of your mind, Jon. How many millions would *I* get for such a trip?"

To George and Hank, he said, "Please excuse us, gentlemen."

Matt despised everything about flying. For one thing, he had to remove his gloves and shoes to go through security. And his bags would be intermingled with other people's luggage. This was no risk to him, as imprints could not be passed, but it was gross. He had to sit in seats previously occupied by hundreds, perhaps thousands, of utter strangers. He also hated New York at any time other than winter. In the winter he could cover up as much as he liked without anyone batting an eye. Walking onto the subway wearing a turtleneck, beanie, and gloves in the middle of summer seemed to incite annoyance, ridicule, or outright suspicion in all good New Yorkers. The short walk from the Forty-second Street station to the New York Metropolitan Museum resulted in no less than twenty concerned looks, four laughs, and three unpleasant comments. As buses, cabs, and delivery trucks zoomed past him, a trip-hammer pounded away at a distant construction site, and the shoulders of strangers grazed against him. Matt realized he despised simply *everything* about this city, whatever the season.

Tuni greeted him on his way into the lobby. He was looking at the giant skeletal *T. rex*, held up by several dozen support cables. He remembered when they were putting it up a few years ago. It wasn't even real—just a bunch of chicken wire, plaster, and plastic resin.

"Right this way, Matthew," Tuni said. It sounded like "MaTYEW"—he liked it.

He only remembered seeing her at the front desk a couple of times, but then it was just her head and shoulders. He hadn't realized how tall she was. As she walked a little ahead of him, he noticed he hadn't fully appreciated a lot of things about her. He also realized that she had kept her hands behind her back when greeting him a moment ago. No attempt at a handshake. Very considerate. Did she know?

She opened the door to the museum director's office, and he saw Dr. Meier stand up behind his desk, a good distance across the room. It all looked the same: impressive books on the walls, antique Persian rugs covering areas of dark hardwood floor. This was the floor he had admired and ordered for his new house. His own was better, though, he noticed.

"Have a seat, Matthew," said Dr. Meier, his voice ringing with triumphant good cheer.

"In one of these antiques, Doctor?" Matt said with feigned umbrage. "I feel that you just don't know me at all."

Meier nodded with a fatuous smile and remained standing.

"It was nice to officially meet you," Tuni said and walked to the door.

"Yeah, you too." Matt waited for the door to close. "I say we cut to the chase, Doc. Let's see the coin."

"Oh, come, come, Matthew. Why would I just hand it to you? You might get everything you need to know in an instant, and then what could you possibly need us for? You get your *quid* with no *pro quo*."

"Why would I believe that this coin exists at all, let alone that it would lead to anything close to what you suggest? I'll need to hold it for at least a couple minutes."

Dr. Meier considered this for a moment, recalling other times he had seen Turner in action. It usually took him a five or more minutes to return anything useful. He also realized that Matthew had undoubtedly thought this through over the past twenty-four hours and would be unlikely to get on a plane to Kenya without a quick sampling.

"Have you brought your passport and whatever else you'll need for our little Kenya safari?"

"I have enough for a few days. I don't plan on staying any longer than that, regardless of what happens."

"More than enough time." Meier opened a low cabinet in the wall behind his desk and spun quickly through a combination before opening the safe. He rose with palm upturned, holding a large silver coin on a square of red velvet. The coin's edges were well rounded from wear, and the face on the front was barely visible.

"Where is it from?"

"France. Napoleon the Third's attempts at 'mediation' between the North and South. Fund the Confederates to even the odds; then force both sides to the table—or at least that's how he spun it. Either way, the silver never made it; the U.S.S. *Hudson* made sure of that—sent it straight to the bottom."

"Cool . . . All right, well . . ." Matt took a wrinkled bedsheet from his duffel bag, spread it on the hardwood floor, and lay down on it while removing his right glove.

"So just touch it to the back of my hand and then remove it a bit later."

Meier knelt beside him and smiled. "Five seconds later."

"Five seconds? C'mon, that's ridiculous! It takes longer than that just to enter the imprint."

"Ten seconds," Meier offered.

Matt rolled his eyes and rested his head back on the sheet, then gave the nod to proceed. Meier pressed the edge of the coin lightly against the back of Matt's hand and looked at his watch. Ten seconds later, he lifted the coin, and Matt calmly opened his eyes and sat up.

"I want a private jet. I'm not riding a commercial plane all that way."

"Already arranged by Peter Sharma. So what did you see?"

"None of your business. Just put my coin back in the safe and leave it there till I get back."

"Very well, but it will have to be returned to me after a week—it isn't 'your' coin. Tuni has all your instructions: where to go, whom to meet, et cetera. She'll be accompanying you."

Matt kept his poker face, though this really was quite a pleasant prospect.

Outside the door, Tuni stood waiting, arms crossed. She raised a single, perfectly shaped eyebrow. "So, are we traveling, Matthew?"

There was that "*Mattyew*" again—he loved it.

"We are. I hope you're getting paid something extra for this. I mean, aren't you just the admin or whatever?"

She gave him a frosty look. "I am the operations assistant. And my only added reward is to be the pleasure of *your* youthful company." They began walking to the staff garage.

"Youthful? You can't be much older than me!"

"I am six years your senior, young man," she said over her shoulder.

"Wow. To see what you've seen in all that time . . ." He inhaled the light perfume trailing behind her. *Subtle.*

"Throw your bag in the boot," she said as the trunk of a white BMW 328i popped open on their approach.

Her car was a few years old, but immaculate as if it had just come off the showroom floor. Even her suitcase, already stowed in the trunk, appeared brand-new. As they drove, he listened to the hypnotic beat music on the stereo and stared out the window at the passing buildings and people. It was nice. He felt as if he were in a bubble of safe and clean.

EIGHT

Peter Sharma hung up the phone and clapped his hands together. Maggie Gwynne, the director of paleontology, looked up from her desk with a start.

"What is it?" she asked.

"Meier has the expert on the jet. He'll be in Nairobi tomorrow morning."

"Well, that's good news." She made a little frown. "Now, remind me— why do we trust this expert's opinion more than the potassium-argon results?"

"He has . . . um, special insights into this sort of investigation. Do you recall the Tarkhan papyrus? He was the one who pointed the field team to the adjacent tomb's location, where the remaining sheets were found."

"And how, pray tell, did he manage that?" she said after taking a noisier-than-intended slurp of tea.

"Can't say. But he's the only one who can confirm its age."

Peter Sharma stood up and stretched his thin legs. Maggie, who was married, liked his lanky physique, though the butt was a bit flat. She also enjoyed the softness of his well-proportioned face and pale green eyes. Of course, the most attractive thing about him was his brain. He was the first Indian director, and the youngest by far, in the Museum Group's history. There didn't appear to be anything he didn't know. If only he were twenty years older . . .

Peter picked up his phone again and dialed Garrett Rheese's satellite number.

"Sharma?" came the abrupt answer.

"Dr. Rheese, I have good news. You'll have the expert on-site tomorrow morning."

"Smashing." Rheese said drily. "And how long must I wait for this expert before we can pack it up here and move on to my next site?"

"There was a pause. Then Sharma said in a puzzled tone, "Actually, Doctor, I had rather assumed you'd want to remain at the site—see what further excavation might turn up."

"No, I'm fairly resolved that there is nothing more to find here. I don't care to have this anomaly, however intriguing, holding up my original schedule."

Peter was shocked at the man's willingness to leave the site of such a pivotal discovery. There could be only one reason.

"Doctor, are you concerned about the artifact's authenticity? We've got quite a sizable team preparing to research this. Is there something I should know?"

"Heavens no, of course not! I mean . . . perhaps we should await your expert's output and then discuss it further afterwards—sound good?"

"Right," Peter replied. "Your guest and his escort will be arriving at Nairobi Airport tomorrow morning. A chopper has been arranged from there to you."

Peter didn't like the sudden backtracking. Perhaps Rheese had staged this whole thing and was now afraid its high profile would blow up in his face. He was now more anxious than ever to hear what Matt might soon discover. Little did Rheese know, if the object was a hoax, the "expert" would know it instantly—and exactly who was involved.

He leaned back in his chair and pinched his smooth, dimpled chin. "Maggie," he said, "I'm going to Kenya."

"Very well—shall I inform Doctor Rheese?"

"Absolutely not."

NINE

Matt pulled the crumpled sheet from his duffel bag and laid it over the leather seat in the Gulfstream jet's passenger cabin, tucking it into the creases and around the armrests. Tuni watched with interest from the adjacent seat. When he was done, he stood up, handed his bag to the pleasant flight attendant, and looked at the seat with satisfaction. He glanced at Tuni and caught her watching.

"Sorry, this probably looks obsessive and freakish—which it no doubt is—but I never get to do this on commercial flights, and it's really sort of a necessity for me if I want to sleep on the plane."

Tuni just smiled curtly and returned to her magazine as the pilot popped his head out of the cockpit to address them.

"You two ready to go? We're all set when you are."

Matt sat down, then remembered the seat belt.

"Shoot," he said. "Do I still have to wear my seat belt?"

The pilot smiled earnestly. "Just during takeoff and landing, sir. I'll let you know as soon as we're at altitude; then you can do whatever you like. Sound good?"

"Perfect—thanks."

Matt pulled his shirt down low and clasped the seat belt over it, then looked all around the cabin, feeling a little tingle of excitement. He saw the flight attendant take her seat at the rear and flash him a nice smile.

The pilot leaned over from his seat in the cockpit and said, "We're going to have to close this door during takeoff, but we'll open it right back up."

"Hey, just one question, sir," Matt interrupted before the door closed. "How much does one of these babies cost?"

"You could step into a nice pre-owned for four-to-five mil."

Matt frowned and shook his head. "New."

"This particular model, a G450, would run you about thirty-five. But there are plenty of smaller models just as nice, just shorter range."

"Hmm . . . thanks." The door closed. He would have to wait a year or two.

He made a mental note to ask the pilot his name before leaving. He would get a gift basket, as well. And perhaps a job offer in a few years.

"Was that for my benefit, Matthew?"

"Huh? Oh, no, not at all. I . . . I should probably tell you something."

"No need, dear. I already know of your extraordinary wealth." She said it with a straight face, but there was something in the way she said *extraordinary.*

"Oh, really? What do you know? What did Meier tell you?"

"Jon didn't tell me anything. Most everyone at the museum knows of your sunken treasure."

"And how I found it?" Matt said casually, fishing.

"No . . . I don't think anyone knows about that."

"You included?"

"Me included, though I hadn't gleaned that there was any big secret, Mr. Mysterious."

"Hm- well, that isn't what I was going to say, anyway. About the money. There's something else. But I need to think about it."

Tuni smiled indifferently, but Matt could tell she was intrigued and trying to hide it.

Do I bring her in? Matt wondered. She seemed trustworthy enough, but that would make how many now? Matt went down the list in his head. Dad, Mom, Aunt Denora, Iris, his ex- Melissa, Uncle J, Dr. Meier, George Miller, Pete Sharma. That was nine. She would make ten. And did she *need* to know? Dad always drilled it into his head: "Keep it tight, boy. If it's not someone that loves you, consider them a threat." Dad had not at all liked Uncle J's suggestion about the museum, but by that time it was out of his hands and Matt had stopped talking to him, or more applicably . . . listening.

Matt wondered about these people in Africa, the ones with the metal arti-fact. Would he have to reveal himself to them as well? He hadn't thought this through nearly enough, and he had to push out his dad's disappointed "I told you" from his head. He peered over at Tuni, flipping through a food magazine. His instincts told him she should know, but he wasn't sure if they were clouded by his other thoughts about her. Was he just trying to *qualify* her? That's what he was doing with Melissa when he first became interested in her. And now she was out there, no longer a part of his life, fully aware of his secret. He couldn't take it back. But wasn't this differ-ent?

It was, or so he convinced himself.

He leaned over and glanced to the back of the cabin. The flight attendant was seated in a little fold-down, reading a thick paperback.

"Tuni," he said quietly.

She looked up with a coy smirk as she returned, "Yes, Matthew?" in the same hushed tone.

"I'm going to tell you something that's difficult to believe."

She turned serious, nodding sharply.

"Very few people know, and you need to make the biggest promise of your life to keep it to yourself . . . forever."

"Yes, er . . . of course. What is it?"

"The sheet here, on the seat? The whole getup, the gloves . . . I'm not a germaphobe. I have an ability called *psychometry*. It allows me to read emotional imprints that people leave on objects."

Tuni's head cocked sideways and her expression shifted to a frown. Whatever she had imagined he was going to tell her, it had clearly caught her off-guard. She made an undecided "mm-hmm . . . " for him to go on.

"I told you it's difficult to believe. But it's how I tracked that sunken wreck. It's what I did for Dr. Meier at the museum. Dating artifacts, verifying historical records, stuff like that. Thing is . . . " he gestured at his beanie and turtleneck's collar. "I can't turn it off. And, as far as I know, it's *on*, I guess, everywhere on my skin."

Another "mm-hmm" and he could see her wheels turning. He guessed she was thinking back to conversations she had overheard, putting pieces together.

"Do you believe me?"

"I . . . I suppose so . . . so, wait. Does Peter Sharma know about it? Is that why he requested you?"

"Yup. He worked with me the most on the *special projects*, as Meier liked to say."

"Does Hank Felch know?"

"He shouldn't," Matt said, almost accusingly. "I definitely didn't authorize anyone else. Only George and Meier, plus my family—and not even my *whole* family!"

Tuni looked to the floor, processing. Matt waited, studying her expressions. He had only had this conversation twice before, and one was George, so it didn't seem as big a deal.

She looked back up at him, seemingly with new eyes, taking in his whole body.

"So how does it work? You touch something with your bare skin, and you get flashes of emotions, pictures, what? I think I saw a movie like that once."

"No, it's not so cinematic," Matt smiled. "There's a brief transition and then I'm essentially *in* the person who touched the object. Every sense is present: vision, hearing, all that. And their thoughts. It could be two thousand years ago and everything is perfectly crisp. The weird part is not being able to control anything; I'm just along for the ride. Also weird when the body is very different from mine."

"Hmm . . . yes, I could imagine suddenly being some obese chap . . . "

"Well, yeah, I guess, but I meant being a woman, or really old or young."

Tuni smiled and nodded, a little embarrassed. She shook it off and sighed as her eyes flashed around before her. He suddenly felt vicariously excited, imagining the questions swimming through her head. She didn't appear to doubt him at all, but how could she be one hundred percent—just like that? He couldn't expect that from anyone. Her eyes returned to his.

"So to make it work . . . you don't have to concentrate, or say some sort of incantation, or what have you?"

"Nope. It just goes, like it or not."

"Hm. Amazing, truly. Makes me wonder what else people are capable of. Are there others? Like you, I mean?"

"Not that I've met. I pretty much know of psychic type stuff the same as you. Those people that say they can communicate with the dead or predict the future? Strangely enough, I'm probably just as skeptical about them as the next guy. It's kind of funny, actually, when I catch myself doing it. Some guy on TV calling out a woman in a studio audience and telling her about her dead father. I think 'no way, that's fake! People can't do that!' But hell, who knows, maybe they've got what I've got."

"That's funny. Hypocrite." She flipped to the next page of her magazine though she hadn't yet looked at it.

"Yeah, I know. Anyway, I needed you to know about me 'cause where we're going, with strangers and everything—I'm pretty paranoid about my ability getting out. I'm not trying to get a TV show, if you know what I mean. I need you to run defense for me. When I'm reading this artifact no one else can be around, however you can arrange that."

"Of course," she said. "I think that's why Jon sent me along with you. He probably knew there would be logistical issues around that. Now that I think back, he did say that he hoped you would tell me something that he couldn't. That it would make my job easier."

"Mmm—figures," *Sneaky bastard. He knew I'd tell her.*

The cockpit door finally popped open, and the pilot leaned back and gave Matt a nod. He removed his seat belt and got comfortable.

"Well, enough about me . . . " Matt began.

"Ah, the old 'enough about me . . .'" She interrupted, but then saw Matt recoil. "It's fine, I'm joking. Go ahead, enough about you."

"Nah, never mind. I'm actually going to try to get some sleep. It was good to talk to you. I feel better about everything now."

He acted normal, but she could tell he was bruised. He reclined his seat, checked the barrier sheet was still secure, and positioned himself toward the window. She felt like a prat, but decided to let him sleep, returning to her magazine. She found her eyes gliding over the words on the page without actually absorbing anything. Could Matthew's claim really be true? Obviously, Jon and Peter believed him, but they were big dreamers, and perhaps necessarily gullible. Matthew's delivery was very convincing though, very matter-of-fact, and clearly apprehensive. Then again, he could be a con artist with a whole act down. *A con artist that can trace a sunken ship?* She rested her head back and closed her eyes, debating both sides.

Tuni awoke several hours later. She drank a sip of her water and took some peppermint gum from her handbag, then looked over at Matthew. He was now facing her, still asleep. She liked that his skin was as pale as a Londoner's, and unblemished. She could tell he had been trying to grow a beard of sorts, probably for the past few weeks. His dirty-blond locks were tousled, though she had a feeling he wouldn't especially care. This was a man with bigger things on his mind than his hairdo.

"Can I get you anything, ma'am?" asked the flight attendant.

Tuni was surprised to feel a little awkward at having just been caught looking as if she were admiring him.

"No, thank you, not right now. Will there be food at some point?"

Michael Siemsen

"Of course, whenever you like."

Right, of course. It wasn't as if there were a schedule and two hundred people to serve. "Very well. I'll wait until Matthew wakes up, and eat with him."

The flight attendant smiled and raised her eyebrows at Tuni before walking away. Tuni felt a vague ruffle of annoyance at the thought that the woman assumed she was smitten with her dozing charge.

Tuni wondered how her cat, Mr. Pups, was getting on without her. She had given her neighbor the key and asked him to feed him and change his litter box. Randall had two kitties of his own, and she trusted him with Pups. Who knew what else he was doing in her apartment, though. Hopefully not going through her skivvies drawer! *Ugh, a wispy little bachelor like him . . .* She wouldn't be surprised. She would have to remember to launder everything on her return.

She did not look forward to her return to Africa. Her last time there, she was a gangly eight-year-old, living with her mum—Dad was out of the picture long before. Their house was no shack, but the menu did often come down to beans and cornmeal *sadza* when times were tough.

Fortunately, after they had moved in with her aunt's family in London, things got much better. In her memory, if not that of others, her awkward phase turned out to be an awkward decade. And standing several centimeters above her classmates, it was impossible to blend into the background. The downfall of many a lanky girl, she used the "hunch" technique to fit in. Mum loved to pull out the old photo albums. "Just look at you *now* . . ." she would say. But Tuni knew what she was really saying: "Good God, look at you *then!*" Blossoming in her late teens seemed to have a lasting effect on her self-esteem. Even now at 31, when a man or group of men gave her the old *reow, hey baby . . .* routine, her first thought was—*If only you knew what I really looked like.*

"Hey, they gonna feed us at some point?" Matt was awake. She offered him a piece of gum. "No, I'm good," he declined.

"Really?" she replied with raised eyebrows.

He frowned and then realized why she had offered. "Oh, sorry—the breath of doom after sleeping, huh? I'll take one."

She smiled, close-lipped.

"They'll feed us anytime we like. I take it you're hungry?"

"Yeah, aren't you?"

"Oh, sure," she said breezily, as if it hadn't really occurred to her. Her belly gave a quiet moan, and she shifted to silence it.

A short time later, the attendant rolled their food to them on two little carts with locking wheels. It was chateaubriand—lovely, nothing at all like airline food.

The pilot poked his head out to say they'd be descending soon.

"Oh, are we there already?" Matt asked, pulling up his sleeve to look at his watch.

"We stop briefly in Accra for fuel and shots and then cross Africa to Nairobi, with no further stops. How is your meal?"

"It's great," Matt replied. "What shots?"

"Oh, the usual immunizations: malaria, hep. B, and so on. You apparently didn't have time back in the States."

Matt felt the icy fingers of panic. He could not do shots. He took a deep, shaky breath and tried to hold back the tears already pooling in his lower lids.

"Hey, you okay?" Tuni reached across and touched his shoulder.

He turned his head so she couldn't see him.

"I'm just not big on shots, is all. Nobody said anything about that. Of *course* your boss wasn't going to bring it up."

"I don't think Jon would have thought to mention it, Matthew. He wasn't trying to hide anything from you. Will the shot . . . uh, can it *affect* you?"

"In quite a few ways, actually." He rubbed his eyes as if they were just sore, then turned to her. "Think about this: up until very recently, most syringes would be cleaned and reused thousands of times. That's just changed in our country so you can imagine what a place like—well, I'm just saying. I mean, you're getting a shot and just think about how many kids have gotten shots with that needle and were terrified and physically hurt by it. Think about a nurse who's been doing this for years, and the irritation she feels every time another damn screaming kid sits down in the pokey chair. All these emotions stick to an object like that. It's gotta be in my top ten worst things to experience, no matter how fast it happens."

"I understand. That makes perfect sense. When was the last time you got a shot?"

"Oh, just a couple months ago. It was no big—my doctor only uses disposables. My dentist still does it old school with everyone else, but he knows I only do disposables."

Tuni looked at him with genuine empathy. *That is genuine bloody emotion, pure and raw. He's the real thing. It definitely hadn't been all roses for him, growing up.* "Can I ask you a personal question? Or . . . well, it can wait . . ." she asked, caressing his shoulder from across the aisle.

"Pssh—fire away. Believe it or not, I'm actually pretty desensitized to things. It probably doesn't seem like it right now, but it's really just the emotions that are forced on me that I worry about."

"Very well. Um, so were you born with your, um, talent? That is, did your parents see you spazzing as a baby when you were, say, wrapped in Grandmama's blankie?"

"Actually, I would *spaz* out if I had to call someone 'Grandmama.'" He chuckled. "Sorry, no. It didn't actually start until I was about eight years old. At least, that's the earliest I can recall. At the time it seemed more like I was blacking out, and when I woke up I'd remember these vivid dreams about being other people. I took quite a few spills growing up. 'Write your name on the paper, Matt'—wait, that's not my pencil, *thunk*. Hold the door open for your mom, *thunk*. I got pretty banged up."

Tuni had taken off her heels. She turned toward him.

"How did your parents react to all of it? I presume they thought it was some sort of narcolepsy."

"Exactly. Doctors tried out all sorts of pills on me. I was already a little hyper, and on the pills I was like an electron, shooting around the house—and, of course, touching everything."

"So when did you put the pieces together and realize the physical contact thing?"

"Well, I had to stay at my cousin's house for a week this one summer. And I slept in the top of his bunk bed. The weird thing about sleeping in a strange bed or with someone else's blanket was that I'd be stuck, basically dreaming all this weird stuff that was always through the eyes of someone else, with all their thoughts and emotions, you know? Super surreal. Well, no one could wake me up. Eventually, my mom and dad were called and one of them pulled me out of the bed, breaking the contact, and I came out of it, groggy, looking like I woke up from a normal sleep. That happened more than a few times. My parents always said how I was the type that would fall asleep as soon as I hit the pillow. As it turned out, it depended a lot on the pillow."

Tuni nodded sympathetically but said nothing more than "Hmm . . ."

"So the day I sort of figured it out, I was in the garage with my dad, helping him mount this bike hanger thingy. I was holding his hammer and screwdriver for him, as I had a bunch of times before, and he would ask me for one or the other of them as needed. So he's up on the ladder and asks me for the hammer and a nail. I give them to him, he smashes the hell out of his thumb trying to drive a nail in, drops the hammer, swears all up and down the garage for a minute, and then it's back to work. A minute later, 'Get me the hammer, Matty.' I pick it up and, wham-o, there I am asking myself for the hammer, smash my thumb (pain and all), and storm up and down the garage cussing a blue streak. All along, I'm seeing myself looking up at myself, all concerned. I wake up, Dad is over me, checking my head for injuries—the usual drill with my 'blackouts'—and I looked at the hammer and understood. He had left a piece of himself in it."

Eyes wide, Tuni nodded. Matt was about to continue when the pilot cheerily declared they were starting their descent into Accra, Ghana.

"So did you tell him?" Tuni asked.

"Oh, yeah," Matt answered gravely as he looked away and peered out the window.

"He didn't believe you?"

"Oh, no, he believed me right away. It kind of made it all fall into place. But that's when everything else started. 'How about this, Matt? Does this one have any memories? What about this? Hey, I don't want you in my room anymore.' Then I became his new project."

"Sort of like a new power tool, huh?"

"Yeah, I guess you could say that."

"What does he do for a living?"

"He was a homicide detective. Retired now."

"No!" She replied with shock. "Would he . . . bring stuff . . . criminal evidence . . . home to you?"

"Yeah, but I'd just as soon not go into it. Let's just say that for something that was wrong to begin with, he went *way* too far, especially toward the end."

Matt looked out the window and saw the lights of a good-sized city, ending abruptly along one edge where it met the sea. They were nearing the ground. The landing was smooth, but as they taxied to the gate, Matt began to worry about the shots again. Tuni picked up on it at once.

"Don't worry, Matthew. We'll make sure they're disposable."

After a short walk from the tarmac, they entered the air-conditioned terminal through automatic sliding doors. Matt had expected a third world airport with chickens and goats and naked, screaming children running around, but now he felt a little guilty about his assumption. Everyone was dressed, no farm animals in sight, and from what he could hear on the way to customs, they all spoke English!

"Inoculations, please," said a woman in uniform at the first counter they reached.

"Yes, I guess that's what we're here for," Matt replied, checking with Tuni, who nodded.

"You have no doctor papers?" the woman asked.

"No, we thought we were coming here to get the shots—and, I guess, papers."

"Very well, please step over there. Next time, you get your shots before you come to Ghana, okay?"

"Absolutely," he replied, as if he planned to visit often. She had directed them to a door with an opaque white window centered with a red cross.

They waited in line for about twenty minutes before their turn.

Tuni whispered in his ear, "What about the chair, if they make you sit?"

"It's fine, I'm covered. Thanks."

Looking around the large room, Tuni wondered what else might be hiding these stories that only Matthew could see. "What about a metal table like that?"

"Doesn't matter what it's made out of. Just can't be a living thing. I'll give you all the 'rules', I guess, later. My father keeps this book about it. All sorts of weird details no one would ever think about."

"You have a manual. That's funny."

They reached the front of the line and Tuni held him back, clearly meaning to go first. He didn't protest. She sat down in the chair and laid her arm on the cold stainless steel table. A large woman in the standard starched white button-down shirt sat on a rolling stool beside the chair.

Tuni tried to see the area through Matthew's eyes. One good thing: the woman wore latex gloves, though some of the fingertips bore yellow stains—they had probably seen a few patients. Another white-shirted woman slid a terry cloth towel to the nurse; on it laid five identical plastic syringes. Tuni looked around the nurse's bulk to see the other woman tearing open more of the same syringes from protective packages and laying them on another white towel.

"Are these syringes reused?" she asked as the woman cleaned her arm with an iodine pad.

"No, missy," she replied with a bit of attitude and little accent. "That is not sanitary. There is an HIV epidemic in Africa, don't you know?"

"Of course. I don't mean to be a bother, but would you mind changing your gloves?"

The nurse lowered her chin and looked at Tuni through her eyebrows. "Gloves are changed every tenth patient—sooner if contaminated. Good enough for you?"

Tuni peered over her shoulder at Matt, who was watching intently from behind the privacy barrier.

"And what number am I?"

"Okay, fussy one. I will change gloves for your pretty arm." She snapped the old gloves off, dropped them in the trash, and slid on a new pair from a package on the table. As the shots proceeded, Tuni looked back at Matt and pointed at the table. He nodded in reply, pulling a pile of napkins out of his pocket to show her. They were the drink coasters from the plane. Tuni suddenly realized that he was probably accustomed to preparing for the unexpected. When she was done, she stood and waited a few feet away as Matt took the seat.

"Do you mind if I put these napkins under my elbow?" He asked the nurse. "I have severe skin allergies."

The nurse looked at him sweetly. "No problem, love. Are you allergic to iodine or alcohol?"

"Nope."

"Any other medications?" She began to clean the injection areas.

"Just penicillin."

"Then we are all good, dear."

The shots had no "complications," and after paperwork and payment, Tuni and Matt were on their way back to the Gulfstream. As they stepped back onto the tarmac, Matt stopped Tuni and turned her to look at her face.

"Thank you. Seriously."

"It is no problem, Matthew," she replied matter-of-factly. "I will take care of you."

She resumed walking to the plane as Matt took a deep breath. He liked this one.

He reboarded the jet, and they were off to Nairobi.

Matt watched a movie on his iPad to kill time. Tuni watched with little interest for the first half hour but had trouble staying with it—she kept mulling over how Matt's father had exploited his son's ability. She couldn't ask, of course, but hoped Matt would volunteer it when he felt comfortable. Her eyes closed, and she listened to Matt softly laughing.

TEN

Dr. Rheese had requested only a quarter of the crew for the site cleanup. Enzi had driven ten men back from the base camp, including Kanu, who would likely need to be interviewed by the arriving expert. Rheese wanted the entire southern half of the pit refilled and the jagged walls smoothed on all sides. Enzi hadn't asked about it—he understood the motivation. It was also why the jackhammers were to be returned to the base camp, and the precision tools—trowels, brushes, screens, and dental picks—brought to the site. Rheese wanted to legitimize the dig.

Enzi was operating one of the backhoes, pushing dirt from the dump pile back into the hole with the front bucket. He had a few men disassembling the lift and winch by the equipment trailer while the rest worked in the pit, dressing the walls with mud and chipping away at jagged ends. Enzi could see that no one wanted to work near the elephant carcass, still present three days after the visit from the officials. He had phoned the office several times and always received the same reply: "Your incident is next in line behind a cleanup near Narok." To which Enzi replied each time: "We *are* the cleanup near Narok!" The call would end after the dissatisfying assertion: "Then the crew should be there shortly."

It seemed that insects and birds from miles around had hit the motherlode, and the stench had reached an unbearable point. The only relief came when it rained, though, of course, this wreaked havoc on the elephant's remains.

As Enzi reversed the backhoe up the new mud slope he had created in the pit, Rheese stuck his bald head out of the motor home and waved him inside. Enzi whistled for another man to take his place on the backhoe and walked up to the RV.

"Our visitor is arriving in forty-five minutes," said Rheese. He apparently just boarded a chopper in Nairobi. I haven't the foggiest where they plan to land. Are there any clearings between here and base camp?"

Enzi frowned and sucked his lower lip. An idea struck him, and he looked around the site.

"We move your motor home to the road there and they have space to land. We done with the backhoe here and park back by the equipment trailer."

"Good idea," Rheese acknowledged. "I'll need to clean up a bit more inside so nothing comes crashing down when we move. How much longer over there?"

"We pretty much done, Professor."

"What about the rotting animal?"

"I call again, but they say same bull to me. They on the way, of course."

Rheese swore softly and shook his head. "I'd just as soon bury the thing if they aren't going to show. Hell, fifteen meters under? I challenge any gravedigger to make a more appropriate resting place for such a behemoth."

Enzi nodded. "Perhaps in a thousand years, people come dig here, find bones and think it millions of years old."

Rheese chuckled. Enzi hadn't been known for his sense of humor thus far. Rheese leaned forward in his chair, resting his elbows on his knees, and looked up into Enzi's eyes. Enzi's smile disappeared as he realized at that moment just how rarely the professor made eye contact with him.

"Enzi," Rheese said softly.

"Yes, Professor?"

"What are we looking for in this site?"

Enzi's brow crinkled in bewilderment. "We look for dinosaur bones and other fossils."

"Yes, yes, but what are we *really* looking for?"

Was this a trap, a test?

"That is all we look for, Professor. What else to find out in jungle?"

"Good bloody answer, Enzi. Don't you forget that."

"No, sah. That is all."

"Bloody right it is. Don't think for a second that I would choose your existence over my objectives. It would take very little money for you to simply vanish—much easier than burying an elephant."

Enzi lowered his head level with Rheese's gaze. His jaw clenched, and his eyelids dropped to half-moons. "That not necessary to say, Professor," he replied with a subtle growl, containing his rage.

Rheese leaned back and smiled, looking off in the distance once again. "Of course not, my friend! We're all in this together, are we not?" He chuckled heartily and clasped his hands behind his head.

Enzi stood there for a moment, glaring at him. He had judged the *mkundu* aright in the beginning. The man had a steel trap of greed in place of a heart. Enzi fantasized about what he could do to the professor with the shovel leaning against the equipment trailer behind him.

"Well, don't just stand there, lad," said Rheese cheerily. "Back to work, then!"

Enzi cleared the images from his head and returned to the men.

Rheese wondered, had he taken it a notch too far? It was important to keep Enzi on his toes. What if he was asked a question that caught him off guard and his natural honesty took the upper hand? There was something in his foreman that Rheese admired: whatever that was that had made him go straight to the broken elephant and lay it to rest. But then, that same impulse might one day turn into a liability, and he suspected that Enzi did not know there was a time and place for doing the right thing.

His teapot whistled him back into the motor home for elevenses. He might have waited for the museum's expert to join him for cakes and tea, but it would likely be some pencil-necked thirty-something, interested only in getting the artifact into his hot little uncallused hands.

Tuni's forehead pressed against the window as she watched the land below them change from tree-dotted savanna to forested hill country. The plastic earmuffs did little more than mute the whine of the turbine engine and the beat of the rotor to a bearable level. She glanced over at Matt, who sat upright in the seat, clearly uncomfortable, with his gloved fingers in his ears. He turned to her when he realized she was looking at him.

"No one said anything about a helicopter, either," he mouthed. She shrugged and spoke an inaudible "Sorry! Fastest way!"

Thirty minutes later, one of their Kenyan pilots pointed ahead, and the other began pressing buttons and flipping switches. In a moment, the helicopter turned and circled a clearing in the woods. Matt and Tuni looked out his window to see a clearing in the middle of the jungle. The majority of the space was taken up by a large pit with a ramp leading up one side from the middle of the floor. The pilots discussed something as the chopper hovered over a flat spot marked only by a pair of muddy tire tracks.

The helicopter descended, rotating slowly. Matt could see some men closing the back of a white trailer while others stood at the walls of the pit, shielding their eyes as they gazed upward.

"Is that a dead elephant?" Matt asked.

Tuni's face twisted and she leaned over to his side and craned her neck to look down through his window.

"Good God! I think it bloody well is!"

Matt got another good whiff of her perfume before she settled back into her seat.

One skid and then the other touched down, and the pilots began flicking more switches before one of them removed his headset and exited through his hatch. He came around and slid open the door on Matt's side. Tuni removed her earmuffs, unfastened her harness, and reached behind the seats to fetch their bags.

As he swung his backpack over his shoulder and climbed down onto the footstep, Matt spotted an older white man in khakis and a pith helmet. The man was walking toward them and waving.

Tuni's lips hovered at Matt's ear. "That must be Dr. Rheese," she said. "Go greet him and I'll grab your other bag."

Matt complied and walked, hunched over, away from the chopper. With the distance between them closing, he saw the man's smile freeze as he gazed past Matt, then back at his face.

"Hi, Matthew Turner," Matt yelled over the helicopter noise. "You must be Dr. Rheese."

Rheese shook the gloved hand halfheartedly.

"Is one of you the potassium-argon expert?"

Matt replied with an extended "Uh-h . . ." as Tuni and a pilot arrived at his side with the suitcase and duffel bag.

"Dr. Rheese, I am Tuni St. James, with the New York Metropolitan Museum."

He shook her hand, appearing no more pleased to make her acquaintance than Matt's.

"A pleasure. Which one of you is the expert I've awaited all this time?" The helicopter grew louder as it lifted off and flew away.

Tuni deadpanned and made a theatric gesture toward Matt.

"You must be bloody joking," he muttered, and walked away.

Tuni and Matt looked at each other doubtfully, as a Kenyan man approached them from out of the big ditch and greeted them warmly.

"Hello, hello, friends. I am Enzi Wata, the site foreman. Welcome to Narok . . . sort of." He gave a slight bow and held out his hand to Tuni.

She shook it, and he dipped his head a little deeper in respect.

"I'm Tuni, and this is the expert you have been waiting for, Matthew Turner."

"Thank you for coming, Mr. Turner," he said, pumping the younger man's hand while subtly wondering about the gloves and watch cap on such a warm tropical day.

"Thanks," Matt replied. "So can you take us to the artifact?"

Enzi peered past Matt's shoulder to the motor home and listened for a moment to Dr. Rheese, shouting at someone on the satellite phone.

"Perhaps you like to rest for a bit? We have fresh water and chips at the food tent, if you like—"

Matt interrupted. "Look, I don't really need a snack. I was actually hoping to get to examine this thing and have the helicopter back before dark."

Tuni touched his arm as if to say, "Easy . . ."

"You will not be sleeping the night?" Enzi asked, confused.

"Well, we *can,* sure, but the sooner we get this done, the better."

Obviously relieved, Enzi said, "Good, because helicopter not return today."

"What?"

"They do not fly here at night."

"So, Mr. Wata . . . ," Tuni interjected before Matt could speak.

"Enzi, please, Miss."

"Enzi," she said, "I think I *would* like to sit down and have a small snack. Matthew, would you like to join me?"

"Sure."

In his RV, Rheese hung up on the "cheeky little tart" at the other end— Maggie something. Why she wouldn't tell him where Sharma had gotten to, he couldn't say. Clearly, those folks at the museum were not really interested in determining the fabric's age. He sat down at the breakfast table and sighed. He had wasted how much time cleaning the little swatch so that a respectable scientist could take a look at it?

Perhaps if he simply humored the young man and that towering amazon of a woman, they'd leave quickly and he could move to the next site on his map. Bingo! That was it: he would apologize for his earlier behavior and welcome them wholeheartedly into his mobile laboratory. That was the ticket—get it done and get them gone. He stopped at the sink on his way out and splashed water on his face.

"So," Matt said to Enzi, "did you know you have a dead elephant in that hole over there?"

"Here he comes," Tuni warned.

Enzi stood, and Matt turned around. Dr. Rheese had put on his best smile and was shaking his head foolishly as if to say, "I'm just a silly old man!" as he walked to the food tent.

"Apologies, apologies, my fellow slaves to science . . . er, no offense." He directed this last to Tuni, who blinked as if she had received a slap. Her eyes met Enzi's, which, by their expression, again appeared to be apologizing for the doctor. "I'm terrible with names—what were they again?"

"I'm Matt Turner, and this is Tuni."

"Of course, Matt and Tuni. Very well, if you'd like to gather your equipment, we can adjourn to our research vehicle and get down to matters of consequence."

Matt grabbed his duffel and followed Rheese to the motor home, where he held the door open for Tuni. On entering, they both looked around the interior.

"If you need to use the loo, it's right there—no need to join the workers in the bushes."

"Lovely," Tuni said drily.

Opening a cabinet, Rheese pulled out a transparent case the size of a shoe box and placed it on the breakfast table. Inside it, several cobble-size rocks sat atop a mix of gravel and dirt. Matt slid onto one of the bench seats and shoved his duffel to the corner, where he opened it and dug for his armband timer. Rheese donned latex gloves, took the largest chunk from the box, and placed it on a white tray in front of Matt. Matt frowned at it and peered into the box and then at Tuni and Rheese.

"Where is your equipment?" asked Dr. Rheese, trying to see into the dark recesses of the duffel.

"Where is the object?" Matt returned.

"This is the sediment in which the object was embedded." Rheese tried to remain pleasant but felt his face beginning to heat. "There, see the pattern, son?"

Matt turned the rock over in his hands and could indeed see the imprint.

"Right," interjected Tuni. "Mr. Turner will be requiring the artifact itself."

"No offense . . . ," Rheese began.

"Of course not," Tuni murmured under her breath.

". . .but the bloody artifact has not a trace of relevant radioactivity. You'll need to measure from this sample here."

"Understood," Matt said as, for perhaps the first time ever, he found himself wishing Dr. Meier were present. "The museum has contracted me to determine the actual age of the artifact itself, not the surrounding rocks. It's my understanding that the museum is already satisfied with those results."

"Well, if you don't mind my asking, how do you plan to determine said age of *my* find, young man?"

Seeing that Matt was about to become unruly, Tuni recalled Meier's instructions. She opened her leather organizer and quickly scanned her notes.

"Dr. Rheese, if I may, Dr. Meier and Peter Sharma have used Matthew's expertise on many high-profile investigations, including A-L two-eighty-eight-dash-one. If you could simply humor us for a few minutes, I think we could make some good progress."

"Lucy, huh?" he replied with apparent interest. "And what did *you* find out about little old Lucy?"

Matt tried to remember the estimation they had given, now that Tuni had put him on the spot. He knew that it was around three to four million years, so he decided to be creative.

"The sample I examined was three-point-seven-two-two million years old."

"Impressive. How could it possibly be so precise? What technology are you using?"

Tuni spoke again, "It's rather difficult to explain, Dr. Rheese. Perhaps if he could simply examine the artifact for a moment?"

Rheese snorted, sighed, and gave a little huff, as if pulling the key from his trouser pocket required considerable exertion, then knelt to open the safe at Matt's feet. *Just get it over with, Garrett,* he said to himself. He took out the container and stood back up, his knees cracking audibly. Tuni and Matt held their breath in anticipation as it appeared. Placing the container on the end of the table, Rheese unscrewed the four screws holding the two plastic sides together, then slid the bottom sheet of plastic in front of Matt. There sat the artifact, fully exposed.

Matt stared at it as Tuni slid onto the bench across from him and looked from Matt's face to the fabric and back again.

Matt thought it looked smaller than in the picture, but somehow much more *real*. Now that it was in front of him, for the first time he actually started to worry about what he might experience. There very well might be nothing— after all, he had never been able to read anything but imprints from other humans, and apparently there weren't any around back when this came into existence. He looked closely at the uneven edges and figured it must have been damaged in some violent act. That would be an imprint right there—if it was the act of a person. He moved it around with his forefinger, marveling at its flexibility. It wasn't quite as fine as window screen; the metal threads were a bit thicker, and woven in such a way that it all moved quite freely.

Rheese cleared his throat. "Is this how you determine your precise dates? Staring and prodding?"

Matt took a deep breath and turned to the professor. "I'm sure you'll find this a little suspect, Doctor," he began. "But I'm going to have to ask you to step outside for about ten minutes."

"Certainly," Rheese replied nonchalantly. "When the hair on my head reappears."

Matt looked at Tuni in a silent plea for help.

"Professor," she said, "perhaps if I could speak with you outside and explain the situation."

"Right. Your request sounds ever so different from his. I will not be leaving either of you alone with my artifact. You will begin your examination now, in front of my eyes, or it will be returning to my safe."

Matt sighed. He didn't trust the professor, and he had made no plans to bring someone new into the circle, let alone someone as sketchy as *this* character. But it didn't appear that he would be getting any private time with the object, and he was still intent on leaving as soon as possible. Matt decided to be mysterious about it—let the man be unconvinced. He didn't need or want him to believe in his ability.

"Fine, Dr. Rheese, I'll proceed. This is a little-known method that few can comprehend. I'm going to have to insist that you not interfere, regardless of what you think. Is that agreeable?"

Rheese nodded. "As long as nothing happens to give me cause to fear for the safety of the artifact. What exactly do you plan to do?"

Matt ignored the question, knowing it would only lead to more, perhaps even resulting in the object's removal to the safe before he could read it. He pulled a clean piece of paper from a notebook in his duffel, slid the fabric onto the paper, and pushed the square plastic piece away from him. Then, taking off the gloves, he gave Tuni a look.

"Just like with the shots, okay?"

She nodded her understanding.

Rheese crossed his arms and, with an impatient sigh, leaned back against a cabinet. Tuni shimmied her bottom closer to the edge of the seat. Her eyes opened wider.

Matt stretched his hands out over the woven metal fabric and pressed them firmly against it.

ELEVEN

Darkness...
    Going . . .
Breathing . . .
We?
Other breathing . . .
Scritching . . .
We walk.
We carry.
Death carry? Death walk?
Feel danger. I feel danger.
I am man. I am wet. It is sweat. Sweat means danger. Need clean.

I see now. I see movement in front of me, and it is nighttime. This is so odd. Who am I? I am a man, and sweat is pouring down my back. Why am I worried about my sweat? They smell it, that's it. He's counting. Yes, I'm counting numbers in my head. Strange numbers. Single plus single plus single plus single plus single plus single plus single plus single, *batch,* single plus single plus . . . *it goes on. It's sets of eight.* Full batch and stop. *Full batch is sixty-four. Sixty-four steps from peak.*

We've stopped. We put him down. Scritching in ears. *Who is him?* Oh, I miss him. There are others around me. I see their hands and arms. We've put down Inni. That's his name. He is naked and dead. I see his skin; it is black. I feel more heat beside me. I hear more now. Bubbling. It sounds like boiling water. I am afraid to put him in. *Faces!* We all make a circle around him and look at each other's eyes. *Those eyes, so huge! Human-like, but so big and very widely set. And the faces, so similar! They look almost like cartoons with those features so exaggerated. Circles of face are exposed, but a headdress surrounds them. It is the scritching sound in his ears. He's wearing a metal fabric headdress. It's called a* top. *The* middle *is the jacket,* lower *is pants, and* bottom *is foot covering. All must wear their* k'yot *when outside at this time. There, that's the whole outfit:* k'yot. *It means protection. Protection from what?*

We push him to melt. *Melt?* Pain! Face burning. There's steam shooting from a crack in the ground. Droplets spray out and burn my face. We think *ylt pwino, ylt pwino.* We think *good-bye, dear friend.* The naked body falls in, and we move away quickly. Back to safe. Full batch steps to peak. Full batch single plus single plus single to safe. To safety.

We walk in a straight line. I know that Pwig walks in front of me. I know that Norrit walks behind me.

Back to structure, Matt. Solidify yourself.

I am Irin. I am old.

What is that, "old"?

My father is *oldest*; I am *old*. When a baby comes, it is *newest*, later it is *new*. I am old; Father is oldest.

I am Irin. I am old. I came new in my house.

Okay, Matt, the usual drill doesn't work here. When is this? Where is this? This is some kind of African tribe wearing the metal fabric all over their bodies, and that was a sort of death ceremony. Now we're walking, and Irin won't stop thinking "single plus single plus single . . . batch!" He has no concept of when. No, wait, he does! The moon. Single plus batch plus batch plus batch plus full batch plus gross batch plus single plus single past. *Past what? How the hell am I going to figure out these stupid numbers?*

Okay, we've reached the peak, and the single pluses continue.

He wipes the sweat from my eyes. They were stinging. Wait—what the hell was that?

Rewind! . . . Wipes the sweat . . .

Rewind . . . I wipe the sweat from my . . .

Four fingers. He's got three fingers and a thumb! And not like one was cut off, either. I feel my hands and they both have four fingers each. I think my feet have four toes, but I can't tell from the feel. Does everyone else have these hands?

Rewind . . . We push Inni into the melting place . . .

I'll be damned! That guy's hands are the same. We think *good-bye . . . Okay, fast forward to end, back to the sweat. I have no idea how to figure out the time.*

Oh, God . . . time.

No! I didn't set my timer! That asshole Rheese had me all distracted! Plus single plus single plus single . . . *yeah, I get it, okay! How long will Tuni let me sit on that bench before she gets worried? How long will Rheese wait until he gets tired of watching this idiot sit there with his eyes closed and his hands on "my artifact"? How long does this imprint last? It should be fading out anytime—unless some other event is coming up that overlaps that dead friend thing back there.*

I see stars now. Wow, so bright! Is that the Little Dipper? Safety is around the corner . . . *I see the silhouette of the mountain up ahead. It looks like we're walking on a path between two small yet steep peaks that converge right up ahead in about half a full batch, I'd say. What's that around the bend? I see light?* The light of safety. *That's where I'm from!* "Safety." Pwin-T. *It means safety. I guess that's the name of the village around the . . .*

Oh . . . my . . . God . . .

It's a city! *There's light everywhere, all a light blue shade, and I am relaxing as we walk down the hill. Pwin-T is huge! There are real buildings down there. We should be there in just a couple of full batches!*

I have to meet in the Center house to have time with Inni's family and friends. Norrit needs to remember to seal the wall when—

"Enough of this rubbish!" Rheese yelled as he replaced the artifact on the plastic and set the second piece atop it. "Where's the bloody screwdriver? Miss Maggie better decide she knows where bloody Sharma is—and fast—or I've a good mind to . . ."

Tuni had leaned over the table and was helping Matt put his gloves back on as he reoriented himself and stared at her with huge eyes. Ignoring Rheese's ranting as if it were no more than the droning of cicadas, she whispered to Matt, "What did you see? Did it work, did you see anything?"

"I saw . . ." He smiled a smile she hadn't yet seen in their short acquaintance. It was like a child walking toward the front castle at Disneyland for the first time. "I saw so little! I mean, I saw these people, so different. They . . . *think* totally different. It's like, sort of a big mess actually, and the numbers, it was like single plus single plus single equals a batch, and that was droning on in Irin's head *forever* and—oh, they were dropping this dead guy into this boiling steam bath fissure thing in the mountains . . ."

He stopped, realizing that Rheese had grown silent and was now listening to his speedy rant.

"So you have a whole bloody story around your five minutes of intimate time with my artifact?" He was obviously unconvinced, though he seemed to be interested in what Matt was going to make up to complete the whole charade. "What's the date, Merlin?"

"Actually, I couldn't really figure it out." *Throw in some bullshit.* "The energies were asynchronous. It didn't make any sense."

"Obviously," Rheese replied with contempt. "I'm going to track down Sharma, and the two of you are going to be on your merry way home shortly, mm-kay?"

He picked up his satellite phone just as the sound of approaching tires caught their attention.

Tuni leaned over and spread open a section of blinds to peer through. Two people in a big black SUV had arrived. Dr. Rheese vultured his head down to see through the window in the door. Tuni jumped a little and turned to Matt with an excited smile.

"It's Peter!"

TWELVE

Peter Sharma stepped out of the Land Rover and stretched his legs. The four-hour drive had been brutal on his back. Only the first half hour had been on pavement; after that, it turned into a jouncing, jarring sickfest.

The air at site 00876-B223KY reeked of death. Peter walked to the top of the slope that led to the excavation. He saw that the remains were still there, obstructing his corner. He heard the RV door open behind him and turned to see Rheese stepping out to greet him.

"Mr. Sharma, a pleasure to have you at the site!"

"I'm sure it is, Doctor. Mind if I ask why that thing is still over there?"

"Oh, the bloody Interior Ministry keeps promising a crew is on its way, and they never quite show. I tell you, I'm this close to having it burned and buried."

"Yes, well, I'm not sure why you've waited *this* long. The thing appears to be well into decomp now, and it'll be a horror show to clean out."

Obviously flustered, Rheese stammered, "Well, I . . . it wasn't . . . if it wasn't for the bloody ministry and their bloody rules about disturbing the remains . . ."

"It's covering up access to that sediment—and possibly further damaging the historic record. I do not know of any law that would keep us from removing it. If anything, there are labor laws protecting the men down there from having to work in such unsanitary and hazardous conditions." He glanced down at the cloud of buzzing insects filling the excavation and noticed the laborers wore bandanas over their noses and mouths. "I'm about to toss my breakfast smelling it from this distance—I'm sure being that close is utter misery. Please, you've got backhoes—get it out of there and bury it away from the camp."

Nodding enthusiastically, Rheese pasted on a smile. "Enzi, dear boy!" he shouted to the food tent, where his foreman was cleaning a scrape on one of the men's knee.

"Yes, Professor?"

"Let's give the men a break, what do you say?"

Enzi shrugged and shouted back, "Sure, Professor, no problem!" He whistled with his fingers, signaling the men to hike out of the stinking, fly-ridden inferno.

"Peter Sharma," Matt said as he walked up to the new arrival. "Good to see you."

Peter turned and smiled.

"Good to see *you,* Matthew! Look at you—you're a full-on *man* now, aren't you?"

"Yeah, I guess I'm all grown up," he said with all the good humor he could muster.

"You know what I mean, man!" Peter replied, swatting him on the shoulder. "Last time I saw you, you were, like, seventeen!"

The driver of the Land Rover moseyed to Rheese's side. Rheese looked up and saw that it was the same driver who had brought the two ministry officials. The man beamed an obsequious half-gold smile, obviously hoping for another manifestation of the Englishman's generosity. Rheese ignored him.

"So, have you, uh, had a moment with the artifact yet?" Pete asked Matt eagerly.

"I have, actually. Just now, but Dr. Rheese ended it abruptly and put it back in his safe." Turning to face Rheese, Matt continued, "I don't think he's all that comfortable with my expertise."

"May I have a word with you in the motor home, Sharma?" Rheese asked, taking Peter gently by the arm.

"Oh, hello, Miss St. James," Peter said as he passed her. "I didn't know you were doing field work now."

"Just caretaking, Peter."

Matt's face flushed. *Caretaking!* And what was that in the way she said "Petah"? Was she interested in him? Had they had a thing at some point?

"Matt," Peter said before Rheese could steer him into the RV, "did you get anything from it?"

Matt nodded, eyes wide. "*Oh,* yeah."

Rheese disappeared inside and Peter stopped, halfway in. He mouthed to Matt, "Does he know?" pointing through the door.

Matt grimaced and shrugged a "kind of . . . "

Peter nodded and gave him a wink. The door closed.

"Mister Sharma," Rheese began, "you'll have to accept my apologies, but as you know, though I am quite intent on proceeding with my work in Africa, I waited a good deal of time for a potassium-argon specialist's assistance in validating the artifact's age. To discover that I have waited this long for an uneducated American to do psychic surgery on it—well, perhaps you can imagine my disappointment."

Peter nodded patiently as his eyes scanned the room in search of the artifact.

"I do understand, Dr. Rheese, absolutely. But I can personally attest to Matthew's ability, difficult as it is to accept. I worked with him extensively and have absolutely no question as to his legitimacy."

"Well, I admire your open-mindedness, Mr. Sharma, but as I mentioned, I am quite driven toward the success of my expedition. Even if I were to allow the lad more time with the artifact, it would not bring us any closer to providing evidence acceptable to the scientific community. I believe the vast majority of my colleagues in the field would agree."

"A valid point, Doctor," Peter acknowledged. "But the thing to understand is that Matthew's ability has the potential to lead us—to lead *you*—to more artifacts. Personally, I am very interested in what he has discovered thus far."

"It was a lot of twaddle, really. He just babbled on about giving some dead person a steam bath. Seriously, Sharma, you give weight to this clap-trap?"

Peter nodded and raised a finger. He had an idea.

The motor home door opened, and Tuni watched the two men step down. Matt had walked off to throw rocks at the crows and kites tugging at bits of elephant meat. The workers were all chatting in the food tent, discussing the forthcoming dismemberment and removal of the monstrous carcass. The work would involve both chain saws and a backhoe's loading bucket. It would not be fun, but they all agreed that in another day the flies and the stench would make the camp unlivable. Tuni could hear Enzi telling them a joke in Swahili. She tried to listen in over their laughter.

"How do you shoot a blue elephant?" he asked. Some of the men laughed at the question alone. "With a blue elephant gun. Now, how do you shoot a *red* elephant?"

Tuni watched Pete and Rheese walk toward Matt as the laborers laughed and shouted "That's stupid!" in Swahili.

Enzi continued. "Hold his trunk shut until he turns blue, and then shoot him with the blue elephant gun. Now, how do you shoot a *yellow* ele-phant?"

"A yellow elephant gun?" One of them guessed.

Enzi replied with the punchline, "Don't be so foolish! When have you ever seen a yellow elephant?"

The men's laughter seemed to irritate Rheese. He was shooting hard looks their way as he and Sharma approached Matt.

"Matt," said Peter, "I was wondering if you would mind a quick dem-onstration of your ability. Dr. Rheese has legitimate concerns that I would like us to dispel, if you're willing."

Matt bristled. Was this a person that he *wanted* to convince? It seemed that Peter had decided so on his behalf. He chided himself for not shaking his head and making clear to Peter that he didn't want Rheese brought it. "I guess . . . whatever it takes. What do you want me to do?"

"I'd like you to do a read on his hat and tell him something you couldn't possibly know."

Dr. Rheese choked. "*Me?* Ah-m . . ." Though he still didn't believe in it, what if the boy's alleged ability should prove real? He couldn't afford to have anyone inside his head, not even for a second. *It's not real,* he repeated in his head as he searched for an adequate alternative.

"Well, yes," Peter replied. "I mean, it wouldn't do much to convince you if he did it with me or someone else, right? Seems that would be like someone else telling you that you just missed seeing a flyby of UFOs, no? Would you not have to see it with your own eyes?"

Matt studied Rheese. What was he trying to hide?

"Tell you what, Peter," Rheese said. "Why not just have the lad tell us the color of my knickers?"

"Nice idea, Doctor," replied Matt. "But this isn't a magic show, and it doesn't work that way. Tell me—without any details, of course—what's the most interesting thing to have occurred here in the past week?"

"Well, it would be difficult to overlook the incident with the beastie decaying in the pit over there."

"All right, good," Matt began. "So don't tell me anything about it, but what were you holding or wearing when it all started to hit the fan?"

Rheese began to stew again. "Well, in actual fact . . . I don't precisely recall, but . . . ah, of course—Enzi had the Mossberg from the equipment trailer." *Good thinking, old boy.*

"What's that?" Pete asked.

"Enzi!" Rheese shouted to the food tent. "Could you fetch the shotgun?"

Now it was Matt's turn to feel uneasy. He had a major aversion to reading weapons, but if it would get him back in the motor home and holding the fragment, he was willing to forego comfort at this point. Enzi jogged past them to the trailer, lowered the tailgate, and ducked inside. He emerged a moment later with the shotgun, and after opening the breech to ensure that it wasn't loaded, he put it in Matt's gloved hands.

Now this guy, too? Things were spiraling out of Matt's control. He needed to pull Peter and Tuni aside and make clear his disapproval. And why wasn't Tuni stepping in? *She must be deferring to Peter, who evidently thinks my ability is a matter of public record.*

"Do you need a chair or anything, Matthew?" Peter asked.

"What I need is to be in a private area, and for people to remember promises they agreed to years ago."

Peter nodded absently, looking toward the RV, then appeared to get it. He glanced at Rheese and Enzi, both with bemused expressions. He looked at Matt apologetically and pulled him aside, out of earshot.

"I am so sorry, man! I wasn't thinking at all. I just thought Rheese was already in and then he suggested his foreman's and the shotgun and I just went with it. The damage is done, I know, but I promise, no more. You tell me where we go from here."

Matt sighed and looked past Peter's shoulder where Rheese had his fists on his hips, staring intensely at Matt and Peter.

"We just have to stop it with these two, Pete. I brought Tuni in on the plane thinking I wouldn't have anyone on my side here. If I had known you were going to be here, it would have just been you and me in that RV. None the wiser for what's going on."

"It was a last minute decision, man. Again, I can't tell you how sorry I am."

Matt brushed it off and they walked back to the group.

Enzi had put the men on the gruesome task of cutting up and hauling away the rotting elephant carcass, piece by revolting piece, to a hole that Kanu had dug with the backhoe. Enzi remained in the RV with Rheese and the visitors, curious why they wanted to look at the shotgun he had used. Was he going to be in trouble?

Sitting at the table, Matt removed one glove, then grasped the shotgun with his other, still gloved hand. He had nothing really to cover the table with, so he had to improvise. Though, with everyone staring at him he felt on the verge of a panic attack, there was nothing for it but to suck in a deep breath, set the timer on his arm to five minutes, and lower his bare hand onto the black metal.

The whoosh filled his ears, and he suddenly felt very wet. It was pouring rain. The ground just shook, and there's a crazed elephant stomping toward the pit.

I am male. I'm thirty-one. I was born in Mombasa, Kenya. I am Jeremiah Enzi, but I go by Enzi Wata. I see my two men skidding away in a Jeep as the professor runs and hides behind the RV. I just got the shotgun out of the equipment trailer. I think of my wife, and I think of little Jomo in his overalls.

The elephant crashes down into the pit, and I am relieved but also saddened. The professor comes to edge of the pit. He asks if it is dying. *This conversation should be enough proof for both of them. How much time left?* I walk to elevator—*hey, that's something! There's no elevator anymore, and the pit is like a giant rectangle instead of the sloped wedge of half that size that's there now. And I see a bunch of jackhammers in there, too, all leaned up against the walls, sitting deep in—*

The timer buzzed his arm, and his bare hand lifted reflexively to push the STOP button. Matt set the shotgun down on the table and replaced his right glove.

"So tell us!" Peter exclaimed. It had been years since he saw Matt work.

Matt took quick note of all their expressions, took a deep, steadying breath, and began. "Well, it was raining . . ."

"Uncanny," Rheese quipped as the rain again began to patter down onto the RV roof.

"There were also two more men—I didn't get to see their faces, but Enzi knew them as Chewy and Zuzuwe. They drove off in what I'm guessing was that Jeep parked outside, while Dr. Rheese ran and hid behind the RV back there."

Rheese frowned and shot a look at Enzi.

"I not talk about any of it with them, Professor. I not know how he know."

"Also, the two of you spoke to each other after the elephant fell in and caved in the whole side over there. You said 'Is it dying?' Then Enzi said, 'Not survive that drop, sir. See his neck.' And then you said 'It made a bloody mess,' and asked where Enzi was going as he walked over to an elevator. And the hole was much bigger, and there were jackhammers all along the walls."

Rheese gulped. Peter frowned and looked at him with confusion.

"*Jackhammers,* Doctor?"

"Yes," he replied dismissively. "We had them brought in just that day for some large stones we were having difficulty with."

Enzi was amazed. His parents had told him stories of wizards that they insisted were true, but he had stopped believing in anything miraculous years ago. Could it be trickery? Could someone else have been there? Chui and Zuzuwi would not have heard them talk.

"What else?" Enzi asked with skepticism. "How can it be real?"

"When you walked out of the equipment trailer with the shotgun in your hands, you thought of your wife and son. You saw an image of him in your head. He was wearing light blue overalls with a black T-shirt and holding himself up with one hand on a glass table."

Enzi felt his legs grow weak, and he sat down on the bench. *Impossible!* He thought over and over again as he stared at Matt.

Matt started to feel uncomfortable again and wondered if he had told a bit too much. He knew how freaky it must feel to have one's thoughts told by a complete stranger. And this guy was looking at him a little too intensely now. Did he need to make that big an impression? Had he lost sight of his need for secrecy in favor of shutting up Dr. Rheese?

Tuni and Peter appeared pretty satisfied by the show, but Matt wanted to see Dr. Rheese's reaction. He was gnawing at the inside of his cheek and tugging his earlobe, clearly conflicted. Peter broke the silence.

"So, Doctor, convinced?"

"I'm bashing it about it my head. How anyone could ever do that . . . ?"

"Well, Doctor," Tuni said, "perhaps you could continue to think it over *and* have an opportunity to judge it some more after Matthew spends some more time with the artifact. Surely, this feat buys him a ticket to another ten minutes," she added with a pleasant smile.

Her cheerful tone infuriated him, but if he didn't agree to it, Sharma would simply overrule him. He would no longer appear to have control over the site, and no one would bother consulting him on *any* of the important decisions to come. It would set the precedent to go over his head to Peter from this moment on. He had no choice.

"I like it, folks," he said with a grin. "Very interesting stuff. Let's give it a ten-minute roll, but the same rule applies, Mr. Turner. If I fear for the artifact's well-being, I pull the plug."

"Right," Matt replied, as if he himself had feared for the thing's well-being all along. It was a good thing, though, last time. He would have been stuck! Best not to advertise that Rheese's boorish behavior had pretty much saved him in the absence of his timer's shock.

"May I stay?" Enzi asked Rheese.

"Of course," he replied affably. "You certainly are a part of this now, aren't you?" Rheese pulled out the most sincere laugh he could muster, while the scheming gears in the other side of his brain were whirring at full tilt. He was also still genuinely curious about the artifact—he merely doubted its ability to make him rich anytime soon, if at all.

"Hey," Peter said to Matt. "Before we get started I'd like to hear what you saw so far. Did you take notes?"

"I haven't had a chance, actually, but it's all still very fresh in my head, and I can always go back to it in a session if I forgot anything. It was all very bizarre."

Rheese handed out cold bottled water to everyone; then, as everyone else listened, Matt relayed the experience to Peter. Peter scratched down notes and asked him to pause a few times so he could catch up. Everyone was enthralled, even Rheese.

THIRTEEN

Fast forward.

Yes, that was definitely the Little Dipper. Light around the bend. Still worried, though; still counting the steps.

Fast forward.

Here we are . . . I must meet in the Center House with Inni's friends and family. We stop walking single file, and Irin stops counting steps. Pwig comes up beside me and grabs my hand to walk with me. Pwig has the same mother and father as I. He is my brother. I had another brother. We're walking, holding hands, toward the Center House.

I see the Center House now at the end of the path. The ground looks and feels like walking on a stone garden, with chunky rocks that are a little too big to feel comfortable walking on. On either side of us are smaller houses, interconnected. Most are dark, but some have the pale blue light coming from them. Are those windows? I wish Irin would actually look at something close-up. I want to see where the light actually comes from.

My timer's set for ten minutes . . . if this imprint lasts that long.

As we approach the Center House, the path splits off in two directions: one to the left that appears to wrap around to the other side of the round structure, and the other curves to the right and then straight to a rounded entryway. The buildings all look like smooth-walled igloos, but this one is huge compared to the rest. I walk inside and see other people. I pull the *k'yot* top off my head and lay it on a flat surface near the door, where several others are already piled. No one inside this room wears the *k'yot,* the shielding clothes, except the men who were with me on the path. Both men and women are bare-chested but for what look like two wide suspenders, perhaps three inches across, going over each shoulder and then connecting to a wraparound skirt piece that starts at the waist and ends a few inches above the knees. The skirts are fairly plain, only dressed up by the overlap of the suspender straps, which, looking around this room, appear to come in many different colors. The skirts, too, are varied in color. I see tan straps with blue skirt, matching purple straps with purple skirt, and dark brown with pure white. Their foot coverings all seem the same: tan material nailed or stapled into large foot-shaped pieces that stick out quite a bit from the actual foot, making everyone's feet look pretty big. Also, judging by the odd feeling when Irin walks, they aren't very comfortable.

That is Oinni sitting on what appears to be a short tree stump with no bark. It's called a *footrest,* but others are sitting on them, too, so I'm guessing these are their chairs. I walk to Oinni and put my hand on her head. Her hair hangs to her ears. It is straight, black, and clumpy, like very thin dreadlocks. It looks as if everyone's hair is like this. Irin speaks to her.

"Inni twyn gin, ylt pwino i pwin opget." Your mate now rests and is forever safe. He feels deeply sad for her and thinks how his own mate, Orin, would feel if he were lost.

I get it now—the names. My name is Irin; my wife is Orin. The first sound is in place of Mr. or Mrs. So is my name actually *Rin?* I wonder what a woman is called before she is married.

Irin looks up and across the round table to some others he knows in the house. In the middle of the table, there! I can finally see one of the light sources! It's a wide tube of liquid that leads all the way up to the domed roof; at the base, inside the tube, something that looks like a lit candle is submerged in the liquid. This tube is clearly made of glass or some sort of transparent plastic. Witno just bumped the table, and now the liquid went into motion inside the cylinder, and the light has begun to dance around the room as if we were under water. Irin steps back and turns toward a man who is talking to him. It's Norrit; he's taking off his middle and tells me I should, too.

Rewind.

That tube of light—how do they get the lit candle thing in there? Some-one must stick it in through a hole in the table, up into the tube, and then something closes on the bottom. The flame in there is huge. It doesn't look as though there's a wick; it's just the whole stick of whatever's on fire in there. Doesn't it need air? Irin steps back . . .

Fast-forward.

He takes off the jacket part of the *k'yot* and lays it on the table by the door. Okay, well, I guess I don't have to wait for the timer. This imprint should fade out quick now that he's not in contact with it anymore.

Back to structure. How am I going to tell what era this is? These people are *clearly* humanlike, but the giant eyes and three fingers thing makes them . . . what? Some kind of unique tribe that started with a couple of three-fingered, odd-faced freaks, and everyone else is an offshoot of them? Irin is stepping outside for air. If this *is* all those millions of years ago, how can I tell? This guy's concept of the date is full of batches and gross batches, and now I'm aware of some "all batch" that works out to four thousand something. Maybe Pete can help with that. Let's hear it, Irin—what's the date again? And I'll try to remember this to write down imme-diately.

Single plus batch plus batch plus batch plus full batch plus gross batch plus single plus single past.

Past *what*? Past the moon. What about the moon? An eclipse or some-thing? No, some *big* moon event. Oh, a big moon event, wow, that's great. Some raging party on the moon. Anything else? Oh, a *t'gyt* will help! That's their calendar. I'll have to hope Irin takes a look at one at some point.

Right now, Irin is looking at the stars and thinking about Inni. That is what he's supposed to be doing right now. This is Inni's evening. Hope-fully the imprint ends, or ten minutes are up soon, or I'm going to forget these numbers. Irin has an image of Inni and another man (who looks just like him), and they're stirring some shiny liquid, like metal, in a huge vat. They're talking about the excitement of the coming gathering—meaning harvesting, I'm guessing by the other images popping up in Irin's head. He gets sad again and closes his eyes.

His eyes are still closed. This is going to get boring. How could the imprint still be going? It's just a wash of emotions now. This keeps going on, let me say the date over and over to remember it: single plus batch plus batch . . . Someone's rubbing his head now and talking to him. He knows the voice. It's Orin. She says it's time to return to house, *i tyg rol*—that means "make safe," referring to a time. It's make-safe time. And be with her inside the house. Finally! This should be good. I want to see inside his house. That Center House seems to be just a town hall sort of building.

Irin steps back into the Center House and grabs his *k'yot* parts. That explains why this imprint went on so long: it's an overlap. We walk around the path from the Center House and then cut left onto a branching trail. I know the way. Three more houses on the left, four on the right, and mine is at the end—it's the only one with the light still visible through the little window opening there. We come upon my house, which is just like all the rest: a small, perfect dome of unknown material. Irin glances through the window as he passes. It's not a glass window, just an opening in the shape of the letter "D" turned so the flat side is on the bottom. The doorways are the same shape, but elongated tall enough for Irin and Orin to enter without ducking.

I turn right just after stepping into the house, toss the *k'yot* to the side, and put my hand at the top of a big door thing. It will fit perfectly into the doorway, but it is not on any hinges. I reach up and turn a metal handle thing out of the way, which allows the weight of the door onto me. That latch was holding it against the inner wall. Irin lifts the door via two bar handles, steps to the right, and pushes it into place. I can tell that the door is really heavy, but Irin is apparently very strong, and it doesn't faze him to lift it. It does indeed fit perfectly into the opening. The two bars twist in opposite directions, and he secures the door in place. We do the same thing for the window opening. Its hatch, I'll call it, was leaning against the wall underneath it.

"Irin," a man's voice says behind me. Irin isn't startled. Odd as Orin and I were the only two in here. I turn around and Orin is undressing on the floor mat. She continues to do so, even though this old guy is standing here. He actually looks really old—the first one I have seen. He's my father, Tillyt. He lives in the adjoining house next to ours, and I see there is a tunnel, shaped like the front doorway. It leads to another house/room behind him. I suppose the whole thing could be considered a house with two rooms, but in Irin's head, this is his house, and his father's house is next door; his brother Pwig's is connected on the other side of his parents' house, but that isn't visible from here.

My father is telling me that his friend, Pret, wants to speak with me next night. Tomorrow night. It's important, apparently, about the *ypritl* he knows is coming. That is a sky stripe. A shooting star? An asteroid? Irin is worried about this. Pret was right about the blood attack a half-full batch before. He had been saying it for many moon cycles, and those who listened made-safe early and stayed in-house for longer the next night. Wil hadn't mentioned anything about it, so Irin had only done make-safe early because Tillyt insisted. Irin is thankful now. Way too many names. I'll have to unravel all that later, if I need to.

Do they have someone with some sort of real clairvoyance ability? This might just be the typical superstition of people, though. There are people today who say something bad is going to happen for months and months, and then when something finally does, they say, "See?" An asteroid is pretty specific, though.

Irin agrees to speak with Pret next night, and his father goes back through the tunnel. Irin turns and looks down at the floor mat bed and sees Orin lying there completely naked. Her body has no hair except for her head. She has the same thin dreadlock thing going on, but longer than Oinni's, spreading out on the mat like a black flower.

We look away and walk over to the candlelight tube sticking up out of the ground by the window. He picks it up with one hand, and the thick candlestick stays on the floor. The tube is pretty heavy, filled with maybe four gallons of the light blue liquid around the edges. He taps the candlestick with the flat bottom edge of the liquid tube a few times until it goes out. Now it's almost completely dark in the room, the only light coming from the liquid in the light tube. There must be residual light bouncing around in the liquid! I am undressing now and throwing my foot covers and clothes toward the other side of the room. That's where the clothes go.

There's nothing else in the room, either. No tables, no containers. Just the light tube, a small pile of clothes now, and the sleeping mat with a thin rolled-up fabric that borders the edges of the mat. Perhaps a blanket of sorts, for when it gets cold. The light from the tube is almost completely gone now as I lie down on the mat and look at the dimming brightness of Orin's eyes. They are not the pitch black everyone has had so far, but a medium brown with little specks of black. Their shine is the last thing we see as the remaining light fades away.

I can feel Orin's arms pulling me closer to her. She wraps them around my head and shoves the rest of her body into contact with mine. She tugs gently at our hair, and I can tell that mine is short—little sprouts of the skinny dreadlocks. I always felt that these intimate moments were a bit of an invasion of privacy, but I found them . . . I don't know, *interesting,* nonetheless. As she continues to play with my head, her toes start messing around with mine. It's fading now.

This is the end of the imprint. I know this feeling well. His thoughts start to pull away into a dark shroud, the vision blurs in and out for about thirty seconds before going completely black, and then I'm out. It was hard to tell at first, since the light in the room was fading out on its own, but now I can't feel her toes or arms around the head.

Matt removed his hands from the artifact, and Tuni and everyone else jumped. He supposed that ten minutes of just staring probably got pretty boring. He pulled off his timer and turned it off to preserve the batteries. Only eight and half minutes had passed.

"What happened?" asked Tuni. "The timer didn't go off, did it?"

"Nope," Matt replied as he shoved the timer into the duffel beside him. "The imprint ended. Actually, they're usually much shorter—this just happens to be a really emotional guy, I guess. He let go of the *k'yot* a minute earlier, so it makes sense it faded away. Normally would have been much quicker though."

"So that's it, then?" Tuni asked. "It's over?"

"Oh, I don't think so. That's just the end of that particular imprint. See, the way this whole thing works is that somebody's holding something when a crazy thing happens or they hurt themselves, or maybe his wife says she's leaving him or whatever—something like that. It leaves an impression on the object of a few minutes leading up to the event and a few minutes after it's over. In this case, Irin had the sort of prolonged emotional period of carrying his friend's dead body to this burial ritual, and then there was a funeral service get-together thing with friends and family. He was pretty upset the whole time and still was at the end there. But let's say something huge happened just then, like someone came and stabbed him in the hand—it would have no effect on the imprint I was reading, because he didn't have the piece on him anymore."

"So what if you just kept touching the piece, Matthew?" asked Tuni. "Would you come out of it still because that particular block of imprint was over?"

"Actually, it would be dark nothingness for a while but would then sort of automatically roll to the next imprint until there was nothing else. Personally, I prefer to take the opportunity for a breather and pull myself out of the session. I need either the shock from my timer or a moment of nothingness like that to find my hands again and move them away from the imprint object."

A loud flush sound echoed from the RV's restroom.

Tuni replied, "I see, so you think you can get more out of it?"

"Yeah, I mean, if he put the thing on again—which maybe he did the next time somebody died. I don't know."

"So . . . what happened this time?" Peter asked.

Rheese emerged from the restroom and dried his hands on a hanging towel.

"Hang on," Matt said. "Let me write something down real quick."

He pulled the notebook in front of him and wrote down the date: "single + batch + batch + batch + full batch + gross batch + single + single."

"Is that the date you were talking about?" asked Tuni.

"Yeah, past the 'moon event,' apparently."

"Okay, so what happened?" Rheese asked, sounding impatient yet interested.

"Well, not too much *happened*, Doctor, but I did see a lot that I'm going to write down real quick, and then we can discuss it all in detail. After that, I'd like to go over this numbering system. I understand the base numbers but can't really do the math in my head."

Matt scratched down a page of notes, muttering to himself sporadically. Pete and Tuni were craning their necks, trying to read as he wrote, but his handwriting was dreadful. When he was done, he flipped back to the sheet with numbers.

"All right," he said at last. "So, Pete, I'm hoping you can help with this—and, of course, anyone else who's good with numbers is welcome to join in. Single is one; batch is eight . . ."

They all simply nodded, wide-eyed.

"Can somebody write this down? You're not going to remember it all."

"Oh, sure—sorry," Peter said as he clicked his pen and began to write.

"Full batch is sixty-four, gross batch is five hundred twelve, and all batch is four thousand ninety-six. Got it?" He went on, explaining how the math worked.

When Matt was done, Pete scratched out some equations and looked up.

"Eighteen-oh-three!" Pete chimed out.

They all sat there for a moment, nodding happily and looking at the number Matt had now written in big numerals on the notepad: 1803.

Rheese and Enzi stood back and just observed it all. Neither understood the numbers just discussed, but both wanted to hear what else had happened in the eight minutes that Matt was under.

"So," Peter finally said, "are we assuming this is eighteen hundred and three *years* past this moon event?"

Matt had no idea. It could have been 1,803 decades, days—heck, perhaps even hours, considering that they counted the very steps they took!

"There was another mention of time," Matt said. "Irin was thinking about something from before, and he made reference to moon cycles."

"What did he say, exactly?" asked Pete.

"Well, they don't exactly *say* anything that I can understand. It's all from the interpretation in his head that I can glean what he or someone else is saying—or if he's thinking something. It's actually easiest with thoughts, because he thinks almost entirely in concepts and images. Some people think words in their head; others think whole sentences at once. I think I could write a whole paper on the ways different people think."

"Yes, interesting," Peter replied, wondering how he thought in his own head, and how it differed from the next person's thinking process.

Matt could tell that Tuni was doing the same thing.

"So anyway, what he 'said' in his head was something to the effect that this other guy had been warning people about something 'for many moon cycles.'"

"So perhaps," Tuni theorized, "it is eighteen hundred and three moon cycles since this big moon event. How many moon cycles are there per year?"

"About thirteen," Rheese chimed in. "But it varies year to year. For the purpose of this exercise, though, thirteen should be more than adequate as an estimate."

Peter did the math on his pad.

"That's twenty-three thousand something. That would be a pretty long time to be able to keep track of the date. I don't know . . ."

They sat in silence, considering the myriad possibilities.

"Well, anyway," Matt broke in, "we've got these numbers written down. Let me tell you what happened."

FOURTEEN

Peter Sharma stopped chewing his mechanical pencil to say, "I think we need to get some research points identified so we can structure this analysis. We could easily get lost in the details here since, frankly, it's all far too intriguing. Matt, I'm going to get on the phone with some good people back at the lab and see if we can't bring on some more specialists. While I do that, did you want to spend some more time with the artifact?"

"I really am interested in doing more," Matt replied, "but I sort of need to break it up. It's a bit of a mental drain, if you recall."

The sun was beginning to set, and Rheese had suggested that everyone ready their sleeping arrangements before the equatorial night fell like a black-out curtain. Though Peter had brought a large tent for himself, Tuni and Matt had supposed that their shelter and bedding were arranged. Rheese had one sleeping bag and a couple of extra blankets in his motor home. With some prodding, he agreed to give up his queen-size bed at the back of the RV and take the fold-down single along the side. Tuni put to rest any thought of her sharing a bed with either of them, volunteering to sleep in Peter's tent outside while Peter and Matt shared the queen bed. Peter called to have a few more tents and bedding brought to the site and submitted a request for another fully outfitted RV.

On hearing Sharma's conversations with the museum, Rheese worried that this distraction was escalating. If they managed to find some sort of concrete evidence from the American's information, as Sharma had said, Rheese would at the very least achieve greater notoriety, which could lead to much easier funding of his personal excursions, with fewer strings attached and questions to answer. But time was of the essence.

Did he want to spend the next three years digging for more pieces of metal fabric? Hardly. He knew where to find his ticket to riches, and it was just sitting there, waiting for him in one of twelve more sites. While mining companies would have no reason to begin exploring those areas, he worried that the Ministry of the Interior could at any time decide to expand the borders of the preserves. They had already done so twice in as many years. He made a mental note to prioritize the potential sites that were nearest the preserve.

Enzi had left two others behind to prepare dinner while he went in the Jeep to drop off the laborers, and when he returned, Tuni was finishing setting herself up in the tent. As she zipped the tent door shut, he approached and walked with her to the food tent.

"*Unasema Kiswahili?*" he inquired as they walked.

"A little. Your elephant joke was certainly interesting."

Enzi laughed hesitantly. "Sorry, miss, I not feel good about shooting elephant. It just, the men . . ."

"You don't need to apologize, Enzi," Tuni replied as they sat down at one of the tables. Smoke rose from the grill nearby, where the two cooks, Wekesa and Zuberi, were working. "I know a joke is just a joke. What is for dinner—*chapati na sukuma wiki?*"

"Hamburgers."

"Ah, authentic local cuisine," she laughed. "I like it."

Pete arrived with Matt in tow. They were discussing the odd features of the Pwin-T people, as they were now being called.

"You don't think maybe they're aliens or something?" Matt asked. "They're really close to humans. It's just the crazy eyes and eight fingers thing I think is so strange."

Pete stopped and faced Matt. Everyone else was already seated at the picnic tables.

"Well, consider this," Pete began. "Let's assume this town really is a hundred fifty-plus million years old. That would mean that, concurrent with the evolution of the dinosaurs we know of, a previously unknown primate-like species existed. That primate would have had to be pretty well isolated from the predators of the day to survive for the millions more years it would take for them to evolve greater intelligence, learn to use tools, develop agriculture, and all the rest."

"So you're saying that we descended from *these* people, and not the whole caveman story you usually hear about?" Matt asked. Rheese rolled his eyes.

"No, not at all. I would think that they had their time. They evolved, died off, and millions of years later the process began again, resulting in us. I also don't believe humans would have survived the mass extinction event of sixty-five million years ago. Half of all species were lost after that asteroid struck."

"But, Peter," Tuni said, "wouldn't scientists have found bones of humans or the primate ancestors you mentioned by now? At least one or two, considering all the other things we find?"

"Central Africa at that time was an extremely volcanic area and believed prone to wildly variable weather patterns and quakes. This is the main reason why fossils are so difficult to find anywhere south of the Sahara—there simply hasn't been enough stability or dryness in the area to preserve specimens. In fact, Dr. Rheese has been one of the few paleontologists to make significant discoveries in the region."

Wekesa brought trays of hamburgers and a steaming pot of beans to the table, and the group began eating.

"These people would have had to remain in the same area where their primitive ancestors had been. Safer, but probably still pretty dangerous in a world with foot-long mosquitoes and hundreds of species of hungry, toothy reptiles out there."

"I suppose," Rheese interjected. "That you find it entirely plausible that these supposedly intelligent, self-aware people happened to evolve in the same exact way that we did, but with different hands and eyes? I would have less trouble with it if it didn't take *us* so long. And what other species could we possibly cite as having evolved from a separate ancestor but ended up, for all intents and purposes, the same?"

"I understand your skepticism, Doctor." Peter's nodded as he raised a finger. "If I was not as sure as I am about Matt's abilities, I would probably be even less open-minded than you on the matter. But to address the first part first—in the grand scheme of history we didn't take long at all. Think about it…six million years of evolution. With the right conditions and starter mammal, we could have evolved to civilized beings and died off twenty-five times since that metal fabric was made. Obviously an unlikely occurrence, but we definitely aren't limited by time in our hypotheses."

Rheese chewed the side of his lip as he made a noncommittal "hrmff" sound.

"As to your like species question, there are actually numerous examples of species being entirely separated and evolving to nearly identical end species over millions of years. In this case, it would not have happened in parallel to us, but that does not change the plausibility of humanoid beings evolving more than once on Earth. All it takes is time, people. And our planet has had more than enough."

Everyone listened to Peter's evolutionary science lesson with great interest. After a bit, he hauled his notebook and set it on the table while everyone continued eating.

"If you all don't mind," Peter said, "I'd like to go over some of the research items I've identified. This is mainly for your benefit, Matt, but everyone should be aware of our direction. Oh, and before I forget, Flip Chamberlain and some others will be arriving late tomorrow to assist with further excavations, and Flip can really help with any lunar cycle questions. He's bringing along an assistant who is an excellent sketch artist."

"You want me to talk to more people about this?" Matt asked. "How do you propose that I explain where the lunar cycle question came from? And a sketch artist? I think you're doing it again, Pete."

Pete slapped his own head and rolled his eyes. "Dammit, you're right! I'm an idiot, Matt. I haven't told anyone anything, though, believe me. We'll figure something out. The vast majority of the researchers I have coming are going to be heads down in the pit."

"And did you say 'late tomorrow?'" Matt asked.

"Yeah," Peter replied. "As you know, it takes a bit of doing to get here from London."

"It's just that . . . well, I wasn't really planning on staying that long. I was pretty dead set on flying out tomorrow morning."

Everyone looked at each other.

"I thought . . . uh," Peter stuttered, "well, I guess I thought we were together on this. Didn't you say you wanted to figure all this out, learn more about the people and some of these other questions that have arisen?"

"I do, I do," Matt assured him. "I just don't really want to hang out in a jungle in the middle of Africa. I've got a lot of stuff going on back home, you know . . ."

Peter flipped his pencil onto the pad. It seemed crazy that a project of this importance should grind to a stop because of the supposedly busy life of a recently made millionaire.

"Hey," Matt said, brightening, "I could bring home a piece of it and give you the same information, you know? I just can't be *here*. I know none of you understand this, but it's very difficult for me to be away from home. Just sleeping tonight, with the arrangements the way they are—it's going to be a huge ordeal."

"I guess I didn't realize how tough this is on you, Matt," said Peter. "I suppose circumstances were different in New York. You got to go home at the end of the day. Tell you what . . . I can sleep outside until the new tents get here if it makes things easier.

"It's not just that," he sighed. "It's everything. I don't know. I could maybe stay through tomorrow and see what comes of a couple more sessions, but after that I really gotta go. I'm not saying I'm done after that, but I need to be done *here,* you know? That probably sounds selfish, but I don't know what else to say."

Peter nodded his understanding. If Matt wanted to go, there was little he could do to keep him here.

Rheese, sitting on a plastic food bin at the far end of the table, said nothing. How lovely it would be if this all just went away because Turner was uncomfortable! Why couldn't it be a remote investigation, as the lad suggested? Then Rheese could carry on with his search, and everyone else could be happily engrossed in this work somewhere far, far away. Toss a hefty bribe the way of the right people in the Interior Ministry, and—voilà!—full authorization to export the historical artifact!

"Well," Peter began again, "I suppose this makes my list that much more important. Here are the points I've identified. Anyone can let me know afterwards if they think I've missed something. One: more details on the lunar event—get a glimpse of that calendar you mentioned. Two: insects and animal life—if you could get a good look at something, say, buzzing around a light source, and maybe some other animals, we could use that approach to narrow down at least the geologic era as a second option. Three: the door—what's it made of? You said you hadn't identified the material, but you could tell that the door seemed to be quite heavy, possibly metal. It seems to me that a door like that—unless it's iron and has rusted to nothingness—might remain preserved over time if the right conditions existed. Four: We want to hear what happens with this *Purrit* guy, who has something to say about a potential celestial event—maybe an asteroid impact. If it's real and was a big enough event, it may well show up in geological strata."

"Excuse me," Enzi interjected. "If Matthew sees mountains that look a certain way, next to another mountain that look a certain way, cannot he find same mountains around here?"

Rheese rolled his eyes but kept his scoffing to himself.

"That's good thinking, Enzi," Pete replied. "Land navigation can be useful, but interestingly enough, the land here looks nothing like it did even one million years ago—which has little resemblance to ten million years before that. In reality, this landscape has probably completely changed dozens of times since the Jurassic period. Even your beautiful Mount Kilimanjaro is just twenty-five million years old. But don't stop thinking, sir—I want your ideas."

"What about the stars?" Tuni asked.

"That's actually number five, thank you. Five: you mentioned seeing the Little Dipper. If there was some sort of unique planetary alignment that happens maybe only every X tens of millennia, or perhaps something else in the stars. I'm no astronomer, so I don't know what could be useful, but if you have another chance to see the stars at night, perhaps try to snap a mental image of anything that might be out of the ordinary. You know what planets look like, right?"

"Uh . . . bigger and brighter?" Matt guessed.

"Sometimes, but the main thing is, they don't flicker. Stars flash; planets don't. You should be able to spot at least one at any given time." Peter stepped outside the food tent's mesh mosquito netting. "Here, come here for a second."

Matt pushed the fly aside and joined him outside. The rain had stopped, and the clouds had cleared to reveal stars like a billion diamonds strewn across black velvet. The temperature had dropped to the point where Matt was finally comfortable in his turtleneck and gloves; the others were already donning sweaters and jackets.

Pete pointed at a bright yellow planet. "See? No flicker—that's Jupiter. That's also what Saturn looks like, just not as bright. 'Venus is white and very bright, but is not visible late at night.' My mom taught me that one. Rhymes nicely, no?"

"Look, Pete," Matt replied, still gazing up at the starry splendor, "I hope you don't feel like I'm leaving you hanging with all this. I really just have a very small comfort zone. True, this isn't as bad as being on a crowded Manhattan sidewalk, but I still have to be constantly paranoid, and I'm still not over that asshole being one of the few people that know about me."

Peter nodded in understanding and said, "Listen, Matt, I do see where you're coming from. I think you know what my motivations are, and I wouldn't ask you to do anything you're not comfortable with."

"Oh, yeah, so it wasn't your idea to bribe me to come?"

"*Bribe* you? No—who bribed you?"

"Well, not exactly a bribe, I guess. Dr. Meier just hung a big carrot in front of me, I suppose."

"Wow. And I hear you're not doing too bad these days, so it must have been quite some carrot. Don't tell me it's Tuni . . ."

Matt gasped inwardly and was grateful for the darkness.

"Hah, right! It would take more than *her* to get me to fly to some god-forsaken jungle half the world away." He paused and glanced over at Tuni in her tight jeans and fleece sweater. She had returned to the food tent and was chatting with Enzi. "So did you two have a thing at some point?"

"Me and Tuni? Only in my dreams, man! Afraid she's a bit out of my league. Besides, my parents are still calling and telling me I have to come to Mumbai and meet the woman of *their* dreams and marry her. . . . So, since you're leaving tomorrow, can I wake you up at sunrise to get going right away?"

"Oh, yeah, sure, no problem. I was thinking I'd do one more short one tonight. At the very least, we need to know that there's more to see. There's a chance that what I've already seen is the only imprint there is."

Matt walked back to the food tent and ate some of the sliced papayas Zuberi had brought out for dessert. Peter went to the RV for his jacket.

A short time later, they found themselves back at the table in the RV, watching Matt prepare for another episode.

FIFTEEN

Irin picked up his k'yot top from the floor in the Center House, where he had left it the night before. He pulled it over his head and attached it to the holdstrip jutting from the top of his k'yot middle. Father had said to meet Pret at the food flat just after dark.

The still air of daylight hours, thick and warm, seemed to linger around Irin's face. He peered around the intersecting paths of the Center House, early risers already milling about in anticipation of the first meal of the night. A few k'yot-clad men stood out in the crowd. Everyone else seemed to think it safe to wander about in clothes, even though darkness had yet to fully clear away the unsafe blues of daytime. Attacks had previously occurred at this time, and even a little later.

Though most appeared tense and watchful, Irin knew why they believed themselves—not just themselves, but their children—to be safe. Screamers had come and gone before sunrise. Many held to the idea that if the killers appeared and then left, that they would not return until the next day. This was, of course, provided they did not catch anyone. In that event, sometimes weeks could pass before another visit. But Irin knew these routines were only considered as such because someone had yet to see otherwise. He thought that if he was a screamer, he would enter the city, make a big commotion, and then hide out of sight.

Screamers, of course, did not hide and wait. They couldn't be silent or still for an instant; it was as if they were on fire. His people believed the creatures to be thoughtless, hunger-driven beasts. Irin thought this misconception would remain until yet another new behavior emerged.

"Screamers *never* come after sunset . . . they only take children . . . they only come in pairs . . . k'yot are impenetrable . . . " How many assumptions had been proven wrong thus far? How many existed before he was born, or before his father was born?

He and Orin had been awakened before sunset, the shrill cackle of one or more screamers outside. They had visited twice in as many days, in search of roaming meat. Finding none, they tested the door of the house next to Irin's, scratching and demanding to be let in. Orin had tried to hold him to the floormat, but Irin had gotten up and peered through an eyehole. The waning sunlight, reflecting off of houses and pale rocks had still been blinding. He squinted against it and saw a gray form streak past. It had made him flinch, and an instant later a crash against their own door.

The screamers were learning. There was a time when they had to smell their prey. But the last attack, the one that killed fourteen people, had been against a house cluster after make-safe. Only one door hadn't been fully secured, but that was all it took. The screamers got in enough to raise the structure out of the ground, flipping the first on its side, the weight twisting the linking tunnel to the adjoined house. There were no survivors.

"You people are foolish to be out right now," Irin said to no one in particular. Nobody replied, not even a derisive murmur. *They are frightened prey animals, like furry crawlers for the flyers that dive from above and snatch up their pick. Only we do not dig holes beneath the dirt, we build our burrows aboveground.*

Irin made his way through the group, onto the path that led to the food flats. Pret, the crazy father of Irin's childhood friend, Wil, wished to speak with him. He remembered the oldest one had always been odd, but the madness had increased in recent times.

The clusters of domes gave way to the vast fields of the food flats. The air always felt cooler out here while heat from the daylight sun still radiated off the domes. Irin inhaled the unique, musty scent of the area as he gazed upon row after row of k'yon stalks. They eclipsed the more distant flats where Irin knew the gwotl vines and dylt grew. Pret was just sitting down as Irin hopped across the main irrigation stream.

"Hello, Pret," Irin said as he approached.

Pret looked up, his wrinkled, leathery face brightening upon sight of Irin.

"You came, you came!" Pret cheered as his feet danced before him at Irin wished he had gone straight to work.

Irin walked to him and placed his hand on Pret's head, the customary greeting for one's superior, or between spouses.

"Your father no doubt told you I wanted to speak with you," Pret said with a two-toothed smile. "And you no doubt said 'oh my, must I go?' because who wants to talk to old Pret out at the fields . . . " Pret's smile slowly morphed to a frown as he seemed to segue from lighthearted banter to incensed complaining. " . . . where no one else spends all night tending the stalks and vines, shooing away crawlers, repairing waterpaths, pruning the . . . "

"Pret, please," Irin interrupted. "I am to work with your son this night. He is surely waiting for me. Is this what you wanted to discuss with me?"

"This? That? What was that? Just the ramblings of a bitter oldest, eh? No . . ." his eyes pensively scanned the sky. ". . . I have to tell you of the death of our people."

Irin's face did not change as he waited for Pret to go on.

"Every last new, old, and oldest, yes that's everyone. All gone. Fwoosh!"

"Because of this ypritl . . . "

"Yes!" Pret's eyes widened. "They are rocks! Some are tiny and put on a show for us when they come over the valley. But this one is like a flying *mountain*! It is going to come . . . faster than anyone can see . . . and it will land . . . " Pret raised his walking stick and pointed at the sunrise side of the valley's mountain walls. " . . . right there! Near the caves. The very caves where . . . well, you know what happened to—"

Irin did not wish to recall his elder brother, but he knew Pret was just being clever. He had mentioned the accident to remind Irin of another prediction—the one that foretold his own brother's death. Though that dream was had not by Pret, but by his only son, Wil, when he was still new. Regardless, Pret always had a calamitous prediction to share. It was why no one ever heeded his warnings.

"Dreams, dreams, dreams," Pret sang. "Sometimes they are only dreams. That is what I thought this one to be, but then Wil came to me two nights ago and asked in his whining little voice if I had dreamt of a giant rock that comes to Pwin-T. That's when I knew. That is when I knew for sure! Dreams, Irin . . . One time I dreamt I was a tiny black stone on a path, and crawlers of all sorts walked upon my back, looking at me as if I were their missing shell. But they had shells of their own, and I knew their ideas were foolish. My one hope as a stone was that I would be lifted and thrown onto stones like me, but bigger. If a bigger stone were beneath me, perhaps a storm might come and—"

"Pret, stop that!" Irin shouted. "You say that Wil had the same dream?"

Pret looked up at him, wounded. He quietly replied, "He did," and went silent, gazing at Irin with scornful eyes.

"I am sorry I yelled."

"It is disrespectful."

"It is, yes . . . you were—"

"Talking crazy, I know. I can hear myself."

"Yes . . . well, Wil awaits me. I will speak more of this with him."

"He has always been better than me . . . with the dreams, that is. When he was a boy, I thought for some reason that he would grow taller than a house. Just keep growing and growing into the sky. He would protect us from not just screamers, but enormous creatures not unlike screamers . . . but now I know it wasn't him I imagined. Look at you . . ." Pret gestured at Irin's k'yot. "Have your own shell now, don't you? Which brings me back to those with shells, and those that only *believe* they are shelled . . ."

Irin walked away as Pret continued. The dome of darkness now sheltered the valley, only the tiny holes—like eyeholes in a house—allowed the sunlight to shine through. Irin stared up at it as he walked, wondering if he could find this mountain-sized rock that Pret spoke of. Could it be true? Could a sky stripe come down to the ground? And if so, why had no one ever heard of such a thing happening?

Irin found Wil waiting for him at the site of the new house mounds. The dirt men had completed their work, shaping the mounds perfectly for the pouring of solid. The protrusions for windows and the door were completed, too, and branches of various sizes jutted from the dirt. The largest, for the air hole, shot up from the top. Smaller ones for eyeholes stuck out from the sides like little arms. On the other side, though he could not see them, he knew there were several in the dotted outline of a door hole for future clustering.

"There you are, Irin," Wil called. He wiped his cheek on his shoulder then inspected the blood he'd left behind. Wil's face had always been covered in little black spots. Many Pwin-T people had them here and there, but Wil's face was speckled with them like no other. He never said so, but it was clear he despised them. When he thought no one watching, he tried to scratch them off, but this just made him bleed, gave him sores, and later scars. Irin pretended to not notice. "Are you going to wear your k'yot every night now that they finally made you one?"

"I came out early," Irin replied as he peered over the lip of the giant vat of steaming solid. "How long has it been heating?"

Wil climbed down from the pouring ladder and walked to Irin, placing his hand on his friend's k'yot top. "Since last night. I already checked it—it's ready."

Irin leaned into the rising heat and inhaled the scent he knew so well. It reminded him of the taste of blood after biting his lip or sucking on a cut. When he was new, he thought he was made of solid, inside. That everyone was, because of that taste and the scent.

"Shall we begin?" Wil asked with a strange tone. He must have thought Irin was behaving oddly.

Irin studied his friend for a beat, then agreed and lifted the end of the pour tube over the edge of the vat, pushing it into the thick, molten mass. Wil hurried back up the ladder and picked up his end of the tube, aiming it. Irin moved beneath the center of the tube where a bar jutted from the bottom.

"One moment . . . " Irin said and unstrapped the k'yot top from the middle and tossed it on the ground. He returned to his bar, clutched it with both hands, and said, "Starting." He thrust the bar forward then pulled it all the way back. He pushed it forward again, back again, and then on the third push the liquid began trickling from the spout in Wil's arms. Wil directed the solid over the dirt dome with well-practiced movements. Irin completed eight thrusts, ducked under the tube to his opposite shoulder, and began another series. As he continued the thrusts, the material began to flow at a faster pace, oozing over the mound and forming a thin layer that quickly dried and hardened as it slid down.

Irin's thoughts drifted back to Pret. Wil hadn't said anything upon his arrival, so it could have been the usual lunacy. But Wil was also known for avoiding discussion of subjects that frightened him. *The caves.* Pret had brought up the caves where other workers extract the teepin and teegrin used to make solid. It was where Irin's brother, Tilleten, had died when Irin was still new.

Wil had dreamt it several nights prior but had said nothing, opting instead to act strange and stare inexplicably at Irin's brother whenever he was around them. When Tilliten finally pressed him, Wil said that he was afraid Tilliten would be "hurt . . . surrounded by solid."

No one listened. They assumed he was mimicking his father's routine of declaring foreboding prophecies. But Irin knew that Wil was different, that if he ever found the courage to actually mention something, it was because it was real. What Irin didn't know was whether the next night could be changed if you knew what was to occur. It certainly didn't change anything for Tilliten. The cave collapsed on him and he died, surrounded by solid.

Irin switched arms again and watched the liquid seep from Wil's end. He looked back at the vat of solid to be sure the other end remained submerged. The vat was almost half empty, but the tube was sinking with it. Irin continued.

A while later they had one full layer completed. The door had formed perfectly over its protruding mold, but the window was only half complete. As usual, its underside would need its own pouring and smoothing to complete the shape, and to join the bottom of the main structure into a single dome.

Irin futilely wiped his head with his k'yot sleeve. Beneath it his skin felt irritated and more sweaty than usual. He thought that clothes under a k'yot would likely help with this. He walked to the edge of the hardening dome and looked down at the border trench. The dirt men had dug it deeper than usual, likely a new rule after the overturned house incident. A screamer should not be allowed to raise an entire house, Irin thought.

"It looks good," Wil observed. "Let me work on your arms."

Irin unfastened the holdstrip from his k'yot middle and let the heavy jacket fall from his shoulders. He kept it on his lap so as not to get muddy from mixing sweat and dirt. Wil stepped behind him and began massaging Irin's swollen arms.

"I spoke with Pret earlier," Irin said.

Wil snorted, "I hope it wasn't too long . . . "

"He told me of a dream he had. You know what I speak of?"

Wil was quiet.

"He spoke of a ypritl. He says there is a giant one that will one day destroy the valley."

"I had the same dream," Wil admitted. "He thinks it real because we both had the dream. You know he grows crazier every night."

"He did mention you growing taller than the valley, or something of the sort . . . "

"Yes, and I protect the valley from screamers the size of the moon. You understand my reservations believing this new dream." Wil switched to Irin's other arm.

"He said you came to him about it first."

More silence.

"Wil?"

Wil moved away from Irin, "It can't be real, Irin. It's . . . it's devastation. Complete. Nothing left."

"And if it's real?"

"If it's real we all die. No new are ever born. Since the last outside tribe joined us, it would mean the end to all people. If it's real, there's nothing we can do about it."

"We could leave the valley," Irin said.

"There would be no time."

Irin stood up. "What do you mean? When does it come?"

Wil looked at him with despair.

"Speak!"

"*If* it is real . . . single half batch full batch. During daylight."

Irin had thought the prediction to be far in the future, that he would have the opportunity to work on the oldest men: discuss new expeditions to seek potential locations for a second city, assemble the smartest and bravest, to *plan!* Panic burned through his head. Sixty-nine nights before absolute destruction.

"Irin, please. It was just a dream. If you tell others, they will either mock me like my father, or be frightened, and with nothing they can do about it. Let us pretend we never discussed it."

"We have to go." Irin said as he paced. "Everyone has to leave the valley."

"And go where? We can't take houses with us! Beyond the valley, it is only screamers! Others have tried to explore further. Everyone learns as they grow from new to old, Irin . . . Pwin-T is safety, but Pwin-T is prison."

SIXTEEN

"**B**affling . . . all of it . . ." Tuni said with a look of wonder.

"What?" Dr. Rheese said from the kitchen area as he took the teabag from his cup. "You didn't grasp all the fascinating details? Beakwings, screechers, and kwottletwigs? It all seems quite straightforward to me." He smiled and tasted his tea.

Pete dropped his pencil along with his till now unfailing diplomatic manner. He turned to Rheese. "Doctor, I'm not exactly sure about the point of your constant sarcasm and belittling remarks. This is *your* discovery, and the investigation into its origin *should* be your highest priority, I would think."

"Absolutely," Rheese replied. "I suppose I'm just not all that excited about the color of the rocks on the ground or the gummed rantings of some supposedly long-dead old man. The point of this Matthew's visit to our humble dig site, as I understood it, was to verify the *age* of the artifact. I do not think we are any closer to that goal than we were before his arrival. Hell, it could be another 'triple-batch-half-batch' before we get anything useful out of this."

"It won't be that long, Doctor," Matt replied.

"You anticipate something of magnitude in your next viewings, do you?"

"I anticipate not being here. Dick."

"I think we all need to get some sleep," Pete cut in. "I've got good notes on all of this evening's new information, and it's nearly midnight. I'm planning to wake Matt at the crack of dawn. Anyone else who wants to sit in, get yourselves together early, 'cause I'm not playing alarm clock for anyone else."

Rheese returned the artifact to its plastic case and locked it in the safe.

"Generator off, ten minutes," Enzi announced, and left the motor home.

Tuni fetched her toiletry bag from her suitcase and returned to wash her face in the RV's sink. As she entered, she saw Matt and Peter standing in the back. Matt had a pillowcase over his head, tied around the neck with a string.

"Tell me honestly," he asked Peter. "Does this look stupid?"

"It's good to know you have a sense of humor about your situation," Peter replied as he shucked off his pants.

"Beg pardon, gents!" Tuni blurted as she averted her eyes.

"Afraid this is fieldwork, Miss Saint James," Pete declared. "We have to get used to the close quarters."

"Are you saying I should feel free to change into my nightdress right here?" she asked in a coquettish voice.

Matt stood still and listened; the pillowcase remained on.

"Absolutely. There's no gender discrimination out here," Peter assured her.

She sighed. "Very well . . ."

Matt jumped into action, fumbling with the shoelace around his neck and ripping the pillowcase off his face. Pete and Tuni burst into laughter.

"Sorry, Matthew," she said. "I'm just washing my face and returning to my tent to get some privacy from you dirty-minded men."

Dr. Rheese poked his head out from the high bunk beside Tuni and said with singsong pleasantness, "Would you all mind shutting your gobs and turning off the bloody lights? Thank you."

Tuni shuddered at the unwanted glimpse of gray-haired chest. Hurriedly drying her face, she turned for the door. "Ta-ta, all."

She spotted Enzi standing by the big, rubber-wheeled generator.

"Are they done in there, Miss Tuni?" he asked.

"I believe so, yes."

Enzi turned a knob and flipped a few switches. The rumbling engine went silent, and the light tower quickly dimmed. A moment later they met halfway between her tent and the equipment trailer.

"So, Enzi, how do I know an elephant isn't going to come rampaging out of the woods and trounce my tent with me in it?"

"No elephants 'round here, miss. That one not belonging, for sure."

"Thanks, I'll take your word for it. . . . So what do you think of all this? The artifact and the people Matt tells us about?"

Enzi raised his eyebrows and shook his head slowly, an expression of overwhelm on his face.

"It is too much, you know," he said. "Like he going to another world and leave his shell on the seat in there. He is like wizard—and he read my mind, too. I hope he will tell me my future before you both go away."

Tuni chuckled. "I don't think he can see in that particular direction." She pointed her thumb over her shoulder and whistled. "Backwards only."

Enzi frowned, deep in thought, and nodded.

"So where do you sleep?" she asked.

"Right over there in the trailer. I keep ramp down and shotgun close by. You safe out here, okay?"

"Thank you, Enzi. I do feel safe with you watching over us all. Night!"

She unzipped her tent and entered as Enzi unrolled his sleeping bag on the metal trailer floor and rolled up a shirt to use as a pillow. He reached up and touched the shotgun on the rack to be sure it was still there. Enzi wondered if Matthew would really leave tomorrow night. And if not, what would the professor do to get rid of them all? Enzi knew that Rheese wished to resume their search for diamonds, and Enzi wanted it, too. But the magic he had witnessed in the motor home—it meant something.

Tuni stared up at the roof of Peter Sharma's tent. Outside, the chirping of crickets and the plaintive call of a nightjar were the only sounds. She hoped Mr. Pups was well fed. He was surely sleeping on her pillow every day despite the stern warning she had given him as she left.

She felt for Matthew—this would be a difficult night. His motivations around the artifact had changed admirably, but he remained adamant about departing tomorrow. If he did, wonderful—she would join him with pleasure. If he decided to stay, though, what would she do? It wasn't just her cat that beckoned her home, but the cleanliness of her apartment and the warm comfort of her bed.

She was proud of herself for keeping up a tough-woman image before the group, shrugging off the bugs, the dirt, the heat, and the residual stench of death, when it all bothered her enormously. She had listened in wonder to Matthew retelling his experiences. She could see it all in her head and had hung on his every word. Matthew clearly was beginning to care about these long-dead people, just as she did. As her eyes watched a flying beetle of some sort bounce up and down on the roof of the tent, she wondered whether there could be a happy ending to their tale.

Was that Matthew's real apprehension? The people were clearly all dead and had been so for ages. Was that what it was? Was it that he didn't relish reaching the story's inevitable end—which could only be Irin's death, however it might come about? Perhaps it was as Matthew had mentioned on the jet: he didn't like feeling forced to use his ability—likely the legacy of his father's selfish, ill-considered decisions.

Tuni turned on her side and closed her eyes. She chose to hope that Matthew might decide to stay for one more night, and then she settled down to sleep.

Peter tried to lie still in the queen-size bed. Staring at the cloth-covered wall just inches from his face, he hoped Matt would be able to sleep. Pete had asked him if he wanted the wall side or the open side, and Matt called open. Though they faced away from each other, giving the other as much space as possible, Peter could feel the presence of another person in the bed. Surely Matt had the same sense of him, though multiplied by ten.

He remained disappointed that Matt would be leaving tomorrow, but he understood—Matt was, after all, an unwilling participant in all this. People were depending on him to experience things that made him uncomfortable, and under conditions that probably felt anything but safe. Matt had said years ago that he had always had this crazy paranoia—one of many—about someone doing something to his body while he was unconscious. That was why he preferred to do his sessions by himself. And here they all were, hovering over him and staring at his bare hands and expressionless face, when he would prefer not to be doing it at all! So it was just a bad situation from beginning to end.

"You still awake?" Matt whispered from behind him.

"Yeah," Peter replied softly.

"I think the asteroid thing is real."

"Oh, yeah?" He liked that Matt was thinking about it in bed and not just fantasizing about escape.

"Yeah. There is no question in Irin's mind. Do you?"

"If *you* do, then I do. You were there. I just hope we have enough time with you to find out."

Matt lay silent and never replied.

The pillowcase over his head irritated his nose, so Matt pulled it forward to make a small pocket of air between his face and the cloth. He had tucked his sweatpants into his long tube socks, and Pete had helped him tie the gloves to his wrists, with the shirtsleeves tucked tightly into them.

As he lay thinking about Irin and his constant intense emotions, he wondered how long the impressions would go on. It was apparent that the ever-present concerns of living in this village ensured a never-ending flow of thoughts and feelings. All were well imprinted into the artifact. When did it end?

If it were Matt's choice, he would take the piece of k'yot with him and read it from the reclined seat of the private jet on his way home. Well, maybe not—eighteen hours in that world would be a little much. He recalled experiencing much worse for much longer, then immediately chided himself for going there and tried his best to shut it out of his head. But her sobbing, dirty face and streaming tears wouldn't leave his thoughts. His breath trembled, and he hoped Peter wouldn't hear or feel it. He could hear her . . . *Think of something else,* anything *else! Think of the silver coins somewhere in the Atlantic!*

There they are: a typical pirate story treasure chest, sitting in white sand, deep under the ocean. A happy little crab scuttles by, and my hand reaches out to open it. Bubbles rise from it, of course, and inside . . . oh, so *shiny.* Are those pearls, rubies, and emeralds in there, too? Delightful. Oh, my, and diamonds? But, I couldn't . . . Okay, if you insist, my little crab friend. Diamonds. Enzi was thinking about diamonds. Why was Enzi thinking about diamonds when the elephant was trampling into the site? Who knows? Back to my fabulous treasure . . .

Rheese, snoring in his small bunk, dreamed of a screeching monster with an ostrich bottom half and *Velociraptor* neck and head, chasing him along the banks of the River Thames and snapping at his ankles. He tripped over a bench and fell into a garbage bin of rotting meat, whereupon the monster began devouring his protruding legs.

Peter's wristwatch beeped three times before he pinched the button to silence it. It was six thirty a.m..

Through the miniblinds of the RV's narrow rear window he could see that the eastern sky was brightening, though the sun had not yet crested the tree-lined horizon. He sat up in the bed, tilting his head so as not to bump it on the ceiling. Matt still had his back to him and was in the same position he had gone to sleep in. Peter reached over to Matt's shoulder and touched it.

"I'm awake," Matt said in a normal voice.

"Oh, good—my watch?"

"No," Matt replied as he slid out of bed. "I didn't really sleep."

"Oh, no way! Sorry about that. Was I snoring or anything?"

Matt tugged the bow knot, releasing the shoestring tied around his neck, then removed the pillowcase from his head.

"Nope. I guess I just had a lot on my mind. So, straight to work?"

Peter looked at Matt's droopy eyes. "I think we have time to get some instant coffee in you."

"I don't drink it—gets me too wired. Bad memories. No worries—let's just do this."

Peter slid down and grabbed his bag from the corner as Matt ran his fingers through his hair and shook his head.

"How about a little breakfast?" Peter asked as he pulled out a fresh pair of jeans. I'm starving."

Matt pulled a knit cap down over his ears before violently rubbing his face.

"Yeah, that'll work. Tumtum's a rumblin', as my mom used to say."

They pulled on jackets and passed Dr. Rheese, snoring away. Outside, they poked through field cases of nonperishables under the food tent and decided on a breakfast of tortillas, honey-roasted peanuts, and raisins.

"Any coffee to be had around here?" Tuni asked, poking her head out of her tent.

"At your service, milady," said Pete. And firing up the propane stove in the cook tent, he put on a pot of water. From across the site, they heard the sound of the generator motor turning over and then putt-putting to a stop. Enzi stood beside it, yanking a pull cord. It started on the third try, and the familiar background rumble returned to the clearing.

As he joined them at the food tent, Pete said, "Hope we didn't wake you, Enzi. Coffee?"

"No, sah. And yes, please, for the coffee." He turned to Tuni. "You sah-vived?"

She smiled at him, "I did. Thank you."

In a few minutes, the sun blazed through the treeline. Looking at Matt, Peter cocked an eyebrow.

"Let's do it," Matt said, grabbing one last tortilla to devour on the way to the RV.

"Hang on," Tuni interrupted. "What time is it in New York?"

"Um . . ." Pete closed his eyes tight for a few seconds, then said, "Almost midnight."

"Do you think we could have a chat with Jon?" she asked, blowing over her coffee. "He was expecting an update last night, but in all the excitement I forgot."

"Yeah, that's no problem," replied Pete. "The sat phone should have a good charge."

"Oh, yeah," Matt piped up, "and don't you have to call for the helicopter to come pick me up before it gets dark?"

Pete and Tuni exchanged a look.

"Yeah," Pete sighed. "I'll do that before we call Dr. Meier. We'll make sure they're dispatched with enough time to return to the airport before sunset.

"Thanks, Pete."

"You going with him, Tuni?"

She nodded guiltily.

"Very well, let's go call it in."

The phone on Dr. Jon Meier's nightstand startled him awake. As he fumbled for it, he realized he had fallen asleep with his glasses on and his book lying on his chest.

"Who is it, Jon?" his wife, Marisol, asked groggily beside him.

"At this hour? Must be the expedition . . . hello?"

"Dr. Meier, this is Peter Sharma."

"Oh . . . Peter." Meier cleared his throat. "Do you know what time it is here?"

"Sorry, Doctor, I'm in Kenya. I've got Matt and Tuni here with me!"

Meier sat up, instantly awake, and asked that they hold so he could switch to his cordless phone and let his wife sleep. "I didn't know you were going there, Peter—but who cares? Tell me everything!"

Peter activated the speakerphone, and Matt proceeded to relay all he had experienced thus far. Dr. Meier plied him with questions afterward.

"Let's try not to get lost in the details, Doctor," Peter interrupted. "We only have Matt until this afternoon."

"Is that right? So you've already determined the age of this civilization, Matthew?"

"No, Doctor. We're hoping I'll be able to get something today."

"But am I to understand that you are leaving regardless of what you discover today?"

Matt sighed.

Tuni leaned toward the phone on the table and answered for him. "That is the plan, Jon."

"Okay, and you understand that your end of our agreement will not have been met—right, Mr. Turner?"

Matt shook his head in disbelief. "If you say so, Doc. If you find the work I've done so far to be worthless, I guess I shouldn't waste my time with any more readings."

Peter saw where the conversation could easily lead, and he well knew that Meier's pigheadedness might actually doom their chances of discovering any more about the *Pwin-T* people.

"Gentlemen, gentlemen," Peter interrupted, "I'm sure we can continue with the existing arrangement. There's also something else I'd like to ask you, Doctor."

Peter switched off the speakerphone and stepped away with the sat phone to his ear.

"I'm having a bit of a problem tracking down some resources."

"Just tell me what you need, Peter," Meier replied.

"We don't have any astrogeologists on staff, and I had my assistant back at the center contact some different research centers. I think you know Gerhardt in Berlin—well, he said he knew of only three that we might be able to work with. One is in Antarctica for the next six months, another is on some other prolonged assignment in Africa, and the third . . . well—"

"You want Felch," Meier interrupted.

"Tell me he's still over there."

Meier considered it for a moment and intentionally let the line fall silent.

"Doctor, are you still there?"

"I'll think about it," he finally replied. "You know he hasn't done any fieldwork in a decade, right?"

"Heck, it's been a few years for me, too, but here I am!"

"I don't know if we can spare him, though, Peter. He's the only one who gets anything done around here."

"Just a few days—I mean it."

"Would he get a private jet, too?"

"I think we've tapped the budget after that first one, but he could certainly ride back with Matt and Tuni. That would work . . ."

"Like I said, I'll think about it."

Pete plugged the phone back into its charger and returned to the table. He could see that Matt looked angry and tense.

"Now, Matt," Pete said, "something to consider: the *greatest* interest in our success is not at the NYMM but at *my* organization in London. I appreciate Dr. Meier's assistance in getting you out here, but in reality, I'm sure I can arrange a similar form of compensation. Okay? Let's not let that be any deciding factor in what goes on out here. You've more than earned your keep in the past two days. Got it?"

Matt nodded and took a deep breath. The last thing he wanted to hear on this call was Meier trying to pressure him to stay and threaten not to loan him the promised silver coin.

"Okay," Matt replied, "how much time do we have? The helicopter's going to be here around four to five?"

Peter glanced at his watch and said, "The charter company said four thirty on the spot."

"So we have about nine hours, minus breaks?" asked Tuni.

Matt winced. "Even just *four* hours in a day is pretty brutal . . . but I'll do what I can."

SEVENTEEN

Irin slid the holdstrip through the loops of his middle and wrapped it around the single loop in his bottom. Turning his head side to side to be sure that the top was properly secured to the middle, he lifted his lightstick from the ground and pulled the two sections apart to access the firestick inside. He turned the bottom portion of the lightstick over until the small pouch fell out into his hand. Then, sprinkling the firedust onto the top of the firestick, he struck the stick against the inner wall of his house, and it burst alight. Tiny bits of the glowing dust flew in all directions before quickly dimming to nothingness on the floor. He then slid the top section back down over the firestick and twisted it securely into place. The bluewater began to glow, and Irin set it down, leaning it against the wall, next to the house light.

"It is getting late," Orin said as she checked over his k'yot. "How long will you be gone?"

"You're coming with me," Irin replied. "I invited everyone: men of all ages, women, new. All need to know what is going to happen."

Surprised, Orin began dressing as she said, "Is that a good idea? I suspect the oldest will not approve. You're ignoring rules, involving women . . ."

"I no longer care what they think. I tried to speak with Twill earlier and he brushed me off like a pest. He'll be there, I'm certain, but I will have my say. I don't expect much, but we are leaving and the more that come with us, the better our chances of survival outside the valley. What we have to do . . . everyone must help."

Orin did not respond, but her face sufficiently expressed her dread. Irin grabbed his lightstick, poked his head into the tunnel to his father's house, and said, "We are heading to the Gathering Rocks."

His mother's voice responded, "We're leaving, too, in a moment, Irin."

Irin worried that few would attend, but as he stepped outside, he saw lines of his people walking the paths toward the Gathering Rocks. He breathed a sigh of relief and he and Orin fell in with the masses. Rumblings of curiosity and confusion buzzed through the crowd. He heard questions followed by hypothesized answers stated as fact. It seemed most thought the gathering, as usual, centered on discussion of rules about screamers and making safe.

As he eavesdropped on these conversations, something occurred to Irin. In their minds, his people were off to find out what new rules were being set for them, not to participate in a discussion. Besides the oldest men, he could not think of anyone that would not blindly follow the lead of someone who spoke with authority. It was the nature of their society: polite obedience. The oldest clearly knew this, encouraged it, exploited it. Sure, close friends and families would gripe in hushed tones amongst themselves, but nothing would ever be publicly challenged. If you longed for change, you just had to wait for seniority and hope that by the time you had a voice, you weren't outnumbered by fierce traditionalists.

Twill was the oldest man with the most power. He had a suave technique for making the other oldest conform to his whims. Irin had seen this in practice with his own father, Tillyt. Tillyt had offered a logical, seemingly innocuous suggestion to place a second gate at the top of the valley entrance, the one from where screamers always came. This proposed gate would be tall enough to delay the screamers, and would be draped with strips of solid to ring out an alarm, providing an earlier warning to those in the valley to take shelter. Twill's subdued response offered praise for the idea, a longing for more men with helpful suggestions like Irin's father, and an indefinite hold on such a project until we better understand the nature of screamers. "But do not hesitate to return with more inspired proposals like this one," Twill had said encouragingly.

As Irin rounded the central path that encircled the Center House, he spotted the tall stone wall that marked the entrance to the Gathering Rocks. A dancing blue glow illuminated the cliff face beyond, and Irin wondered just how many people had shown up. The din of a massive crowd grew louder as they walked through the tunnel.

Orin leaned close to his ear and whispered, "You brought . . . *everyone!*"

Emerging inside the Gathering Rocks, Irin peered up and around at the tiered walls, nearly filled top to bottom with blue-lit eyes and cheeks. Bombarded by thousands of lightsticks all around, he was relieved to see that many were being extinguished. Orin took a seat on the ground level as Wil stepped tentatively from the tunnel's darkness. He paused and leaned out, examining the crowd with a stricken expression. Irin gestured for him to come in and join him in the center, but Wil refused. Irin turned to Orin for help, and she went to Wil's side.

"Come, sit with me," as she took him gently by the arm.

Irin felt his sweat trickling beneath his k'yot. It streamed down his neck, chest, and back. He was the only person wearing one, and this was clearly apparent to the masses currently staring at him. A preponderance of curiosity spotted with reproachful glaring.

It appeared that all who were coming had arrived, so Irin took a deep breath and prepared to greet them. *Speak with authority*, he reminded himself. He stepped to the center of the circle and several people took notice, hushing those near them.

"I am Irin," he announced. His name echoed off the cliff and through the mouths of his audience.

The clamor of the spectators lowered to near silence.

"Most of you do not know me—"

A familiar throaty voice interrupted from the lowest tier, behind Irin, "Yes, yes, my old friend, Irin . . ." Helped by his youngest son and his polished walking stick, Twill rose and shuffled his way toward the center. He spoke loud enough for all to hear, "I can help you to convey this very important message—perhaps a bit faster than you intended, but in light of the time, we must speak with haste and release everyone home for make-safe."

Irin glared at the oldest man; he wished he had prepared for such a predictable coup attempt. "I thank the oldest man for his generous offer, but will continue, unaided."

Twill and his son, Ilter, positioned themselves in front of Irin. Ilter had always been large and intimidating, surely encouraged by his father to establish himself in a leadership role since a young age. Ilter leaned close to Irin and whispered, "You should go sit down."

Irin gave him nothing but a quick glance before turning around to face the people seated on the cliff side.

"I am no one of consequence, I know," Irin began, and ignored the hiss from behind his back. "I simply pour houses with my friend, Wil. You all surely know Wil's father, Pret."

A high-pitched cackle burst from Irin's left and he spotted Pret, slapping his knees and doing his little leg dance on the second tier. Hushed murmurs spread around the circle. With the audience distracted, Ilter placed a hand on Irin's side and dug in his meaty fingers. Irin winced and stepped a pace away.

"My friends," Twill resumed. "There are a very tiny few who believe that—"

Irin interrupted, speaking in a booming voice that drowned out Twill's, "Again, thank you, Twill, but if you would, please wait until I am finished before sharing your thoughts."

Irin would not allow another second of silence for Twill to fill, so he continued immediately as an anonymous voice called to, "Let Irin speak!"

"Pret and Wil sometimes have dreams," Irin said as Twill and Ilter moved a short distance toward the tunnel. Twill feigned amusement to save face.

"These dreams in the past have foretold events that have touched many of us currently present. The recent blood attack that took fourteen people . . . we were warned of this event several nights before it occurred, but we did not listen. My own brother, Tilliten, for those that remember, was lost in a cave collapse. At that time, Wil was new . . . a very small new, in fact. I do not speak of this event. I have not spoken of it since it happened. But I will tell you, my father and mother can tell you, as well as a few others that were there—that Wil came to us and warned my brother that he would die, surrounded by solid."

He let this last bit settled in as quiet chatter resumed around the Gathering Rocks. He walked in a circle, nodding. "Yes, I think of him every day. I think if only we had *really* listened to Wil, Tilliten would still be here this night, probably speaking to you instead of me. As I said, I am no one of consequence. But Wil . . . " Irin waved to Wil. Orin tried to nudge Wil up, but he resisted.

" . . . is afraid to stand!" Twill said, and many chuckled.

Irin scowled at Wil and waved more insistently. Wil finally stood and reluctantly walked forward.

"Wil wished to share with all of you what he and Pret have recently dreamt. Wil?"

Wil said to Irin's ear "You say it, I can't say it."

"You *will* say it. It can't just be me."

"There are too many . . . "

The spectators began talking amongst themselves and Irin noticed Twill preparing to take over again. Wil clearly wasn't going to speak.

"My friend is afraid he will not be believed yet again," Irin said just as the thought came to him. "He believes it pointless, just as the previous tragedies went on despite his warnings. Well, I can understand this," Irin put his hand on Wil's head. "So I will speak on his behalf. There is a *yPretl* coming to Pwin-T. These beautiful stripes we see above are in fact rocks—

some big, some small. And there is a large one, the size of a mountain, flying toward us right now."

Eyes moved to the starry sky above as murmurs grew to an uproar.

"You cannot see it," Irin shouted over the commotion. "It is still too far away. But believe him when he says it is coming."

Pret howled from the audience and jovially said "Oh, it most certainly is!"

The noise level continued to grow as people shouted questions "where will it strike?" and "what will happen?" and "when?"

"Everything will be destroyed," Irin boomed and the people were finally silent. "Everything in the valley will burn. But we do not have to stay. That is why we have called you here, because we have so little time to prepare and go. We have more than two moon cycles before it comes . . ." but a clamor had arisen the moment Irin mentioned not having to stay.

Dominating the frantic dialogue, "Leave the valley?" and "Screamers . . ." stood out above the other rumblings. But Irin was satisfied by this discord. It meant they had taken the warning seriously, and that his anticipation of majority skepticism had been wrong. He let them go on, but noticed immediately as Twill dragged himself back to the center with Ilter in tow. The surrounding noise kept anyone but Irin and the oldest man's lumbering son from hearing Twill's next words.

"I hope you are satisfied," Twill spat. "Now step aside so I may repair the damage you have wrought."

Irin nodded and presented the floor to Twill. Ilter raised his lightstick to regain the crowd's attention. Quiet slowly returned.

"My friends, these are frightening times," Twill said. "And we must heed the words of Irin, a most skilled pourer! The oldest men and I have been conferring on this very quandary for days now, and fortunately, have had more time to consider the best course of action than my brawny friend here, Irin."

Irin seethed. He saw what Twill was doing. "He's not much of a thinker, but he sure is strong!" he may as well have said.

Twill continued, "And while we oldest would probably have opted against a citywide announcement, we now see it was the right thing to do, so we thank Irin for bringing us all here this night."

Where is this going? Irin thought.

"Now, since make-safe time draws near, I will speak quickly, and then we must all hurry home. First, we know that our houses—the very houses that this stout man pours for us—have withstood screamers, floods, and avalanches. A rock from the sky would not penetrate them. This is a fact. Despite this, we will increase the extraction and production of solid so that our able pourers can place another layer atop every house in Pwin-T!" Approving mumbles from the audience. "Second, we will need look-outs at all waking hours to keep watch at the sky and to alert the city when and if this rock is coming. This way, everyone will have time to make-safe."

"Twill, this is ludicrous—" Irin began, but Ilter stood in front of him and held his ready hands out before him. Irin could see Ilter wanted to fight him in front of the spectators. He would probably let Irin win, too. It would make him look like a simple-minded brute. Irin put his own hands up in a sign of peace.

"Third—and this was already planned—our biggest threat is the same we have always had. We will immediately begin construction of a second gate, all the way up the path to the canyon, to slow the screamers whenever they come. We will craft noisemakers and hang them from this new gate to provide us all with ample warning of an imminent attack. Now, with all these new projects, every hand in Pwin-T will be busy for some time, but I believe that we can not only accomplish these tasks, but complete them faster than we ever thought possible!"

The crowd was jubilant. Irin was horrified. Twill told them what they wanted to hear. Everything will be all right, no extreme measures necessary, but we will do something so that we are not doing nothing.

"Now, the safety of dark's dome will leave us any moment. Get you all home and make-safe as quickly as you can!"

Irin stepped out and spun slowly around in dismay as his people stood and made their way to the tunnel to leave.

EIGHTEEN

"**W**ait!" Irin shouted to the crowd. They paused and looked back at him. "This is no solution! Pret and Wil's vision sees the *entire valley* destroyed. There are no more houses. There is *nothing*!"

The murmur resumed, and many retook their seats.

"Listen to me. Listen to Wil. We *melt* the solid to make your houses. My brother, Pwig, mixes and melts solid for the pouring of k'yot threads. And all of us can tell you for certain that the solid that blocks rain and keeps out a screamer *cannot* keep out fire."

More people sat, and Irin seized the opportunity. Some were growing frightened again, and that was a good thing. Ilter grabbed Irin's arm, but his father stopped him and gestured for his son to sit. Ignoring them both, Irin turned to Wil, gesturing once more for him to come forward. For whatever reason, this time he did not receive the same resistance from Wil.

"Now, please, ask your questions of Wil and he will tell you what is coming."

Wil walked to the center and looked around him at all the people. A newest cried, and a woman tried to put it to her breast. His gaze held on her for a moment, and Irin hoped that his friend would think of Owil, back at his house, and her growing belly.

A man on one of the high rocks stood and spoke.

"Where does this rock come from, and why does it come to us?"

Wil glanced at Irin and then back at the man.

He said too quietly, "It comes from the stars . . ."

Irin leaned close, "Louder. And speak with strength. This may be our only chance."

Wil nodded nervously and repeated, this time with a power Irin had never heard from his friend. It may have been contrived, but it was perfect. "It comes from the stars . . . and the reason it comes to the valley is . . . well, that is where it is pointed. Like a stone that is thrown, this is simply where it lands."

The man sat back down, and another rose from a lower rock behind Wil.

"I want to know why you think this dream is real. I dream of running along the tops of these mountains, but it never happens—probably never will!"

"It is hard to explain," Wil replied. "But a dream feels like one thing, and a vision feels like another."

Questions like these came for a while, some merely repeating those already asked. Finally, Twill swung his walking stick in front of Wil.

"That is enough. My people do not wish to leave their homes. Most of them clearly do not believe this is going to happen, and those who do are more afraid of the screamers that will surely kill them if they leave."

Irin stared at the back of Twill's head and imagined what might happen if he struck him. He guessed that it would work against his goal, people seeing him as more tyrant than savior. He waited for the feeble voice to fall silent.

"I ask this," Twill continued, "and afterward let there be no further discussion of the matter. Those who believe the ridiculous dream of this killer rock, stand now."

The people remained seated, looking around them. Irin could tell that some wished to stand but did not want to be the only ones. A new murmur began, and Irin saw some people pointing behind him. He turned and saw one person standing. Orin.

Irin closed his eyes and raised his chin to her. When he opened them again, he could see that Oinni had stood as well, along with her eldest new, now called Inni after his dead father. Irin watched as an oldest woman, Olin, also stood up. Her oldest man had been taken in the recent attack. Many more people began to speak among themselves when they saw her stand. Soon all the families of the attack victims were on their feet, and others, who had not found it in them to stand before, rose as well.

Irin watched with relief as more and more stood. In the end, half the gathered were now on their feet. He stepped forward to speak, but Twill again swung the stick in front of him.

"Now . . . very well," the oldest's thin voice cried out, "you are believers. But the more important question is this. Who, of those standing, does *not* wish to leave Pwin-T? It is fine to fear the dream coming true, but sit back down if you have no intention of following this . . . this *old* into certain death outside the valley."

Irin stepped around the upraised stick and looked out on the throng. He raised his chin to them all. No one who had stood sat down.

"Fine," Twill concluded. "Those who leave, we hope some of you survive to return to the rest of us. Let us make-safe and discuss tomorrow how we can help the travelers."

As everyone began to leave, Irin spoke again. "Those who are fleeing with us, please stay for a moment. The rest can go ahead. We have plans to discuss."

Irin's new followers sat back down as the rest made their way from the circle.

Twill moved close to Irin. "Hear me, Irin," he said quietly. "Have your talk while those with good sense make-safe, but think hard on this: do you *really* believe I would allow you to take all these foolish believers to their deaths? No one will be coming with you. Be sure of that—it will not happen."

And he shuffled away, with Ilter assisting him into the tunnel.

What could Twill do to stop it, Irin wondered. The oldest had tried to convince them all, and it didn't work. But the man was a wise and influential manipulator and may very well disrupt his plans. Irin continued to ponder this in the back of his mind, hoping that the process of planning would solidify his people's decisions.

The last of the nonbelievers exited, and Irin raised his hands to hush the low whispers of the group. "I know the risk you take in doing this," he began. "And I promise you this: we *will* make it out of the valley. When the day comes, we will watch the skies in daylight to see the rock come down. When it comes, we will grieve for those left behind. They will not be forgotten."

"What if it does not come?" asked a man near the front.

"If it does not, we will return immediately to the valley and rejoin the people, thankful that they are still alive. Now, here is what we must do . . ."

Irin called on several people to lead various aspects of the preparations. Norrit would lead a group of men and women to visit every house and borrow k'yots from those who had decided to stay behind. Pwig, Irin's brother, would gather rope and cutters. Every household would bring its lightsticks. Wil volunteered to gather dylt, gwottle, and k'yon seeds to replant elsewhere. Irin asked if he could lead a group to create bundles of food for the journey as well. Other people shouted out other ideas.

"We need plenty of firedust . . ."

"Firepots for cooking . . ."

". . . and for melting solid!"

"Sleep mats . . ."

" . . .more clothes for the coming cold . . ."

The meeting went on until the eastern sky began to brighten, prompting everyone to depart quickly to make-safe.

Irin called out as they left, "Bring everything back to the Gathering Rocks for the next two days. We leave on the third." Then he walked to Orin, who looked at him with eyes wide. "Orin," he said, "return to the house and get Tillyt to help you make-safe."

"What? Where are you going?" she gasped, terrified. "The daylight comes!"

"I'll come quickly, before the sun reaches the mountains. I will tap on the door three times with a stone. Wait for me."

She looked at him in fear, but he squeezed her head and pushed her away. She loped out of sight around the bend in the path.

Wil looked at him, confused. "What are you doing?" he asked.

"Go to your house and make-safe. I must get something."

Irin jogged down the rightmost path, leading to the Clothes House, as Wil ran off in the other direction, toward his own house. Irin felt nervous as he trotted alone through the city. Not a single other person could be seen; every house had already made-safe. He came to the Clothes House, its doors left open as usual, for no one slept there. Inside, he found what he needed, picked it up, and stepped outside.

He checked the horizon; daylight would come anytime. The mountain paths were all fully visible now, and he scanned them to spot any sign of screamers coming. Seeing none, he ran up the main path to the city center, then cut left. He stopped outside the house, picked up a stone, and gave three light taps on the door. He looked around nervously as he waited, listening for any movement outside. Screamers had been through the city at this hour many times.

He heard the door's pushlocks turn, and the door pulled away from the opening.

"Irin?" Twill said, bewildered. "What are you doing at my house with the sun rising?" Behind Twill, Ilter leaned the door against the inner wall. "Are you so foolish that you wish to be ripped apart by screamers before you can even *try* to take away these foolish followers?"

Ilter stepped in front of his father and grabbed Irin's middle. "You had better run to your house now," he said. "Do not worry, we will end this tomorrow."

Ilter's face suddenly changed. His eyes rolled backward and showed only white as his hand dropped from Irin's middle. A ribbon of blood trickled over his lower lip.

The cutter had sunk so deep beneath the jaw, Irin supposed it had reached the inside of Ilter's head. He withdrew the weapon and let Ilter fall to the floor, clutching at his neck and gurgling blood.

Twill saw the blood and took a step backward in horror. "What have you . . ." He fell to the floor, and something gave way inside his midsection.

Leaping forward, Irin dragged the cutter across the oldest's throat until he felt it hit bone. The mouth opened wider than Irin thought possible, and Twill briefly moved as if trying to cough. His body slumped.

Wiping the bloodied cutter on Twill's clothing, Irin poked his head out the door opening. When he saw nothing moving in any direction, he dashed up the path toward his house. His eyes darted about. Acute fear buzzed in his head. Fear of being caught—no one had ever done what he just did. To intentionally end another's life. Fear of screamers—they could run three times faster than a person and his house was not yet in sight. Fear of Orin, his father, his mother, finding out what he had done. *It had to be done.*

At the door to his house, Irin picked up a stone and tapped on the door three times. Behind him he heard a barking squeal from the mountain pass, and looked back to see the sunlight fire the tops of the mountains. Three screamers were galloping toward the city. He had never before seen one in its entirety. His heart pounded in his ears as he imagined seeing all three— close up and very soon.

Again he tapped the door three times, but not a sound came from within. The barking continued, and he looked back in panic. He could see each creature galloping on all four of their long, thin legs. The one in front, the largest, was about as tall as his house. *Where is Orin!*

He sprinted around the corner and rapped on his father's door. Peering back around the corner, he saw that the screamers were clambering over the gate with ease. One of them spotted him and squealed, twisting its long neck toward him. As all three came at him, he slammed the rock continuously on his father's door. When they were just four houses away from him, Irin heard Orin scream from around the corner. He darted back around to his doorway, where she stood with his father. Both wore expressions of terror. Irin knocked them out of the way and grabbed the door as the largest screamer reached the opening and darted one of its front legs at him. Irin dug in and slammed the door shut with his shoulder, smashing the clawed foot against the jamb.

Orin and Tillyt rushed forward to lend their weight just as a tremendous blow from without flung Orin to the bed mat and opened a gap between the door and the wall. Two massive sets of claws snaked in from above the door. Irin released one handle, grasped the cutter tucked into his waist, and swung it blindly over his head. Feeling it sink into flesh, he twisted; then it was ripped from his hand. A fearsome screech sounded from mere inches away, and both long legs withdrew, taking the cutter with them. Father and son wedged their feet against the floor and pressed forward again with all their might, and the door sealed. Irin immediately twisted the handles.

Two huge slams struck the door again before the clawing and scritching sounds began. Gasping for breath, the two men sank to the floor. Irin looked back at Orin, panting heavily on the mat and pressing her hand against a gash on her forehead. He rushed to her side and moved her hand away to see. There was a large bump on her head, and he could see that the cut came only from the impact of the door, not from the terrible claws. He grabbed a piece of clothing from the pile and pressed it against the wound, tilting her onto her back.

His father shouted, "What were you doing out there?"

In the hallway, Irin saw his mother, weeping. He replied, "I wanted to make sure everyone had made-safe since I kept them all out so close to sunrise. I walked all paths."

"Foolish," his father replied. "Your woman could have perished along with you."

They paused and listened. The screamers had run off in search of easier prey and could no longer be heard.

"I know that. And I thank you for helping, Tillyt. And you as well, Orin." He stood and walked to his mother, steering her by the shoulders back to her sleeping mat. "I am sorry, Otillyt. You are safe now; you may sleep."

Returning down the hallway to his house, Irin lifted the top off his head and removed the rest of the k'yot.

"The screamer bled all over your k'yot," observed Orin.

Irin did not respond but just lay on the mat beside her and held her head to his chest. He breathed deeply and felt her body quiver in his arms. He hoped that the screamers would smell the blood, find Ilter and Twill's bodies, and take them away—it would look as if they had been caught before they could make-safe. He lay awake for a while, wondering what the next night would bring.

NINETEEN

Peter pressed the disconnect button on the sat phone and set it on the counter. "They landed in Nairobi about two hours ago," he said to Matt and Tuni, "and they've been on the road since. I'm thinking they'll be here within the next two hours."

"So who's this Flip guy?" Matt asked.

"He's an astrophysicist—works half-time at the university and the other half in our lab," he explained as he sat back down on the bench seat beside Tuni.

"Actually," Rheese said with that smirk that so annoyed his companions, "He's an astronomer who *thinks* he's an astrophysicist."

"I'm sure you'd love to tell us the difference . . ." Tuni said.

"Well," replied Rheese, "Flip would tell you that anyone can say they're an astronomer these days if they've studied the skies and know all the classifications of celestial objects and phenomena. He would say that an *astrophysicist,* however, is someone who actually understands how all the aforementioned phenomena work based on physical laws."

Tuni yawned and said, "Uh huh. So, then, what are they really?"

"Oh, that's exactly what they are, all right," Rheese clarified. "And he's still just an astronomer."

Peter gave Rheese a long-suffering look and said, "Whatever hairsplitting you want to do with titles, Flip is the foremost authority on lunar and planetary cycles at the research center. He should be a helpful addition."

"Back to business, then," said Tuni. "Matthew, your good friend Irin is a murderer."

"Yeah, so it appears," Matt replied as he munched a fistful of wheat crackers. "I was pretty shocked as he planned it at the gathering place. It was interesting, though. He was cold about it—I mean, in his head. It wasn't as though he hated them or was bloodthirsty or anything; he just *needed* to get Twill out of the way. I've experienced the mind of a murderer before, and it's very different."

"How so?" Tuni asked.

"I'd prefer to not go into it, but Irin didn't feel good about it; he just knew it needed to be done. There was no other option—in his mind, anyway."

A brief silence stole over the cramped motor home as everyone imagined various scenarios of what Matt might have experienced with a murderer in the past. Pete broke the silence when he snapped open the leather folder containing his well-scrawled notepad.

"Doctor Rheese," he began as he scanned his notes, "I'd like to get your archaeologists back from that base camp of yours. We'll need them to resume digging out from the artifact corner as soon as the new team arrives."

Rheese nodded as though he had anticipated this perfectly reasonable request, but his mind was awhirl with uneasy thoughts. The idiots he had smashing away at the site would obviously be inept at any sort of proper excavation. He needed them to disappear immediately from the base camp. He also realized that he needed to get the story straight with Enzi, who was outside at the food tent helping with lunch.

"There's a bit of a problem with that," Rheese admitted. "I only had them on loan up until yesterday. They've already returned to their . . . um, university."

Peter looked at him with disbelief. "They're *gone*?"

Rheese nodded with regret.

"Were you planning on sharing this tidbit of information with the rest of us anytime soon?"

"Well, I . . . I tried to say this was all a waste of time! I thought you realized that every hour counted."

Annoyance and disappointment clouded Peter's face. "Okay," he said, I'm not sure why this wasn't discussed over the phone a week ago—or, actually, well before that." His frustration was evident in his tone, but he managed to maintain his professionalism. "Well, we at least need all the survey equipment returned to the site: sonar, magnetometer, gridding string and stakes, flags—what else did you have? We'll need it to make sure we don't damage anything after we remove the topsoil with your backhoes."

Rheese inhaled sharply through his nose and appeared to be searching the RV's ceiling for an answer to the question.

"Doctor?" Pete persisted.

Rheese scratched his chin. Equipment? Besides the jackhammers and pickaxes? How to explain that he had never had a single piece of legitimate survey equipment during the past six months.

"They . . . ah . . . all the equipment was theirs as well. We'll, uh . . . we'll need to source it from someplace else. We probably have some spools for gridding, though."

Pete dropped his head into his hands while Matt and Tuni looked on in silence, feeling as if they were watching their parents argue. Rheese excused himself and went outside.

Enzi laid the pile of knives and forks on the first table after counting out enough for all. Hearing the trailer door shut behind him, he glanced back to see Dr. Rheese headed his way, an expression of urgency on his face. Enzi stood upright, waiting.

"Walk with me, Enzi," Rheese said through his teeth.

In the RV, Peter was on the phone with Maggie, outlining a list of needed equipment. He found himself getting a little snappy with her, and she told him to calm down if he wanted her help.

At the breakfast table behind Peter, Matt and Tuni sat discussing Pwin-T and some small details from the last session that Matt had left out during the note-taking session with Pete.

"What exactly did the screamer look like?" she asked. "From what you said earlier, I'm picturing a giant dog with a long neck."

"No, they're pretty nasty-looking, actually. I'd crap myself if I saw one of those things coming at me."

She looked at him with sleepy eyes. "Tell all, Mr. Turner."

"Okay, well, I can't really draw, but . . ." He slid a blank piece of paper in front of him and began to sketch. "See, they're really tall, and they run on all fours. This is the back—all bumpy and spiny like this. And the neck's kind of long, like a . . . What are they like?" He looked up for help.

"Ostrich? Giraffe?"

"No . . . uh, wait—you know what a monitor lizard is?"

"Yes. That's like a Komodo dragon, right?"

"I think so." Matt went back to his sketching. "Like a monitor lizard's neck, but a little longer and I think *way* more flexible. That one was twisting it around crazily. It looks like they can turn all the way around backwards just with their neck . . . There." He slapped the pencil down and turned the paper around, sliding it in front of her.

She frowned at it and bit her lower lip.

"See it now? Oh, and I think there's feathery things jutting backwards around the neck and sort of around its ass. Forgot to draw that—gimme." He quickly filled in the missing parts before returning the paper to her. "Oh, yeah, and sorry—I forgot the big, jutting chest bone thingy. Just imagine it there."

"Well, honestly I wouldn't be able to say it was missing from your artwork. Or where I would imagine inserting it."

"What do you mean?" He tilted his head to look at the paper.

"I mean, I can't really tell what this is. At all."

"It's a frickin' *screamer*," he said. "What do you want?"

She looked at it as though deep in concentration, but her chin began to quiver as she resisted laughing.

"Matthew, it looks like a five-year-old's attempt at a disabled horse with sharp teeth. I thought you said they don't have tails." She began to laugh.

"That's supposed to be feathers. I told you before, I don't draw." Matt flipped the paper back around and looked at it again. He saw what she meant, and joined in the laughter. Tuni leaned over the table to see it again.

"And why is its head on fire?"

"That's the neck feathers!" He had to laugh.

"Do you two mind!" Peter shouted, covering the sat phone mic. "These calls are over a hundred pounds per minute!"

They stifled their glee immediately. Matt felt bad, but when Pete resumed speaking and turned his back, Tuni mimicked his stern face and shook her finger at Matt, prompting more snickers. She gestured for them to go outside and leave Peter alone, so they scooted off their seats and tiptoed out.

"We're such children," Matt said then spotted Rheese and Enzi on the far side of the pit, walking and talking. It looked suspicious, and he elbowed Tuni to have a look.

"Dodgy . . ." Tuni murmured.

From the food tent, Wekesa called to them. *"Karibu, tafadhali!"*

"C'mon, food's ready," said Tuni.

They walked to the food tent, and Tuni asked Wekesa what was for lunch.

"Humburg," he replied over his shoulder.

"You'll never guess what's for lunch," she said to Matt.

"I caught that—burgers. Joy."

They sat down across from each other, and Tuni looked at Matthew's face. She had studied his features at length, both on the jet and during all the sessions. She thought he looked better awake and alert.

Peter burst out of the trailer and let the door slam behind him. Looking over Tuni's shoulder, Matt could see that he looked cross. He was coming toward them and muttering things under his breath.

"What's for lunch?" he asked curtly.

"Hamburgers," they answered together, looking at each other with cautious smiles.

"Oh good. I don't know what I was expecting out here . . ."

"So, Peter," Tuni said, "do you find it odd that Dr. Rheese doesn't have any equipment for excavations at his excavation site?"

"Yeah, what an imbecile. But I did tell him before to halt everything, so it makes sense if he was trying to save the grant money. It's just that usually, when we know how long a project will go, we buy equipment or make long-term lease arrangements with the owners."

"I don't trust the guy," Matt declared.

"I know where you're coming from," Peter replied. "But just because he's an ass doesn't mean he's dishonest. You'd be surprised how much he's done for the Cambridge Museum of Natural History. I suppose he does get a little leeway from our side of things because of that good record. If I had to like every person that worked for me, I'd have a fairly sparse staff. The nature of genius and all that . . ."

They all looked back as an engine started. Enzi was in the Jeep, near the equipment trailer. Dr. Rheese was walking away from it, coming toward the group, as the tires skidded in place for a second and then caught, before the Jeep took off up the road, the sound of its engine fading after it.

Rheese approached as the burgers and buns arrived on the table.

"Where's Enzi going?" Tuni asked him.

"He's off to the base camp—thought there might be some men left over there that he might convince to come back to the site and help out. I told him it couldn't hurt, if he didn't mind taking the long drive yet again. Good man, Enzi." Rheese took off his pith helmet and began to prepare his hamburger. "Believe it or not," he said, "you'll grow tired of these after a while."

TWENTY

Word spread quickly through the city: Twill and Ilter had gone missing. The trail of blood leading from their house was the only clue to their fate. As Irin walked the paths, he maintained the same look of shock and despondency that he saw on everyone else's faces. The horrible event had clearly slowed everyone down, though much remained to do.

With dark clouds looming over the sunset mountaintops, and gusty winds bowling through the valley, Irin hoped for the weather to come and go quickly. He visited the Gathering Rocks several times to monitor progress, biting back the impulse to hurry them, so as not to appear indifferent to the tragedy. His sense of hope found new strength as people who had not attended the gathering approached him and announced their plans to follow him. There were even some who had attended and sat in favor of Twill's "solution" who asked if they could still join.

"Of course," he told one and all, and reminded them of what was needed. Would they have converted if not for Twill's death? Irin wondered how many more would be convinced as they watched neighbors and family members prepare for the journey.

Irin found Wil with Pret at the food flats. They were arguing with Trig and Gen, two oldest men. Many people were busy gathering crops from vine and stalk, and Irin immediately understood what the oldest must be worrying about.

"They must stop, Pret," said Trig. "There is no way this much food will sustain the thousands remaining in the valley."

Irin saw the genuine fear in Trig's eyes. "Excuse me," he interrupted, touching the heads of all present. The four men looked at him; Trig and

Gen's faces bore sour expressions. "Wil, how much food has been gathered so far?"

"Only enough for a week," he replied. "And that's not accounting for all of the people joining in this morning.

"You keep going, old ones," Pret insisted. "You could take five times that and there will still be more than enough food for those remaining behind to sustain us until the rock arrives."

Irin nodded and then realized that Pret had said, "sustain *us.*"

"Then you will not be coming, Pret?"

"Oh, no," he responded with a toothless smile. "I don't believe there are any oldest who will be leaving. We would simply slow you down, and to be sure, most of us wouldn't even make it over the first two ridges."

Understanding completely, Irin closed his eyes to him. It was true; they would slow the rest.

"Hold it," Gen said. "Not everyone believes this thing is even coming. When it does not, the food will all be gone, and we will starve within a week when the seeds, roots, and mothers' milk run out."

"Is this true, Pret?" asked Irin.

"Yes, it would be true if the rock did not come to greet us. But it will, so, you see, there is nothing to worry about."

Trig and Gen were about to take up the argument yet again when Irin raised his hand in respect.

"Do not fear, oldest men. Your concern is a true one, and I make this vow: we will leave two weeks of extra food for you all. From our distant encampment, our eyes will face the valley during the daylight of the rock's arrival. If it doesn't come by nightfall, we'll immediately send a batch of the fastest old men to return to the valley with enough food to sustain all until the rest of us return days later. Pret, how long until next harvest?"

"None will be complete before the rock burns the flats, kills us all, burns the valley to ashes . . ."

Irin interrupted, "I understand. No, let us *pretend* the rock does not come—how long after that day before the next harvest?"

He thought for a moment. "The first will be the dylt in the far mountainside flats. They would be complete in the second week . . . after the sky stripe destroys the entire valley." He looked at the other two oldest as he said this, smiling with wily stubbornness.

"And after that?" Wil persisted, nudging his father's gaunt shoulder.

"After that?" Pret burst out in laughter, pulling at his long, white cords of hair.

Trig and Gen were growing more incensed than ever.

"Pret, please," Irin prodded.

"Yes, yes . . . of course. So important, all of this . . ." He chuckled a little more and then wheezed. "After the dylt, there will be short k'yon stalks. They will not be complete, but certainly edible and more than enough for the city even if it were closer to full."

Irin turned to the two oldest.

"Is this acceptable, wise oldest? You will have enough new harvests, *and* we will have food returning."

They accepted grudgingly and shuffled away, grumbling.

Irin waited until they were out of earshot, then leaned to Wil's ear. "Leave just enough food to sustain half the city until the rock arrives."

"But you said . . ."

Irin cut him off with a gesture, and Wil shouted across the flats to one of the gatherers. He passed on Irin's instructions, and she ran off to tell the others. He sighed and turned back to Irin with a concerned expression.

"Wil," Irin said quietly after another glance over his shoulder, "I thought of something new that we may not have considered. What if the teepin and teegrin doesn't grow in the rocks outside the valley? We will not have anything to mix into solid."

"Yes, it is possible. If we could find just one or the other, we could still melt and pour it, but it would not be as strong as solid. They have found a new t-lit, a yellow-brown one—like sunset—in the mines near the Gathering Rocks. No one has tried to use it yet, because it is too soft, but it makes me wonder if there might be other types in the faraway rocks. We have only every known what we have in the valley."

"We have to believe there is *nothing* outside the valley. If there is, it is a greatness, but we must plan as if there were nothing at all. The biggest unknown, of course, is water—beyond the Great River, we have no idea if there is more. We can only hope."

"So what will we do if there is no t-lit?" Wil asked.

"And what if there are no trees?" Irin added.

"We will have to find caves or dig houses under the dirt."

"Yes," Irin agreed. "We will need dirtpulls. We'll need them for other things as well, especially if there is no solid to make new ones. I'll tell Pwig he has a new task."

Irin left as Wil walked through the flats to speak to the food gatherers. Progressing through the city, Irin grew more confident that they could leave in two nights.

There was still much talk of Twill and of doubts about their safety outside the fence. Several times people stopped him to inquire about screamers. Did he think the killers would be satisfied if they took just a few people? Or were there countless screamers outside the valley—perhaps one for every fleeing person? Did the screamers *know* they would be leaving? Were they even now lying in wait beyond the second ridge, so that no one would be able to run back to the city? Irin tried to calm these worries, saying there were probably but a few screamers in the world and that if they attacked a group of such size, the men could defeat them by their sheer numbers.

He was unsure if they really believed his answers, but at least they returned to their preparations and allowed him to continue on his way. Indeed, he was unsure whether he believed his own answers. But the choice was simple: certain death in the city, or a fighting chance outside.

When he passed the trail of blood from Twill's house, a strange feeling settled in his belly, and he wondered, for the briefest second, if what he had done was wrong. But no. They would have been dead in a couple of moon cycles anyway. *Rid your head of such thoughts.*

As Irin arrived at the Hot Place, he saw Pwig speaking to Orin. Men and women sat on the floor, guiding solid through the thin channels and raising the frames of screening at the last moment before they hardened. In the next section, the lengths were scraped clean of burrs and then spun around sticks.

Pwig touched his brother's head when he arrived beside him.

"I think we must stop, Irin," he said through the side of his mouth, the way he always spoke.

"Why is that? We need hundreds more k'yot of all fittings."

"I have everyone who knows how, and they work at full speed. They say they will have only three k'yots completed in that time."

"*Three!*" Irin exclaimed. "Where is Opwot? Mine was ready in one day from the time it was requested."

"Yes, Irin," Opwot said from behind him. He turned and saw her sitting at his feet, placing a stick roll of solid on the ground beside her. Her clouded eyes stared sightlessly at his legs. "Yours was done in a single day. The rest of the old who were with you already had theirs, so we had to hurry to complete yours. Your middle took us the entire night, while Onorrit and Nitt cut and adjusted your top and bottom—they were Inni's."

Irin looked down at his k'yot bottom, only now realizing that he wore pieces of his dead friend's k'yot.

"So the middle alone took a whole night? Why can't we get everyone threading them right now and see how many can be made?"

"It normally takes three nights for an entire k'yot to be made," Opwot said as she resumed stitching from the new stick jutting from the ground. He watched her wrinkled hands work nimbly as she spoke. "We are all working as quickly as we can while teaching others how to stitch. It is not an easy task, but you are welcome to join us if you wish to add to our numbers."

"That's all right," Irin said disappointedly. "It's a greatness that you all work this hard."

He raised his chin to Pwig and ran his hand over his forehead to keep the sweat from his eyes. Orin took his arm and pulled him out of the area.

"It is halfnight," she said. "You should take this off."

Irin thought about it and realized what a relief it would be. He wanted to get used to wearing it always, but he knew that after another night, he would have no choice. Better to take the last opportunity to be free of it, as Orin suggested.

He disconnected the holdstrip from the bottom and slid them off, exposing his thickly muscled legs. Irin saw that women in the Hot Place watched with interest, smiling at each other. He pulled the top and middle off over his head and handed them to Orin.

Orin tried to hold the k'yot with one hand while helping Irin slide the shoulder straps of his clothes back on. The women were looking at him like never before. Orin was surprised to find that she liked their looks. Her man was known to be the strongest in Pwin-T. Though he was not the tallest, his arms, chest, and legs were thicker and harder than any other man's. He had grown this way when he had begun pouring. She walked away with the k'yot to return it to their house.

On the way, she decided to stop at Owil's house and check on her. All the women were most worried that with her belly so large and her pains growing more frequent, she would not be able to travel.

Orin stopped on the path and swayed, pressing her hand against the side of a house to stay upright. This was the third time. She felt the foodrise feeling in her stomach, but somehow she held it down. She swallowed and closed her eyes, taking a deep breath to calm her insides.

No time to be on the mat, she thought. She wouldn't tell Irin, not now— he had too much to do and too many worries. She would wait until the day her belly began to grow enough for him to notice, and it would be a surprise for both of them. But where would that be? Somewhere far away. Somewhere colder? Hotter? Somewhere that screamers lived, or perhaps, as Irin was fond of saying, somewhere screamers would *never* go.

She continued walking until she reached Owil's doorway. Her friend was lying on her side, munching dylt seeds without a hint of enjoyment.

"Are you well?" Orin asked her.

Owil moved only her eyes to look up at her and smiled. "I am fine, Orin, but I cannot seem to stop eating."

Orin knelt down on the mat, moved Owil's hair out of her face, and tied it behind her head. "When do you think the newest will crawl out?"

"Thank you. I don't know. If you had asked eight nights ago, I would have said next night. You ask me now? I say next night." They smiled, and Orin considered telling her that she had been feeling foodrise and that her belly, too, would soon grow. Probably best not to tell her as she might tell Wil, and he would certainly tell Irin.

"Do you need anything more that I can get you?" Orin asked, looking at the waterbowl. It was still full.

"I am fine, Orin, thank you . . . but how are *you*? Your skin looks tired."

"I'm fine as well." She stood up, hurriedly rebundling the k'yot under her arm. "I'll see you later."

As she walked the last path to her house, the foodrise feeling overtook her, and she clapped her hand over her mouth and fell to her knees. Her belly seized a few times, and she lost control of her throat movements. She forced a deep inhalation and held it. *Do not come, do not come, stay inside, stay inside,* she chanted to herself.

After a moment, Orin won the battle, and her food settled without coming out her mouth. Continuing her deep, slow breaths, she stood up, walking past the last few houses before entering her own. She dropped Irin's k'yot on the floor, lay down on the mat, and curled into a ball.

TWENTY-ONE

Matt raised his hands from the k'yot piece and opened his eyes. He looked around the RV and realized he was alone. His stomach churned, and he felt the same violent nausea Orin had suffered. He swallowed, and his eyes began to well up as he realized he did not have her same ability to fight it. He slid from the seat and rushed to the toilet, his hand over his mouth. He made it just in time and spewed into the stainless steel bowl. His eyes teared and his nose ran until, several heaves later, he was done.

Sitting there on the floor, he breathed through his mouth and cleaned his face with toilet paper. He stood and looked at his hands to see if they were clean, and realized he was gloveless. He flashed back to everything he had touched. The table? The counter as he passed, the door latch, the rim of the toilet, the floor. Fortunately, they had all been "clean." He yanked a paper towel from the roll and turned on the faucet to wash his hands and face. After carefully using the paper towel to flush the toilet, he left the bathroom and returned to the table to fetch his gloves.

Through the RV windshield, he could see a large group of people outside and two older silver-gray vans. They were the European sort of van with the unique, pointy front.

Matt pulled off his timer armband and returned it to his duffel before proceeding outside. Men and women were unloading the second van while Dr. Rheese and Peter showed two other men and a woman the corner of the pit where the artifact had been found. Matt looked around for Tuni and found her carrying cases from the second van with the new arrivals. She had just set the two cases down in the growing pile beside the equipment trailer when she spotted Matt. Jumping up, she smacked her head with her palm and jogged over to him.

"I'm so sorry, Matthew! We left you all alone!"

"It's okay," he replied casually. "I . . . er, needed the privacy..."

She looked at him questioningly. "What happened?"

"Orin's pregnant."

"Oh, my, she is? And you said Irin didn't want a child before."

"Yeah, well . . . I came out of the session and yakked."

"Yakked?" She looked puzzled. "Oh, you tossed! Poor dear! I'll get you some water."

"I'm okay. Thanks, though. I take it these are all the research lab folks that Pete called for . . ."

"Yeah, they just got here about ten minutes ago. There were too many names to keep track of, but . . . um, the guy down there with Peter and Rheese is Flip."

"Which one?" Matt said, squinting.

"The one with the spiky red hair. You can't see it from here, but he has a face-full of freckles and big black plugs in his ears."

"Ah, a punk rock scientist, eh? And who's the other guy down there? And the woman?"

"I don't recall his name, but he's the sketch artist gent. And the woman with the ponytail and implants—she's an anthropologist from Paris—Colette something."

"Implants?" Matt asked with an accusing smile.

"Obviously—her frame's much too petite for those monsters."

"Hm, you could be right there . . ." Matt said, shading his eyes with his hand. "What about the rest of these people?"

"You know, I met them all, but I can't recollect. There was a Geoffrey and an Allison, and I think that tall gent with the brambly beard is Rodney."

"Matt!" Peter yelled from the pit as he scrambled up the slope with the others. "We left you alone in there—sorry about that! Let's get you back inside to go over your last session, but first I'd like you to meet everyone." He leaned to Matt's ear and whispered, "I told them you're just a lab monkey. Be sure to avoid getting sucked into any work conversations with these folks. Hey, I forget—do you shake hands? "

Matt replied, "It's no problem when I'm nicely sealed." He held up his gloved hands.

"Good," Pete replied. "You'll notice all these field folks are pretty touchy-feely." Pete stepped aside and held out his hand toward the freckle-faced, spiky-haired man. "Matt Turner, this is Flip Chamberlain."

Flip reached out his hand. "Nice to meetcha, Mr. Turner," he said with a thick Scottish accent.

"Same here," Matt replied.

"And this is Colette Vioget, from the Anthropological Studies Department."

"*Bon soir,* Monsieur Turner," she said. Matt shook her hand while making a conscious effort to look her in the eyes and not down to the swell of décolletage emerging from the half-buttoned khaki shirt.

"Matt, this is Graham Hillary."

A short man with a ready smile stepped forward and said "'Ello!"

Peter continued with the introductions as Matt found himself in the same boat as Tuni on name/face recognition. As Peter finished off with the last of them, the tall bearded fellow walked up to them carrying two cardboard boxes.

"Where do you want these, Mr. Sharma?" he asked.

"Ah, yes . . ." Peter glanced at Matt and said loud and theatrically, "Why, Rod, is that a brand-new tent and sleeping bag you have there?"

"Yes, sir," he replied. "I have a sealed new pillow and air mattress back in the caravan as well."

"Great. Well, I'm not sure if we'll need them now." He turned to Matt. "They were for you, so you'd be more comfortable sleeping. Sorry, I requested them before I knew your plans."

"No prob—that would have been cool. Thanks."

"Just put them back in the van, would you, Rod?"

"Sure thing, Mr. Sharma."

Peter turned to the group of new arrivals and said, "I'm sure you all know what you're doing and what you need for prep, so have at it, folks." The group dispersed and remerged into smaller clusters of specialists, some heading to the equipment trailer for supplies, others down the dirt ramp of the pit. Pete turned to Matt and Tuni and cocked his head toward the RV. "Shall we?"

Inside, Matt described the most recent events, ending with the new Orin perspective and her era-spanning nausea. From their surprise, it was apparent that no one but Matt had considered that anyone else might have imprinted on the artifact. In Matt's experience, most artifacts had countless imprints from various people from wildly different ages. There would be a short flash here and there from the original owner, say, an Egyptian priest, then some other priest, maybe a wife or child after a death; then there were the burial people, all very intense with their ceremonies, and finally, flash forward a few thousand years to the archaeologists discovering it. Then there were the researchers and maybe a conservator or two handling it, and that was where the imprints typically ended. That was the usual situation, but Matt had experienced numerous other patterns and the occasional unique imprint. In the last session with the artifact, for example, he had experienced something new—he had never "been" a pregnant woman before.

Pete continued scrawling notes for a few minutes after Matt had finished, then the three of them returned to the oppressive afternoon heat. Peter instantly spotted someone working on something they apparently should not be, and he excused himself with a "Silly prats . . . pardon me, be right back."

Matt heard Tuni say "Ugh" behind him and he turned to face her.

He asked, "What's up?"

"I think I'm getting smelly. I'm going to go take a quick shower in the RV while I've got it to myself."

"Uh, okay, I'll come with you," he said with a smirk.

"Right, cheeky man, and guard the door—keep me safe, right?"

As she walked to her tent, Matt pushed up his sleeve to check the time. *Final countdown,* he thought. *Two more hours and I am out of here.* Hearing crunching footsteps behind him, he turned to see Tuni returning, but with a strangely angry expression on her face, narrowed eyes fixed squarely on his.

"What?" He took a step back and put up his hands, fearing that she just might take a swing.

"What have you done? With *me,* I mean."

"Uh . . . ya got me," he said, truly baffled. "What the hell are you talking about?"

"Have you read anything of mine? Gotten a quick peep at me through my own bloody eyes?"

He blinked in surprise as he tried to form the words to defend himself.

"I—I can't believe you would even *think* that of me!" She crossed her arms, and her eyes held not a scintilla of humor. "Seriously? I wouldn't— Tuni . . ." He tried to marshal his thoughts, but she had him raddled. He breathed. "Listen to me, okay? For one thing, I would *never* do that. It's a total invasion of privacy, and I would no sooner sneak into a women's bathroom and peep over the stalls—it's the same thing. And second, I would never . . . I mean—*you* . . . you're . . . you're *you.*"

"What the bloody hell does that mean?" She was still serious.

"*Meaning* . . . of all people, I would never do anything to damage . . . forget it."

"Your chances?" she ventured.

He nodded sheepishly. "Something like that."

Her face softened a degree, and she regarded him for a moment, chewing her gum. His face radiated innocence and desperation.

"I believe you," she finally said. "I'll be back."

Tuni walked off to the RV, and Matt shook his head with disbelief. He looked at his watch again and then at Peter and the new team, pointing at this or that, sticking little wire things into the ground with yellow flags at the tops, others unwinding string and stretching it between wooden stakes. The site had really come to life. He was melting in his turtleneck and decided to seek shade back at the food tent.

A short while later, one of the new women had driven a backhoe to the far side of the site and was expertly digging up the area above the corner. Tuni had appeared from the trailer in a fresh pair of cargo pants and a tank top, her hair still dangling in wet strands.

"I'm sorry about that, Matthew," she said as she approached. "I really don't think you're a perv. I just went barmy and paranoid for a moment when I was looking at everything in my tent and thought how I must have imprinted on it all . . ."

"I understand," Matt said gravely. "You glance around at your things and suddenly I'm a deviant. Makes sense." Though overcome with relief, he played up the hurt.

Peter jogged up to them, clapping his hands as if shooing pigeons from the ground.

"Let's get going, people! Tell me, what are you up for, Matt? You think one more long session, a couple of short ones? Your bird will be in the air in an hour. Clock's ticking."

"I think I'll ride it out. My stuff's all packed, so I'll just set the timer for an hour and pass up the breaks if there are any."

"Wonderful," Peter replied. "They just flip to the next 'clip' if you don't release the object, right? I don't recall you ever going so long in New York."

"Yeah. It's just dead air—kinda spooky, but I'm used to it. Sometimes it's long, sometimes just a minute or two. Though there hasn't been any dark space since the first time he took off the suit. Just keeps rolling."

Walking to the RV, they saw Enzi arrive in the Jeep, alone.

"Jambo, Enzi!" Tuni waved. He searched for her voice and smiled when he found her.

She pointed at the trailer door to invite him into the session, but he declined with a polite gesture and jumped out of the Jeep, clearly on a mission to see Rheese.

She followed Peter inside, and the door snapped shut behind her.

"Oh, wait—we need Dr. Rheese," said Peter.

"Ugh, do we really?" Matt quipped.

"Hah! Yeah, we actually do. The key to the safe."

Peter disappeared outside for a moment.

"So," Tuni said, "less than two hours and we're out of here, huh?"

Matt nodded. "Yep. Home sweet home—after thirty-something hours of traveling."

"What will you do?"

"What do you mean? When I get home?"

"I mean, it's going to kill *me* not to know what happens next in the story. I sit here and wait for your eyes to open, and it seems like forever! I lean over and read your timer and sit and doodle on scratch paper. And this one—an *hour*? I don't know what I'm going to do—go bloody insane, I suppose. I just imagine that you—I mean, when you're there, essentially you *are* Irin. You said you feel his emotions and everything. I just don't know how you could stand it. Leaving, that is."

"Honestly, I've never experienced a single person this long. I usually dread sessions of *any* kind because it's so invasive to my mind and—well—my body." He gestured toward the bathroom. "But I really just need to see what's next, like you said. This time it's different. Even though he's . . . you know, he . . . " Matt sighed. "He's *dead*. Man, weird, but it's hard to say. And I *know* it happened—millions of years ago! But right now, he really isn't. He isn't dead to me. I'm stuck."

Tuni nodded enthusiastically. "That's exactly how I feel! I know he's been dead so long, he's not even dust anymore! But his story's a bit like a movie to me. How you start to get invested in someone—a character—emotionally, I suppose." She paused and peered into his eyes. "Can I tell you something daft?"

"Always."

"When you tell me what's happening, I picture him as being you. He looks exactly like you, but black and with little dreadlocks."

Matt laughed, "That is funny. What's weird is, I actually just saw him for the first time. I mean, I knew basically what he looked like, because they all have the same sort of features, but it wasn't until I was seeing him through Orin's eyes in the last session that I got to see his face. She sees him as beautiful, too. I told you: their emotions are very intense. And not just because of everything that's happening—they feel even simple things with this crazy intensity."

"Perhaps that's just love and you've never felt it before."

"Uh . . ."

"Nothing against you. I don't believe *I've* ever been *in* love, but I know the love I feel for my mother is intense. Do you have that for your parents?"

"Not really. I think just my sister. I don't know, maybe my mom."

"You mean you don't love them at all?" she asked, looking a little shocked.

"No, no. It's not that I don't love them, but my feelings around them are all twisted up and ruined by other crap. My dad, for . . . well, I mean, it's obvious how awful he was, and my mom, she didn't do anything to stop it."

"She didn't protect you."

"Not even a little—too busy being a good wife."

Tuni looked at him and felt a touch of his sadness. She felt bad that she had brought the conversation there.

"I'm sorry, Matthew. I really am. That's what mums are—"

"It's all right," he interrupted. "Let's drop it. No big."

She nodded, and in walked Peter and Dr. Rheese.

TWENTY-TWO

Orin's face appeared in front of him, and she tilted her head to indicate that everyone was ready.

Irin walked around the tall rocks and climbed to the tallest one. From up high, he saw the glowing line of women, new, and k'yot-clad men, stretching from the Gathering Rocks all the way to the Center House and then disappearing along the paths toward his house and, eventually, the gate. Only the tips of lightsticks were visible over the houses.

Wil and Pwig had completed the final count, and Irin had been speechless at the increase. He scanned the line and saw all the fully packed n'wips. Their triangular frames of young trees, with cloth bundles suspended between, would be pulled by their two extended front poles. Most of the weight rested on the smooth, up-curved ends at the back of the n'wip, to minimize the strain on the puller's back. Only having used n'wips in the food flats and over relatively short distances, everyone agreed they would alternate pullers along the way. Irin worried about fatigue during the initial ascent up the hillside, so he had instructed the men to take turns frequently and even double up to pull the same load when the going was especially steep.

All along the line, oldest and others who had decided to stay were saying their good-byes to the travelers and bringing them extra waterbags and clothes. Irin had waited a short while, but he knew they needed every bit of the dark hours to get through the mountains and then scout for a safe, suitable encampment. Climbing down from the rock, he made his way to the gate. He felt it deeply, in his throat and head, when nearly every person he passed thanked him or uttered words of confidence or support.

He had assigned three scouts and put them near the front of the line, behind those he called fighters. Not all the male old had k'yots, so those without were in the middle of the procession with the women and new. All men were given cutters, and many women carried them as well. At the front, nearly a full batch of fighters matched roughly the same number at the rear. Some had longer cutters, the length of a man's arm from fingertip to elbow, curving slightly, with the sharp edge on the inside for harvesting k'yon stalks. Wil had thought they might prove useful should things turn bad.

Near the middle, where the women and new walked, Irin stopped with Orin, and they wrapped their arms around each other's heads. She pulled his forehead to hers and looked deep in his eyes.

"I have no more doubts, Irin," she whispered. "You're doing this. And you're my man."

He felt the intensity from her for a moment, and then she turned his head, pulled his ear to her lips, and whispered, "You are *everyone's* man now."

She smiled at him, and he continued toward the gate while she remained at the front of the women and new. As he reached the front, the fighters all saw him, and some touched his head. He climbed atop the gatepost, where the screamers had come over two nights ago, and tried to think of something to make the people believe. All those in sight had hushed and looked up at him. He inhaled deeply and tried to imagine what they would want to hear. Another proclamation that they would be safe? A reminder that everyone must help one another or that they all must move quickly? A final good-bye to Pwin-T?

He reached to his waist and pulled out his two cutters, one long and one short, and raised them high over his head. The people stared at him in silence, each interpreting the gesture as they wished. He put the cutters away and climbed down, picking up the lightstick he had placed there.

He turned to find Wil, his cheeks—except for the spots—aglow from the lightstick.

"I must tell you something," Wil said in a concerned voice.

"Of course," Irin replied. "Let's just get everyone moving. We'll have plenty of time to speak on this journey." He touched Wil's head and nudged him to the gate handle.

Wil slid the gate all the way open, and the line began to move forward and stretch out. No one spoke, and he could hear only the tramp of shuffling feet and the scuff of n'wips dragging on the path stones. The n'wips quieted to a smooth swish once their skids reached the dirt beyond the gate. Irin watched his own foot coverings as he marched up the first hill, and realized he was stepping in screamer tracks. A deep breath and a long blink pushed the images from his head once more.

After a short while, the front of the line had reached the first peak, and it continued ahead while Irin trotted off to the side and climbed up a small outcropping of rocks. He peered down the hill and saw that the last of the convoy was just now passing the gate. It was an awe-inspiring sight: the plain of domes that he had seen but a few times from this vantage point. He watched the shifting, bouncing blue stream of lightsticks curving below him as if the Center House's giant light tube had cracked and this were the leakage. The journey had truly begun.

Irin rejoined the line and walked quickly to the front. He could identify Wil's back from the way he walked. Other than their gait, all the men at the front looked the same: all k'yot-clad and holding lightsticks.

As they approached the second peak, Irin felt the heat of the Melting Place. Few had ever seen it, and seeing the steam rising over the heads of the people beside him, he cut through the line to have a look. The crack in the ground extended to a narrow fissure in the mountain, and there the mist rose up as well. Both sides of the inner wall were soaked and gradually crumbling away, with little cobbles of smooth rock tumbling down into the boiling water. Irin imagined that the mountain grew bit by bit with everything that fell into its boiling center. His people had been feeding their dead to the mountain for generations, as long as they had lived in the valley.

He recalled, just a half batch of nights before, when they rolled Inni into this very crack. Inni would have been a good fighter to have along now; his strength and courage would be welcome. Irin had to wonder: if Inni still lived, would he not be leading this trek instead of Irin? Inni had always been the leader until he fell ill. It had only been a couple of weeks before the bloodless death took him. Aside from Inni, Irin hadn't known of any other old, men or women, who had died in the manner of the oldest. No one had understood it. As he peered down into the crack where Inni's body had fallen, he wished that his friend would rise from the steam and take this burden away from him.

He turned to see the women and new watching the steam rise behind him as they passed. Some had placed their newest on the n'wips. A good idea, he thought, for their arms were surely tiring by now. He looked at the passing faces, trying to measure their fatigue. Though he was not yet breathing heavily, he reminded himself that others would likely need to rest before he and the fighters might think to pause. For the moment, though, all seemed to be doing well. He would check again soon.

The front of the line had moved around the Last Turn. Irin had never seen beyond the Last Turn, and he knew only a few oldest who had. He trotted ahead, squeezing between the people on the left and the cliffs beside them, but finding more room on the right side of the trail, he cut back across the k'yotless men and women and hurried to the front.

He finally found Wil and Pwig in the lead and joined them there, walking along the narrow defile until the trail dipped and widened into a broad, diamond-shaped opening. Pwig glanced at Irin; all three were keen to see what lay ahead.

Irin inhaled a strange, bitter scent and looked all around. The sides of the gorge rose so high around them that the moon was no longer visible and only a thin strip of stars lit the blackness above them. This must be the Last Canyon that the oldest spoke of. But they had never mentioned the immense pile of rocks that now blocked the way forward. Irin looked up and saw where the rocks had come from. Far above the great blocks of talus, an overhanging buttress of stone suddenly ended—an arch that, before giving way, had once connected the two sides of the gorge.

"How do we get everyone past this?" Wil asked. "The n'wips and the new?"

Behind them the convoy slowed and stopped, and a murmur of voices wondered why.

Irin gestured for Wil, Pwig, and some of the fighters to come with them down the short hill to the rock pile. As they approached, a fighter named Nitt said from behind them, "Screamer tracks."

They stopped and looked where he held his lightstick to the dirt.

"I know," Irin replied. "And their scat—don't you smell it?"

The men all shot looks where Irin had pointed. The big, globular droppings lay all about them. The men all peered into the darkness, trying to see everywhere at once. Would the creatures leap from above? This would be a good spot for an ambush, coming from both sides. Irin moved toward the rocks to have a closer look. With every step, the smell grew more acrid—it must be their urine, too.

Approaching the largest rock he could find, Irin kicked the sticky droppings off it, then worked his fingers under one side of it. He looked back at the other men for help.

Nitt noticed first and jogged to him, grabbing hold of the other side of the rock. They lifted it and shuffled up the hill sideways, heaving it away from the path. Wil and Pwig followed their lead and rolled another block, too heavy to lift, off to the side. Others joined in, and soon they had cleared away the stones down to a layer of mud that reeked of screamer scat and urine. After moving the stones, the men had to take great care not to wipe the sweat from their brow with an unclean hand, for as Nitt discovered, the rank liquid burned the eyes like fire.

Wil thought of using dirtpulls to bring down fresh soil and gravel from the sides of the bowl so that the others would not have to track through the foul mud or soil the n'wips. Soon they had a dry, firm trail.

Irin gazed back at the waiting throng and then ahead just as the scouts reappeared. This territory was unknown to all, he realized. Even the oldest knew of nothing that lay beyond the Last Turn or even the whereabouts of the old city. Some called it Pwin; others called it Kytin Gyor. It was where their people had lived thousands of moon cycles before the trees ceased to grow there.

"The trail continues the distance of three k'yon furrows," the scout known as Woggir panted, "and then dips down before another steep rise." Both men wheezed and sipped water from their bags.

"Will the women and n'wips make it up this rise?" Wil asked.

"It is no steeper than the rise to the first peak from Pwin-T," Woggir replied, still breathing heavily.

Irin let the two scouts return to the front and waved for the march to begin again. The first rise had not been too arduous, but everyone was much more fatigued now. He posted fighters at both sides of the diamond-shaped opening as a precaution. Screamers clearly frequented this spot, and no one could climb the steep, scree-covered walls to see what lay beyond. He waited until perhaps a hundred people had crossed the cleared and filled area safely, then returned to the front.

Trudging along, the fighters in front found themselves walking into a dark and progressively narrower canyon, whose walls closed in until finally joining overhead, so that the taller men had to duck to get through. Irin wondered, could a screamer fit through an opening this size? It would have to crouch down low, and even then it would not be easy. He stepped through the narrows, and a while later the canyon walls opened wide once again. The trail was not as clearly defined by the surrounding terrain, but the stars shone in a clear sky, and the light of the rising moon glowed above the far ridgeline.

Irin turned and let the men by as he waited to see the first n'wip clear the opening. Below him, the men at the bottom of the ravine were pulling off their foot coverings and shaking out the gravel after sliding down another long, scree slope.

After telling those behind him to wait, Irin began to work his way carefully down the slide. Despite his caution, he lost his footing twice, sliding and nearly sprawling headlong before he reached the bottom. The scouts had failed to mention this part—he would have to send the others the longer but gentler way around the side.

"Irin," Wil called out, pointing to a fighter who waved from the path above.

Irin raised his arms in response.

The man kept his arms up but spread his fingers and made clawing motions. Screamer? Irin and the others at the bottom reached for their cutters, but the man waved no, then pointed at his own backside. Irin understood at once: he meant they had encountered more droppings.

Irin gestured for those above to hurry up. He understood why everyone was so uneasy, but it was well known that the creatures had never once shown themselves at this time of night. Still, they must move along—no one wanted to discover just how early the killers rose from their slumbers.

The line continued, wrapping around the safer slope to reach the bottom. It was good that they had had a short rest, Irin thought, because the hill ahead would be a bit of a push.

Wil fell into step beside him. "I still have something to tell you, Irin. I had a new dream last sleep."

"Yes, I had forgotten . . . hold a moment."

TWENTY-THREE

Matt pressed the STOP button, ending the buzzing of his armband. His hearing cleared, and he noticed a new ordering of sounds: activity outside—a backhoe, most likely—and people shouting back and forth across some distance. His eyes adjusted to the light as he fumbled for his gloves.

"Matthew," Tuni said softly, "Peter and Dr. Rheese are outside, but I'm afraid you'll have to tell me everything quickly—right now." She spoke bluntly but with a playful note in her voice. "Peter said you could write everything down on the jet and e-mail it to him, but the helicopter will be here any minute, and it will be far too loud in there for you to tell me anything—and I simply will not wait."

"Yeah . . . ," Matt said groggily. "I gotta go."

"Damn! Well, hurry it up, sir."

Matt slid out and walked unsteadily to the loo, closing the door behind him. When he returned a few moments later, he said matter-of-factly, "They're already on their way over the mountains. Lots of monster poo everywhere, and Wil had another vision."

When he said no more, Tuni said impatiently, "Well, go on—what's it about?"

"Don't know. The timer buzzed before he could tell me."

"Well, um . . . crap!" she muttered. "Can you jump back in real quick and just get that part?"

"Hmm . . . it's a good idea," he said. "I'm a little shaky, though. Well, actually, no—it'll take too long."

"Why? Can't you just set your timer for a minute, hear what he's got to say, and buzz right out?"

"No. I have to fast-forward through everything I've seen. It's quick, sort of like jumping through chapters in a DVD, but it still takes a couple minutes just to get back to the last part. Reads always start with the strongest imprint."

"What if we take the artifact with us?" she said half jokingly.

"Right. Then we get put in some scary Kenyan prison basement to eat rats for the rest of our lives and pass each other notes through a little crack in the wall between our cells. Not for me."

"You're no fun."

They heard the approaching helicopter, and Matt and Tuni hurried outside. The new team was bustling about all over the site, and a backhoe had taken off most of the topsoil over the corner of the pit where the artifact was found. Several team members were clustered in the corner, carefully picking away at the rocks with small hand tools.

As the helicopter came to a hover overhead, Enzi came trotting up to move the RV so the bird could land. Matt and Tuni were walking toward the pit to allow the helicopter a wide berth, when Peter came up behind them and clapped his hands onto their shoulders, making them both jump.

"So this is it, huh?" he said with a hangdog look.

Matt nodded gravely.

"'Fraid so, Peter," Tuni replied for them. "Time for me to get the lad home."

"Nothing I can do to convince you to stay another night, right?" They looked at each other and shook their heads as the helicopter began to descend into the clearing. "I've got all sorts of tents and sleeping bags—all *new* stuff, Matt, so you'll be comfy . . ."

Tuni watched Matt carefully.

"Just one more night?" Peter shouted over the deafening *whop* of the helicopter rotors.

Dr. Rheese came toward them and reached out to shake Matt's hand. Matt shook, then leaned forward to yell near Peter's ear, "I'm really sorry, Pete!"

"It's okay," he shouted back. "I didn't really think you'd change your mind, but I had to try. Hopefully we can get you and the piece back together again soon so we can find out what happens. And please don't wait to jot down everything from this last session, okay? I need notes for all of it."

"Mr. Turner, Miss St. James, it was lovely having you out here," Dr. Rheese shouted without a hint of sincerity.

Matt nodded dismissively and leaned forward to Pete again. "Don't forget, it doesn't have to be the whole artifact. To keep reading, all I need is a tiny piece of it, okay?"

"Understood," Pete replied. "We'll see if we can get clearance from Nairobi. It would still be considered destruction of historical materials, though. And who knows when—or *if*—we can ever get it out of country."

Peter turned and looked back toward the pit, where some sort of commotion was going on. Colette and Graham were waving their arms and shouting, "Pete! Pete!"

They were pointing excitedly at the corner as the others hurried toward the pit from all over the site. Rheese turned and hurried away to join them. Dust and particles filled the air as the helicopter descended nearby.

"Did they find something new?" Matt shouted, his head cocked away from the onslaught of debris.

"Looks like it," said Peter. "Well, I've got to go—you guys have a safe trip, okay?" And off he loped down the slope to see what the stir was about.

"Sir, miss, we must be going," the Kenyan pilot shouted from behind them.

"Matthew?" Tuni said in a mother's admonishing singsong.

"Yeah . . . let's go. *Damn.*" He shook his head. As Tuni jogged to her tent to get her suitcase, Enzi appeared with Matt's duffel bag in hand. Handing it off, he shouted in Matt's ear, "It was crazy have you here, Mr. Matthew. I hope you come back, meet people. You nice man for a wizard!"

Matt smiled and patted Enzi's shoulder, then handed his duffel to the pilot, who stowed it behind the seats. Tuni handed her bag to the pilot and pulled herself up, and they buckled into their harnesses. Hands over his ears, Matt leaned in front of Tuni and tried to peer down into the pit.

"What do you think it is?" she asked. "Another piece from the k'yot?" She, too, was trying to catch a glimpse of whatever had the camp in such an uproar. As the pilot slid their door shut and stepped up into his seat, all they could see was Peter, holding his hands to his head, crouched down and leaning into the corner.

The pilots began flicking switches, and the chopper shook as it lifted off. The ground slowly descended below them.

Matt and Tuni saw through her window that the entire team was now crowded into the corner, and Peter was no longer visible. The chopper rotated northward, and Matt could see now. Pete was standing away from the group, waving up at them! What was he trying to say? He held something in his hand. It glinted in the sun.

Matt's eyes grew wide with awe, and he turned to Tuni, who had her face plastered to the window, trying to see down. He smacked her leg, and she turned to him and mouthed, "What the . . . !" as he leaned over and pulled her neck to him.

He shouted something to her, but she couldn't hear. The site was no longer visible, and the helicopter accelerated northward over the forested hills.

He shouted excitedly, a single word. She lifted one of her ear protectors and leaned in.

"One more time!" she shouted.

"Cutter!" he yelled into her ear.

She snapped the ear protector back on and grabbed his shoulders, her face alight. "A *cutter*?" she shouted back to him. "The knife thing?"

He nodded.

She shook her head in wonder and tried to look back out the window, but they were already miles away.

Matt was gazing outside and thinking. Tuni put her hand on his knee, and he turned back to her. He mouthed, "What?" and she turned her palms up and gave him a questioning look.

"Well?" she mouthed.

Matt looked at her and groaned, then let out a little defeated laugh. He tried to reach forward to tap one of the pilots' shoulders, but his harness was too tight. Tuni touched his knee and pointed up at the red call button above them. Matt pressed it, lighting a button in the pilots' center console.

The pilot on the right looked back at them. Matt mouthed "Sorry" as he twirled a finger in the air, then pointed backward with his thumb. The pilot stared at him for a moment, then made the same gesture with his hand to verify. Matt nodded.

Speaking into his mic, the pilot turned forward again. Now the copilot's head popped around. Looking hard at his two passengers, he shook his head in annoyance.

"Unbelievable!" Rheese shouted as he watched the helicopter descend. "Bloody Yank."

"I knew it!" Peter shouted as he ran up the slope. "No *way* he could resist a new find!"

The skids touched down, and Tuni gave Peter a smile and a wink as he ran to the door. One of the pilots got out and gave his two passengers an evil look as he set their bags down. Peter shouted in the pilot's ear that he'd call when they were ready again.

"Not tomorrow or Thursday," the pilot replied. "Schedule booked till Friday."

"Fine, fine," Peter replied, and apologized for the wasted trip.

"No problem," he replied. "You pay either way."

As the chopper rose away, Peter clapped Matt on the back a little too exuberantly. Matt smiled and nodded a "yeah, yeah." Feeling a tap on the shoulder, he turned to see Tuni beaming at him. She threw her arms around him and planted a quick kiss on his mouth.

She pulled away from him, her light brown eyes shining. "I'm going to go claim a tent of my own so Pete can have his back," she said, and dashed away, leaving him with an intoxicating minty taste on his lips. He suddenly felt like a thirteen year old.

Peter gave him a crooked little knowing smile. "Come and see!" he said, waving eagerly. "It was only another foot in, just a meter from where the original artifact was found."

Kneeling down by a Plexiglas box, Peter took something from it and turned toward Matt. "The handle's gone, of course," he said as Matt marveled at the find.

"Go ahead, man, hold it! I know you'll be careful."

Matt took it from him and rolled it over in his hands. Its surface was pitted but free of rust. The cutting edge was dull, and the metal no longer held any luster. The blade was straight rather than curved, though it had been kinked in two spots, so that it bent in a slight zigzag.

Could this be Irin's, too? He looked at the thin cylindrical section at the butt end of the blade. Apparently, the craftsman had bored a hole in the wooden hilt and slid it over this part.

"The tang is broken," said a voice with a working-class English accent behind him.

Matt turned to find the tall, hairy fellow—what was his name? Roger?

"Rodney," he said as if reading Matt's thoughts. "I don't b'lieve we met formally, Mr. Turner."

Matt shook his hand. "What's a *tang*?" he asked.

"It's that part you're touching there. Never seen a cylinder like that before, though. The hilt would go over it and be secured with pins or the like. See there?"

Matt held the base of the tang up. It was somewhat rough and angled ever so slightly. Perhaps an inch of it was missing.

"Yeah, I guess you're right," he said. "Cool."

Peter smiled and nodded. "So you get what that means?"

"Um . . . that it broke—what about it?"

"Well, normally when you find a weapon or implement with no handle that's really old, you assume that whatever material it was made from simply deteriorated over the centuries. In this case, there's no question that the handle is long gone, but *how* it got separated from the blade—that's the interesting question. Some sort of violence, no doubt."

"Well the blade is crooked, too, so it just seems to me like the whole thing is jacked."

"Um, sorry, sir," Rodney interjected. "Actually, that 'crookedness,' as you call it, is warping from the weight and pressure of the rock it was in. Lots of shifting and compression. It's actually nothing short of amazing that it's in such good condition. Must be a superior alloy."

"Interesting stuff," Matt said, trying not to sound as uninterested as he felt. "So, Pete, can we . . . er . . . talk about this in the RV?"

"Man after my own heart, Mr. Turner," Pete replied with a clap.

They climbed out of the pit to find Tuni wrestling with a tent. Two unshaven young men, one with his hair pulled back in a frizzy ponytail, stood by, chuckling over something.

"You need some help over there, Tuni?" Peter called out.

"No, thanks. Your friends here have been gracious enough to offer, but I will have the bloody thing licked on my own in just a moment—it's become a point of pride." Then, as they continued to the door, she called out behind them, "Wait—are you doing it now?"

Matt grinned. "Time's a-wastin'."

Dropping the tent pole, she joined them at the RV's doorstep. The door swung open, and they could hear Dr. Rheese speaking to someone on the sat phone.

". . . to thirty strong men, and Enzi will start it all off. He knows ev . . ." Rheese shot a glance at the faces in the open doorway and paused. "Right . . . yes—sounds great, sirs. Have a lovely time." He pushed the END button and set the phone down.

"You find us some more men, Doctor?" Peter asked as he, Matt, and Tuni filed in.

"Oh . . . excuse me. Um, ah, no—no more men. Just discussing distant plans."

"Well, nothing wrong with keeping an eye to the future, but we might have just hit the motherlode right here in this spot."

"Right," Rheese replied, looking a bit distracted. "If you'll excuse me . . ." And he stepped out the door.

"Okay, buddy, you ready for this?" Peter said to Matt.

"I'll do a minute just see what it's all about," Matt said as he pulled on his timer and set it.

"Great," said Peter, eager to get started. "Let's see what we've got!"

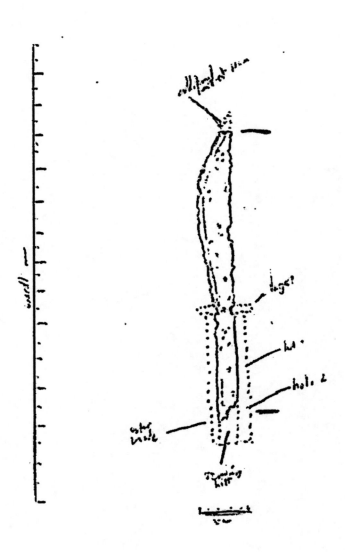

TWENTY-FOUR

"**Y**ou are too new, little one," Olo said as she rolled the cutter from side to side in the cloth. She could still feel the heat from it.

"I won't touch the sharp part, Mama," Opwot said, bouncing impatiently.

Looking at her daughter, Olo marveled at how similar they were. When she was new, she, too, had always wanted what she could not have.

"Well, even if I were to let you hold it, it's too hot to touch right now. Your skin will burn, and you'll cry."

"I won't cry, Mama. Boys play with cutters at the Clothes House all the time!"

"Watch . . ." Olo dipped her fingers in the waterbowl and splashed a few drops onto the blade. The water popped and sizzled and disappeared.

Opwot jumped and laughed. "I want to do that!" she cried. And plunging her whole hand into the waterbowl, she shook it over the blade, getting more water on her mother than on the metal.

Her mother frowned and wiped her eye with her shoulder strap.

"You got it in my eye, Opwot—be more careful."

"Why don't we just put the cutter in the water so it's not hot anymore?"

"Because it will break the blade, newest. We can put it in the water in a little while. Now, why don't you go play with Gleyer and Pret? Let Mama work."

"They just throw rocks at other rocks. It's stupid."

Tapping the blade with her finger, Olo determined that it was nearly cool enough. She let it slide into the waterbowl.

"Can I touch this one?" Opwot asked, pointing at a complete cutter with a handle attached. Not wait for an answer, she wrapped her fingers tightly around the blade, then shrieked as she felt the razor edge slice deeply into her fingers.

"No! Opwot! What did you . . . ?" She grasped her daughter's hand and squeezed it into a tight fist. Opwot screamed again from the pain as Olo's eyes darted over the room, looking for a bit of cloth.

TWENTY-FIVE

Matt shut off his timer.

He gave his two companions a perplexed frown and shook his head. "Nothing we can use right away," he said.

"What do you mean?" Peter asked.

"It's too far back. I mean, there's probably plenty of stuff on the way to where we are now, but this is years and years before Irin was even *born*."

"How do you know?" Tuni asked.

"I was this woman I've never seen before—she must be long dead by now—and her daughter is Opwot. She was just a little girl, maybe six years old."

"And who's Opwot?" Peter asked impatiently.

"Sorry, one of the oldest women—blind—she makes the k'yots. She made the middle—the shirt—that we have a piece of. The imprint goes all the way back to her mother making this blade. It could take months going through it all just to get to where I am now with the k'yot."

"Right—got it," Peter said, giving the table a slap. "Well, probably plenty of fascinating data we could get from it after you've run out of k'yot stories, right?"

"I'm sure," Matt sighed. "Speaking of which . . ."

"Ah, so eager now," Peter said, "but it's going to be dark soon and you need to get your tents squared away. I have to go help out in the pit for a few—it's going to rain again tonight and maybe all day tomorrow."

Tuni gave Matt a look of chagrin. "Bloody *torture*," she moaned. "I think there are laws against this." Matt loved the way her words sounded: "*. . . lors agaynst this.*"

"I know. Let's go handle our tents before we beg Dr. Rheese to get it out for us."

They left the RV, and Matt went to the back of the van, where he had seen Rodney pitch the new tent, back when he and Tuni were boarding the chopper. He looked fondly at all the beautifully sealed, brand-new equipment: air mattress, sleeping bag, tent, pillow, pillowcase, even sheets! Grabbing what he could in his arms, he went to where Tuni's tent and poles lay strewn on the ground, and dropped his burden. He peeled the tape from the tent box, opened the flaps, and inhaled the pleasant smell of the new nylon fabric.

In minutes he had the tent up and the rain fly staked down. He threw his sleeping gear inside and went back to the van for the pillow. Beneath it lay a shopping bag with a stack of new jeans, assorted turtlenecks, T-shirts, underwear, and socks. He shook his head in surprise. How could Peter know he wore boxer briefs? And the jeans: twenty-nines with button fly— just what he would have bought.

Turning, he saw Peter looking at him. Matt raised the bag in acknowledgment, and Peter gave him a knowing look before ducking under the awning of tarps that covered the pit.

Tuni was trying to slide a shock-corded pole through a sleeve in her tent and cursing under her breath. Matt tossed the bag in his tent, then grabbed the other end of the tent pole, pulling it down and seating it over the pin. Then he pinned the other pole in place while Tuni figured out what to do on her side. The tent popped into shape, and Matt put the stakes and hammer at her feet while he shook out the rain fly and flung it over the top.

After pounding in the last stake, she said, "See? Now, that wasn't so difficult, was it?"

"Yeah," he said drily. "I don't know what my problem was."

The equatorial night came on quickly, and stars winked through the patchwork of scattered clouds as the team gathered under the food tent. Now there were twenty or more at the site, conversing and joking with the ease of people who had known one another for years. Matt noted how different this felt from the quiet awkwardness when it was just the five of them at the site. The energy of such a large and voluble group overshadowed even Dr. Rheese's annoying superciliousness.

"Tell me, Matt," an American girl named Felicia said to him from across the table, "What makes you so important here? What's your degree even in?"

Tuni turned to Matt, and he felt her look but decided not to return it.

"I'm just here for the food," he replied.

Felicia looked thrown, apparently unsure if he was trying to be funny, was simply a jerk, and whether he was actually going to answer the question. A retort neared her lips when Matt interrupted.

"Hey Pete."

Peter finished his sentence to Flip, at another table, and raised his eyebrows in inquiry to Matt.

"So, think we can *chat* in the RV again?" he said to Peter as soon as they were a few yards from the mess tent. "We didn't turn that whirlybird around to just hang out . . . as awesome as all of you guys seem."

"Of course, of course. You're not going to eat dinner, though?"

Matt made a face. "Seriously?"

"Doesn't appeal to you, huh?" Peter laughed. "Well, yeah . . . then, how about you and Tuni—if she's not interested in eating, either—head back in there for a little bit."

Matt looked uncomfortable. "Uh . . . ," then he mouthed, "can you have Rheese get it out?"

"Oh . . ." Pete smiled, realizing no one seemed to want to ask Rheese for anything.

TWENTY-SIX

"**W**hat was this vision, Wil?" Irin asked as they headed toward the next rise.

Wil looked around, but no one was within listening distance. "It was about you."

Irin looked at him from the corner of his eye. "What about me?"

"I saw it . . . that is, I saw what happens, and . . ." He paused and rubbed at a face spot on his cheek.

"Say it, Wil—say what you saw."

"I saw . . . your death. It was a vision, too, not a dream—I know the difference."

Irin looked ahead of him as he walked, wondering whether he wanted to hear any more. He held the new fear in his belly and kept his voice strong and confident.

"Only tell me one thing, Wil," Irin said, still not looking at him. "Is it soon? I don't want to know when, but is it soon?"

Wil was silent. Irin turned, and the expression on his friend's face gave him his answer. They remained silent to the top of the hill and long after.

The group snaked its way through the mountain pass, where they came across more screamer droppings, though most were dried out and clearly very old. Irin began to realize that they may have passed the screamers' burrows or caves or dens or wherever they slept. Why, they may have been as close as five house-lengths away when his people walked through the diamond-shaped opening.

How much more time in the night remained? They would need to find a suitable encampment soon. The procession moved slowly, and it would take time to make safe with whatever perimeter they could throw up to protect themselves as they slept. He would keep fighters awake, a few at a time, taking turns guarding.

This thin strip of a trail with walls on both sides would be a good make-safe for a couple of reasons, Irin thought. First, they would have to protect only two sides, front and back. They could use n'wips, turned up and lashed together, as fences. Second, the high walls would keep it mostly dark during the daylight. Babies and new would be better able to sleep, along with anyone else who had a difficult time withstanding the brightness.

There was only one problem: they were far too close to the screamer-frequented area they had passed. Their scent would likely be picked up quickly, and he had seen how fast the killers could run. They would also see how their droppings were disturbed and would know at once that people had been there. He needed to keep everyone moving a while longer, but they would need enough time before dawn to find a suitable area, get everyone fed, and make safe.

And what about Wil's new vision? Irin wondered. Would his death come to him as he tried to defend the encampment of his people? He wanted to know more, but he feared doing something in his own interest instead of his people's. He thought of Orin and realized he had not checked on her for a while.

He stopped walking and leaned against the hard rock wall while the procession plodded past. They looked tired and probably hungry, and he realized that his own belly was complaining. Would everyone wait for his word before even asking to stop? A woman passed him, holding her new as she walked. She looked haggard and only half awake, but she smiled at him with a look of gratitude. He was surprised she could still feel so kindly toward him despite all he was putting her through.

Orin was talking to one of the men pulling a n'wip, and they passed Irin without noticing him. Irin let them pass, then fell in behind to listen to the conversation. The man was complaining about his shoulders.

"I think you should let your k'yot middle hang off your arms," Orin suggested. "The solid is tearing at your skin—let your clothes straps be your cushion."

"It's a good idea, thank you," he replied. "But Nilpen has fallen behind, and I can't stop and hold up everyone behind us."

"Here," she said to him as she put her hand on one of the n'wip poles. "I'll pull it as best I can while you take your k'yot down."

The man looked at her strangely, then started to hand her the long poles, when Irin stepped in front of them.

"Here, let me," he said.

"Oh, Irin . . . ," the man said in surprise.

"It is all right, Irin. I can pull it for a moment while he fixes his k'yot," Orin persisted.

"You are a good woman, Orin, but I would not be a good man if I allowed it. Go ahead, my friend," Irin said, taking the poles.

Orin looked at him with frustration. "Well," she added, "I think you'll need to let all the n'wip men make this adjustment, for the k'yots chafe the skin and will rub their shoulders raw before much longer."

"A good thought," Irin said as the other man fumbled with the holdstrip. He had clearly never worn a k'yot before this journey. "How do you feel? Are you in need of food?"

"Yes, I think everyone is, but they will continue until you think it safe."

"Yes, but they'll slow," Irin sighed. "I'm afraid I don't know what is best: stop and let everyone eat as the daylight draws near, or push on and eat when we arrive."

"When do we arrive?" Orin asked him.

"I don't know," he replied. He glanced at the other man, who now had his k'yot middle down and was poking tentatively at his shoulders and grimacing. Irin felt the way the k'yot threads rubbed against his own shoulders, and realized that it had been a mistake to have them don the protective wear. How many other decisions had been mistakes? There had been so many, he couldn't think of them all.

"Orin," he said, "please go quickly down the line and tell every man pulling a n'wip to open his k'yot as he has done." And moving aside, he let the man back under the n'wip poles.

The man grimaced with pain, but he looked at Irin and sighed. "Much better," he said.

Irin pulled Orin's ear close to his mouth and whispered to her, "I think there may be other problems like this. I can't . . . will you help me?"

She turned and spoke soothingly into his ear, "You have done well, man of mine, but I'll go and help with the little things. You have a much larger n'wip on your shoulders."

He looked at her eyes and believed her words. No one had died or even been injured, they had lost no supplies, and they had come a great distance. But what of Wil's vision? if Irin should die, would others as well? Wil would have mentioned it, wouldn't he? But he didn't want any more details; he wanted it out of his mind. He wished Wil hadn't told him.

"If your second doesn't return soon," Irin said to the n'wip puller, "you must tell someone to find him or find a replacement. Do not wear yourself out, understand?"

"Right, I won't," he replied.

Irin continued ahead at double speed and told the other two n'wip pullers at the front to adjust their k'yots as Orin had suggested. He had the seconds change theirs first before relieving the pullers.

A short time later, he had passed all the fighters and was reaching the front, when he saw that the trail split in two. One path curved off sharply to the left, and the other veered slightly right. Irin wondered which way the scouts had gone.

"Which way do you suppose they went," asked Pwig as they approached the fork.

They heard footfalls, and a scout appeared from around the left bend, jogging toward them. He was pointing with his lightstick toward the right path, waving that the left was no good.

"That path ends after only a few turns," the scout panted between breaths, "so this is really our only choice."

"Good work, Iwwi," Irin told him. "Why don't you rest for a bit while Owwi and Iwwint catch up to you?"

He raised his chin to Irin and dropped back.

"Do you hear that?" Wil asked as they walked. He turned his head to listen.

Irin heard it: running footfalls. A few seconds later the other two scouts appeared, lightsticks bouncing in the air as they ran over a small ridge where the canyon walls finally dropped away. Shrubs and small trees grew in the hollows, and outcrops of stone like the Gathering Rocks rose here and there.

The scouts arrived, panting, and Irin and Wil gave them water from their bags and let them catch their breath.

"Over . . . the ridge," the first scout finally gasped. "The mountains continue, but the stone is rougher and pitted."

"Yes," the other agreed, "and small caves everywhere."

"Little creatures," the first continued. "Like big crawlers, but bigger and with hair…they run around in the caves and brush—there!" He pointed to the right, and they all spotted a long, sinuous animal with dark hair, scurrying from one bush to the next as they passed.

"They *are* like crawlers," Pwig agreed, and he walked toward the shrub.

"Leave it, Pwig," Irin said. "There may be an all batch of them hiding behind these plants, just waiting to feast on you. That one was the bait, luring you in."

"I think not," Pwig replied humorlessly, but he returned nonetheless.

"Tell me more of these caves," Irin said to the scouts.

"There is a large one some distance up from the ground. It looks like we could climb there, but we didn't try."

"Did you look inside any of the smaller ones?" Irin asked as they continued walking.

"I poked my lightstick in one," said the first scout, "but it ended after only a house-length."

"And were there many of these smaller caves?"

"They are everywhere, just over this ridge, where it grows rocky again.

"Very well," said Irin. "Thank you. Take a rest and rejoin the line before the fighters at the rear."

Irin had an idea about these small caves. Perhaps he could divide the company into smaller groups, perhaps two houses together, and put them in different caves with two fighters guarding each. If an attack came, they would all be separated, and the losses would be minimal. He would tell all fighters to go to the cave where the attack was happening and combat the killers there; the other caves would be safe. But then, they might attack more than one cave at once, he thought. He had enough men ready to fight them if that happened. Irin just hoped there would be no more than three screamers, perhaps four at the most. Any more, and it would be hard to fend off an attack—if, that is, they could fight one off at all. No one ever had; he was only guessing.

The front arrived at the beginning of the "rough rocks," as the scouts had described them. There was no visible trail through the area, but it looked as though they could get the n'wips through. The surface was still covered in dirt, and though the ground sloped steadily downward, the grade was hardly noticeable.

Irin pointed to those behind him to branch out and have everyone rest along the rocks while he, Wil, and Pwig surveyed the area. He told Norrit to have everyone unpack the night's meals from the n'wips.

"Get *everyone* eating and drinking their water. Even if they say they are not hungry or thirsty. They may just be too tired."

"And when will you eat, Irin?"

"We will return soon—don't worry about us."

TWENTY-SEVEN

"He's going to die soon," Matt said to Tuni as Rheese put the artifact back in its case.

"When?" Tuni said breathlessly. "Is he hurt? Did you feel it? What *happened*?"

"Wil's new vision—he said he saw Irin's death and that it's soon. But I don't know if that means in an hour or a few days . . . if we're to continue believing Wil's predictions."

"Oh . . ." Tuni lowered her head. "So that's going to be it, then. . . ." She took a deep breath. "How do you feel about that, Matthew?"

"I'll tell you how *I* feel," Dr. Rheese interrupted, standing up after closing the safe. "That this fellow from a hundred million years ago—who *croaked* a hundred million years ago—is going to die? Well, I've gotta say I'm pretty bloody torn up. I thought we might be able to track him down on Facebook after this was all said and done. P'raps meet for tea . . ."

"You're a bloody arsehole, *Mister* Rheese," Tuni replied, aware that being called "Mister" instead of "Doctor" would infuriate him far more than "arsehole."

He paused in the doorway and sniffed, "Realists are often considered such, Miss St. James." The door swung shut behind him.

Tuni slumped back down in the seat, her face compressed with fury. Matt said nothing, writing down his impressions from the session and waiting for her to relax a bit.

"To answer your question," he finally said, "I feel kind of sick about it. I'm afraid of how it happens—well, happened. I'm afraid of *when*. And I also feel the same drive now about this that he does. I don't know if it's just from being in his head and feeling it for so long, but I really *need* them to be safe. I *need* them to rebuild their city someplace else. It's stupid. Rheese is a dick, and I hate to say it, but he's right."

"I don't think it's stupid," Tuni replied. "I feel it too, what you said . . . Though I'm sure I don't feel it as strongly as you do. I'm actually more interested in Irin living on. If Shinehead hadn't ruined it, it would have been nice to imagine that I could one day have met Irin in person. Obviously impossible, but one can imagine it, no?"

"Yeah." Matt smiled a little. "I wish I could introduce you."

"Oh, you have, dear. You have, absolutely."

Their eyes met for a moment. "I guess the campfire's going," Matt said to fill the silence.

Tuni nodded absentmindedly.

"Hey, you awake?" Matt said, standing up.

"Sorry, dear," she said, snapping out of her daze. "I was just thinking something." She stood up beside him.

"Tell me, then," he replied.

"No, just thinking about . . . what might happen. C'mon, let's go."

They stepped outside as Tuni asked for more details.

"Just a lot of walking. Right now they're stopped and are looking at a bunch of little caves. He wants to split everyone up to sleep during the daylight."

"Matty, Matty, Matt-Matt!" Peter shouted from the fire. Someone had made a ring of rocks a short distance from the food tent and put benches around it, and a fire was blazing merrily away.

"Petey, Petey, Pete-Pete," Matt replied with somewhat less enthusiasm. Peter was drinking a beer.

"Man, *every*one here keeps asking about you!" Peter continued. The new team laughed. Matt tried to settle Pete down before he said something he shouldn't. "We could learn soooo much more if we had everyone on the same *page* if you know what I'm talking about . . ."

"Not sure I do, Pete." Matt leaned close to Pete's ear and whispered. "And you need to cool it. They're all staring at us."

Pete flipped around and inspected the group—indeed they looked like an audience waiting to see the magician open the box.

"You people are bloody nosey!" Pete barked, only half-joking.

Tuni put her arm in Matt's, in what, for the briefest second, he took to be an affectionate gesture.

She whispered, "He's a bit tilted." Matt nodded, and her arm disappeared.

"Yeah, hey, everyone!" Matt said cheerfully. "Nothing mysterious here, please move along, talk amongst yourselves . . ." The others made convivial gestures and comments of "no worries," and their various conversations resumed.

Moving closer to the fire circle, Matt realized it was getting pretty cold. His mind must have been getting accustomed to being warm outside at night, so that in contrast, it seemed especially cold here. He looked around at all the happy, naive faces glowing in the firelight, heard the babble of apparently worry-free conversations, and felt as though the others had no idea what was going on right now. But it wasn't going on *right now*, exactly, though it certainly was for him. He thought he should be back where he belonged, with Wil and his brother, Pwig, finding a safe place for his people to sleep. How meaningless this campfire was, he thought, and then he felt a sudden twinge of guilt that he was going to abandon them for his own distant, safe retreat in North Carolina.

A muffled buzzing interrupted his thoughts, and he felt for a second that his timer was pulling him out of himself. Rheese had begun telling a story, and most of the team appeared to be listening. Peter popped up off a bench and fixed his eyes on the RV. Matt heard the sound again and realized that it was the sat phone ringing. He saw Peter get up and jog to the RV.

The door closed behind Peter, and Matt turned back to the fire. He caught Tuni's eyes, and she waved for him to come and squeeze into the small space between her and one of the new guys. He hated being crowded between people, but then, when would he get to be forced so deliciously close to Tuni again? He walked around the benches and excused himself as he scrunched in next to her.

"Hello?" Peter said into the sat phone.

After a brief silence, a deep voice said, "Who is this?" in an accent that might be Kenyan.

"Um, this is Peter Sharma. Who's this?"

More silence.

"Where is Rheese?" the voice finally replied.

"He's around," Peter answered curtly. "Who is speaking, please?"

"You work with Rheese?"

"Rheese works for me," Peter said, his annoyance obvious.

"Ah-h," the man said with a chuckle, "you tell Mistah Rheese we have what he need. But the price will be double."

Peter frowned. What the hell was this about? "Sure, I'll let him know," he said. "And what exactly are we talking about? *Which* need, exactly?"

"The equipment . . . What you say your name again?"

"What did you say yours was?" Peter countered.

The deep voice paused for a moment, and the line went dead.

Was Rheese trying to source the lost equipment from some questionable source? Peter had already said he would take care of it, but maybe he was trying to make points by getting it faster. But for *double* the price? Well, it was still grant money, and Peter wasn't going to let it be squandered to pay off some mysterious Kenyan godfather just so Rheese could kiss some asses.

Rheese poked at a flaming chunk of wood with his stick as he continued his tale. "Now, don't think this was going to be an easy excavation simply because we had millions of pounds to blow!" Everyone laughed. "None of you have ever met him—he's just an old codger nowadays—but bloody Dan Mitchellson . . . that was his full name, see, Bloody Daniel Mitchellson . . ."

Peter slid into his seat across the fire from Rheese.

"Mitchellson was an angry bastard," Rheese continued. "This man would shout at you and tell you things about your mum that you wondered how he would know, if you get my meaning. So . . . Mitchellson and me, we're hiking up the little sand hill and we're gonna raise the balloon again to get a better overhead of the Sphinx. Bastard loses his footing, and I see him fluttering backward with his pipe still clenched between his rotty choppers. I reach out for him—kinda half-effort, though, if you know what I mean . . ." Here Rheese winked and smirked left and right. ". . . but mainly 'cause I don't want him taking me with him on a lovers' roll down to the bottom. It was all soft for the most part, but knickers full of sand wasn't what I was looking for. I watch his legs and then his thinning hair, and there's his bloody feet again, until finally he starts to slide on his back, headfirst, the rest of the way. I'm having a spit of a time holding back my laughter at this point, not knowing if he's hurt or not, and then his slow slide stops suddenly as if his head hit something. I start sliding down on my boots until I get to him, and sure enough, his eyes are open, pipe still in his mouth, and he's shaking his head at me as if I'd *pushed* him."

"And was that it?" Colette asked in her breathy French accent.

"Was what what?" Rheese replied.

"What stopped his slide—was that the entrance?"

Rheese nodded. "It was the upper right corner, yes. And crafty bloke later says how his instincts had guided him to the spot, and there you have site seven-four-four-three-tango-X-ray, the famed Sarcophagi Preparation Chamber. His story got better and better over time."

"The one I heard," a bearded young man said, "has Professor Mitchellson searching the area alone with a garden trowel for two years before he came upon it."

Rheese threw his head back and laughed out loud. This made others laugh, though they could not say precisely why.

"I hadn't heard that one yet," Rheese chuckled. "But I'll tell you some-time what he was *really* doing for those two years, young man. . . ." He raised his cigar to his lips and puffed.

The campfire was quiet for a moment as everyone's eyes returned to the flames. The sounds of pops and crackles seemed to begin again, as if they'd been paused.

Peter stood up and walked around the fire. He tapped Rheese on the shoulder and nodded for him to follow. A short time later, shouting erupted from the RV. No one could really understand what was said, but it was pretty clear that something had happened on the phone call that annoyed Peter greatly.

Tuni looked for Enzi's face and found him sitting on a folding stool some distance back from the fire. His eyes were locked squarely on the RV, and he appeared deep in thought. She hoped he would look her way, but moments later he got up and walked away.

Then the blonde American girl, Felicia, blurted out, "Nature hike!" and hopped up. There were a few groans, but several seemed to welcome the proposition and trundled off to their tents to fetch flashlights and jackets. Now alone on the bench with Tuni, Matt realized that his close proxim-ity to her had been appropriate only when forced by the lack of room. He scooted away nonchalantly, wondering how long she had sat there on the end of the bench, hoping he would move.

"What, do I smell or something?" she said in feigned injury.

"What? No . . . shut up. Just getting hot."

She raised an eyebrow at him. "Really?"

"Shut up." He looked around the benches to see who was left.

Graham, the sketch artist, was sitting close to the fire, putting the toe of one of his boots into the fire and then pulling it away repeatedly. One of the women sat with a headlamp on, reading a book. Towering Rodney lay sprawled across one of the empty benches, using his clasped hands as a pillow.

Peter and Rheese appeared from the trailer, and both looked surprised to see nearly everyone gone.

"Nature hike," Matt explained, and Peter nodded recognition, then hurried off to his tent for his flashlight.

Rheese approached the fire, hands in his pockets, and stood behind the benches for a moment. Finally, he shifted his eyes to Matt. "So, young Turner," he said, "guessing you'd like another go before lights-out?"

Matt sat bolt upright, but before he could speak, Tuni said, "Yes, please!"

TWENTY-EIGHT

I rin held his lightstick out in front of him to illuminate the cave. It was as the scouts had described: a small hollow in the rocky escarpment. This one was far too small to accommodate even a few people; also, they would be easily visible from outside. He wanted deeper caves, and perhaps higher up the cliff to give them an advantage.

"There are some larger ones over here," Pwig called out.

They stepped down from the rocks and looked where he was pointing. Indeed, two wide-mouthed caves could be seen farther along the rocky slope, one atop the other, and both elevated well above the ground. From where the three stood, the interiors were completely black. They walked to the base of the mountain and saw that a wide ledge of rock led to the lower cave. If this was a large enough cavern, it would be an easy climb for women and new.

Wil scaled it first and leaned in to look around. He turned back to Irin and Pwig. "It looks big," he said.

Irin and Pwig stepped up to the opening but could not see in at all. The ledge on which they stood was wide and flat, perhaps three houselengths, and the roof of the cave was as tall as the Center House at Pwin-T. They stepped in, but even with their lightsticks held before them, they could see little. Pwig remained close to the right wall, illuminating the coarse rock beside him. Wil tripped over something and gasped, and Irin lowered his lightstick to the floor of packed dirt to find a little pile of bones, perhaps those of a hairy crawler such as they had seen in the brush.

Irin inhaled the cool, damp air, thinking it smelled somewhat bitter. The people would have to deal with it, he thought. He could not see how far in the cavern extended, but even if it had ended where they now stood, it would hold forty, perhaps more. Pwig moved closer to his two companions, taking small steps and watching the ground to keep from tripping. The walls and ceiling were so far away that the lightsticks did little to provide them with any sense of scale.

Wil stopped, and Irin and Pwig looked back at him. He was holding his lightstick up over his head, trying to see the ceiling, which was much lower here than at the entrance.

"Irin," he whispered. "Look!"

Irin and Pwig both stepped beside him and looked up. They stood in awe as Wil moved the light from side to side to illuminate more. Above them they could see, carved into the rock, crude images of people. Some were bigger than others, and some of the figures held small, roundish creatures in their hands. The three men looked at one another in silence, grasping the significance of what Wil had found. Long ago, their people had been in this cave! Perhaps, when they moved from the old city, they lived in this very cave for a time. The carvings continued into the cave and spread out beyond the reach of the lightsticks. The men walked slowly, heads high, trying to read the events depicted.

Irin held his lightstick to a section of jagged rock that had a carving of a face with a large, oblong thing on its head. Beside it, a big arm held up another of the small round animals. He could see that the artist had given more detail to this one: big teeth in its mouth, and a wide tail with points at the end.

"*Tsst!*" Wil hushed, and no one moved.

Irin rolled his eyes down at him and opened them wide in inquiry. Wil pointed at his ear: *listen.* Pwig pulled back his k'yot top, exposing his ear. He heard it, too: a soft whistling that went for a few seconds, stopped, then came again. It continued for a moment as they listened and held their lightsticks out to see where it might be coming from. The sound was very small and thin, like that of a sleeping newest with a stuffy nose.

Irin looked behind them and realized that pitch black surrounded their compact bubble of pale blue light. They must have rounded a bend in the cave and could no longer see the entrance. Searching for the source of the noise, Pwig walked forward again, holding his lightstick out before him. The melted top of the firestick inside oozed down, and the flame fought to stay alight at the awkward angle. He swung the stick to the left, and the flame flickered a final flash before it was extinguished under its own melt. Irin hissed at him, and Pwig moved closer to share the light. Wil stumbled again and found more bones at his feet. He knelt down to shine his light on the remains and discovered the source of the whistling.

The nostril was wet and oozing. A single tooth poked out of the mouth, pinching back a scaly upper lip. Wil stopped breathing and slowly moved the light behind him. A closed eye was only half an arm's length from his face. Irin touched Wil's neck slowly and gave it the slightest pull backward to get him to move away. Wil's chest shook as they both looked down and saw that his toes were under the foot's three claws, glowing blue and each as long as his entire hand. He tried to inhale slowly, but it only made the shaking more pronounced.

Irin gradually turned his head sideways and saw that Pwig was squinting toward them, not yet grasping what lay near the wall. Pwig suddenly gasped, and Irin's face scrunched in fear that the sound would awaken the slumbering screamer. He glanced back and saw that it still dozed; the whistling continued at the same pace.

Irin gestured for Wil to move his foot away carefully as he handed his lightstick to Pwig and drew the cutter from his waistband. Wil complied, but now his entire body shook, and his eyes were closed tight in fear. Irin's feet scratched on the dirt and gravel floor as he positioned them on either side of the massive head. In the silence of the cave, the sound seemed as loud as a ravening screamer clawing at the door. Surely the killer would wake at the noise.

He leaned right to find the best place to insert the blade and kill the beast before it could awaken and attack. There, behind the jaw! He would thrust it in and pull it down to the throat. But what if the cutter was not long enough? It might be only a trifling wound to such a huge, thick neck. He reached to his other side and slowly drew the long cutter. The solid made a high-pitched tone as it rubbed his k'yot bottom on the way up. Irin took a slow, deep breath and forced all fear from his head. He reached out to hand the short cutter to Pwig but could not find his brother's hand. He turned and saw that Pwig had moved a few more steps in and was shining Irin's lightstick around the area. Three more shining noses appeared in the dark as the blue light flickered across the rest of the cave.

Irin clenched his fists tight and realized he could not fight the fear any longer. He squeezed his eyes shut and tried to push thought in front of fear and drown out the sound of his own inside beating. It began to fill his ears, and he could no longer hear anything else. He felt something touch his back, and he flinched, his fright almost sending him headlong into the sleeping beast. He turned to see Wil with his own two cutters in his hands. The look of fear still shaped his face, but his eyes looked intense and ready to do whatever was needed. Irin drew strength from his friend and turned back toward Pwig, who was looking at him in desperation.

Four screamers, three men. With his foot coverings nearly cradling the jaw of the nearest one, he tried to figure out how they would kill them all—and not, themselves, be killed.

He gestured for Wil to come close, and they leaned together. Irin pressed his lips into Wil's ear and spoke only with his breath.

"You . . . over there . . . tell him . . . two cutters . . . either side of middle . . . stab neck deep . . . same time . . . move fast to middle one after—both of you."

He pulled away and looked at Wil's face. He had understood. He closed his eyes and raised his chin to Irin, and Irin returned the gesture. He watched as Wil moved ever so slowly across the cave to Pwig and spoke the instructions silently into his ear. Pwig turned and said something back, and Wil had to return to his ear twice more. Irin was growing impatient and worried. Did Pwig understand? Would they kill them right, or would they be fighting a barely-wounded and enraged screamer a few seconds from now? He realized he might need to get to the other side to help them after killing his.

Irin watched as the other two took their positions between the killers. Just as he had instructed, it was now screamer, Pwig, screamer, Wil, screamer. They had the only two lightsticks, so he wasn't sure if they could see him anymore. He readied his blades and watched the others to be sure they proceeded at the same time. He saw them look at each other and look toward him . . . but not *at* him. They couldn't see him! Irin hoped they would realize that he could see them and would go quickly with their cutters. Who knew when the creatures would wake on their own, eliminating the men's slim advantage.

Irin watched as Wil waved a hand to Pwig. He had decided—he would proceed! Wil's empty hand moved slowly in a chopping motion; he raised it and did so again. Finally he raised it higher, held it for a second, and dropped it quickly. Irin saw both men turn and fist their cutters with both hands, reaching back to swing them in. He turned to his own and swung back, held it for an instant, then plunged the long cutter into the sleeping screamer's neck. It made a gurgling sound, and its head began to rise as he twisted the cutter down to the ground. Blood jetted over his hands and face. The killer began to thrash and move and make sounds like choking and drinking, and Irin turned to see that the other two had plunged their cutters home as well. His eyes began to sting, and he tried to wipe the blood out, but his hands were more covered than his face.

He dashed across the floor as the other two turned to the middle screamer. Wil's had rolled to its side and was thrashing with its great hooked feet, violently kicking the middle screamer several times. The unharmed creature's head rose quickly, and it released a piercing shriek just before Pwig's and

Wil's blades plunged into its neck and they pulled them down together, opening long gashes down the front. It shrieked again and, as it continued to rise, swung a foot toward Pwig with blinding speed. Irin watched as his brother was flung deep into the darkness, his lightstick crashing to the floor and winking out. The bluewater briefly held its glow before darkness overcame it.

Irin leaped at the standing screamer and swung his long cutter across its neck. He felt a rush of liquid fall over him again, and the head dropped onto him, bringing him to the ground. He could only see the dim flicker of Wil's light behind him as another shriek, powerful and healthy, echoed through the cave.

The screamer on top of him quaked slightly every few seconds as the one stabbed by Wil lay dying beside him. He could hear but not see both his and Pwig's prey squirming and quivering in their final throes. The shriek pierced their ears again, and they heard scritching from the dark area where Pwig had been knocked.

The fifth screamer padded forward with quick lunges until its dripping mouth entered the edge of the blue light. Its bulging eyes seemed to search the darkness. Irin tried to wriggle his way free, but the weight of the head on his back, and the twisted neck over one of his legs held him fast. He couldn't see Wil on the other side, nor could he hear Pwig moving in the darkness. As the screamer moved, its head turned toward Irin and released a series of barking chirps near his face. Irin recoiled as the monstrous face lurched toward his several times until it finally twisted all the way to one side, its eyes now below its mouth, and pressed its nose against his shoulder. It snorted. The nose pushed violently and slid up to his neck, just under his chin. Irin knew that it would be nothing for the creature to bite his head off. The thought made him go stone still. He wasn't sure whether it thought he was part of the dead beast trapping him to the floor, or was preparing to feast on him, but the blood burned his eyes, so that he could not keep them open for more than a second before squeezing them shut again. He wondered what Wil was doing or whether he or Pwig was even alive.

The huge nose snorted repeatedly, inhaling all over his face and smearing around the thick ooze. He felt a sharp tooth scratch against his face, cut his cheek, burning, stinging pain, thoughts of imminent death, his own, his brother's, Wil's, his people returning to Pwin-T in defeat and fear, pain again. The head continued upward to sniff the dead screamer's neck above Irin. As he choked back any moans or grunts of pain, he felt the warmth of his own blood begin to pour out of the gash that ran from his cheek all the way up to his right eye. Irin suddenly became aware of his left hand again and realized that it still clutched the short cutter. He could make only a pitiful swing at the creature from where he lay, but perhaps if he held on tightly, the killer's own retreat would extend the damage.

The screamer's head pulled back and turned in the opposite direction, exposing the area under its mouth. Irin noticed that the blue light on the ceiling was beginning to move slowly away, toward the back of the screamer, and he wondered whether it was simply the lightstick rolling on the floor, or Wil suddenly finding the courage to attack. Irin looked back at the pale area half-circled by the lower jaw and recalled that it was through that same soft opening that he had delivered the killing thrust to Ilter with this very blade.

He decided to wait no longer, and bringing the hilt of the blade to his own chin, he put the palm of his right hand behind it as well, then shoved it forward with all his strength. It pierced deep, and even the cutter hilt and the tips of Irin's fingers penetrated the killer's flesh. It twisted away and shrieked again, swinging its legs furiously at Irin and the head of the dead screamer. Irin felt several smashing blows to his legs, and he turned his head aside as the pummeling and the horrible screams continued for a few seconds longer. Then it released a new squeal of pain, and the glow of the last lightstick winked out. Now all was black. He heard the struggle continue in the dark, and finally something heavy landed on his legs and remained there, writhing.

The cave grew silent again except for the sound of heavy breathing above him. He felt something on his face and realized at that moment that the fifth screamer had taken his cutter with it.

"Irin . . . ?" He heard Wil's voice above him.

"I'm here, Wil . . . alive."

He heard Wil's sigh of relief, but he had only one thought now. "What about Pwig?" he asked.

"Here, Irin," came Pwig's voice, from the same spot as Wil's.

Irin felt his eyes well with tears, and he reached for their legs or arms or whatever was nearest him. They huddled in close to him, and all three cried and laughed together for a time.

"Is either of you injured?" Irin asked as his thoughts and emotions began to clear.

"My belly and side, between k'yot," Pwig replied from the darkness.

"My hands sting with their blood," Wil said. "I think I opened them with my cutter. What about you, Irin? Can you get out?"

Irin tried to pull himself free, but he felt separate weights holding his legs and his body fast. The three of them groaned and heaved the head away, and Irin was able to drag his legs from beneath the last screamer to die, then slid out from under the monstrous head of the middle one. He heard them drop it back down as he tried to stand up, and a pain shot up his lower leg. Still, it was bearable—for the moment, at least.

"Tell me, what happened?" Irin asked. "I saw your light, Wil, and Pwig, I thought you were dead in the darkness.

"I landed on the legs of the fifth one," Pwig replied excitedly. "It shoved me away like nothing, and I felt the claws in my back, but the k'yot did its job. I stayed there and watched its shape in Wil's light. It seemed only interested in the one on top of you, so I slowly got back on my feet and walked around behind it, where I found Wil."

"I thought that my vision was wrong," Wil interrupted. "I thought you dead, and I had lost my cutter on the ground somewhere. I found it as I moved around the last screamer, and that is when I saw Pwig. We agreed with our faces to attack it, but then it suddenly turned on us before we could start, and we had to stab at it until it finally dropped."

"That was me," Pwig said. "I sent the cutter through its eye, and then it was over."

"Very well, my friends," Irin said with a sigh. "You'll have a story to tell the new for the rest of your lives. Now, let us get out of here and return to our people. We don't know, but these caves could be teeming with screamers. This is the only one that we *know* is safe now. We must return with new lightsticks and more men."

They held one another's arms and shuffled in the dark, Wil and Pwig on either side of Irin, their free arms outstretched and feeling for the walls. They finally made it around the bend and could see the light at the mouth of the cave, far away. Irin hadn't realized how far in they had gone. As they approached the entrance, they could see that the sky was beginning to brighten. Only a short time remained in which to get everyone sheltered before sunrise.

As they climbed down the wide rock path to the dirt, Irin saw that most of his body was covered in blood, and he felt the stinging along the side of his face. They would need to pack the cut to stop the bleeding, he realized. He looked at Pwig's face and then turned to Wil.

"Wil . . . ," he said, his voice quaking a little, "I thought that was it."

Wil looked at him oddly, then realized that he was speaking of the vision. His mouth curled as if the idea was absurd. "I was worried also, for a time, but I knew that wasn't your time."

"How?" Irin asked.

"It's during daylight."

Irin turned and peered ahead at the masses awaiting them. Daylight? Would it be in the coming daylight, or the next? He still did not want to know.

As they neared the band of travelers, his face and blood-covered k'yot became visible to those nearby, and a panicked whisper shot through the crowd. Orin gasped and came running to him as thunder rumbled in the distance. She tried to examine his whole body at once, then pulled her hands away when she felt the thick wetness.

"I'm well, Orin," he said. "We killed them all . . . There were five."

She stared at him in awe, and Irin peered up to see a sweating Owil clutching her man's head as he rubbed her swollen belly. He heard the tale pass through the group and back toward the rest, who still sat waiting on rocks all along the mountain.

"Five screamers!" . . . "Irin killed them all!" . . . "Covered in blood—three men against five screamers!" . . . "We are stronger than they" . . . "Irin promised . . . five!"

Irin touched Orin's head and moved away, climbing up the rocks to see everyone. He saw that all had eaten though not everything had been repacked into the n'wips. He wanted to shout out to them in his loudest voice, but he feared waking and attracting more screamers. Instead, he climbed down from the rocks and called for all the fighters nearby to come forward and surround him.

"Listen to me, because we must work quickly . . ." Irin spoke quietly and quickly. "We need to empty two of the least-packed n'wips and carry them to this cave—Wil and Pwig will show you. Bring others, n'wip pullers, and many lightsticks. You must go inside and remove the carcasses from the cave. Throw them over the far edge where the cliff is highest. Try to cover any blood inside with dirt from outside. Anything you see inside that might frighten a woman or child—or yourself—get rid of it. There are also shards of broken lightsticks and cutters on the floor. We need it all cleaned out. Don't grow distracted by the screamers. They are dead, understood?"

Some of the faces appeared frightened, but all agreed, and off they went to work.

TWENTY-NINE

Matt awoke to the sounds of a thousand birds. The warmth inside his sleeping bag held him there. He poked a hand out and ran it down the cut on his face, but, of course, the cut was not there. That had been Irin's face, not his. And he was not asleep inside a dark cave, but in a bright red tent. He felt his body shudder as he remembered the night before, as if the ordeal with the screamers had happened to him and not someone else, millions of years ago.

Someone was at the food tent, making coffee. Two people, at least. He could hear an unintelligible conversation and occasional laughter. He rolled onto his side and tried to rest a while longer. It was nice to be wearing a T-shirt, he thought, his skin rubbing up against something with no worries. He wondered, would he be home yet if he had left yesterday? Probably not. They would be somewhere over the Atlantic by now, nearing the East Coast.

He listened for a little longer to the crunching footsteps of people passing his tent, before braving the morning chill and slipping out of the bag. Dressing quickly, he donned a fresh pair of jeans, gray turtleneck, and black watch cap, all from his bag. Tomorrow he would need to dip into the bag of new clothes that Peter had gotten him.

After zipping up his tent door, he went to the food tent, where a dozen people were already congregated.

He found some cold wieners in the big metal ice chest and decided to have a couple, along with a can of pear halves in syrup. Tuni arrived as he was dipping his bare fingers into the can.

"Ooh, that looks tasty," she said, and reached into the can after him, snatching the last one and slurping it down. "Sorry, dear, was that repellent?"

He smiled in reply and glugged down the remaining syrup in the can.

"Gross," She slapped his shoulder. "You don't know where my hands have been!" Then she nodded and puckered her lips toward the RV.

"Yeah," Matt replied. "That was intense last night, huh?"

"I dreamt about it. But in my version, the screamers just kept coming and I was running and running into this endless cave. Woke up soaked in sweat with my heart racing like a coke fiend."

"Sorry . . ."

She waved off his apology and stirred the steaming coffee in her Styrofoam cup.

The whine of a car engine announced the jouncing approach of an old, rusty Subaru. It stopped a little too close to the tents, sending a cloud of dust drifting over the pit.

Matt and Tuni watched Peter jog over from the pit. "Who d'you suppose this is now?" Tuni asked.

A man stepped out of the car and stretched. He wore black sunglasses with the curved leather flaps on the sides. His long khaki cargo shorts and tan button-down made him look like a travel clothier's representation of an explorer. Matt thought all he was missing was the safari hat.

"Now, *that* is some large hair," said Tuni. "Wait, I know that hair! That's Hank Felch from the museum. I didn't know he was coming—actually, I didn't know he ever went outside."

"I don't think we ever met," Matt said.

Peter jogged up to Hank, and they shook hands, with Peter patting him on the back repeatedly. It looked to Matt as though Hank was not altogether enjoying all the glad-handing and physical contact. Peter ushered him about the site as the driver unloaded four large duffel bags from the trunk.

Matt and Tuni watched the interaction in silence as the recently-caffeinated crowd around them grew progressively louder. The current conversation was a six-degrees-of-separation exercise based upon the intimate relations of people both present and absent. Tuni and Matt shared a shocked look as it became clear that no more than two degrees of separation appeared necessary.

Matt heard a whistle and found Peter, alone, waving him to join him near the light tower. Hank Felch was busy with his gear on the opposite side of the site. Matt excused himself from Tuni and walked to Peter.

Peter said, "I have to request something of you that I have no business requesting, and you have every right to say no, but I'm going to ask it anyway in the interest of this project." Matt raised his eyebrows in anticipation. "I would like you to bring Hank into your circle."

The request was not unexpected. "I take it you trust him?"

"Implicitly. And I'm not just saying that. In fact, if you agree, I suspect he will receive the information in such an impassive manner that you will think he doesn't believe you. But his brain will start working away, and he'll put all the pieces together." Pete smiled. "It'll quite simply *make sense*. As for trust, he would have no interest in revealing your secret to another soul for the rest of his life."

"Tell you what, I wish I could trade him for Rheese." Matt peered across the site to the bouncing mop of hair, sighed, and said, "Yeah, all right. But why him, exactly?"

"When you've got a puzzle in front of you, sometimes you want everyone else to shut up and go away so you can figure it out yourself. Other times, you wish there was someone smarter than you around to just solve it. Hank is smarter than everyone else. I tried to hire him away when I was first promoted but he told me that the museum would crumble if he left."

"Well, great. So you just want me to tell him my story, tell him what I've experienced thus far, and let him work on it? What's he even going to try to figure out at this point?"

"He'll tell us the questions we should be asking, too."

Tuni watched Peter and Matt interrupt Hank as he separated his tent pieces into piles of like parts. Hank and Matt nodded at each other. Hank's hair continued to nod for several seconds after his head stopped. Matt spoke for a while, held out his palms before him. Telltale hand gestures.

He's telling him.

Hank cleaned his glasses on his vest, nodding. Hank asked a question. Peter and Matt shared a look, and then laugh. Hank doesn't appear amused. A few more words and Hank was left behind to resume his setup.

Tuni stood up and intercepted Matt on his way back to her. Peter broke off and joined the raucous bunch at the food tent.

"What did he say?" Tuni asked.

"Huh, who . . . Pete?"

"Hank, after you told him."

"Ah, you caught that, huh?" Matt smirked as he remembered. "He nods and blinks and then asked me if I can at some point help him with three artifacts he hasn't been able to figure out."

"That's Hank," Tuni chuckled. "So . . . what are you and me waiting for, exactly?" she said.

It took him a moment to understand. He looked around. Peter was leading a bunch of the new arrivals over to Hank for introductions, and Dr. Rheese sat in his chair under the RV's canopy, sipping tea.

"Right, let's go. He doesn't look busy, so he might not snap at you."

"At *me*? *You're* asking!" she replied.

"Not fair—I did last time!"

"Lies."

"Whatever . . ."

THIRTY

Orin held the k'yot top and middle out from under the rock overhang and let the pouring rain saturate it. She watched as the blood-pinked water trickled from the bottom and ran down the small rock cliff at her feet. She had washed screamer blood from this k'yot before—or so she had thought. But this was not the same stuff at all. She knew now whose blood it had been.

Gazing out at the broad rolling hills and plains that stretched out below and into the distance, she wondered if their new homeland lay somewhere in that vast expanse, or if they would travel even farther yet. All she knew from Irin was that they would stop where it was both safe and near a water source.

When they awoke, Owil had complained that she could not walk any further. Though the pace had been slow thus far, her pains had been nearly constant, and two men had had to pull her on a n'wip for the last leg. Orin hoped that the newest would fall soon and that Owil would not be taken by newest death.

Stepping backward, Orin shook the k'yot several times to force off as much rain as possible. Others were outside around her, capturing water from the rocks and in outstretched clothing, refilling waterbags. Turning back to the cave, she took a lightstick from a row on the wall and walked in. She looked at all the faces along the sides and on the ground; some still slept, but most had either awoken or had failed to fall asleep at all. The majority did seem refreshed, though, and not as frightened as during sunrise. They ate cold gwotl and seeds, though perhaps a bit too much—Irin might need to pass along a reminder to save food and eat only enough to keep up strength.

She found Irin seated where she had left him. He stood up and thanked her for cleaning the k'yot.

"It was not as easy to clean as the last time," she said, and Irin held her gaze for a moment. Did she know? If so, she apparently had nothing more to say of it.

As he pulled the k'yot over his head, Irin felt safe again. It rested against his gashed cheek, though, and he wondered if this might become a problem later. One of the oldest women had packed it last night with underdirt mixed with bluewater, which at least stopped the bleeding.

After strapping the k'yot from top to bottom, Irin walked to the wall, where Norrit and Pwig were studying the carvings. They had discovered the night before that nearly every surface of the cave had some sort of carved or painted image except for the floor.

"It seems that they ate the small crawlers," Norrit told him. "They burnt them with fire and ate everything, including the bones."

He pointed to a painting, and Irin leaned closer to look. Indeed, there were five people with bones in their hands, and one with a bone in its mouth.

"Perhaps it was a remedy for sickness," Irin said.

They pondered this for a moment, and then Irin pulled them away to get the group up and moving again. Perhaps they would return to this cave one day to learn more from the drawings.

"Let all n'wips be repacked and secured. Keep one of them lighter to carry Owil. Who are the other ones with growing bellies?" said Irin.

"Owwi is," Pwig answered, "but hers is small and she has refused help."

"Otwip is as well," Norrit said, "but she does not even show yet."

"Very well. If there are those who haven't yet eaten, have them do so—just a little—quickly."

They separated, and Irin stopped beside Orin to touch his head to hers before walking out to check on the others. Most of the men had slept in the large cave above because the climb up was too treacherous for many of the women and new. The rest of the group was in a cave they had found around the other side of the mountain. It was wide and not very deep, but the single entrance—a narrow ledge that no screamer could negotiate—made for the most secure sleeping spot.

Irin looked up the rock face to the cave above. One of the fighters had thought to lower a rope for people to descend safely. A good idea, Irin thought, relieved that he could depend upon others. For a while he had felt the weight of the entire journey in his head. He watched a few people climb down with the rope and, after being sure all was safe, he left them for the third cave.

"Hello, Irin," a man said as he came off the ledge. Irin returned the greeting and felt odd for a moment, realizing that everyone now knew him even though he seemed to know so few.

He moved carefully along the ledge and into the big, wide cave. The wind pushed the rain well past the overhanging ledge above, and Irin realized that there was very little cover from it inside. When had the rain begun? Had any of them been able to sleep? The fatigue on the faces here told him. Another mistake.

He returned to the ledge and hiked down to the ground level, where the n'wips were being prepared. In the distance, lightning flashed across the sky, illuminating thick gray clouds and a barren plain. If screamers preferred caves and mountainous places, he thought, they would not be out there.

"Irin!" Wil called to him from the screamer cave. "Owil says she won't move!"

Irin had feared this. The newest would come soon, and Owil would bleed and have to stay.

"Is the newest falling yet?" Irin shouted back.

"No, Gwyn just felt inside; it has not come yet. But Owil says it's on its way."

"If the newest isn't falling out, we move now. Get her onto the n'wip."

Wil stared at him through the falling rain and saw his soaked face and his resolute expression. "She will not be moved," he repeated.

Irin stood like a stone jutting from the ground, and they stared at each other for a moment. Finally, Gwyn appeared from the gloom of the cave.

"The newest falls!" she shouted, and pulled Wil's arm. He looked at Irin with bitterness as she drew him back into the darkness.

Irin turned and looked at the assemblage. It was the right decision, he said to himself. He must do what was best for all, not just a few.

"Pwig!" he yelled. His brother turned away from a n'wip and jogged to him through the mud.

"Yes, Irin."

"We need scouts to see if this hill is safe to descend. Are any near?"

Pwig searched the area for familiar faces and found Tryt and Iyo. He called them forward and sent them down the slope.

THIRTY-ONE

As the sound returned to his ears, Matt realized that there were many people in the RV, and some sort of commotion going on. His eyes quickly unblurred, and he tried to take in all the activity—a stark contrast to the usual silence and Tuni's lovely features and look of anticipation.

". . . just bloody got here and . . ."

". . . *not* your decision . . ."

". . . not sure what's the big deal . . ."

Matt searched for Tuni and saw that she was on the other side of a heated exchange between Peter, Rheese, and Hank Felch. She looked as though she was trying to explain something but could not be heard above everyone else. Finally, Peter shouted and chopped sideways with his hand.

"Enough!" And as the others grew silent, he continued, "This is ridiculous. I understand your point of view, Doctor, but in the end it really doesn't matter. We're all here to get work done. Some of us are more eager than others"—he indicated Hank—"and may not yet be accustomed to some of the more *considerate* ways of doing things here—"

"Made a bloody mess is what he did—"

But before Rheese could launch into a new tirade, Peter cut him off. "Yes, yes, yes—we don't need to rehash it."

Matt slid his gloves back on and inched up on the bench to survey the damage. Rolls of papers were strewn on the floor and on the table in front of him, and Rheese's wooden case of little calipers and compasses and other measuring instruments was spilled upside down, its contents spread across a map like paperweights, holding it unrolled.

"It didn't look like this before, that's all I'm saying, Peter," Hank said. "This is basically ninety percent of Doctor Psycho guy . . ."

Rheese threw up his hands and began to shout again, and Peter shot an angry look at Hank for reigniting the fireworks. He stood between them, waving for silence, while Tuni stood, arms crossed, staring at the ceiling.

"It's done, okay?" Peter shouted. "Done! Now, what I'm hoping is that we can clean this up exactly as Dr. Rheese would want it—in the right bins or whatever—and keep out just the map you were looking for, Hank."

"Yeah, that's no problem," Hank said, still with an air of *I didn't do a damned thing wrong*. "The one I needed is spread out right there on the table. . . . Oh, hey, Matt—you're awake."

Peter turned to Matt. "Sorry about that, pal. Did all that screw you up?"

"Oh, no, just a little weird to come back to. My timer was up."

"Right, right . . ." Peter tried to organize his thoughts. "Well . . . so . . . Hank is here . . ."

"Yep, I see that." Matt replied. "Hiya, Hank."

Peter continued, "I've mostly filled him in on your findings thus far."

Rheese was picking up paper rolls and looking at the tags on the ends to organize them back in their bins. Peter knelt and picked up a bundle to help.

"So anyway, Hank," Peter began, "I'll help Dr. Rheese with this, and you finish whatever you were doing with the maps."

Hank nodded and turned back to the map in front of Matt. He straightened it out and spread his hands over it, studying the spot in Eastern Kenya where they now were. His index finger traced a swirling path and stopped.

"Here, right? We're right here?"

Rheese shot an annoyed glance at the map. "Looks about right."

"Great. So, then, Matt, do you know what direction these people traveled from their city?"

"Um . . . well, they were in these canyons for a while, which might have zigzagged some . . . but, um, in Irin's mind they're following the sun. It's

Michael Siemsen

kind of funny, thinking about it now, actually, but he thinks that because they follow the sun it gives them extra darkness, whereas, if they had gone the other way, they would meet the sun sooner."

"Interesting," Hank mused. "They'd have to be doing a couple hundred miles per hour for there to be any noticeable gain. Logical theory at the core, though . . ."

"Yeah, um . . ." Matt said, hoping to refocus him.

"Right . . . they're traveling west, then . . ." Hank took a ruler and placed it flat on the map, on an east-west axis. "If we're here, and the sun—their destination, let's say—is over here, then this alleged asteroid would have had to strike somewhere from here to here—approximately, of course."

Rheese was looking over his shoulder now with annoyed interest, "You're estimating based upon *current* east-west?"

Hank kept his eyes on the map as he said, "This continent's east-west has remained basically the same since the Triassic, Doctor. Perhaps five to eight degrees rotation, but nothing significant over the distances these people would have traveled on foot in such a short time."

Peter leaned over and looked at the map and said, "So we should go retrieve some sediment samples along that path until we find, what, some sort of odd mineral deposits? I doubt any crater would remain after that many years of erosion and shifting."

"You'd be surprised, actually," Hank replied. "An object of a good size, though not large enough to cause any major global catastrophe— there could still be subtle land markers, that is, if you know what you're looking for."

"I seriously doubt that, Mr. Felch," Rheese quipped. "The Earth's face has changed so much in only the past sixty-five million years that they were barely able to locate the K-T event impact. And that asteroid was ten kilometers across!"

"I'd be happy to show you some examples, Dr. Rheese, along with the recovered shocked quartz and tektite glass that are *only* associated with impacts."

"Well," Rheese huffed, "I wouldn't know anything about all that, but I have surveyed this land thoroughly and have seen neither hide nor hair."

"I'm sure you have," Felch replied, trying to keep an atmosphere of civility. "You wouldn't happen to have any satellite topography or InSAR maps, would you?"

Rheese turned to Peter and snapped, "Look, Sharma, I don't have time to play research assistant to your friend here. No offense, but we have quite a bit going on with the excavation, and, frankly, to pore over maps I am already well acquainted with in search of an ancient asteroid impact seems an unjustifiable waste."

Peter nodded and tried to play it diplomatically. "I understand, Doctor. Why don't you go out and see how they're doing out there?"

Rheese looked around at all his map rolls and instruments. "Well, I don't want . . . that is, my system . . ."

"I'll stay with him, Doctor," Peter assured him. "We'll make sure your documents are all kept in order and put back exactly as they were found."

Rheese sighed, obviously flustered at the idea of leaving Hank alone with his things, but finally he stalked outside. The group released a collective sigh.

"Sheesh!" Peter exclaimed. "That man . . ."

Tuni sat down across from Matt after moving a protractor and compass back onto the table.

"Hey, Peter?" Matt said, pointing at the artifact, which still rested on the table in front of him.

"Oh, right! Well, let's get it back in its box, but we can leave it out of the safe. 'Scuse me, Matt," he said, squeezing in beside him. "So tell us, anything new and exciting happen?"

"His friend's wife is giving birth in the cave. They haven't continued on the journey yet. I think I need another hour for them to get going again."

Hank hmm'd over the map and moved the ruler around. He spoke without looking up, "Peter, as fascinating as all of this is, it's essentially academic. Do you mind if I ask what your end goal is?"

"*Our* end goal . . ." Peter said. "*Ideally*, is to find where these people ended up. If we could locate that spot or spots, there could be a treasure trove of artifacts within twenty or thirty feet of the surface somewhere out there, just waiting to be unearthed. We have no idea at what point this piece of fabric and the knife were dropped. It could be a hundred feet from another Pwin-T village . . . or inside that cave they slept in, or it could be kilometers from anything or nothing. Sadly, this could very well be it."

Hank reached behind Peter and sorted through the rolls of maps protruding from Rheese's bins.

Peter went on, "I'm going to go work with Flip and Graham for a bit. Hank, you go to town on this stuff, all right? Don't mind Rheese—I'll handle any fallout." The RV door slammed behind him.

"So is that guy always such an ass?" Hank asked as he peered through his glasses at the labels on the tubes.

"Rheese?" Tuni replied. "Oh, yes, all that and much, much more."

"Well, I thought this was his project, so I'm not sure why he's so hostile. You saw him slap those tubes out of my arms, right?"

"Yup, I was stunned," she replied. She turned to Matt. "You should have seen it, Matthew! You were still under, and he walks in and takes one look at Hank before blowing a bloody gasket." She turned back to Hank as he pulled a roll from the bin. "You're lucky Peter came in when he did."

"I guess . . . ," Hank replied, distracted. He turned the roll sideways and peeled back a corner to see inside. "That jerk! He *does* have satellite!"

Unrolling the map so that it overlayed the Kenya map, Hank spread his hands over it, scanning, while Matt and Tuni looked on in fascination.

"What are all those circles?" Matt asked, pointing at one. They were marked with red pencil and did not appear to encircle anything in particular.

"I don't know," Hank replied. "Dinosaur sites, maybe? Let's see where we are on this one . . . where's the road?"

He ran his finger over the glossy surface for a moment, then pulled back the corner to compare it to the map underneath.

Suddenly, Tuni jabbed her finger at a point on the map. "Isn't that the highway before the road?"

Hank nodded, "Mm-hmm . . ."

"Well there is a T like that on the satellite one. Look . . ."

Hank released the corner and let the map flop back down. Tuni pointed it out. It was much bigger now, in the upper right corner.

"I think you're right, Tuni," Hank said. "So this circle . . . here would be our site, where we are right now. I guess it was covered in trees when this photo was taken." Frowning, he adjusted his glasses. "Wait a second . . ."

He turned around and began rooting through the other rubber-banded tubes as Matt and Tuni shared an amused glance. After rummaging about for a minute, he finally emerged from the bins with a loud "Aha!" and unrolled a third map atop the other two. This was a much larger view and had red circles all over, each bearing a number: 218, 227, 241, 223.

"Isn't this site two-two-three-K-Y?" Hank asked, but got only blank looks. "I'm assuming these are his site identification codes, and we are right here—see this? Same picture, just smaller."

All three gazed at the small circle. They found the T that Tuni had identified, and the small red circle lay just below it. They nodded, feeling as though they were getting the hang of this—whatever "this" was. Hank stared at the new sheet: a combination of hundreds of satellite photos, all patchworked into a single map of the country.

"This is . . . hmmm," he mumbled to himself.

"What?" Matt prodded.

Hank waved the inquiry away as if it were a gnat. Tuni and Matt sat back down and waited while Hank carried on an unintelligible conversation with himself, moving from red circle to red circle.

"This one is definitely . . . I mean, so blatant . . . and that one . . . well, if not for the obvious water source . . . those ones, too . . . well . . . ha-ha, I would have made that mistake, like, ten years ago . . . yeah, yeah, these . . ."

Tuni coiled her hair around a finger and sighed. Matt caught her eye and pantomimed a yawn, then nodded toward the door. She smiled and agreed, and they scooted from the benches.

"Excuse us, Hank," Tuni said as they moved by him.

"See you in a little bit, 'kay?" Matt added.

Oblivious, Hank continued, ". . . but why dig them all up? Why . . . I mean, minerals? Or . . . hmm-m, what dinosaurs . . . bones . . ."

He was still muttering away as the door closed behind them.

Matt and Tuni spotted Flip and Peter on their way from the pit, which was beginning to look more and more like an inverted pyramid, with elongated steps rising out in three directions. The ramp of packed dirt remained the same, though Fozzy and Jesse appeared to be digging out a narrow set of steps along the near edge—a safer way in and out than the loose, precarious footing of the ramp.

Peter called to Matt, "An hour break then back at it?"

Matt thought he didn't need that long, that he could just use the bathroom and jump back to it, but realized the break was probably in his best interest.

THIRTY-TWO

I rin helped pack the n'wips as women came and went from the cave. Two were rinsing out blood-soaked cloths in the downpour and wringing them out. At last Orin emerged and came to him.

"The newest is out and its rope cut," she said. "Owil continues to bleed, though. We have blocked her with cloth to make it stop, but she has many pains."

"Can she be brought onto a n'wip so we can get everyone moving?" Irin replied impatiently. "We'll lose this entire night if we don't."

Orin's eyes flashed, and she turned sharply back to the cave, and Irin felt his frustration grow as the rain continued relentlessly drenching everyone and everything. He surveyed the scene and saw that most of the people were looking at him, waiting.

He deliberated for a moment and then walked along the scattered line, telling one and all that they could retreat into the caves for shelter, for they'd be here a while longer.

Others could be heard talking around the corner, below the rocky outcropping of the caves. Irin rounded the wall and slid down a short drop to find several men and a couple of older new poking at the screamer carcasses. One of them lay splayed upon the others, its toothy maw agape and pooling with rainwater. They greeted Irin.

He moved about them, easily identifying the three beasts with single slashes across their necks, though he could not differentiate among them. The two others, bearing multiple stab wounds and gashes, were clearly the last two to be killed. He had a thought and began lifting the heavy front legs, one by one.

Sure enough! He found a wound, perhaps from a cutter, healing at the underside of the one with the ruined eye. Could this be the monster whose enormous claws had gotten inside his house? It had happened quickly, but that was the spot where he had stabbed the screamer only a few nights ago. And this wound was sealing itself—plainly not from last night's clash. What could this mean? If not a coincidental wound, it meant that the screamers had traveled a great distance to reach the city. On the other hand, it just might be that these were the only screamers in the area.

The stench from the beasts was quickly growing unbearable, and he dropped the huge forelimb and turned to go, wishing only to put some distance between himself and the ghastly charnel heap. The muddy slope was too slick to ascend, so he pulled himself up a series of rock holds to the area above. The others followed his path.

Above and to his left, people sat around the edges of the screamer cave; others waited near the mouth of the upper cave, their faces raised to the cooling rainfall. He climbed to the ledge and watched steam drift from the cave's mouth. Entering, he could feel the moist heat of too many people. The air was thick. The crowd parted as he made his way among them, in search of Orin and Owil.

The cave was well lit now, with lightsticks positioned all along the walls. People were pointing and discussing the carvings, making more noise than he would have preferred.

When he finally reached the wider area at the end, he found a pocket of space where Owil lay resting on her side, atop a pile of clothes. Orin looked up at him as she patted a wet cloth around Owil's head. Wil sat beside them, holding the newest. Other women looked on as Owil rocked gently, humming in a low moan.

"Owil will not let her feed," Orin said to him with a grim expression.

"Why not?" Irin asked.

Orin sighed, answering with only her face as Irin saw Owil's eye open just a slit, then close again. Irin looked back at Wil and saw the despair in his eyes. The newest twisted and cried and let out small coughs between.

"Can it not feed from another's breast?" Irin asked.

"We have tried on some, but all the most recent births stayed behind in Pwin-T. These women are dry."

"Then she *must* feed it," Irin responded sternly, more to Owil than to anyone else.

Owil moaned louder in response as she continued rocking.

"The melodrama doesn't change anything. It is not your choice, Owil," Irin said, kicking her foot. "Wil, put the newest on her breast—she can hum and whine all she wants."

"Irin!" Orin scolded him.

Wil looked up at him. "She will, Irin; she only needs a little more time."

"Can the newest remain empty for long?" he asked, and most of the women gave him the same look as Orin.

"If this goes on much longer, I say this to you, Owil," he said in a loud voice, "I will return, and the newest *will* feed. I know your ears hear me."

And turning away, he wrestled again through the heat of the masses. He needed fresh air.

THIRTY-THREE

Dr. Rheese strode through the forest, his boots crunching against dead leaves, twigs, and desiccated beetle shells. As he walked, his eyes darted from the ground to the canopy overhead, half expecting every vine or aerial root to morph into a lurking python or boomslang. He hated snakes—hated their way of hiding in plain sight. At the moment, though, he had more pressing problems.

In the distance behind him, a man's voice called out, and for an instant he wondered whether his plan had been discovered. Probably just one of the new idiots calling to one of the other new idiots, all happily wasting their own time and his at this useless site. In fact, since Peter Sharma's arrival, he had felt a rising unease that now bordered on panic. Sharma seemed to delight in coming to him with the ambiguous and ever-annoying preface: "We need to discuss something." *But of course, my swarthy young friend. My time is yours, always.* A plague on whatever equal opportunity program had recruited the interfering little wog and put him in charge of the museum's paleontology department!

Rheese parted the leaves in front of him and found himself looking out at the dirt road. So where the hell *were* the bastards? He looked at his watch, then stared back into the thicket. He had heard something. Had someone followed him? But . . . why would they? These were scientists, not detectives. But nosy, to be sure—an inquisitive, meddlesome bunch, examining and pondering his every move and motivation. *Well, not for long.*

He heard the truck, then saw it crest the rise a half mile away, pulling a plume of reddish dust behind it. *Slow down, you fools,* he thought. *They'll bloody well hear you!*

An older American pickup that had once been white approached, and Rheese stepped out from the trees, waving his hat.

"Garrett Rice?" the driver said.

"No, you idiot. I'm someone else meeting you in the bloody spot where I said to meet. And what's the goddamn meaning—"

The metallic *cha-chink* of the rifle's bolt silenced his rant. The passenger was armed as well.

"Ah, yes, well . . . ," he said, his tone suddenly affable, "I see you have your equipment. Good."

"Money," the driver said.

Rheese didn't like being unable to see the man's eyes through the black sunglasses. Would he be shot dead here on the side of the road, leaving his killers ten thousand dollars richer? He reached behind him under his shirt and pulled out the bound stack of bills. Flipping through it in front of them, he could almost see them salivate.

The driver took his hand off the gun and held the eager palm out the window. "Give it."

Rheese considered saying something tough like "Just remember what you're being paid for," or "Don't screw it up," but thought better of it and simply handed over the money. He watched as the truck whipped around in a three-point turn and roared off in the direction it had come.

Turning back to the woods, he chided himself for being such a coward. For all he knew, those two could be driving off to Nairobi for a wild night of debauchery with HIV-infected prostitutes. Not that there was much he could do about it if they were, though their boss, the Gray, would certainly disapprove—he had as much invested in this as Rheese, and they knew it. They also knew that the Gray would burn their homes and remove their manhood with a broken Tusker beer bottle should they be fools enough to cross him.

Rheese walked back to the site, ever mindful of snakes and more nervous than ever about what lay ahead.

Enzi caught his eye as he came out of the forest. Rheese gave a single nod of inquiry, then watched Enzi make a subtle gesture toward the RV. *Damn!* He speeded up his pace, rounding the excavation while doing his best to look composed. The door swung open in front of him, and out stepped the buxom Collette woman with the Turner brat in tow. Behind them, he could see Hank Felch rolling up more of his maps and replacing them in their bins.

He glanced back at the pit, looking for Sharma, and there he was, of course, getting his hands dirty so he could feel like a real field scientist. And what about the dusky Amazon? She and Turner were seldom apart. Very soon he would have to find something else to occupy her interest. Entering the RV, he heard the toilet flush and realized that it had to be her. Felch turned toward him and gave him an accusing look. *What's on your mind, sheep-head?* Rheese wanted to say, but instead he gave him a cordial sneer and looked casually at the maps still on the table. What the hell would he be looking at on that one?

The door snapped open behind him, and Tuni came out, drying her hands. "Oh, hello, Mr. Rheese," she said.

"Hi, there," he replied cheerily, seething behind his smile. *Keep calling me "Mister," cheeky little slag—soon you won't be so perky.*

She walked out the door, leaving the two men alone.

"So, Doctor Rheese," said Hank, "I was noticing the circles you have on some of the satellite imagery—"

"It's lunchtime, lad," Rheese interrupted. "Let's discuss your fascinating observations later, shall we?"

"Oh . . . well . . ." Hank hesitated and began to move one of the maps.

"I'll take care of putting those back in their proper bins, Mr. Felch—you needn't bother, m'kay?"

Hank sighed and handed Rheese the map. "Fine," he said, "but we need to discuss something after." And donning his leather-lined shades, he left Rheese alone in the RV.

Discuss something—a line from Sharma's book if ever there was one. They would do no such thing, of course, for soon there would be ample goings-on to distract them all.

Rheese picked up the sat phone and punched in a number.

Matt sat hunched over at the food tent, his chin resting on his gloved hands as he munched on peanuts. The dark bags under his eyes were growing. Gazing absently toward the pit, he saw the silhouettes of Hank and Peter chatting. The lowering sun hung just behind their heads.

A girl's voice behind him, "So . . . why are you here again?"

Matt spun around and saw the American girl—Felicia, he thought he'd heard. She was cute, though the generally flirtatious type.

"This and that," Matt smiled.

She squinted accusingly while still smirking. "Funny, I haven't seen you do either. You just disappear into the RV and talk to Peter and that tall chick."

"Pretty much."

"Are you and her . . . like, together?"

"Often."

Felicia sighed and appeared flustered by him: clearly not something with which she was accustomed. She plopped down right next to him, a little too close for strangers or familiars.

She looked him over. "What are you, twenty? Twenty-one?"

The RV door swung open and Tuni stepped down. Matt watched her survey the site. Was she looking for him? *Well, this is an interesting opportunity . . .*

He turned to face Felicia directly. Her face was only a few inches from his. "Twenty-five," he replied. "You're what, seventeen? Eighteen?"

Obviously offended: "Twenty-two." She looked him over. "So seriously, what do you do?"

"I'm just looking over the artifacts. Offer theories, stuff like that."

"Okay, but what's your field?"

"Matthew?" Tuni was right on top of them.

"Oh, hey," he said. Her face didn't reveal anything as he had hoped.

"I was waiting for you," she said, nodding pleasantly toward the RV. She turned to Felcia, "Mind if I steal him for a bit, dear?"

Felicia wore a saccharin smile, "Not at all, dear." She got up and walked off toward the pit.

"She seems to like you," Tuni said.

Matt shrugged. Still nothing to read from Tuni. He wondered why he thought she would have cared. *Deluding yourself*, he thought. "I'm on break. Gotta get my head clear. Starting to not feel so good."

"Oh—I hadn't realized . . . sorry if I've been pushing or anything . . ."

Hand and Pete spotted them and made a beeline for the table.

"Hey, Matt," Peter said as they approached. He was even more animated than usual. "We're getting a helicopter brought over tomorrow to map out a proposed site path. We're going to start doing small sample sites in a broad line from here west. Radar units coming in the morning, along with some other cool stuff that will let us find underground anomalies without having to dig anything up."

"Yeah," Hank added. "If this site is representative of their migration path, we might be able to find more artifacts along the way."

"Sounds great," Matt replied. "Do you need me . . . you know, to *do* anything?"

"Oh, no, not really," Peter replied. "Just do as many sessions with the k'yot as you're comfortable with, and keep track of any directional changes as they go. Oh, and uh . . ." Peter smiled apologetically. "I didn't want you to think the chopper was for you."

"Got it . . . so, about that, when do you think would be a good time for me to go? By Saturday?"

"Oh, yeah, Saturday, definitely! That'd be great if you stuck around that long—I really appreciate it."

They walked away, enthusiastically discussing their plans.

Tuni said quietly, "Don't feel pressured by him, either. He's eager, but if you're not feeling well . . ."

"Thanks, no, it's fine. I'll be fine after a long break. Maybe after dinner."

"I was wondering about that—what if you were to eat something ghastly and rotten and then do a session? Would you still vomit?"

"This is the kind of stuff you think about?"

"It's a serious question, Matthew."

"Yeah, I would probably puke my guts and drown in it. It would be a horrendous tragedy."

They turned to the table as Wekesa slid stainless steel bowls of unknown foodstuff in front of them.

"Speaking of . . . ," Tuni murmured.

"Absolutely!" Rheese answered when Matt and Tuni asked for the artifact from the safe. He squeezed his cigar into the ashtray by his folding chair and popped up on his feet.

Tuni and Matt exchanged a skeptical look as he opened the door and bounced up the steps into the RV. He pulled the artifact from the safe and placed it on the empty table.

"Enjoy," he said, and went back outside, whistling.

"He seems a little too happy," Matt whispered.

"He's faking it, dear. I bet you Peter gave him a stern talking-to after the episode with Hank."

Matt sat down and pulled the timer from his pocket. "What do you think?" he asked. "An hour?"

"You said you were feeling ill . . ."

"Oh that passed quick. It's really annoying doing short sessions now. It used to be, I'd only get the *good* stuff, so to speak, but with them, they have to leave the k'yot on the floor for there to be a gap—you know, the dark space. He's *always* wearing it, though not in his sleep yet, thank God. It'd be hours of dreams, I'm sure."

"Well, I'll be here for the next hour, then, dear."

He frowned. "You have to stop that," he said. "Not with me, okay?"

"Stop what?" she said, obviously puzzled.

"The 'dear' thing. I'm sorry . . . It's just that it'll keep bothering me until it means something."

Her face changed and she put her hands in her lap, looking at him for a moment before saying quietly, "Okay. Sorry."

THIRTY-FOUR

Matt's senses returned to him quickly as he felt his shoulder being shaken. He heard garbled yelling. He hadn't felt the timer's buzz, but Irin had more than likely gone through an hour of walking around caves and talking to people. It had been utterly uneventful, and he was ready for the hour to be up. He realized that the k'yot was no longer under his hands and that it was Tuni's voice yelling at him for "missing it." But, missing *what*? Her face came into focus, and her expression was very different from the one she had worn when he went under.

"Sorry," he said. "Say it again—I didn't quite catch what you were saying."

"Hank is missing!"

"*What?* Where . . . he was just . . ." He paused, realizing he had no idea where Hank just was, because he had been unconscious for the past fifty-four minutes. He pulled off his timer and slid his hands into his gloves as Tuni stood over him, looking out the blinds. Outside, Matt could see flashlight beams bouncing about and could hear people yelling, "Hank!"

The door swung violently open, and Rheese appeared, with Peter right behind him. Peter looked frantic, but Rheese exuded only anger.

"God damn it!" Rheese barked as he picked up the sat phone and began pushing buttons. "This is what happens when you treat a bloody jungle like a summer camp! Bloody nature walks in the dark . . ."

"Who are you calling first, Rheese?" Peter said as he riffled frantically through his notebook. "I think we should call the American embassy—that's his embassy."

"Waste of bloody time, Sharma! You think they're going to care about someone who's missing for an hour? They have no idea what that amount of time means out here in the jungle. Besides, they don't have searching resources themselves—we have to go right to the source."

"And who is that?" Peter asked.

"Law enforcement, lad—the bloody law enforcement. They'll be far more responsive to an American missing in their country than the Americans themselves. They'll also understand that an hour's no joke out here. We need dogs; we need choppers . . . hello? *Hello!* We have an emergency here! English—need English, not bloody Swahili!" He listened on the line for a moment, shaking his head, then glanced at Tuni. "You speak their damned jabber, don't you?"

She nodded and took the phone.

"*Hebu?*" She began. "*Habari za jioni . . . jina langu ni* Tuni Saint James . . . *ndiyo . . . ndiyo. Samahani, kuna mtu anayesema Kiingereza? Ndiyo . . .*" She turned back to Rheese. "She's getting someone who speaks English for us. She's just the cleaning lady."

He took the phone back from her and gave her an almost polite nod of thanks.

"Hello? Hello, yes, English. Yes, *I* am English, too. We have an emergency out here. We are scientists . . . yes . . . researchers. We are in the forest and we have an American citizen *missing* out there. Yes, American . . . Ah, a couple of hours ago, but he is not answering our shouts. Yes . . . yes . . . I have GPS coordinates I will give you. Okay, we'll do that, but we need dogs out here, too, and spotlights . . . You have helicopters, yes?" He cupped the receiver and turned his head to Peter. "They said to turn on any lights we have so he can see us from afar. It's a good idea—can you tell Enzi to raise the floods as high as they go?"

Peter nodded and dashed outside as Rheese stayed on the phone, describing the location and Hank's physical description. When he was off the phone, he told Matt and Tuni, "Go outside and bang on the equipment trailer with a wrench or something else metal. People shouting gets lost quickly in the woods, but a loud clang like that resonates—he could follow it back to the site if he hears it."

They ran out into the night and headed to the trailer to find something to bang on. Through the tree line, they could see flashlights and hear the team shouting "Hank!" from all sides. Near the trailer they found Felicia, pacing back and forth and sobbing.

"He was right behind me . . . ," she wailed.

Matt found what he was looking for: a four-foot length of steel pipe and a heavy adjustable wrench. He handed the pipe to Tuni, and they began banging away on the sheet metal wall of the trailer.

Felicia turned to them. "What are you doing?" she cried, "That man is out there somewhere! He could be hurt!" She ran to Matt. He recoiled, but not fast enough, as her arms flew open and wrapped around his neck in a desperate embrace.

He collapsed and slid to the ground.

I am Felicia McWharter. I am twenty years old, from Anaheim, California. I'm anxious and spinning around. Trees surround me. My flashlight beam plays across the wall of trees. . . . "Omigod where's that Hank guy?"

Matt blinked and saw the faces above him. Felicia was crying harder than ever. He sat up with Tuni's help as Felicia cried out, "What's *wrong* with me!"

Matt brushed the dirt from his hair and tried to tell her it was okay, that she didn't do anything wrong. Her jacket had touched his neck, but he wasn't about to explain what had happened. She wasn't hearing anything, so he just found the metal pipe, stood up, and began banging on the trailer again. Felicia screamed and covered her ears.

"Felicia," said Tuni, grabbing her arm forcefully, "why don't you go try to calm down at the food tent?" Felicia stared at her for a second, holding her ears, pigtails bobbing as she nodded. "Go, honey, go," nudging her in the direction of the food tent and watching her shuffle away.

Peter and Enzi were cranking away at the floodlight tower, raising it above the low canopy of trees. Tuni rushed over to them.

"Peter," she said, "isn't there a risk of someone else getting lost out there while they look for him? We should get everyone back and pair people up together. Perhaps have everyone search for a time, maybe ten minutes, and then come back to check in?"

He nodded, despair written on his face.

"Yeah, that's a good idea . . . um . . . *Crap!* How do we get them all back?"

They pondered this for a moment, and then Peter shouted out to the bobbing flashlight beams nearby, "Hey! Everybody! Everyone come back to the site to meet! Pass it on!"

Ten minutes later, most of the team stood at the food tent. Rheese was inside the RV, calling more government agencies, while Enzi banged on the trailer with the pipe every twenty seconds or so. Peter took a head count—all present but Hank. Assigning the searchers to groups of three, Peter instructed them not to separate for any reason. They were to walk out from the site in as straight a line as possible for ten minutes, turn right and walk for two minutes, then walk back to the site.

Rheese stormed out of the trailer and stomped to the tent, swearing all the way. "Goddamn bureaucratic bollocks!" he snarled.

"What's the deal, Doctor?" Peter asked.

"Well, we supposedly have two helicopters on their way, but get this: only one has a searchlight. Backwater idiots. There is also a truck full of Defense Forces troops with bloodhounds on the way, but it won't be here for four bloody hours."

The teams had gone out and come back twice, not only calling out for Hank, but also searching the forest floor for a body.

The helicopters had arrived, and the one with the searchlight blared from a loudspeaker to get everyone back to the site while they searched. From the food tent, they all watched as the choppers flew in straight lines, back and forth, until it seemed that the whole area had been covered. In the distance, the gathered team could hear them still calling from their speaker, "Move to a clearing and wave your arms." The choppers had flown much farther than the searchers on the ground had been able to walk, and everyone tried to keep up hopes of finding him before the dogs arrived. If it did come to that, no one wanted to think about what the dogs might find.

A little after three a.m., the police arrived in two unmarked SUVs, a crime scene van, and a small patrol Jeep, while the soldiers, who had arrived with their dogs, combed the woods. Their dogs had gone straight to the buried elephant remains and had to be taken some distance away before they began sniffing for anything else

The policemen moved recklessly over the site, tripping over gridlines, tossing gear from tents, and treating the three Kenyans—Enzi, Wekesa, and Zuberi—rudely and accusingly. By five a.m., they had spoken to most of the team. Rheese and Peter had explained several times why there was a decaying elephant in the woods, but the detectives could reach no one at the Interior Ministry to verify their statements. The stress on everyone present mounted as it became clear that Hank's disappearance was being treated as a crime.

The policeman in charge, a Detective Chitundu, sat in the RV with Rheese, Peter, Matt, and Tuni. He rubbed at his large, round head as if it ached. He had large bags under his eyes, and when he opened them they were droopy and red-rimmed, much like those of the hounds that the soldiers had brought.

"You surprise me, all of you," he said in a slow, deep baritone. "Your friend is missing, and you first look for him for an entire hour before calling anyone. Why would that be?"

"As we said, Detective," Peter explained yet again, "we're all field researchers. Most of us are used to environments like this. We didn't get concerned until after a half hour; then we grew more concerned when everyone came back in and said they couldn't find him anywhere." The others nodded agreement.

"Of course," Chitundu laughed. "You thought he had been eaten by a snake." More laughter. Then all the merriment left his voice. "You know what concerns me?" he said, fixing each of them in turn with those droopy, doleful eyes. "It concerns me . . . that someone has made a mistake." Again, he regarded each of them. "You know what that mistake was? It's so simple, ha-ha-ha. I can see how you forget this."

Everyone just stared at him in confusion. Matt and Tuni thought he was doing typical cop tricks from TV crime shows, watching to see who got nervous at suggestion that their plot had holes.

He slapped his hand down flat on the table. "Everyone say Mr. Felch had a flashlight!"

His weary eyes moved over their faces as if he had just found the smoking gun that each of them had fired. When they did not respond as he had expected, his eyebrows rose, creating three gleaming black cigars in his forehead.

"You know the easiest thing to find in the forest?" He began again. "A flashlight." They nodded; it made sense. "So did the hungry snakes drag Mr. Felch to their underground lair, sure to bring the flashlight along so as not to leave evidence? Smart snake was sure to click off the power?"

Matt understood his point. It would make sense if something had attacked him, but not if he simply got lost and kept walking. He was probably still out there, walking in the wrong direction for nearly seven hours now. He wished a flashlight had turned up, for he could have learned what happened merely by touching it—but there was no trace.

"Sorry," Matt interjected, "but do you know if the helicopters are coming back anytime soon?"

Chitundu turned to him and blinked. He glanced down at his notepad. "Matthew Turner," he said in the same accusing tone. Tuni thought he might as well have added "*if* that is your real name!"

"Yes, that's me."

"You are curious about helicopters? I wonder why that is. You think there is a chance they will still find him out there? That is funny, ha-ha-ha."

"I don't think it's funny at all, Detective," Peter interrupted. "We want our friend found—safe! None of us were even out there when he disappeared."

"Yes, *disappeared*. That is the interesting part, Mr. . . . ." He consulted his pad. ". . . Sharma. To answer your question, Matthew Turner, the helicopters will return after sunrise. They will widen their perimeter. We *all* want to see Mister Felch okay . . . okay?" He smiled blandly and got up.

Another of the officers came in the door, glanced at them, and called Detective Chitundu outside. They spoke mutedly for a moment before Chitundu nodded and peered over at the food tent. The two then walked away in that direction.

"This is ridiculous," Rheese blurted out. "They're going to waste time playing Sherlock Holmes while one of our people is lost out there."

"Yeah," Peter replied, "we just have to cooperate as best we can to get this part over with. I'm sure this is standard procedure for them."

"The dogs are coming back," Tuni said, peering through the window behind her.

They stood up and went outside. The soldiers were appearing on all sides of the tree line, their flashlights clicking off as they reentered the well-lit site. None seemed to be giving any hint of a discovery. Over at the food tent, five policemen huddled around Enzi. Wekesa came walking toward the RV, and Tuni asked him what was going on.

"*Polisi . . . weka rumande Enzi,*" he replied, and continued walking.

"What!" she replied, shocked.

"What did he say?" Matt asked.

"They're arresting Enzi!"

The four of them hurried over to ask what was going on, but the policemen kept them back while they handcuffed Enzi. Two uniformed officers walked him from the tables. As he passed by, head hanging low, he looked up at Tuni and then back down again.

"What did he do?" she called out to the remaining police. "Did he say he did something?"

Chitundu chuckled to himself, finished what he was telling the other men, and then walked to her.

"This man is your friend?" he asked.

"Yes. For the past few days only, but yes."

"You know his name?" he said as he looked down at his notepad.

"Of course—Enzi . . . Enzi . . ."

Rheese finished for her, "Wata. It's Wata."

"Yes, yes, good name, Enzi Wata. Ha-ha-ha. His name is Enzi, yes. Jeremiah Enzi. This man is a criminal." He walked leisurely toward the vehicles.

"What has he done?" Peter called to Chitundu's back.

"He is a thief, sir. You check you bring any jewelry with you here. Let us know what is missing, yes?" He smiled and continued to the vehicles.

"What's that have to do with Hank?" Matt called out after him, but he received only a dismissive wave from Chitundu.

"This is bullshit," Tuni said. "Complete nonsense. Doctor, how long has Enzi worked for you?"

"More than a couple of years now, I'd say," Rheese replied, looking up as if the information might be found in his hatband. "Must have been September . . . yes, over two years. *I've* never had anything come up missing. Had no idea about the lad—hard worker, for sure."

Rheese sat down in his folding chair and took off his hat, shaking his head and mumbling, "Bloody shame . . ."

Tuni was about to follow Matt into the RV, then suddenly stopped and blurted out, "Bollocks!" and stormed toward the police and military vehicles crowding the entrance. She found Enzi in the backseat of the small patrol Jeep. The front passenger door was open. Brushing past the crowd of police and soldiers in camouflage, she plopped down onto the seat in front of him.

"Did you have anything to do with this, Enzi?" she asked. "Tell me now."

Enzi looked up at her, expressionless.

"You *did*? Did you do something to Hank?"

He frowned and shook his head.

"What *did* you do?"

He sighed and looked away.

"Step out, miss," a uniformed officer said, and held his hand out to her.

"Unbelievable, Enzi. I thought . . . I thought you were good man." She stood up, ignoring the officer's hand, and walked back through the group.

Matt stood just beyond them, waiting for her. "Did he say anything?" he asked, falling in step with her.

"No, but he's obviously guilty of something. I don't think he did anything to Hank, but he knows something."

THIRTY-FIVE

By ten a.m., most of the group had gotten only a few hours' sleep before crawling out of their tents. Nobody *wanted* to sleep, or perhaps they had felt guilty about doing so with Hank's fate still unknown, but each had eventually succumbed to exhaustion and slipped away. The police had departed, and the soldiers had left only one platoon of men to resume the search after sunrise.

Matt crawled out of his tent, wearing the same clothes as yesterday, and shuffled over to Peter's tent, where he stood listening for any sound of wakefulness.

"Who's that?" a crackling voice inquired.

"It's me. Did I wake you?"

Peter yawned, "Nah, I couldn't really sleep. Those damn birds in a full-scale *riot*. Is anyone here?"

"Like, anyone new?"

"Yeah—cops or whatever. C'mon in—I'm decent."

Matt crouched down and unzipped the door, "Nope, those soldiers are just now coming out of their truck." He sat down on the foot of Peter's poofy orange sleeping bag.

"Dude," Peter said, "I don't know what the hell to do now."

Matt shook his head. "I know. I'm probably just as lost."

"I just hope they find him, that he's just sleeping somewhere in a pile of leaves, pissed off that he, of all people, got lost out there. The thing is, he would have heard the helicopters, right? Started walking back our way? Wouldn't the dogs have found a scent trail or something?"

"I don't know," Matt replied solemnly.

They sat in silence for a moment, until Tuni's voice greeted them. "Hey," she said.

"Hey," they replied together.

She poked her head in the door. "You men think you can eat? I've scrambled some of the eggs, and the coffee's fresh."

They agreed that it sounded good—no one had eaten much of last night's dinner, and they were hungry.

They went to the food tent and served themselves the eggs from the pan, and were eating in silence when Dr. Rheese descended from his RV in worn black jeans and an oversize flannel shirt.

The whole team was present, and no one had much to say. If they did speak, it was in hushed tones and brief. Longer conversations were taken away from the food tent.

Felicia broke into silent, quivering sobs periodically and sought reassuring hugs from whoever happened to be closest. She sat next to Matt at one point, keeping a few inches away, and apologized for "whatever happened last night," then asked if he and Hank were friends. Not wanting to set her off on a fresh crying jag, he said, "Sure, yeah."

Soon they heard a helicopter approaching. Most stood up to watch it search, but instead it flew directly over the site and hovered, the pilots looking down at them and making hand gestures no one understood. Finally, Peter realized that it wasn't one of the search choppers and that they wanted to land, but there was nowhere they could go.

"Well, if they have to bloody land," Rheese announced, "it'll have to be at the road junction—it's the only spot wide enough."

Peter pointed toward the road, and the pilots looked in that direction, exchanged a few words, and turned and made for the road.

"Why are they landing?" Matt asked as Peter started off to meet them.

"It's for the survey. Hank and I were going to . . ." He waved his hand as if that explained it, and jogged away.

"What do you think he's going to tell them?" Tuni asked Matt.

"I don't know. I doubt he'd go on the survey thing by himself—especially with Hank still missing."

A few minutes later the helicopter reappeared, with Peter visible in the rear. He waved to them and pointed in the direction where everyone thought Hank had gone.

"He's going to go do his own aerial search!" Matt said.

"Are you sure?" Tuni asked.

"Yeah, they said they were going to go survey west of here. That's like . . . northeast, he's headed."

They watched the chopper sail slowly away, zigzagging over the forest.

Tuni whispered to Matt, "Come with me, wouldja?" She shifted her eyes to Rheese, behind them. Matt got up and followed her to the RV. She glanced back and opened the door quietly, waved him in, and clicked the door shut.

"What's up?" he asked.

"Hank was buggered out over those satellite maps and all the circles and such, right? What if Rheese had something to do with him disappearing? None of us said anything when that detective asked if Hank had any enemies or recent arguments, but you know what all of us were thinking in the back of our minds."

Matt bit at the back of his thumb. "I don't know," he said. "He looked pretty pissed last night. My guess is, that's how his type would respond when worried. He's in my top ten list of assholes, but it seemed genuine to me."

Tuni gave him a disappointed look and turned to sort through the rolls of maps in the bins.

"I mean, " Matt continued, "he's obviously peeved with everyone being here, and that argument he had with Hank was no worse than he'd had with us or Peter or anyone else."

Tuni held up one finger. She glanced out the window again and unrolled the large satellite map on the table.

"Holy crap!" she whispered.

"What?"

"They're gone! All the red circles that Hank was so flipped out over—Rheese *erased* them!"

"So what? It's like dry-erase marker or whatever. It's supposed to be drawn on, then erased, and all that. Hell, *Hank* might even have erased them. Actually, how do you even know that's the same map?"

She leaned close to it and turned her head sideways, scanning till she found the angle she sought.

"There . . . look from here. You can see where a circle was."

Matt leaned down and saw what she meant. A faint circle was visible at a certain angle, the map's glossy surface dulled ever so slightly by the erasure.

"I don't know, Tuni," he said, standing up. "I still don't know what one thing has to do with the other."

"You don't feel like he's been up to . . . shit, here he comes. Sit down!"

She whipped the map back into a roll and stashed it in the bin she thought she had taken it from. They slid into their usual seats and tried to look glum as the door swung open.

"Ah . . . dismal morning this is, eh?" Rheese said in a suitably grave voice.

Tuni nodded, and Matt answered, "Yep . . ."

Rheese looked around the room casually and asked if the sat phone had rung.

"Nope, not in the last few minutes." Matt answered as he gazed out the window. He felt Rheese looking at him and heard the map rolls being moved around.

"This is interesting," Rheese said to himself but clearly for their benefit. He pulled out the satellite map and slid it back into the bin where it belonged. Matt drummed on the table with his fingers while Tuni examined her deteriorating manicure. "Were you waiting for something, folks?" Rheese asked finally.

"Hmm," was all Matt could muster.

"Of course," Rheese answered himself. "What better to take one's mind off the uncertain?" He pulled out his key, knelt down to the safe, and got out the k'yot piece. He slid it onto the table and unscrewed the case. "Have at it, lad. No use letting it just sit there, eh? You kids knock yourselves out."

Rheese paused outside the door to light a cigar, and Tuni waited until he walked away before speaking.

"You see that?" she hissed. "Tell me he wasn't involved now!"

Matt nodded, "Yeah, didn't it seem like he was trying to tell us he knows we know . . . or something? Or are we just suspicious of everything now because you were talking about it? Ach, I don't know . . ."

"He's bloody guilty, Matthew. We don't have to understand why to listen to our instincts. That said, what do we do? Peter's up in the whirlybird for who knows how long?"

"I don't know. The sat phone's right there, but who would we call?"

"And what would we say?"

"Hey, wait a minute," said Matt. "You said you thought Enzi knows something, right?"

"Yeah, he *definitely* knows something he's not saying."

"Well, the cops have him now. Don't you think he'll talk? That detective seemed pretty determined. Maybe they'll beat it out of him."

"Matthew!" she scolded.

"Yeah, sorry—um." His eyes wandered over to the artifact and lingered there.

"You're going to just let it sit there?" she asked. "We have our suspicions, but there's not much we can do about it right now. Don't worry, I won't think you're insensitive and selfish if you want to have a go."

"I was just wondering . . ."

"Well, he's an arse, and a bloody guilty one at that, but he's right—there's no use in just letting it sit there. There's nothing you and I can do to find Hank right now. Just do an hour and then you'll be able to take my mind elsewhere when you're done. Do it for *me*."

He decided not to prolong it. He'd been thinking about Irin all morning, between thoughts about Hank. He slid the case in front of him, pulled up his left sleeve, and took off his gloves.

The door popped open, and they both jumped as Fozzy popped his head in and looked at Matt.

"Hey, you seen Tuni?"

Matt pointed across the table, and Fozzy leaned in farther, spotting her.

"Oh, hey . . . um, the rest of the folks were wondering if you could hook up some more of those kickass eggs. That Wekesa guy said it's cool to use the rest as long as you turn off the propane this time—or at least that's what we think he was saying. I was like 'I'll make 'em,' but everybody started putting their fingers in their mouths and made puking faces, sooooo . . ."

"Right," Tuni said, and smiled for the first time today. "I suppose." She looked back at Matt and waved at him to carry on. "Just hang on, I'll be back in a jiff."

Matt found his timer band twisted up in his pocket, and straightened it out before sliding it onto his forearm. The LCD screen showed "60:00." He slid off his right glove and put it on the table beside him. He thought about doing it alone but decided it probably wasn't a good idea without Tuni or Peter present. He didn't want Rheese walking in and finding him alone and in a vulnerable state.

The sat phone rang, making him flinch. Sliding over, he took it from the counter with his still-gloved left hand, searching for the button to answer. All he could find was a button that said ON, and he pressed it as the third ring ended.

"Hello?" He answered, holding the handpiece close to his ear.

"Is this Peter?" an English-accented woman's voice blared into his ear through the speakerphone. He dropped the phone but caught it as it bounced off the corner of the table. "Peter?" she repeated.

"Uh . . . hello? No, this is Matt—Matt Turner."

"Oh! Hello . . . Matthew, yes—Peter has told me all about you. This is Maggie Gwynne, and I've got Danielle here with me. I work with Mr. Sharma here in Cambridge."

"Hello, Matthew," another English-accented voice said.

"Okay, cool . . . hi." He set the phone down on the table beside the k'yot fragment.

"Is Peter available?"

"Actually, he's on a helicopter right now . . . uh, doing a search."

"Ah, yes, I received his voice mail this morning. Awful. I take it, then, that there has been no progress?"

"No, not really. I guess there are more people coming and some more helicopters."

"Very well. Now then, I wanted him to know—though it probably seems rather callous and unsympathetic under the circumstances—that Danielle received an update on the survey of other experts on impact events that she had originally compiled. Just let him know to call her when it's a better time, and they can discuss it if he wishes."

"Okay, I'll let him know. Impact event experts."

"And tell him that I do wish him and Dr. Rheese luck on finding that Felch gentleman."

"Rheese?" the other voice questioned. The phone on the other end rattled a bit, and Matt could hear a muffled conversation. After a moment, the receiver was apparently uncovered.

"Quite baffling, really . . . Matthew, sorry about that—are you still with us?"

"Yeah, I'm here."

"Well, Danielle was just informing me of a funny coincidence. Her counterpart in Berlin gave her Dr. Garrett Rheese as one of the experts from their roster."

"Oh?" Matt didn't catch the significance.

"Yes, quite strange that out of the three they consider the foremost authorities on the subject, you've got two there with you. Or—sorry, terribly insensitive of me—that you *had* two."

"Yeah . . . well, okay . . . so did you need me to tell Peter that, too?"

"No, no bother. Just have him give me a ring when he has a free moment. Lovely speaking with you, Matthew."

Danielle also said good-bye, and Matthew pressed the OFF button and laid the sat phone back on the counter.

"Let me help you with that, lad," Rheese said as he stepped into the RV. He took the phone and plugged it into the charger. "Did someone call?"

"Yeah, a woman from the museum, for Peter." He looked at Rheese and saw an odd expression on his face.

"Oh? And what did they have to say?" He stepped a little closer to the table, looming over Matt.

"She just wants him to call her back."

Rheese smiled at him and nodded with accusing eyes.

"And you're going to tell me now that that is all dear Maggie had to say, are you?"

Matt frowned and looked through the window in the door to see if anyone else was near. His mind raced. Was there something he had missed? What had Hank said about impacts? They had been arguing. Hank said something about glass, and Rheese replied, "I wouldn't know anything about that." Rheese glanced outside. *What's he doing?* Matt wondered, alarm bells sounding. *Seeing if the coast is clear. What's he going to do, kill me right here? Tuni'll be back any—*

Rheese turned back to him and, without a word, slapped Matt's bare hand down onto the artifact. He watched Matt's eyes roll back and then close. Careful to not move the hand off the artifact, he adjusted Matt upright, into his customary position while reading, and then slowly let go of his shoulders. Leaning back, he peered out the window again to be sure no one was coming. Still clear.

Now, then, you American pissant —should have left the phone alone. Rheese snapped his fingers in front of Matt's face; the eyes did not flinch. Putting his knee on the bench beside Matt, he bent down to his ear.

"Can you hear me, nosey bastard?" He whispered. "Your dearest Tuni is outside twisting tongues with her shadowy brethren, the cooks. You should see where her hand is right now." He moved back and flicked Matt's ear. Nothing. He looked down at the timer and saw that it had not yet been started. He scolded himself for almost making such a silly mistake. Then he reached across himself and pressed the start button with his fingernail, and it began to count down: 59:59 . . . 59:58 . . . 59:57 . . .

One more test, dear boy, then it's down to business. Rheese turned around and opened a drawer, pulling out a safety pin. He opened it and, reaching behind Matt's head, jabbed it into his scalp, drawing blood. Nothing flinched; nothing moved.

After taking another quick look out the window, Rheese dropped the safety pin back in the drawer and withdrew a set of needle-nose pliers with a wire cutter, squeezing them closed and open again. He climbed onto the bench beside Matt and, placing his hand over Matt's, brought the tool down, clipping a tiny length of metal thread, no longer than a couple of millimeters, from the artifact. Picking it up with the tip of the pliers, he brushed aside the hair where he had stabbed Matt with the pin, and found the dot of blood. With luck, there would be time to clean it later. He moved in close and used the pliers to slide the tiny wire into the puncture wound. He twisted it and nudged it and finally got it to slide under the skin. Releasing it from the pliers, he saw the dull gray tip protruding like a splinter. It was bent; he needed to get it all the way in. He tapped it with his index finger, and it slid in a little farther, but now it was bleeding a bit too much. Turning, he reached for a paper towel over the kitchen sink—and gasped.

Tuni was leaving the food tent and coming this way. He tore off a piece of paper towel and quickly dabbed the blood from the back of Matt's head, feeling a rising panic. Tuni was perhaps ten steps away. He rubbed violently, tousling the hair back into its usual state which pushed the fiber of k'yot all the way under the skin.

When the door clicked open, he was at the sink, pretending to wash his hands. Tuni looked at his back, then over at Matt. She stepped up and into the trailer and leaned over Matt to check the timer. He had been under only four minutes. Rheese must have just come in—Matt would never have begun a session with just the two of them in the trailer. She sighed and slid onto the seat across from him.

Rheese tucked the paper towel into his shirt sleeve and turned off the water. He wanted to dump it in the loo, but he was just washing his hands. Would that look too suspicious? He cleared his throat.

"Well, huh," he said, "have to drain the weasel."

Tuni rolled her eyes, "Ugh, charming."

With a sophomoric snicker, he went into the loo, closing the door behind him. For Tuni's benefit, he let out a long sigh, then dropped the wad of paper towel into the bowl and flushed the toilet, watching the blue liquid soak it before it slithered down the hole.

When he came back, Tuni was doodling with pencil and paper; Turner was still upright and playing his part. He would have another fifty minutes of quiet before anyone noticed something amiss.

Enjoy your coma, Mr. Turner.

Soon, with these last two pests removed from his pantry, he could regain control over his own destiny. Sharma, for all his big talk, had been a pushover—couldn't think about more than one thing at a time. After the heat died down about Turner and Felch, Rheese would recall that he knew a little something about asteroids and perhaps, with a bit of prodding, would help Sharma track down the precious location of his much-ballyhooed city-killing asteroid, a mere fourteen kilometers directly east of the site. It hadn't been the next red circle he planned to visit, but definitely in the top three. He chided his prior foolishness, seeking not the most significant impact sites, but instead focusing on the most plentiful limestone deposits. Re-examining the satellite data after Turner's proclamation of an easterly impact, Rheese had looked at the maps with new eyes.

I'll be damned to hell, he had thought. *Not only is Turner for real, so is this precognitive fellow he spoke of.* At that moment, and for who knew how long, Rheese was the sole living being on earth that knew the location of a devastated, pre-human, intelligent civilization. This fact buzzed and throbbed in his head for only a moment before he had moved on to what it really meant to him.

Massive dolomitic limestone deposits hid beneath this entire area for kilometers in every direction. Dolomitic limestone that, when subjected to the extraordinary heat and pressure of an asteroid impact, turned into something much more rare and precious: diamonds.

Of course, there was nothing wrong with surveying for precious stones, but not on the dime of a non-profit organization. He also had no intention of sharing the find with the Kenyan government. The Gray would help him smuggle the stones out in return for an ungodly cut.

If Felch wasn't already onto him, he surely would have been, and in short time.

THIRTY-SIX

The downpour began to ease, but the wind had picked up. Now, though there was less rain, it came almost horizontally, stinging the eyes and face in intermittent flurries. Across the way, several new played on the rocks, clambering in and out of the little bowl-shaped caves. Irin watched with mild interest as he sucked on a gwotl half. He wondered about the time of night and whether the dark clouds to the east would allow them much warning of impending daylight.

He tossed the gwotl husk to the ground and wiped the sticky pulp on his foot coverings. Beside him in both directions, others sat and watched their new at play. Those without such concerns enjoyed the protection of the caves. Someone asked him if this was to be their new home. No, he explained, they were still too close to the valley, and also, there would be no water here once the rains ended. He said nothing about the ongoing threat of screamers. Let them believe there were no more—only the fighters need remain on guard.

He stood and walked back up to the stifling, packed screamer cave. The air was even worse now with the smell of hot, damp bodies.

Owil seemed to be asleep, and Orin nodded that indeed she was. Wil lay beside her, eyes open and staring at the back of her neck. The newest was in another woman's arms, wriggling and making small crying noises. Irin gestured to Orin to put the newest on Owil's breast now, while she slept.

Orin made a face, not liking the idea, worried that Owil would wake. She decided to try it, though, and reached around to the other woman, taking the newest and pulling aside Owil's coverings. She slid the tiny, wrinkled thing into contact with Owil's body, and its behavior changed immediately. The newest began opening and clinching its tiny fists while its lips and tongue seemed to sense food nearby. Its head turned from side to side until it found the object of its search and locked on. Irin watched the little legs kick out, and the hands punch at Owil's breast as if in battle. Orin tried to calm it and held the arms close to its body so as not to wake Owil.

Hearing the newest make a choking sound, Wil rose up on his elbow to see what was happening. He saw the newest trying to feed and looked around at Orin and Irin and at his woman's face, terrified she would wake and do something to the newest. Irin gestured for him to remain calm, but the newest pulled away from the breast and released a dry, throaty wail. Orin looked up at Irin and shook her head; it wasn't working.

Owil's eyes opened suddenly, and she looked down at the newest as it gnashed down again on her nipple. She flinched, and Irin prepared to restrain her, but Orin put her hand on Owil's arm as she looked down at her newest with an odd expression. Owil took quick, panting breaths as she watched its desperate motions, kicking and nestling into her. Wil saw her hands become fists, and moved his own hand to hold back her wrist if it should move.

Then her eyes softened and her shoulders appeared to relax, and she let her head drop back down onto the bedding. Owil's eyes slowly closed, and the newest calmed as loud swallowing sounds could now be heard from its throat. All sighed and relaxed.

"How long must it feed?" Irin asked.

"Until *she*'s done, Irin," his woman answered.

"We'll begin reloading and forming the line. That should give it—*her*—enough time, yes?"

Orin nodded, inwardly pleased.

A short time later, the wind had mostly calmed, and light rain fell. Wil and three women, including Orin, helped Owil out of the cave and down to the awaiting n'wip, filled only with bedding. They sat her facing rearward and handed the newest to her.

Irin stood atop the high ledge and watched as the line stretched off in the distance. He sent Pwig and Norrit down the sides to count.

"And don't forget to add one," he told them.

They both looked at him strangely for a second, then smiled and went about their task.

"We are missing one," Norrit told him as he approached.

Pwig had counted in the opposite direction and was just now walking up to them, shaking his head.

"We have one extra," he said.

Irin looked at them both with annoyance and waved them off to count again. Time was growing short—they must be off.

A bit later, Pwig and Norrit returned with the correct count.

Irin stood and raised his arms to get the people's attention. From his perch atop the higher cave, he cupped his hands around the sides of his mouth and shouted to them. "Pwin-T! Let us continue as we did last night! Fast . . . safe . . . helping each other!"

They nodded, and some raised their hands up to him—a rather muted response, but he did not mind. They had been cramped in a hot cave for the entire first half of the night and now stood soaking in rain. They needn't be excited; they need only walk.

He climbed down from his rocky perch and went to the front as his people began to make their way down the hill.

THIRTY-SEVEN

A coil of circles bordered the top of a circle of equal size. Two more circles, for glasses, surrounded two smaller circles: the eyes. It wasn't making *fun* of him, Tuni reflected; it was just that, above the neck, Hank was basically a cluster of circles of various sizes. She drew a flashlight in his hand and added sharp eyebrows to make him look more formidable.

Outside, the beat of a helicopter grew louder, then quieter, as it paced over the forest canopy, searching for the missing man. Feeling a growing knot in the pit of her stomach, Tuni wondered if Enzi could have done something to him. Or was it Rheese? She wouldn't be surprised if it turned out that all this was a product of her overactive imagination. Rheese was clearly a coward, shrinking and groveling before anyone with any real authority. Would someone so spineless be capable of actually following through with something like that? And *why*? Circles on a map in the middle of Africa . . . more circles. She sighed at her own foolishness. Right, it was a bloody message: *circles. Pull your head out, Tuni girl.*

She looked up at Matt's expressionless face and recalled how interesting she had found it the first time she watched him do a reading. Not even his eyes moving behind his lids, as someone in a dream would do. It was truly as if his spirit had left his body and traveled back in time, returning only after he released the k'yot. She looked at his lips and wondered. Twenty-five years old. If only he were thirty.

They would soon leave this place and return to New York. But then what? Could they remain friends? What if he ever made a move on her? Would he even try? Could he even try? How exactly did that work, she wondered. What matter? He didn't even live in the city, not even in the state. *North Carolina?* She considered for a moment why he would move there, and then remembered that his sister attended the university there. He also probably enjoyed being away from a huge city with so many people, so much history, so much untidy human baggage. She imagined what it might be like living in a small town. It seemed as though there would be nothing at all to do, but then, it probably had that beauty that only smaller towns seemed able to possess.

What are you doing? she chided herself. Away from this place, these circumstances, there could be *nothing* between them. So what *did* she like about him, aside from his boyish good looks? Besides his insightfulness and his quick wit? Chemistry? *Do I believe in chemistry?* Was it that she felt sorry for him? *Eh eh, no mothering.* She chuckled to herself—*though, he is extraordinarily clean . . .*

Hearing the buzzer vibrate on his timer, she sat up, excited. Her eyes moved to his hands, to watch them pop up, the right one zooming to the timer to press STOP. They popped up for a second, then fell right back down. His eyes didn't open. What the hell was that? Did he not lift them enough?

She leaned up and craned her neck to read the display: it flashed "00:00," with a lightning bolt beside it. It was definitely buzzing, but he wasn't lifting his hands again. She hadn't seen this before, but maybe it was normal. Maybe something important was happening and he was choosing to ignore the timer until it was over. Could he do that? She remembered what he had said about the timer. He had started using it at the museum when he was seventeen, training himself to withdraw his hands when the buzzing sensation jostled his nervous system. It was his only way to get out with no outside intervention. Did he need outside intervention now? What if the timer wasn't working right? She decided to play it safe, since he didn't appear to be in any danger. *Wait five minutes. The thing's still buzzing— give him a chance.*

She stared at his unmoving eyes and hands for two minutes.

"Bollocks!" she said out loud. "That's it . . ." And reaching across the table, she pulled the artifact from under his hands. "Oops, shit!" she said as his bare hands flopped onto the tabletop. Quickly grabbing his gloves, she lifted his hands and gently laid them on the gloves.

She swallowed, and her stomach began to tighten as she watched his eyelids.

God damn it . . . "Matthew?" she said with a quiver in her throat. "Matthew," a little louder. She felt her leg begin to tremble, and her heartbeat quickened. "Matthew!" she shouted, throwing a balled up piece of paper at his face. It bounced off his chin and fell on the table.

She leaned across and began slapping his face repeatedly. Still no response. *Oh, God, don't panic, don't panic, don't PANIC! He's okay, he's okay . . . he's . . . oh, my God . . .*

Her eyes welled with tears as the thought struck her. She pushed it away as idiotic. *He is not dead, Tuni. Shut your brain, idiot.* Her eyes shot down to his chest and watched for ten seconds. It wasn't moving. She slid off the bench and around beside him, putting her hand to his neck in search of a pulse. *Oh, God, no pulse. No, no, no, no, no, no.* Where was the pulse supposed to be? Where on the neck? It was on the wrist, too! She grabbed his wrist and waited. Was that it? *Yes! That's it, I feel it! He's alive, definitely alive. Oh, God, yes. But is he breathing?* She put her hand across his chest and felt it expanding and contracting—faintly, but nothing to be worried about. She put her finger under his nose and felt the air come out.

Okay, so he's just stuck. That's what it is. He's stuck and he can't get out. She thought for a moment and dragged the artifact back, placing one of his hands on it. She looked at the timer on his other arm, still flashing zeros. Wondering if the buzzer part was really working, she slid her finger underneath the fat part of the timer and found a dull metal point.

"Ow! Son of a . . . *ugh!*" She pulled her finger out and stuck it in her mouth. "Bloody hell!" If a shock that intense wasn't waking him up, she couldn't imagine what would. *Holy crapballs!* she thought. How could he deal with that shock so calmly?

Tuni sighed and looked at his hand, atop the k'yot piece where she had placed it. Her hand wrapped around his wrist and pulled it sharply from the metal fabric. Still nothing. She slapped it back down and lifted it again. *This is ridiculous,* she thought. *He's being bloody electrocuted by a band on his arm, and I'm trying to touch his hand to this thing.* He must be touching something else . . . or something else was touching *him,* rather. She looked at his sleeve and felt inside, around his arm. As she pulled his left arm to her to check it, his back began to slide slowly away from her.

"Oh, bloody hell," she moaned. He had slumped all the way to one side, his bare cheek resting on the seat. She pulled his arm to straighten him out and began to feel a sense of dread again at how limp his body felt. She pushed the term "dead weight" from her head as she righted him. With him steady again, she slid out from the seat and poked her head under the table. Something touching his ankles? She pulled his pant leg up and saw a white sock. She reached in, past his calf—so his socks were the long sort that went nearly to the knee. It made sense. Something in his shoe, maybe? But then, how would he have walked over here?

She needed help.

She crawled out from under the table and, after another look at his motionless face, ran out the door.

"I think we should strip him down bare in his tent," Peter said. "We've tried everything else. We know he was fine in there last night—everything is definitely new. Something could have slipped down his shirt or some-thing."

Tuni looked at him in despair. They had tried everything, and the timer apparently wasn't doing its job.

"How long does the timer take to charge?" she asked.

"I'm not sure," he replied. "Meier had it made several years ago as an upgrade to the one his father had put together. It uses some special lithium battery to give him enough juice, but like I said, that's beside the point. The timer is for waking him up when he's *in* a reading. If we've taken everything away from him that he would be reading, the timer should be irrelevant. Come on—let's get some more people in here to help move him."

Rheese moved out of their way, and Tuni glanced at him. He seemed to be somewhat concerned, but she had lost any shred of trust she might have had in him.

"I'll wait with Matt," she said to Peter's back as he hurried out the door.

She sat down beside Matt's inert body, his head now lolling back against the seat back, mouth agape.

"Perhaps you should try pouring cold water over his head," Rheese suggested, leaning against the cabinets.

"Hmm," she muttered, not looking at him.

A few minutes later, Peter returned with Rodney, Jesse, Fozzy, and Graham. Tuni moved and allowed the five men to get their arms under Matt's armpits and thighs, raise him over the table, and muscle him awkwardly out the door.

"Go open his tent," Peter said to Collette as they shuffled past.

She darted ahead and unzipped it, tying it open. Hunching down, they pulled and scooted the limp body into the tent and set it down gently on the sleeping bag.

"Okay," Peter began, "I'd like everyone out, please. We need to minimize the chance of something else touching his skin."

Peter ignored the question from Graham, "Why does it matter if something touches his skin?"

As they all piled out, Peter saw Tuni crouching over outside the door.

"You want to help me with this?"

"Ah . . . I—I don't think I should."

"Great," he huffed. "So you're going to stand there and watch me strip him, but you won't cross the line and help?"

She swallowed and sighed and finally came into the tent as Peter began pulling off Matt's boots.

"We should leave him a bit of dignity, don't you think?" she said, nodding to the doorway. At least fifteen sets of eyes gawked back at them. "Especially if he wakes up right now."

"Whatever," Peter replied peevishly. "I think there are certain things we stop worrying about in emergency situations, but if it'll make you feel better, go ahead."

"I got it," Rodney said, and he untied the door flap and began to zip it up. "Let's go, you lot. Bunch of gawking wankers, every one of you . . ."

The voices trailed off.

As Peter shucked off Matt's bright white socks, Tuni turned to the gray turtleneck. She pulled the bottom up, exposing an undershirt, which she wrestled over his arms and head and tossed in the corner. As Peter unbuttoned his jeans, she untucked the undershirt and pulled it off as well. Peter moved to Matt's feet and slid the pants all the way down and pitched them in the corner.

"Last bit..." Peter said as he slid off the black boxer briefs. "Okay, let's make sure there's nothing else touching him besides the sleeping bag material."

Tuni gulped and pulled up a wrist, checking one armpit and then the other. Peter examined between the toes, then glanced around everywhere else.

"All right, let's him roll him over," he said, and got his hands under Matt's legs.

Tuni turned away as she pushed against a shoulder until Matt lay facedown.

Peter sighed. "Damn it . . . okay, you might want to look away again— I'm gonna spread the cheeks to be sure . . . yep, nothing out of the ordinary there. Now, check his ears and hair."

Tuni tilted Matt's head to one side and looked in one ear as well as she could. Then, after lifting and turning it the other way, she examined the other ear. Then she slid her fingers into his hair, shaking it out. Nothing fell out.

"This sucks," Peter finally said as they plopped back down beside him. "Well, let's roll him back over and cover him up with the sleeping bag, at least a little. It's going to be roasting in here in a couple of hours."

As they struggled, moving him around and unzipping the sleeping bag, Tuni began to lose hope. "What if it was too much?" she asked.

"What do you mean?"

"He was so against longer sessions, but then he started doing them on his own. He had said he always tried to avoid it. He even said he was feeling sick last night before dinner. That he needed a break. What if it's just too much for his mind? Like . . . maybe he could get *stuck* there."

After tossing a flap of sleeping bag over Matt's lower half, Peter sat back and looked at her with a solemn face. "I don't think he's *there*, Tuni."

"What does that bloody mean?" she said with a quavering voice, her eyes beginning to well up again.

"I mean, he's not touching anything, so he *couldn't* be there. I'm not a doctor, so I'm not going to say the word, especially not this soon, but I think he's just on his own right now—you know, dreaming his own dreams."

"The word is 'coma,' Peter. There, that wasn't so hard, was it? Well, I tell you what—he is *not* dreaming any of his own dreams right now! I've seen this face when it's dreaming." She stroked Matt's cheek and held her hand there as she looked at him through blurry eyes.

Peter looked at her and decided not to reply. He straightened the sleeping bag a little more and crawled to the door. "You stay with him, okay? I've gotta call for some help."

She turned and gazed at him, her cheeks shiny with tears. "How is *anyone* going to know what to do with him? No one will understand."

Peter took a deep breath. "I don't know, but we have to get him out of here fast. I don't think we'll have much luck getting water into him, and he'll dehydrate within thirty-six hours. He needs a hospital, and you'll go with him. *You* make sure they understand."

Tuni nodded and sobbed, unable to restrain her emotions any longer. As he opened the tent and jogged away, she heard Felicia begin to cry outside. Tuni contained her anger and didn't scream at her, though she wanted to. Instead, she crawled to the door, gave the gathered team her best smile, and zipped the flap closed again.

THIRTY-EIGHT

As the clouds began to drift apart and stars reappeared above, Irin began thinking about the next sleeping place. He moved from the front of the column and walked backward beside Pwig. In the distance, the rocky encampment had shrunk, and the mountains surrounding it appeared no taller than the Center House.

Around them, the surface was flat, and one could see all the way to its ends, where the stars disappeared. The small shrubs seemed to be houses for an endless number of the hairy crawlers, skittering about the dirt and eating small berries and things they dug from the dirt.

Irin turned around and walked forward again. His brother kept wanting to talk about the fight with the screamers, but Irin was no longer interested. He had seen a pair of flyers sail over a short time ago. Flyers had never attacked anyone in Pwin-T before, though they were known to pull a k'yon stalk from the food flats and fly away with it. Pret had told them that the flyers never seemed interested in eating the k'yon, but only in taking them off to the mountaintops to build their houses. He had also seen them in the trees, breaking off dying branches with their long beaks or picking up those that had fallen to the ground. If that was the case, though, Irin thought, what *did* flyers eat? Norrit had spotted them gliding off in the distance, and they had clearly sailed closer to the ground when they flew over the line of people, as if to have a look.

"Don't you think?" Pwig said to him.

"Sorry, Pwig, what did you say?"

"Which part?"

"I don't know. I wasn't hearing you."

"I said, the screamers will probably eat the dead ones when they find them. Don't you think so?"

"I don't know. If there are more, I suppose it's possible."

"What do you think Tillyt and Otillyt are doing right now? Do you think they're good still?"

"I think so," replied Irin, distracted.

"You don't think they are, do you? Do you think their food ran out?"

"What? No . . . no, they are fine. There is plenty of food. Not even two nights have passed. Don't be thick."

"Do you think—" Pwig began.

"No, Pwig, be silent. Let's just walk, please."

Pwig muttered to himself and then fell silent.

As Irin walked, he could feel soreness in his legs, and a sharp pain nagged at him from under his arm with each step of his left foot. He had felt something pop inside when the screamer's head dropped upon him.

Eventually, the sky behind them began to change colors—the early signs of sunrise. They had made little progress toward any better terrain for daylight sleeping. He knew it would be very difficult for everyone to get any sleep with the light of the sun reddening their eyelids from without. He had considered it before they left Pwin-T, not anticipating the good fortune of caves, but hoping they might at least find a forest or some sort of sheltering area. Peering off into the distance ahead, he saw no sign of any cover. He had also contemplated walking during daylight, perhaps shielding their eyes with scraps of clothing.

He watched a crawler scurry in front of him and dart into its cave in the ground. Perhaps they could dig their own crawler holes—they had brought many dirtpulls. He thought about it for a moment and dismissed the idea. Perhaps they would proceed with such a plan when they reached their destination, but it would take far too much time to dig enough holes for everyone now.

He moved aside again and stopped walking, allowing the group to pass him by. He studied their faces as they passed, and again wondered at their strength. The fighters all looked strong and unfazed by the journey. Farther down the line, the men pulling n'wips were a different story. With their k'yot middles hanging behind them, they looked worn out, even on this flat land. The women, too, appeared fatigued and no doubt hungry. He reminded himself that none were accustomed to this much walking. Only the new seemed truly cheerful, chasing crawlers to their holes while their mothers scolded them.

"Those may be only the babies, Gillen," he heard one mother say to a laughing girl. "The old may be the size of screamers, waiting to leap from a giant hole in the ground and gobble you down!"

Orin approached, and he walked to her. Behind her, Wil, his face dripping with sweat, pulled Owil and the newest.

"Do you have a second to help you, Wil?" Irin asked.

Wil looked up at him with a guilty expression. Irin tilted his head. Wil nodded in Orin's direction.

"Orin?" Irin said in disbelief. "Are you pulling this n'wip?"

She looked at him, untroubled, "Yes. What of it?"

"What of it!" he replied angrily. "I don't want you becoming exhausted before everyone else! You mustn't deplete your legs of their strength."

Another woman moved close to them as they walked.

"She's been helping others with their n'wips as well," the woman confided in a disapproving tone.

"What do you care, Oinilyg?" Orin snapped, and pushed her face so that her jaw made a clopping sound. Oinilyg stalked angrily away, cradling her cheek.

Irin put his arm around Orin affectionately. "I like your strength with her," he said with a smile.

"She is useless—with no higher purpose than silencing the new and stealing food from the n'wips."

"Well, it's good that you stand up, but I want you to stay away from the work of a man, understand?"

"I understand what you are saying, but look at me and then at Wil and the other pullers. Do I appear as weary as them? When you see my shoulders scraped and raw and my eyes drooping, then you can tell me to stop and I'll be happy to perch atop a n'wip as you would have me do."

He didn't like it, but he had to admit, she did not yet appear exhausted. Eventually, though, she would tire, and when she did, he would return and embarrass her by doing exactly as she said: sit her in a n'wip and pull her himself. Until then, perhaps her insolence would work to motivate, whether by shame or by example, any man tempted to complain.

He allowed the travelers to pass him until the rear guard caught up. Now that they were no longer confined to a narrow path, the line had widened.

The sky grew brighter behind them, and Irin decided it was time to stop and ready an encampment. Marching ahead, he found Pwig and Norrit having similar thoughts, and so they stopped and surveyed the area after sending word back to circle the n'wips. Irin also sent scouts out forward and to the sides to see what lay just beyond their sight. People voiced their concerns over how they would sleep under the sun, and he suggested huddling together and using clothes to shield their eyes, as the new did when playing blind-eyes. All complied, though the prospect of being caught in full sun frightened them.

Shortly after the n'wips had been arranged in a loose circular enclosure, long daggers of sunlight shot out from between the distant peaks. People began to groan in pain and also in fear. Many of the smaller new cried and huddled behind their mothers as the sun climbed higher in the sky.

Irin saw one of the men unstrap his k'yot top and turn it around with the face hole in back. He tried it himself and found that, though it hurt against his face wound, it did a good job of shielding his eyes from the light without blinding him completely.

Most of the people had finally succumbed to their exhaustion, while others rolled about uncomfortably, squinting in the dazzling light. Checking on the sixty fighters who stood guard outside the barrier of n'wips, he found several trying vainly to shield their burning eyes with their hands. After showing them how to turn their tops around backward, he returned to find Orin, asleep beside the n'wip that had carried Owil. Beside her, Owil slumbered, the sleeping newest a shrouded lump beneath her blanket.

As he knelt down between Orin and another woman, he saw Wil's face appear from beneath the same blanket. Wil squinted at the faceless k'yot before him.

"Irin?" His friend's voice sounded anxious.

"Yes, Wil," he replied, and turned the k'yot top around just enough to reveal the side of his face.

"No . . . don't," Wil breathed with dread.

Irin turned the k'yot fully around and held his hand before his eyes to block out the unbearable, blinding light.

"What is it?" he asked, troubled by his friend's behavior.

"Your k'yot . . . that's how you wear it . . ."

At first Irin didn't understand; then it hit him: Wil's vision! He must be wearing his k'yot top backward at his death. It made sense—now that he had discovered a good way to filter the sunlight, of course he would be wearing it in this way. Wil had said it would be during daylight. But when? Did he even know? He had said only "soon."

He turned the heavy protective garment backward again and stood peering round the group and beyond the n'wips. He could see nothing of concern—no approaching creature, no building storm to flood them, no rocks that might fall on them.

Placing his hand on Wil's shoulder, he said, "Sleep, my friend, and don't worry—there's nothing in this moment that we can do.

As Irin's racing mind slowed, he drifted off to sleep and fell immediately into terrible dreams. A flyer swooped down and snatched him up, only to drop him from a great height. He landed on the ground and felt crushed, as he had when trapped under the screamer. The flyer came again and dropped him over and over again. After a while, he could no longer move any part of his body. The flyer lifted him by one foot and flew him far away from his people. As he hung from the monster's beak, he felt himself melt into a brown liquid, like thin mud, and drip down to the ground. As his melted face sank into the dirt, he felt that he could no longer breathe. In the darkness, his body tried to come back together, but the soil was too hot, and he began to merge with it, losing himself in it, so that he could not say where his body ended and the dirt began.

He awoke to the cries of Owil's newest beside him. Seeing the faint blue of a lightstick, he realized that his k'yot top was still backward. He turned it around and saw a black vault of sky, strewn with stars. Relief washed over him—he had lived to see another night! No danger had awoken him; no creature had come to kill him. He inhaled the cool air and closed his eyes, savoring the sensation.

Sitting up, he realized that he was one of the last few people still asleep. How long had the sun been gone? There was certainly no sign of sunset light in the distance. He looked for Orin, but she was not in sight.

He stood up, his side aching, and felt his neck pop and crack as he rolled his head around. Looking about for Orin, he saw a crowd of people around two displaced n'wips. Words and arms were flying; there appeared to be a problem.

Irin stepped over to a crowd of some fifty people, with Orin standing in the center, shouting at Gwilt.

"You think Irin would allow this? This is foolish, and you're endangering all whom you gather."

Gwilt, short and thick and missing a front tooth, shoved her away from him. "Do not speak to me as if you're a man, Orin!" he roared. "You have no special stature just because you're Irin's!" He jabbed the heel of his palm into her chest, and she tripped backward, just stopping herself from falling.

Irin held back for a moment and watched. He remembered, long ago, knocking that tooth from Gwilt's mouth. They were younger, and Pwig was still new. Gwilt was making Pwig and another new eat dirt, telling them that it was what the oldest men had decreed. Seeing Pwig's lips covered with dirt, and tears dripping down his dirty face, Irin had smashed Gwilt's face with his fist. Gwilt had spat blood and run off, screaming that he would kill Irin. Now he had just struck Orin.

"Don't you touch me, coward!" Orin shouted at him. Other men nearby began to grumble, and Irin knew he must put a stop to it, for she was definitely speaking out of line and in front of too many.

"What is the problem?"

The grumbling stopped, and all eyes were on Irin.

Breathing a sigh of relief, Orin stepped back. "Go ahead, Gwilt," she said calmly. "Tell him."

Doing his best to remain defiant under Irin's cold stare, Gwilt said, "We're going back."

"Are you really? Back to the city to be killed?"

"No, back to the caves, where it's safe and where people can sleep in the dark, where they're supposed to."

Irin nodded coolly and gazed around at those behind Gwilt.

"And who are the 'we' who you think are going with you?"

"Everyone you see here," he said, gesturing at the downcast faces around him.

"You all wish to return to the screamers' house?" Irin yelled to them. "To wait for more to come and tear you to pieces? Or do you suppose you can fight them and win because I and two others were so fortunate?"

From the crowd, an anonymous voice bellowed, "There are no more screamers!"

Nodding, Irin took a deep breath and looked squarely at Gwilt. "You wish to bring many people back with you, I see. And these n'wips?"

"Yes, we'll need food and supplies," he replied.

"I cannot allow it," said Irin quietly. "The food belongs to the group. You leave the group, you leave the food and the n'wips."

Gwilt's face soured, and he looked about him for support. "I pulled this n'wip half the way here! And these men pulled the other one. They are ours."

"I cannot allow it," Irin repeated, looking calmly at the enraged Gwilt.

Someone in the group behind him muttered, "Just forget it, Gwilt," and Irin watched as the people began to disperse.

"I need no one's permission to save my family and friends!" said Gwilt, turning toward the n'wip. Anyone who's coming, let's go!" And he placed the poles on his shoulders.

Some people hesitated, looking to Irin for a cue, while others, with determined expressions, grabbed their women and new and began to follow Gwilt as he dragged the n'wip away. Others sat back down or busied themselves with other tasks, as if they had nothing to do with the mutiny.

Orin's face went to Irin's ear, and she whispered, "Twill."

She knew! And not only did she know, she was telling him he needed to do something. He looked into her brown eyes and saw the stony resolve behind them, then looked over to see the back of Gwilt's n'wip sliding away, with perhaps twenty followers joining him. Unfortunately, Irin thought, he wouldn't be able to dispose of this problem in secret, as he had with Twill.

He overtook the n'wip and stood facing Gwilt.

"What're you going to do, Irin?" he snarled. You can't stop us merely by being a nuisance. Move out of the way!"

Irin put his hands on his hips and sighed with disappointment. "I can't convince you to stay?" he asked.

"Never," Gwilt replied. One of the men beside the n'wip added, "So move!"

Irin nodded and stepped to the side, and Gwilt hauled again on the poles.

The cutter pierced deep into Gwilt's side, causing him to slump against the poles with a startled yelp. Amid the horrified screams of nearby women and the gasps of stunned mutineers, Irin stepped over him and plunged the blade into his back. Gwilt gave a guttural scream, begging him to stop.

Raising the cutter a final time, Irin said, "I told you, I can't allow it." And the blade struck again.

Gwilt shrunk to the ground. It appeared that he was trying to say something, but when no words came out, Irin wiped the blood from the blade onto Gwilt's clothes and turned to the gawking people.

"Now, one of you take this n'wip back to the circle. We don't have time for any more of this." And he walked away to find Orin waiting for him just outside the circle. He could hear the word spreading faster than he could walk. He hoped his decisive act would not work against him—perhaps a blade thrust between his shoulders when his back was turned—but then, his death was imminent, however it came. His hope was that the people would receive the message that everyone needed to stay together—not that a heartless tyrant was ready to kill them if they spoke against his wishes.

As he followed Orin back through the crowd, avoiding the frightened eyes and disapproving stares, he realized that he probably would have let Gwilt go if not for Orin's whispered spur to action. He would have taken the n'wip from him—beat him, perhaps, if he continued to resist—but let him leave. The only risk was that more would see him leaving and decide to follow. Acting as if nothing had happened, he signaled for everyone to get moving.

The travelers marched on for several more hours before stopping briefly for food and water. Small trees grew in scattered stands, some of them bearing hard, black pods the size of a closed fist. When one of the men cracked one open with his cutter hilt, he found a slime-covered creature inside, waving a pair of large, wickedly pointed pincers. It had been damaged when the shell was crushed, and green goo oozed from its underside. Irin watched the man throw it away in revulsion.

As they walked through the night, Irin was relieved that no one spoke about Gwilt's death. Not even Pwig or Norrit breathed a word; it was as if it had never happened.

Finally, they stopped in a vale where the trees were thicker, offering shade from the coming daylight.

There were not as many black pods on these trees, but no one wanted to sleep with such fearsome little creatures hanging over their heads, so Irin dispatched several men to remove every last one and smash them far from the encampment. The rumor among the new was that the slimy things came out in the daylight to pinch off and eat the flesh of sleeping people.

With the meal over and the sun still below the distant mountains, Orin suggested that the people start small fires using fallen branches, saying that it might help calm the new and let them find sleep more easily. The idea worked wonderfully, and for the first time since leaving Pwin-T, a hint of cheer drifted through the people as the new scampered about excitedly gathering sticks.

Irin sat beside Orin. Though it was not at all cold, he enjoyed the warmth of the crackling fire. He put his arms around her and thanked her.

"Who knew the fires would do so much?" she responded modestly.

Irin turned and pressed his forehead to hers. "No," he continued. "Thank you for everything, not just the fires."

Smiling, she returned her eyes to the fire.

As the horizon brightened, Irin sent people around to see that all were covering up and preparing for the sun. Then, turning his top backward again, he lay down beside Orin. As he lay there, listening to her breathing, he wondered again whether someone might come to stab *him* in the back. Daylight would come soon, and many of the men who had planned to follow Gwilt were fighters, armed with cutters. Were any of them brothers of the man he had killed? Irin kept his cutter close to him, lest someone approach while he slept. He believed he would have fair warning as he now always slept in his k'yot, his only exposed area the back of his head. Only a fool would try to stab someone in such a hard area, but if anyone did, or tried to pull open his k'yot to expose a vulnerable spot, he would be ready.

When at last he drifted off, his dreams were no better than before. Now the slimy pincered creatures were huge, the size of a small new, and chasing after him. He also dreamed that someone had set his eyes on fire and that he could see nothing but a brilliant, burning whiteness.

THIRTY-NINE

Tuni awoke with a stiff neck from sleeping in the hard plastic chair. The hospital ward was a long, wide dormitory with a row of beds on either side, like those she had seen in old films. Sick or injured people filled all the beds. Though some had a sliding curtain for privacy, she and Matt had not been so fortunate. Placards identifying HIV-positive patients hung on the ends of perhaps one-quarter of the beds.

The nurses gave Tuni stern looks every time they passed her. Her insistence on a new gown and bedclothes for Matt had not gone over well, but she had fought long and hard and eventually won.

Sitting in the bright-orange molded plastic chair, she looked over at Matt. He had an IV with two tubes dripping fluids into his arm, and a feeding tube ran down his throat. The Nairobi doctors all seemed apprehensive about touching a foreign patient, or perhaps it was just Matt who made them nervous. He and Tuni had been here four days, and all anyone had done after hooking him up to life support equipment was to check him for changes.

Tuni had no phone number for Peter or anyone else in country who might be able to help, so she had finally called Dr. Meier to act as a go-between. Meier had Matt's old emergency contact card from when he first joined their payroll. He was supposed to call Matt's parents and find out if he had ever had an episode like this before, and whether they had any suggestions. A friendly voice mail recording was all he could get, so he had left the urgent message with his contact numbers. Tuni had yet to hear back for an update. She was to call him on every odd hour.

She had also asked Meier to call Peter and arrange for Matt to be transferred somewhere else, preferably back in the States. The best he could do was arrange for a medical airlift service to take Matt to a specialized facility in Germany, but it would be a few more days before that happened. Meier assured her that it would be a much easier matter to return him to the States once they were in Europe.

As the days went by, Tuni would stare at Matt's eyes and wait for them to pop open as they always had before. She found it ironic that her place had always been to wait for him to wake up, just as she was now doing, though now with the fear that those eyes may never pop open again. She struggled with the idea of leaving, knowing that she could not sleep in a chair beside his bed for the next month, three months, three years. How could she leave him, though? He might be ready to emerge from his coma in a week, but if someone stuck an old, imprinted sensor against his skin, he would stay under. He could end up lying on an old set of sheets with *years'* worth of miserable stories stuck in them!

She tried to clear her mind of the endless horror scenarios and take things one day at a time. If she had to go, she would figure it out. Meier wasn't firing her anytime soon, she had checked on Mr. Pups, called her mom with a brief update, and Peter had pulled strings at the museum to have the medical bills paid. All that aside, she truly cared about this man lying here in front of her.

Dr. Garrett Rheese sat in his chair and watched the van leave. *Yes, go,* he thought as five more people left the site for good. Only the diehards remained now: Peter, Rodney, Collette, and the two fuzzy-wuzzies. The soldiers and police had given up their search for Felch, and no foreign media frenzy had arrived to egg them on. Turner and St. James were both out of the picture, and now it seemed that Peter had decided to carry on the project without Felch or the brat, because "that's what they would have wanted." Things were definitely looking up.

The sat phone rang, and he picked up.

"Hello Dr. Rheese, this is Detective Chitundu. How are you doing today?"

Rheese sighed and pulled out his best defeated voice. "Just trying to get through the days, Detective. What can I do for you?"

"Ha-ha-ha," Chitundu laughed. "Days are difficult now, aren't they? Yes, of course they are."

Rheese waited for more but heard only the sound of Chitundu busying himself with something nearby.

"Well, Detective, how can I help you today?"

"Oh, yes, Doctor, I *do* need your help—oh, let me see, now, is it 'Doctor' or 'Professor'? Your good friend Enzi refers to you as 'Professor.'"

Had Enzi been talking? *Ah, of course, clever plodder, keep fishing.* "Either one is fine, Detective."

"Good, good," he continued in his jolly tone, "I think I will call you 'Doctor.' It seems the more respectable of the two, don't you think?"

"Sure," Rheese said curtly. *Get to the bloody point.*

"Well, I do not want to take too much of your time, but I wanted to ask you a couple of questions. Is Mr. Sharma available as well?"

Rheese hunched over and peered out the window. Peter was standing with Rodney in the mess tent, looking at a chart spread out on a table.

"I'm afraid he's indisposed at the moment, but I can have him ring back at his earliest convenience."

"Ha-ha-ha. 'Indisposed'—I like that, Doctor. I always think of a food disposer in a sink, as though someone is *in* the *disposer.*"

Rheese sat silently, waiting for the tedious man to get around to whatever he had to say.

"Have you ever heard of anyone called 'the Gray,' Dr. Rheese?"

Bloody hell. "I'm sorry, you said *the* Gray?" Rheese replied with feigned confusion. "I'm afraid I don't know anyone with such a theatrical moniker, no. Should I?"

"Hmm . . . are you *sure* about that, Doctor? Think hard."

Nice try, Officer. "Sorry, Detective, but it's unlikely I would forget such a unique name. What does this have to do with our work out here, if you don't mind my asking?"

"Ha-ha-ha, I was hoping *you* could answer that one for me, Doctor. But I suppose not. Excuse me for . . . just a moment."

Rheese heard the phone clack down onto a desk, without being switched to HOLD. He could still hear another phone ringing in the distance, and various indistinguishable conversations. A metallic squeak and a grunt later, the phone rattled around, and Chitundu's breathy voice returned.

"Apologies, Doctor—my shoe was untied."

Silence.

"Doctor, are you still there?"

"I'm here, Detective. Just waiting for the second question—and then I really must return to my work."

"Second question? Ha-ha-ha, did I say I only had two?"

"Yes, I believe you did."

More laughter. Rheese was growing angry. The laugh moved to a series of choking coughs and wheezing.

"I'm sorry, so sorry, Doctor," he finally said. "Your time is very precious to me."

"It doesn't appear to be, Detective, but I'm pleased that I can at least amuse you."

"Oh, don't be so offended, Doctor. I can skip the questions if that is what you wish."

"Well . . ." Rheese softened. "If it is something that can help our cases, I'm more than happy to assist where I can, but as you said, time is precious."

"Oh, no, no, don't worry, Doctor. I can ask Mr. Felch—when he arrives."

Rheese clenched his teeth and tried to breathe deeply without making any noise. *Appropriate response? Eager excitement!*

"I beg your pardon!" Rheese exclaimed. "Did you just say Mr. Felch? Where is he? What's happened? Is he all right?"

"Ha-ha-ha! Oh yes, Fit as a fiddler! He is understandably shaken up, but he will be here soon and we will have a long conversation, he and I."

"Well, that's just smashing news, Detective! When can we retrieve him? Where will he be?"

"Give us some time with him, Doctor. Ha-ha-ha, you seem so excited . . . it's funny. Did you think he was dead or something?"

"Well, I don't see what is so amusing about our friend and colleague disappearing. We have been worried no end, Detective! Of course, the worst enters one's head in a situation like this—one can't help it. But I do *not* appreciate your making light of it."

"Ha-ha-ha, yes, of course. I will call back tomorrow, Doctor."

"Wait . . . Detective . . ."

The phone clattered a bit before finally being disconnected at the other end.

Hank Felch had listened to his captors argue for the past few days. He rolled his head around to try to relieve the soreness in his neck. All his joints and his back hurt from sitting in a wooden chair for three days and nights, with perhaps a half hour off for bathroom breaks in all that time. At the moment, their argument seemed to be about money, since one was shaking a fistful at the other as he yelled.

Though Hank couldn't tell what their real names were, he seemed to have two choices for each. The smaller one, who always wore sunglasses, called the other "Jon-Jon" most of the time, but occasionally just "Jiji"—perhaps because he didn't think Hank was listening. Jon-Jon/Jiji would call the other man "Gabriel," though with his thick accent it sounded like "Gah-vril." The other name he used was "Mkundu," though, again, he couldn't tell which was real and which was just a handle.

The arguments would range from who had to untie him so he could use the nonfunctioning toilet, to fights over custody of the TV remote control. Hank pretended to ignore them and avoided eye contact. His ear had dried blood crusting on it from yesterday, when, unable to understand what Jiji was saying to him, he had raised his voice in reply. Jiji's blow had ripped the top of Hank's ear away from his head, and it had bled profusely.

He also had a cracked rib or two from when they snatched him in the woods. He had been walking behind the Felicia girl. Just after she ducked a low-hanging branch, he had heard a crackle on the ground beside him, and a hand slapped over his mouth to silence him. The two men had dragged him a short distance as he struggled and kicked, until one of them slammed a knee into his ribs. No one had heard his muffled yelps, and he was eventually tied up, with a smelly T-shirt pulled over his head, and tossed into the back of a pickup truck on the side of the road.

As Jon-Jon shook the wad of cash in front of Gabriel's shaded eyes, he yelled louder and louder, and Hank could hear the neighbors upstairs banging on the floor again. He could tell he was in an apartment building with noisy people on all sides, but apparently his captors were going too far this time.

When a teacup or some other ceramic object flew just over Hank's head and shattered on the wall beside him, he glanced into the kitchen to see that Gabriel had drawn the small pistol from his belt and was waving it in Jon-Jon's face. As they continued shouting, Jon-Jon shook the money hand toward Hank, and Hank looked away. The tones of their argument, and the repeated words and gestures, made it easy to imagine what they might be saying:

"If you want some of this money, you go kill him now!"

"Why do I have to kill him? Why don't *you* kill him?"

"Too scared?"

"*You* scared!"

"Kill him now!"

"I will kill him now!"

"Then stop talking and do it!"

Or, Hank mused, maybe they were discussing something else altogether:

"I have a lot of money in this hand and I want to buy doughnuts!"

"If you get doughnuts, then I get half of them! I want doughnuts!"

"Some for him?"

"None for him!"

"Get the doughnuts!"

"I will get doughnuts!"

"Hurry and get the doughnuts!"

Or why assume that they were so simple? It could be a quite scholarly argument, for all he knew. Perhaps the fistful of cash had inspired a social sciences debate.

"Keynesian economics has not withstood the test of time!"

"Nor would Marxist economics or . . ." *Uh-oh* . . .

When Gabriel stomped across the room and jammed the barrel of the gun to Hank's temple, he realized that his first scenario may have been the correct one after all. They were both still shouting, and Hank closed his eyes and waited for the boom that, if it came, he would never hear. He began to pray in his head, though he did not actually believe in God.

God, we both know I don't believe in you, and I am sorry about that. But if you are real, then I do believe in you and I will always believe in your . . . greatness . . . holiness! I will go to church or temple or mosque or all three, but I need to keep living right now. Please let this be over, and I will do your good work or whatever it is you want. Oh, and I'm sorry again for not believing in you until I required your intervention. That probably doesn't rate too high on your list of criteria for saving people. Amen.

The gun pressed against his skull as Gabriel shouted louder and louder. Hank felt the spittle hitting his face. *Is he yelling at me? Should I say something? Where is Jon-Jon/Jiji?*

A horrible smashing sound ended the shouting, and Hank opened his eyes as Gabriel fell and rolled over Hank's knees, landing on the floor. The crash had consisted of two distinct sounds, that of breaking glass and plastic and the grisly crunch of a human skull being bashed in. Hank saw the destroyed microwave oven, and the blood spreading out from under Gabriel's head. He lifted his feet from the floor as the pool widened toward him.

Carefully looking up at Jon-Jon, he saw the man's chest heaving as he stared at the body sprawled on the floor. Jon-Jon said something to Gabriel, presumably telling him to wake up or get up. Moving closer, he kicked Gabriel in the side.

Jon-Jon began to pace all around the apartment, sobbing and talking to himself. Hank imagined that the repeated words were something to the effect of "Oh, no; oh, no; oh, no," interspersed with "Gabriel...Gabriel....Gabriel..." He hoped Jon-Jon might now somehow forget all about him and just run out of the apartment to escape. Instead, Jon-Jon remembered that Hank was tied to the chair and had just watched him murder someone. He went to the kitchen and returned with his rifle, which he pointed at Hank's head. The man glanced down at the dead body then turned to Hank, sweat pouring from his temples.

He spoke in a quiet voice. Hank heard "*Ju ju way sah may . . . ju ju way sah may.*"

Jon-Jon poked Hank's forehead with the gun a couple of times, then tossed the rifle to the couch and ran to the door. He began to unlock it, then returned to the table, where the rest of the money lay. After stuffing it all in his pockets, he left the apartment.

After a moment, Hank twisted his head around and realized that Jon-Jon had left the door open. Several minutes later, a neighbor poked her head inside and shouted something before disappearing into her apartment.

When at last he heard the sirens approaching outside, Hank closed his eyes and took a deep, quivering, breath. *Thank you, God,* he said. *I thank you for ending this. I'm really going to try to do the church thing or whatever. Thank you, thank you, thank you.*

FORTY

Halfway through the fifth night of travel, some began to feel foodrise, and the procession had to stop. On investigation, it turned out that a young man had picked some red berries from a bush and, finding them sweet, pointed them out to others near him in the column. A short time later, a hundred people were losing their midnight meal, and their skin grew hot.

Irin decreed that no one eat anything but the food they had brought; after all, who knew how many poisonous things grew in this new and strange place? He was anxious to journey on, but Orin said it might be best to sleep where they were. As she pointed out, there were trees for shade, with none of the black pods, and also, far too many had fallen sick than could be pulled in n'wips. Irin grudgingly agreed, and they passed the rest of the night and the next day where they were. By next night, the afflicted had fully recovered, and the people marched on.

Five more nights of travel passed, and water grew scarce. A tally of n'wips revealed that they had several weeks' food remaining but only three nights of water if they rationed well.

Camping twice in arid, treeless plainland, they slept only fitfully. They moved slowly now, and Irin did not push them to go any faster. Wil had told him three nights ago that they were more than safe from the coming sky stripe—the task now was to find a suitable place to build their new home.

They found water just in time, reaching the banks of a small stream toward the end of the eleventh night. As they filled their water bags, some of the fighters studied one of the flowering plants growing along the banks, whose seeds they had seen hairy crawlers gathering as they approached.

Irin rubbed the seeds between his fingers and sniffed them. He asked the fighters, "Who's willing to try one to see if it's harmful?"

A burly fellow named Plit stepped forward, bit it tentatively, then munched it down. He raised his eyebrows. "The taste is good," he proclaimed.

"Good," said Irin. "We'll wait a while, and if your belly doesn't complain, three more can sample them."

Irin found Wil kneeling by the water. "How are Owil and the newest fairing?" he asked as he filled his own small water bag.

"Both much better. Owil wishes to begin walking on her own."

"Good. I need you back with me at the front."

Wil raised his chin to him.

"Have you had any new dreams?" Irin asked.

"About you?"

"No—any at all."

"No, nothing."

Irin fought back the desire to ask more about the vision of his death. He stood up and surveyed the sky to the sunset side. He could see the outline of small hills in the distance. Could that be their new home, he wondered? Hills often meant trees, and perhaps watercourses like this one.

The seeds, which grew in abundance downstream, proved safe. Some people went on a gathering mission, filling empty food bags with what seeds they could find. Though there was no shade to sleep in, they could go no farther before sunrise, and so they set up the n'wips in a half circle, closed on one side by the stream. As the sky brightened to the pale blue of a lightstick, Irin settled to sleep under a n'wip, beside Orin. No terrible dreams haunted him for the first part of the day, but soon after the sun had passed its highpoint, he was awakened by a woman's scream.

Through the back of his k'yot, he could see five fighters running toward him, trying to dodge between the sleeping forms, stumbling over some. Heads began to pop up, awakened by the noise. Irin stood and pulled out his long cutter. Were they coming to kill him?

But the men running toward him kept looking back, and now more were shouting from the far side. It was difficult to see much through the k'yot top, but suddenly Irin saw what had caused the commotion. His cutter fell from his hand as he stared, dumbfounded.

Beyond the n'wips at the far end, by the stream, Irin had seen an earthen-hued hump and assumed it was a distant mountain. But then it shifted, and beside it a spike-covered neck rose up from behind the n'wips. When it stopped rising into the sky, the head was higher than ten Center Houses—so long that the creature's feet stood outside the circle while its head waved above the middle of the group, most of whom were now awake and screaming and running helter-skelter.

Irin had no idea what to do. Before him stood a creature big enough to eat every one of them and still be hungry. Its tail rose up behind it as it plodded into the circle, knocking over two n'wips and crushing one utterly. The ground trembled with its every step.

"RUN!" Irin shouted out, and picked up the waking Orin at his feet. Blinded by the daylight, she covered her eyes, though still catching a glimpse of the monstrous animal coming at them. They ran past the n'wip as more and more people got to their feet and fled for their lives. Glanc-ing back, Irin saw the enormous foot come crashing down on a cluster of people who had somehow managed to sleep through the uproar around them. Where were Wil and Pwig? The scene became a blur of people run-ning with hands or clothes covering their faces, scattering in all directions, tripping over one another—and there was nothing Irin could do to stop it.

He looked back and stopped running. The thing had paused in the mid-dle of the circle and was swinging its head around, apparently searching for something. Several people who had been hiding beneath n'wips seized the moment to get up and flee.

The beast's head hovered above a n'wip full of food, then descended and began to chew the covering blanket and rope. It seemed not to like the taste of it, and its head rose up again as a tongue the size of a half-grown new tried to remove the rough, fibrous stuff from its mouth. The neck curled backward, like a screamer's, and the rest of the body followed, the tail swinging around behind it and clipping the tops of a half-dozen n'wips, knocking most of them over.

As he watched the n'wip cover drift to the ground, Irin noticed that the huge beast quite ignored the people it had crushed, as well as the ones still hiding and trying to remain quiet.

"It doesn't eat us," Orin said, squinting through a small hole in a cloth she held against her face.

"No," Irin agreed. "But it wishes to destroy us."

Behind them, people began to walk cautiously back toward the n'wips. Irin turned and looked past the river, where the giant thing was heading, and saw that hundreds of its kind were slowly making their way across the land ahead. They did not seem to be going anywhere in particular, though many stretched their necks to the tops of the tallest trees and examined them, most likely for food. Even if these giant screamers did not want to eat them, how could the people possibly walk among such creatures and make it to those hills?

In the sky, over the heads of the distant long-necked animals, flew hundreds of flyer-looking creatures. This land belonged to others, Irin thought—perhaps he had brought his people too far.

As the destructive beast moved farther away from them, people began to run back to the scene to see who was killed, who was injured, and who still hid. Many new were crying, and the tears spread to others when word traveled about who had been crushed: Dit, Odit, and two others who could not be easily recognized. Dit and his woman had been friends to many.

After another count, it became clear that the other two killed were Dit's brothers, Pwint and Dyngit. Five others were missing, though, and in the still-bright sky, with people moving about, it was hard to keep track of who had been counted and who had not.

Weeping faces surrounded Irin, asking what they would do next. The sun would soon set, but where would they go? Back to the caves, as Gwilt had wanted? Should they have listened to him?

Irin took a deep breath and tried to answer their questions, but he quickly found that he had many of his own that he could no sooner answer than theirs. Better to remain calm; better to behave as if all were going as planned—just a small tragedy here that they must overcome.

"Hear me!" he shouted over them, and the voices died down. "We must repair the n'wips. Protect your eyes as best you can until the night comes again. We must be ready to move quickly. Fighters watch for any more of those things approaching, Mothers, calm your new, and everyone stay close."

Wil came and spoke in his ear.

"Wil is right!" Irin continued. "These beasts move very slowly. Guards will keep watch, as I said, and will have plenty of warning if another approaches us. They don't seem interested in people—it came only for water."

A hundred questions came back at him, but Irin raised his hands and gestured for them to go quickly and repair the damage. He followed to the chaos of overturned and smashed n'wips. Beneath one, a grisly scene awaited them. The five missing were there, broken and pulverized, held together only by the blankets that had covered them. Two had been clothes makers whom Irin knew; the other three he barely knew. The tears began to flow again, and everyone longed for the safety and darkness of their houses.

By sunset, all the n'wips but two were repaired and repacked. The travelers gathered around Irin, lightstick held high over his head.

"We won't forget those who have lost their lives along our journey to find a safe new home," he shouted loud enough for all to hear. "Our destination is the hills beyond the field of walking giants. Scouts have gone out and surveyed the path we'll take, and it appears that the giant creatures have left the area to sleep somewhere else. There are other, smaller creatures running about on two legs. Like the giant, they don't appear interested in us. We'll walk quietly until we reach the hills."

Many people murmured among themselves, but no one spoke against the plan, perhaps for fear of Irin's violent wrath. The line reformed and began to move, splashing through the stream.

After they had traveled some distance, the small animals that the scouts had reported could be seen scampering about. They were perhaps half the size of a man, but had powerful legs that enabled them to run with long, bounding strides. They had pointy mouths, and their eyes glowed when looking in the direction of the moon.

Wil walked beside Irin and pointed at one that stood crouched behind a bush, watching them as they passed. It had tiny little arms with clawed hands and made soft clicking noises, rocking its head from side to side on its long neck. They continued to walk past it, but Irin had a few fighters stop and stand side by side between the creature and the line of people, in case it was looking to snatch a small new. Irin glanced back at that side of the line a few times as they progressed, and felt relieved when at last he saw it running off in the other direction.

Irin asked for three new scouts to run ahead and check what lay before them.

Far above them, Irin and the others nearby heard a screech. They looked up, unable to find the source at first, but then Pwig spotted it: an enormous flyer circling above. Though quite high in the air, it still appeared massive.

They continued walking, wary of everything around them, as the flyer still circled above, screeching periodically.

"Irin!" Wil shouted to him.

Turning Irin saw his friend pointing above and behind them. The flyer was swooping down, directly toward him, descending along the line of travelers, its broad, dark wings spanning the length of six houses built side by side. As it came close, they could feel the wind from its huge, flapping wings and saw the two legs swing up, bearing hooked, shiny claws many times longer than a screamer's. As the creature approached, the people ducked to the ground and covered their faces. One last gust from the wing-beats pounded them, and Irin looked up to see it sail overhead and pass them to the open ground ahead. He popped his head up and saw it glide just above the ground, then rise up with something writhing in its talons. A loud squeal drifted back to him, and he saw that the flyer had caught one of the small two-legged runners and was carrying its squirming prey toward the same hills that Irin sought.

Irin got his fighters on their feet again and set a faster pace. The hills were well within reach, though they did not appear so inviting as from afar. Even as he pressed on, Irin grew uneasy about these new flyers—it had been nothing for one to snatch the small runner and vanish up in the air with it. What would keep one from taking a person? Worse, it attacked at night—the time when his people had always known peace before. Would this new threat force them to keep hidden in moonlight as well as by day?

He could hear the talking behind him: doubt, fear, even anger.

"Life grows more dangerous with every step" . . . "We'll soon be food for them" . . . "Not even Irin can protect us from creatures so large" . . . "Go back."

He and Wil flinched at the same time as they saw two small runners charging for them from directly ahead. Irin reached for his cutter just as he realized that it was only the returning scouts. Breathing a sigh of relief, he looked to Wil, amused that they had both thought the same thing.

But why were there only *two* scouts?

"Irin!" they shouted as they approached.

"Where is Oten?" a scout behind Irin asked.

The two returning scouts panted for breath, barely holding back their sobs.

"He was taken!" one of them gasped.

"It was a giant flyer, but dark . . . so much bigger . . . it took him."

Irin reeled inside. They would have to move close together—appear as one giant beast. No new would be allowed to play along the edges of the column. He sent his instructions back. Must *everything* go wrong this night?

Irin closed his eyes and tried to breathe normally. He heard the screech echo across the mountains. The flyers were calling for them to enter their land.

FORTY-ONE

The Learjet's twin turbines hummed behind Tuni. Beside her, Matt lay motionless, bound to a stretcher. When they rolled him on four hours ago, the wheels had dropped into four slots in the floor and locked with a loud click.

The feet of another man faced Matt's; his stretcher, too, was secured in the floor panels. The other patient had an oxygen line to his nose, several IV bags hanging above him, and a stack of electronic devices behind his head. He was conscious, though, and his drooping eyes roved over every inch of Tuni's body before moving on to the two nurses.

Tuni watched the black accordion rise up and drop down in opposite sync with the man's chest. Tired of his ogling, she gave him a goggle-eyed stare to embarrass him, and after a slow blink, he moved his expressionless gaze elsewhere.

In front of her sat two other men she did not know. One, clearly the son of the gawking man on life support, appeared terribly inconvenienced by the whole affair. He also seemed to think that the nurses were his personal flight attendants.

The other passenger, sitting in the front seat, just behind the cockpit, was a skinny African man with smooth shiny skin, who had started reading his copy of *Town & Country* for the third time. Tuni had noticed him right away at the airport and wondered if he was getting free transport via a relative in the company—why else would anyone tag along on a medical flight? He wore a cream-colored silk shirt tucked into expensive black slacks, Gucci loafers with no socks. *How eighties,* Tuni thought—like the thick gold bracelet dangling from his wrist.

Tuni decided not to bother trying to sleep. Peter had arranged for a hotel room near Matt's hospital so she could start getting some real sleep. She had decided that it was okay to leave him alone with people she trusted, but she would stay with him at least the first night to make sure the staff understood his special needs. The big paycheck Jon Meier had promised her would post to her checking account at midnight, so she could get some new clothes and other essentials, and she looked forward to a long, hot shower in a clean, private room. With a tired sigh, she nestled into the seat and closed her eyes.

"Hello—Sharma," Peter answered into the sat phone.

"Mr. Sharma, Detective Chitundu," said the deep voice on the other end.

"Yes, Detective, how are you?"

"Me? Well . . . I suppose I am a bit blue," Chitundu replied in a tone of exaggerated melancholy.

"Oh?" Peter rolled his eyes to Collette, who stood beside him in the RV.

"Oh, yes. It doesn't matter, though. You've decided to answer the phone this time, so I will have to find some happiness in that small act."

"Um, yeah—sorry about that. I guess you've tried calling before and no one answered?" The man's melodrama was beginning to pall.

"No, no one answered. I believe this is eleventh attempt, but we needn't dwell on that. My perturbation will no doubt pass."

"Okay, great. So, um, tell me what this is about."

"Ha-ha-ha . . . yes, *cut to the chase,* as they say. I suppose I have a tendency to ramble on. Yes, let us."

Peter waited in silence.

"Mr. Sharma, are you still there?"

"Yes, Detective, right here—go ahead." Peter mouthed *HO-LY CRAP* to Collette, who looked at him questioningly.

"Ah, there you are. I was wondering if someone would like to know what time we would be arriving. No one has called or anything to check on your friend's status. He has not said so, but I'm sure he is quite shaken inside, as I would be in his position."

"Friend? What friend . . . ?" He looked out the window and realized that the Jeep was gone and that he hadn't seen Rheese all morning. "Is Dr. Rheese there with you?"

Silence on the other end. When Chitundu finally spoke again, the slow, dramatic affect was gone and he sounded like an entirely different person.

"What are you talking about, Mr. Sharma?" he barked. "Dr. Rheese is not there?"

Peter had had enough. "No! He isn't—and if you're not talking about him, *who* is with you? Did you—did you find Hank?"

"Of course. Mr. Felch is in the office beside mine. You were not told? I informed Dr. Rheese late yesterday. Have you seen him since then?"

"What! Hank's alive! Jesus!" He paused. "But . . . Rheese was at dinner—he never said a bloody *thing*!" Peter looked around the RV, then stepped quickly down the hall, and checked in the closet—no clothes, no bags. "Yeah, he's gone. All of his things, too. But is Hank *okay*? I mean, where did you find him? Is he okay?"

"You asked that twice, Mr. Sharma," Chitundu replied. "If not for your Dr. Rheese further incriminating himself, I would normally have found that suspect. I'll be there with Mr. Felch in under four hours. And yes, he is okay. Yes, he is okay."

"They found Hank!" Peter shouted to Collette. "He's alive and fine!" As she bounced out the door to spread the joyous news, he put the phone back to his ear. It sounded as if it was still connected. "Detective, are you still there?"

"You shouted in my ear, Mr. Sharma."

"Oh . . . um, sorry. So, are you coming or what?"

Silence. The call had ended.

Rheese swung the Jeep into the small car park beside a farmers' market. Nakuru looked fairly well maintained and tidy, he thought. Indeed, one might forget one was in the heart of the third world. He blended well with the other white tourists—only the oversize camera swinging from his neck was missing. He threw a dirty tarp over his bags in the back—one couldn't be too careful.

He walked along between the mounds of corn, melons, and bananas, ignoring the calling, waving merchants. Beyond the market, he spotted a canopy and, beneath it, a bank of telephones. How pleasantly modern, he thought, inspecting one. Credit card scanner, digital display, a small port for some electronic device or other. He dialed the number, and the display requested one shilling, which he dropped in the slot. A moment later a woman answered in Swahili.

"The Gray," Rheese said behind a cupped hand. He heard the phone drop, and the woman shout. The phone clattered, and another woman's voice came on.

"Who is these?" she said.

"*These* is looking for the Gray. No one else."

"We no hear of no Gray. Who is these?"

"Bloody brilliant!" Rheese spat. "Look, I've used this number before. Is there another number, perhaps?"

"These number?"

"No, another phone that I can call. A mobile? Cellular? Cellie?"

"Cellie phone?" she answered as if that had clicked.

"Yes, the Gray—cellie phone."

"These Rheese?"

"Yes, damn it! Yes, this is Rheese! Give me the number, please."

"I have message for you."

"Well, give me the bloody thing! What is it—what did he say?"

"Say you dead." *Click.*

The phone fell from Rheese's ear, and he turned and scanned the area around him as he felt dread knotting in the pit of his stomach. *What have I done? I paid him! I did nothing wrong!* His eyes darted to every car, every face. With hurried steps, he walked behind the vegetable market to return to the Jeep, fighting down the panic. *Where now? He was supposed to get me out. I could have kept that bloody money and done it myself! What was I thinking, dealing with a bloody scoundrel like him?*

He needed a disguise—a wig. A white man with a bald head was surely the first thing they'd be looking for. But how would they know he was in Nakuru? The Gray didn't even know he had left the site. But now . . . caller ID? Would they know he had called from that pay phone? Were they that sophisticated?

He started to get in the Jeep, then stopped. He had seen this before. A bomb? Brakes cut?

Dropping to the muddy ground, he peered up into the undercarriage. But what to look for? He knew nothing about bloody cars! Everything he saw could be a bomb, for all he knew. But he had to get away from here. *Bloody hell with it!* Getting up, he dusted his knees off and climbed into the Jeep, closed his eyes, and turned the key.

After the engine caught and he realized that he still existed, he reversed and drove away to the north. He needed as much distance between himself and the site and Nairobi as possible. He mentally totted up his cash on hand: fifty-five hundred U.S. dollars and a few hundred Kenyan—enough to get him to Egypt or Morocco. But from where? Kampala? Addis Ababa? Too far—perhaps Torore, right across the border. There should be an ample population of corrupt airport personnel he could bride on the cheap.

Turning onto the highway, he followed the signs pointing to Uganda-Lake Victoria.

Blast that bloody Gray! It was his own fault for losing Felch, however the hell it had happened. They were supposed to keep him for a week, and now they were coming after *him*? He wished he were a crime boss and could order a hit on the Gray and the fools who had bollixed the job—no doubt those two idiots in the truck.

Behind him a siren wailed. Rheese peered in the rearview mirror and cursed in a steady stream until he had stopped on the shoulder. He kept his hands on the steering wheel, breathed deeply and slowly, and prepared his face for a jolly smile. He considered trying an American accent, but it might not be convincing enough.

"Hello, sir," the officer said, his face impassive behind reflective sunglasses. Rheese turned and smiled. "Where you from, sir?"

"Dublin, m'lad!" He opted for Irish. "'Ow can oi 'elp ye?"

"You forget something, sir." The officer sounded angry. Rheese's mind raced with all the things that could mean. Forgot the speed limit? Forgot to stop at a red? Forgot that police in Kenya were smart and knew which way you would travel?

How about, forgot that cops were corrupt and could be paid to put a bullet in your head by order of the Gray?

"Yeh?" Rheese smiled innocently.

The officer held up his hand, clutching a blue tarp. Twisting around in the seat, Rheese saw that the tarp covering his bags was missing.

"Oy!" he exclaimed. "So sorry, lad! Can't be dairtyin up the beautiful land out 'ere, now, can we?" He took the tarp from the cop and stuffed it deep behind his seat. "Oi unnerstan if oi 'ave to pay a teckit. Where do oi soign?"

The policeman stared at him for a moment through his big mirrored shades, tapped the door of the Jeep twice, and walked back to his car.

What does that bloody mean? he wondered. *Can I go?* As he watched in the mirror to see if the man was leaving or getting out a ticket book, the police car made a U-turn and headed back the way it had come.

With a gasp of both relief and annoyance, Rheese shifted the Jeep into first gear and continued on his way.

FORTY-TWO

I rin led the group cautiously through the last of the foothills. Behind them stretched a continuous woodland canopy; ahead rose mountains, with no obvious way up.

Irin had decided to send no more scouts ahead, for fear of another flyer swooping down on them. The travelers moved in a tight pack with light-sticks held high, for Wil had suggested that the unfamiliar blue glow might dissuade the flyers from grabbing someone in the group.

As they continued down the final slope before the first mountain, Irin drank in the cool, moist air. He could smell the sweetness of the soft soil beneath their feet and hoped there would be more like it wherever they landed. Though he had never worked the food flats, the earth looked rich and fertile, and luxuriant plant life grew all around.

Following a weakness in the foothills, they reached the steep watershed between two mountains. With no easier path in the direction of sunset, Irin turned up the valley, walking along the streamlet with his feet on either side of the water. The others followed, and with some pushing from behind, the n'wips moved slowly along. Irin was relieved that none of the monstrous screamers or the small fast-running creatures seemed to occupy this terrain, and that no new ones had made themselves known.

Two challenging mountain passes later, they stopped to camp in a flat meadow, like a miniature version of their own valley but carpeted in soft, hair-covered plants as tall as a man. To flatten the plants, Pwig had two n'wips unloaded and dragged back and forth over the area. The mountains on all sides would provide shade for much of the day, allowing direct light for only a few hours when the sun was overhead. Soon all had eaten and were lying down for the day on comfortable beds of soft vegetation.

The next night they awoke and continued upward, making many winding twists and turns to avoid the steeper slopes. And in this way they passed another night, another sleep, another night. With each night, the feeling grew that they were close to a new home. What about this spot? Too small for houses. And this? Too far to water. The next night, one of the new, Gritten, went missing. No one saw anything, but all assumed that a flyer had taken him. His mother, delirious with grief, wished to stay in that spot and be taken as well, supposing that at least she might get to see her new one more time. Irin did not have to convince her to carry on, for her man promised her that another newest would come to them and that it would be *another* Gritten, as if nothing had happened. She eventually allowed herself to be lifted to her feet and led along.

One evening, after Irin had lost count of the nights, he, Wil, Pwig, and Orin stood atop one of the mountain peaks, looking out at the distant clouds. Though they could see flat land in the distance, the nearby mountains were hidden in the clouds. Below them, three thousand people sat spread across the slopes, eating their midnight meal.

"How many nights before the asteroid comes?" Irin asked Wil as he re-strapped his foot coverings."

"I've lost track of how many have passed, but I think not many more. It comes during daylight."

"Irin," Pwig began, "do you think we'll still return to Pwin-T when the fires are gone?"

Irin looked at his brother in disappointment.

"Do you wish to make that journey again?" Wil answered for him.

"But . . . you told everyone we would go back and rebuild."

"Pwig, I said that to convince people to leave," Irin said, placing his hand atop Pwig's head. "To save their lives."

"So we will never return?" he persisted.

"The city will never return, no," Irin confirmed. "But that doesn't mean a small group couldn't one day return to see it. Perhaps, when you find yourself an Opwig and a newest is made, you'll want to take your new to see where his people came from."

Wil added, "But you know the dangers this journey holds. You may not want to risk it with a new."

"Would you, Irin?" Orin asked him as she walked closer to him.

"Would I travel back to Pwin-T? I think not."

"What about when you have your own new? Two or three boys who want to go and see where their father killed screamers and where he poured houses?"

"No, they don't need to see what they can hear from my mouth. And that is, *if* we ever receive any new."

Orin was silent as Irin looked at her.

"You believe we will, of course," Irin said with a snort.

She continued to look at him and moved her hand over her belly. He looked down and frowned at her hand, then back up at her face.

"What? You want one now?"

"I think she *has* one now," Wil interjected. "Orin?"

Pwig smiled and ran to her. "Is it true?"

She looked up at Irin, waiting for his frown to disappear. She clearly did not want that face to be the one to receive the news. He relaxed it a little as the idea floated around his thoughts.

"Is it true?" he echoed.

She leaned into him and curled her hands and arms around his head.

"It is," she finally admitted.

He pulled her close to him, unsure how he felt about the revelation but not wanting her to think him unmoved. Pwig and Wil touched both their heads in congratulations.

"Will it be Irint or Orint, I wonder," Pwig said. "Do you know, Wil?"

"No, I didn't even know a newest was coming to them," Wil said with a hint of sadness before he walked away.

Irin wondered what thoughts his friend was having—likely dark ones, since he well knew that Irin wouldn't be going anywhere with new ones he would never live to see.

Irin and Orin looked into each other's eyes as Pwig descended the slope beside them, following Wil.

"We should eat, I suppose," Irin told her. "How long has it been?"

"Since last I ate?" she replied.

"Since you knew."

"Just before we left Pwin-T. I didn't want to disrupt your thoughts."

He nodded and guided her down the hill, his thoughts disrupted.

Irin led the people of Pwin-T over mountains and through canyons to a wide plateau. Short, dense trees covered the high plateau. From a distance, they appeared to be round balls of foliage that clung to the sloping ground without rolling, but on closer inspection, within the balls were thick trunks rooted deep in the reddish soil. Irin and Orin lay beneath one of the strange trees. The rigid branches scratched them whenever they moved in their sleep, but it was shade nonetheless, and all were grateful for it.

Wil shook Irin's arm until he awoke with a start, wincing when he sat up into the branches above him.

"What is it?" he asked when he saw his friend's veiled face. Thin rays of sunlight pierced the crown of leaves, dappling Wil's k'yot top so that it looked much like the dark spots on his face.

"It is now."

Irin's breath paused in his chest. What had come to kill him?

"Now . . . what . . . how?"

"Not you," Wil explained, "the giant rock."

Irin breathed once more. "It is coming now? Do you see it?"

"Not yet, but hurry if you wish to."

Irin slid out from under the ball of leaves and sat up, turning his k'yot backward to shield him from the searing light. Pwig was also there, his k'yot covering his face, ready to go.

"Should we wake others?" Irin asked them.

"*It* will wake them," Wil replied. "But the daylight will blind them—if they walk near the cliff's edge when it happens, some might fall. Come."

"Irin?" Orin's voice came from the green ball. "Where are you going?"

"The sky stripe comes," he answered. "Do you wish to see?"

"Of course! Oh . . . our people—this is their end! Wait a moment." She slid out from under the tree, her brown eyes peering through a thin slit in the clothing wrapped around her face.

They walked around more of the ball trees, carefully stepping over people, and stopped at the sunrise side of the plateau, where Wil held his arms out to halt them. A precipice dropped off directly in front of them.

"Be careful," Wil told them. "Pieces slip off." Leaning back, he stamped his heel onto the edge, and a section of the ground fell away into space.

"Where is it?" Pwig asked, scanning the landscape around them. "I don't—"

"It'll come from that side." Wil pointed to his left.

In the distance, all they could see were more mountains; not even the plains they had traversed were visible. A panorama of clear sky lay before them, bright blue from the sun behind them and all but free of clouds.

All four stood and waited silently. Had they missed it? Had they come too far to see it now? And then they heard a sound like thunder in the distance. It echoed through the mountains.

"Was that it!" Pwig blurted. "Did it hit?"

But Wil snapped a hand in front of him to be silent. The hand curled shut, with one finger outstretched, and moved from Pwig to the sky where he had pointed. Half a breath later, an enormous ball of fire appeared at the tip of his finger, trailed across the sky, and disappeared in silence, all in an eyeblink.

All four had sucked in a sudden breath as they had watched the sky stripe's split-second flight. But still it made no sound. Irin wondered if it somehow had missed the surface, but then they heard the rumble—very soft, but long and with a deep waver as if someone were humming. Was that it? Their city destroyed that quickly? Tillyt and Otillyt now dead, burnt to ash? The houses melted in a flash like lightning? Was Pret awake and watching it come to him? Did he make it to the hill so it would hit him first, as he had boasted?

The ground beneath them rumbled slightly, and small pieces fell from the edge of the cliff and bounced their way to the bottom.

"Was that it?" a new voice asked behind them. Irin turned and saw many heads, shielded from the sunlight by arms and clothing.

Irin and the other three moved away from the edge. Walking up to the man who had asked, Irin told him quietly, "Yes."

The last living people of Pwin-T were understandably distraught. Most were unable to return to sleep, and Irin envied those who still slept. They wouldn't know until they awoke, after sunset.

Looking back toward the sunrise side, he saw a giant cloud rising and growing in the distance—smoke from the fires, he supposed. He and Orin returned to the ball of green and lay there, unable to return to sleep.

After darkness finally arrived, Irin allowed people the time to let the event sink in. They would not travel this night, he decided, and he sent word around. The plateau was an acceptable place to sleep through another daylight.

The following night they packed up and resumed their journey. A sensation of numbness seemed to afflict one and all; no one moved quickly, but neither did anyone argue, and no complaints found their way to Irin. He understood that most had eaten little or nothing before they left, and he kept the pace leisurely.

The next four nights were difficult ones. During one, they encountered a rocky area where a mountain had apparently lost half of its peak, filling the lower lands with enormous boulders too difficult to pass with n'wips. Irin led them all the way back around a mountain to find a different way. Another night, a man broke his leg after slipping and rolling down a hill and had to be carried in a n'wip.

At the close of the fourth night since the destruction of Pwin-T, as people assembled to eat the last meal, Irin discovered that the dylt and k'yon were almost completely gone—no one had told him. After scolding the men he had placed in charge of the food supply, he pondered what to do. There was hardly enough even to feed the group tonight, let alone the next. And if they consumed everything, they would have no seeds to plant in a new food flat. As the sun rose on the other side of the mountain, Irin heard some new complaining of hunger. He told Orin to give half-portions of gwotl only, to save the dylt and k'yon and get everyone to sleep quickly.

When Orin asked him what he would do, he told her that he would take some men out during the daylight to scout for seeds, nuts, berries, or anything else they could find. They had filled up water bags at a mountain brook nearby; they would start their search there. He assembled his group of men, including Wil, leaving Pwig and Orin in charge of the group. He knew now that she could handle most problems much better than he himself could.

The eight men, all carrying cutters and with their k'yot tops turned backward, set off traversing around the mountain. Each carried food bags for gathering samples. If they found an appropriate food in good supply, Irin would send back hundreds of people the next night to gather all that they could pack into n'wips—at least he *hoped* there would be such a discovery.

Arriving at the foamy, rushing river, they surveyed the plants that bordered it. Wil pulled up a bush and sniffed its thick, twisted taproot. Nibbling off the tiny tip, he told Irin it was sweet, almost like gwotl nectar.

But Irin said not to pull up more of the plants yet; thousands grew along the stream bank, and they could come back for more later.

"That is, if you don't get foodrise in a short while," Irin told him.

The men explored farther up the river, to a point where the sides were too steep to walk and they had to trudge through the water. Walking against the flow proved difficult, and they progressed slowly, wading through areas where the water almost reached their crotches. It was also very cold.

They continued around a bend in the stream until Nitt cried out. Irin turned to see him hopping about in the water, as if he were avoiding stepping on fire.

"What is it?" Irin shouted to him.

"Something in the water!" He kept dancing about and sloshed to the edge of the stream, pulling himself out and onto the steep bank.

The rest of the men's eyes shot downward, and then another felt it, then two more, and they all began scrambling to get out of the water. Irin saw something long and silvery slide past him. He moved up onto a teetering rock, with only his feet still under the water, and tried to see more. Wil and the others were retreating to the banks, at once amused and uneasy about what this strange thing might be.

Irin balanced on the unstable rock and knelt down, cutter in hand. There it was again! This time he got a good look. It was very long, like a big lightstick, with two large wings spreading out at the bottom. When it moved, its body curved like a twisting rope.

"It was trying to bite my legs!" Nitt told him. "I could feel it through the k'yot bottom. Its mouth was strong, like a person's hand."

Irin poked his cutter into the water and spun it around. The rock beneath him rolled forward a little, and he had to arch his back and throw his arms behind him to keep from falling. It worked, and he steadied himself. Then, without warning, the rock rolled backward and he rolled with it, his head plunging beneath the cold water. His nose suddenly burned as he inhaled, and his arms floundered for something to pull himself up. His cutter fell from his hand, and his back struck the rock he had been standing on. The water was pushing him down the river. He was able to flip himself over and get a foot planted on the ground. His head broke through the surface, and he coughed and spat, hunched over and standing in water that was well over his knees.

Wil and another grabbed the back of his k'yot middle, pulling him up onto the bank. Shaking the water from his ears, he pulled his k'yot top away from his face and felt himself begin to laugh.

"Wil?" he said with a heavy sigh.

Wil said nothing, just touched Irin's head.

"Did one of them try to bite you?" Nitt asked, fear still in his voice.

"No, I think the thrashing scared them away, but I lost my cutter in there."

"You can have Nitt's," Dill joked. "He won't use it anyway—he just runs."

"And what did the rest of us do?" Wil replied. They all chuckled.

"Come on," Irin cut in. "We have to keep moving. I don't know about the rest of you, but I'm *very* awake now."

Moving along the sloping bank, they heard a low rumbling somewhere up ahead. Around two more bends, they arrived at a wider area, where a waterfall dropped from high above them. In the distance a vast gorge appeared, surrounded by enormous cliff walls. Below them, the ground was wooded with tall trees, and ferns and deep-green moss seemed to cover the rock walls. The waterfall roared and pounded, making the ground tremble. They looked up, marveling at its power, trying to see the top through the misty air.

Irin took a few steps back and inhaled the moist air, hoping they would find another gorge like the one down there, but bigger. The beautiful green bowl beneath them looked very appealing, he knew, but it would never hold the houses and food flats for so many people, nor did it have an ample tree supply. He hoped that a larger one existed nearby so that he could return to this spot often with Orin.

There was a sudden lurch, and he felt his stomach rise as the ground beneath him disappeared. With a gasp, arms swinging wildly out in front of him, he watched the backs of his seven companions rise above him. One arm landed on hard ground, and his chin hit, slamming his jaw shut, teeth gnashing into his tongue. Blood spread across his mouth and down his throat, so that he could not shout. He choked and grappled for a hold on the smooth rock.

The others, still gawking at the noisy waterfall, had not even heard the collapse. Irin watched his hand sliding toward him and realized that this was it; the moment that Wil had envisioned: daylight, k'yot top backward, as he had said. Did Wil know right now? As his hand slid on the smooth, wet rock, his other unable to find purchase on the remains of the crumbling soil, he twisted his head and peered down below. A long drop. Sheer cliff. If one of the monstrous long-necked beasts should stand down there, its head would not reach nearly this high.

He felt his hand leave the wet, smooth stone, and the rough surface scratched his face; then the others disappeared from view and he slid down and away. He closed his eyes as he felt the fall truly begin. His fingers scratched the last few pebbles and clods of moist earth, and then he was all alone in the air, touching nothing. He tried to take a final deep breath, to let the smell of this place be the last thing he thought, when his head flew back and his body slammed against something hard. He felt something in his chest pop, relieving whatever had happened to his side in the fight with the screamers.

He felt his legs still dangling, and when he opened his eyes, Nitt's voice was shouting "Irin!" right in his face. Irin's eyes grew wider still as he saw that Nitt's k'yot-covered face was sliding with him. He didn't know that Irin was *supposed* to die here. He shouldn't have tried to stop him; now he, too, would perish. Nitt's hands clutched at the back of Irin's k'yot middle, and he was shouting more things at Irin: to hold on, to grab him, not to worry. They stopped dropping, and Irin realized that someone must be holding Nitt's legs. He glanced up but could not see anyone else. Of course not—they would fall as well.

Irin wished that Nitt would just let him go. They apparently had a good hold of him and could probably raise him back up if not for Irin's added weight. Irin's ears began to function again, and for the first time he truly heard Nitt's words.

"Reach up! Hold on to my middle! I am going to grab my cutter and put it in the wall!"

Irin threw his hand up and grasped the k'yot tightly, not quite understanding the logic but going along with it all the same. What good would a cutter wedged in the collapsing rock do? Nitt released one of his hands, and Irin felt himself drop a little more. The fear had reentered him, and he began to grow angry that he hadn't been allowed to fall and die while he had found peace a moment ago. Now he was thinking there might actually be a chance to survive, and again he was terrified of falling. What would it feel like when he hit?

Nitt's hand disappeared above and came back down with a cutter. They both looked at it as Nitt slammed it into the wall. But it had slid too easily into the mud, and Nitt pulled it back out.

"What are you trying to do?" Irin shouted at him.

"I'll get it strong in the wall, and then they'll give me more cutters to make handholds for you to climb up!"

Irin felt his arm burning with exhaustion. Looking at Nitt's eyes, he spoke calmly, "Listen to me. You're a good man for trying, but you need to let me go. Let them pull you up."

Nitt's faceless k'yot top said no, and he tried to jab the cutter into another spot. Irin heard another of the men above shout, "Hurry! . . . Too slippery on these rocks!"

That was it, Irin decided. He looked up as Nitt pulled the blade out of the wall the second time. He closed his eyes and took another deep breath as he opened the hand holding Nitt's k'yot. He dropped down more and felt

Nitt's other clutching hand give way. With a groan, Nitt tried to improve his grip, but the k'yot slipped from his fingers.

"No!" he heard Nitt scream, and he felt himself fall for only a second before his body lurched forward again, his head once more banging against the rocks. He opened his eyes and, through the filter of his k'yot, could see both Nitt's hands. They were gripping the wall and not touching him at all.

Nitt turned back and shouted, "Give me another! I've got him!"

Irin looked down and saw the cutter. It was stabbed through his k'yot middle and stuck deep into a section of rock. Nitt had done it! He still dangled precariously, but he certainly wasn't falling. Nitt's face disappeared as they pulled him back up.

In Nitt's place, Wil's face appeared just over the ledge. He had removed his k'yot top altogether and squinted at Irin. His face drooped with somber despair.

"Not this time, either, Wil?" Irin called to him. "How many times must I practice dying before the real thing?" he joked.

Beyond Wil, Irin heard one of the men shout at another to go back for rope. Wil glanced out of Irin's sight and then looked back down at him.

"No . . . this is it, Irin. Just close your eyes."

And then Irin felt it. The k'yot was ripping. Nitt had stabbed it in the cliff with the edge up, and it was cutting the threads! His body lurched down, tearing it farther. And then only the knife and a small piece of k'yot stuck to the cliff while Irin's body flipped backward. He felt his hand grab for the cutter handle, and his fingers, as if acting on their own, wrapped tightly around it. As his body dropped straight down, his arm became fully outstretched, yanking at his elbow and shoulder for but an instant before he felt the hilt break away from the blade.

Irin's body began to flip backward as the rocks before him disappeared, and he soared through the air.

FORTY-THREE

Irin landed hard, his hands and head slapping down on something soft. His eyes opened and were blinded by the bright of the sun. His k'yot top must have come off during the fall. Closing his eyes, he tried to raise his arms to cover them, but his arms would not move. He tried to move his legs, but they, too, were immobile. Was he alive? Where was he? He managed to move his fingers and felt something soft, like clothes, beneath him. He tried to move his tongue, but it hit something and he realized that something was lodged in his throat. He began to choke, and his mouth filled with saliva and he choked more.

Since his arms would not move, he tried to turn his head, and it moved a little. He felt the thing in his mouth, sticking out and leading somewhere else. He opened his eyes again, and the light was still too bright, though he could see other things above him. He began to feel desperate, unable to move the thing from his mouth. He tried to make himself breathe through his nose—that felt better, and he kept it up. What was that smell, though? Like alcohol or something else medicinal. He blinked again. What was this feeling at his fingers? Soft like a sheet. Wait . . . *alcohol.* Not Irin! *I'm me! But . . . where?* He waited for his eyes to adjust to the light. *I'm in a hospital room somewhere. What am I touching? What's touching me? Obviously, nothing imprinted—I'm conscious.*

He rolled his eyes around the room and again began to panic as he realized that a tube was down his throat. *Someone, get in here quick. Call for someone!* Matt let out a small groan, choked a little, inhaled through his nose, and let out a louder cry, a garbled try at "Help!" Hearing the clip-clop of footsteps passing outside, he let out a good, loud bellow, then promptly began choking on the tube.

He heard a woman's voice shout, "Doctor!" She had heard him, thank God. "Doctor, thirty-five is awake!"

More rushing footsteps, and faces came into view. He was still choking, and someone was saying, "Hang on . . . just relax . . . just relax." He felt the object coming out of his throat. Dear God, that thing was long! He gagged and choked more and felt the burn of vomit in his throat. He couldn't swallow, couldn't get rid of the pain!

And then the tube was out. He could finally swallow, but it hurt like hell, as if he had the worst sore throat in history. Four or more bodies busied themselves around him, saying just to relax, everything was okay, *blah blah blah,* while they shined lights in his eyes and put cold things on him. His feet were *freezing*! He tried to wiggle his fingers, and they responded slightly.

"Matthew," a doctor with silver hair and bright, white smile said to him, "can you hear me okay?"

Matt nodded a little and was able to manage a "Yeah" with his thick, dry tongue.

"Do you know your last name, Matthew?"

Matt nodded again and said, "Tuhna." He thought it sounded as if he were talking underwater.

"That's very good, Matthew. You have no idea how happy I am to hear that."

"W'cut mm'ms mff?"

The doctor just shook his head. "It's okay, you'll be able to speak much better in a couple of hours, and *worlds* better in a couple of days. You probably have a lot of questions."

Matt nodded. "Nuh shht."

"I'm going to answer some of the easy ones for you, so you don't have to try to strain yourself trying to form the words. First off, 'Where am I?' Always a good thing to know, right?"

Matt felt one side of the bed sink where the doctor sat down. *Don't touch me, dear God, please.*

"You're currently a patient at the Gribbs Foster Dunham Center in New Rochelle, New York," the doctor began. "I am your attending, Dr. Ofle. No jokes! Ha-ha. You can call me 'Matt' when you are able—should be an easy one for you to remember. Next question: how long? A very short time, relatively speaking—just over a month. Well, a month with us, anyway. You went through a couple of international transfers before we got you. I believe your total length was around two months."

A nurse lifted one of his legs, bending it all the way to his chest, pushing the wind from him, then put it down gently and moved to the other. A nurse beside him was flexing his arm up and down.

"What happened? Well, we're not really sure about that, but you are not injured in any way as far as we can tell. You are not paralyzed, in spite of the way your body feels right now. Here, feel this . . ."

Matt saw him reach for something from beside the bed. He came back with a metal instrument and lifted Matt's hand.

"Nnnuh!" Matt groaned at him. "Dnnn't!"

"Oh, it's quite all right, Matthew," the doctor said cheerfully. "You've had a sort of guardian angel here almost every day, and . . . well, let's just say the point was well taken, long ago. Everything in here is new and has never been used on anyone but you. Perhaps when you're better able to communicate, you can tell us all about these allergies of yours."

Guardian angel . . . Tuni! Was she here? Matt felt the object poke his finger.

"See? Full sensation. Let's see, other questions—how long until I can move around some more? Get up and about . . . feed myself? Well, I'd be a liar if I didn't tell you you've got some work ahead of you. The body needs to be moving around; those muscles and tendons need flexing. When they don't, well, they sort of go to sleep right along with you. We've had a great staff in here taking care of you, making sure you remain limber, don't lose any flexibility, and also to keep you free from any of the other nasty problems that pop up when the body's immobile."

"Wrrrs Tnnneh?"

"Sorry, Matthew, but like I said, we're gonna get that mouth working real fast. It'll come around long before the rest, trust me on that."

Outside, he heard a new voice ask, "he's awake?" English accent . . . no South African twist—not Tuni?

A woman with red hair appeared over him and smiled. "Good to see you awake, Matthew," she said. "I'm Dr. Sylvan, and I'm sure we'll be talking a lot in a couple of days. For now, a simple nod yes or no will do—don't fight to get everything off your mind, okay? Let's try a 'yes' nod right now."

Matt nodded.

"Very good; how about a 'no'?"

Matt moved his head side to side.

"No? You can't do that? Ha-ha-ha, just kidding. Old joke."

Strangers streamed in and out of his room, all very excited to see him. Another woman came in a little later and introduced herself as Breeze, the physical therapist. He wanted to ask her if that was her real name or if it just seemed soothing to her broken patients. She said they'd be seeing a lot of each other in the coming weeks.

So where the hell was Tuni? Did she really come almost every day?

A couple of hours passed, and Matt had begun exercising his tongue and lips the way Doctor Sylvan instructed him. She said it would not only help his speech improve but also help him drink and eat his first real meal a little later.

They had propped him up on his pillow so he could see the room around him. He looked around—no TV, but he did have his own bathroom. *Wait . . . how have I been doing* that? He slowly reached down and felt the tube under his gown.

A nurse he had seen before appeared in the doorway and said "knock knock." She smiled and tilted her head to the side.

"Hello again, Matthew. Your visitor has returned! I have to say, when you're able, you've got many thank-you's to bestow on this one!"

Tuni!

"Hello, son," Matt's father said as he entered the doorway. "Can't tell you how good it is to see you awake."

FORTY-FOUR

Kyle Perkins set the phone down and stepped outside Peter's RV. He scanned the field for Tuni but spotted only Peter, sitting at a console while DeMotte carted the ground-penetrating radar unit around. In the distance, he saw several people huddled over another monitor. No Tuni there, either.

"Hey, Pete!" he shouted, but Peter didn't hear him. "Damn it . . ." He would have to jog out. He walked past the tables and the giant baobab and called him again.

"What's up, Kyle?" Peter replied over the bleeping of the radar pulses.

"Phone call from the States."

"You keep going, Jack," Peter called to DeMotte. "Same pace. It's recording. I gotta take this." He jogged over. "Who is it?"

"Not sure. They wanted to talk to Tuni, but I don't know where she is."

"She went with Hank and Miles to B site," Peter told him as they walked to the biggest of several motor homes on the site.

After wiping his feet on the mat, Peter stepped inside.

"Hello, this is Pete Sharma. Tuni is currently off-site; may I ask who is calling?" He listened for a moment. "He *is*? Holy shit! Is he okay, though? This is so wonderful! I'm sorry, who is this again? . . . Oh, okay, hi. Nice to meet you . . . yeah . . . Okay, I'll tell her as soon as she gets back. Yeah, okay, thanks for calling!"

Peter hung up the phone and slapped Kyle Perkins on the back, shouting, "He woke up!" as he dashed out the door.

"*Who?*" Perkins asked as Peter ran off.

Peter ran across the field to tell Collette, Rodney, and the others the news about Matt. "Rodney, has Hank got a radio?" he asked, breathless from excitement as much as from the run.

"I think he charged it this morning," Rodney replied. "I imagine he would have taken it." He handed his radio to Peter.

Peter depressed the button. "A site to Hank, A site to Hank—you there?"

The radio crackled quietly for a moment.

"Hank here—what's up?"

"Hank, please tell me Tuni is there with you."

"Tuni? Tuni who?" Hank said, but Peter could hear Tuni's voice in the background, shouting, "Silly fool."

"Can you put her on, please?" Peter persisted.

A few seconds later, her voice came through the speaker.

"Yes, Peter, how can I help you?"

"Matt woke up."

The radio crackled. Everyone huddled around Peter, waiting to hear her response. It cracked again, but Hank's voice was back.

"Hey, Pete, did you just say Matt woke up?"

"That I did, Hank. Where'd Tuni go?"

"Uh . . . she's still in the backseat . . . just—you okay? Hey, you want to go back to A site? Hang on, Pete. She's a little, um—hang on."

"Is she crying?" Collette asked. "I bet she's crying."

"So, Pete," Rodney interjected, "you going to fly him back out here to see what we've found so far?"

Pete smiled and nodded. "I wish. I don't think Matt Turner's gonna be visiting Africa anytime soon, though. They said it might be a couple months before he's out of the hospital, and even after that . . . you think he's going to *want* to come back? He couldn't wait to leave!"

"Peter?" Tuni's voice cracked through the radio. She was sniffling.

"Yeah, I'm here."

"Can I go? Can I see him?"

"Of course! They said you're the first person he asked for. Wouldn't shut up about you, or so I gather from the nurse there."

"Okay . . . coming back . . ." They heard the sound of Hank crunching around a U-turn before the radio cracked off.

Tuni dropped her two duffel bags near the RVs and waved to the others at the tables under the baobab. She had really gotten to know only perhaps forty of the sixty-odd people now working the A and B sites. Pete had assembled specialists from all over the world, and more were on their way. No television vans were parked outside just yet, but that would change soon. Peter had told her that the crew would bide their time and keep mapping until the documentary folks arrived next week. He wanted to be sure they captured everything significant.

She stepped inside Peter's RV. Her request was a simple one, but she feared that his by-the-book mind-set would shut her down. He stood as she entered, while Collette remained seated, munching at her sandwich.

Peter swallowed and said, "So this is it? Tell me you won't get too comfy over there and leave us out here to rot."

"Of course not."

"Great. Well . . ." He leaned forward awkwardly and hugged her.

"So, Peter . . . ," Tuni said with an innocent glance upward. "I have a teensy favor to ask, and you will be simply unable to refuse."

"Tell me—anything."

"I want to bring it with me."

"Uh, okay, I should have said, anything but that! C'mon, how could you even *ask*? You know the laws and everything. We *just* got the okay from the ministry to send that package to Meier, and that was like pulling teeth! The inspections alone took a week."

"I'm not hearing the emphatic yes I had hoped for, Peter."

"Emphatically, no," he replied.

She moaned and rolled her eyes. Peter's face told her the same as his words, and he sat back down at the little round table to finish his chips.

"Very well. I had to ask. Tah-tah, all! I'll hopefully be back within a fortnight." She turned and opened the door.

"Hang on a sec," Peter called behind her. She paused on the step and glanced back. "You know that package is going to be in Meier's hands tomorrow. It might be a bit easier for you to convince *him* to let you take it on a field trip."

Tuni smiled. Jon? Oh, *very* easy.

"You're out of your lovely mind, Tuni," Dr. Meier told her twenty-six hours later. "The freedoms of the field have clogged your once logical mind."

"It's six hours, tops, Jon. Don't be a fuss-pot. By the way, is that a new sweater vest?"

He shook off the compliment and hugged the open box closer to his chest.

"Do you have any idea how long I've waited for this package?" he said. "I woke up at five this morning to get here early just to *wait* by the dock for FedEx."

"You are a great man, Jon. I understand the sacrifice. Not quite the magnitude of *Matthew's*, of course, but definitely agonizing. Let me cure your pain again in six hours, okay, dear?" She stepped closer to him and leaned down, prying the box from his hands.

He made a halfhearted attempt to hold on to it, but he knew it was useless. Had she intentionally given him that glimpse of cleavage? She didn't have to, but he was appreciative nonetheless.

As she sauntered away like a runway model, he called behind her, "You take care of that thing as if it were Matt Turner himself, understand?"

"Cheers, Jon. I'll send your love to Matthew."

Matt sucked his lemonade through the straw and pretended his father wasn't staring at him. He reached for the plastic fork and began to shovel mashed potatoes into his mouth. While he ate, he hummed nervously and rotated his ankles beneath the sheet. The awkwardness became unbearable, and he reached for the remote, pointing it to his new room's corner-mounted LCD television.

"That's pretty rude, Matthew," his father said. "I'm not here to watch you eat and flip through channels."

"Hmm, no?" Matt replied sarcastically. "Why *are* you here?"

"I'm here to help you . . . and to talk to you."

"Right," Matt nodded exaggeratedly. "I'm just not sure I'm in the mood to help you clear your conscience."

"Boy, I was here every single day, making sure they—"

"Yeah, yeah, yeah, I got that the last few times. You fluffed my pillows, you yelled at helpless nurses. Admirable. You should be knighted." He stuffed a chunk of meatloaf into his mouth.

"Boy, I know you despise me, but I didn't do any of that for myself, understand? You think it's all some sort of atonement for . . . *ahem* . . . my guilt." Matt nodded and smiled his agreement. "But I—that's why you need to . . . ah, damn it, forget it. I told her you didn't want to hear any of it."

"Mom was right. Listen to her, please."

"I'm not talking about your mother, son. I'm talking about your *girl-friend.*"

Matt swallowed a half-chewed bite of meatloaf.

"Tuni?"

"Yeah, the black girl."

"Oh, Jesus," Matt exclaimed. "You're still such a racist."

"How is that racist? Is she not black? I've had many conversations with her, okay?"

"Right, Dad, awesome. That's almost as rich as having black friends."

"This is ridiculous," his father said, standing up. "I came here to try to fix what I did—fix it for *you*, not for me, okay? I . . . I know what *I* got. It can't . . ." He reached up and shielded his eyes, his voice cracking. Matt let him continue. "What I got inside me, it can't be fixed. There ain't no 'clearing my conscience,' okay? There's nothing I could do to fix that."

"Look," Matt said without venom. He tried to keep his chest from quaking—*not in front of him*. "Mom and Iris are in the cafeteria. Go find them and get yourself some lunch. I don't want to argue."

His father dropped his hand, revealing his reddened eyes and tears. They looked at each other; it was hard for Matt not to look away.

"When I saw you every day—all the tubes and crap going into your veins and everything—well, I couldn't help thinking about Jessica Harris . . ."

Matt stiffened. "Nope. I don't want to talk about that. *At all,* okay?"

". . . and how I did that to you. I didn't give you any choice. You . . . your little arm with the IV jabbed in it. I thought it was the fastest way—the *only* way . . . let you get to the end of the imprint. Son of a bitch was doing who knew what to that little girl, and you could save her. That's all there was to it. I never put it together, you know?"

"Look, I said no . . ."

"She was twelve; you were twelve. I see it now. For a while now. I know I was just as bad as him, the kidnapper, you know? Except I was doing it to my own goddam son. Four days, I had her torn shirt on your hand. *I* put you through that. I knew what you must have been experiencing. And you came out of it; you tried to be strong. You had seen the other house and told us where to go, and we got her. Bullet in that piece of shit's head. We got her out of there."

Matt began to lose his composure and began squeezing his face and ears.

"And what did we do while she was being taken care of and fawned over and going through all her therapy and loved by everyone? We took you out for pizza. Goddammed *pizza*. I think about it every day. There's nothing I can say or do to undo it, son. So no, my guilt will stick with me until I die."

He walked out, and Matt screamed inside. He had let him get in his head. *Now I feel guilty about him feeling the way he should about what he did!*

He rubbed at his eyes and tried to get his breathing under control. He was shaking with every breath, and he realized he hadn't been overcome like this since he was thirteen—when Dad thought it would be a great idea to have Matt and Jessica Harris meet in person so she could thank her savior. Yeah, that would show Matt how it was all worth it! He'd stop complaining and help with more cases!

Matt pushed the food tray away and reached for a tissue. He blew his nose. *Ugh, that was horrible,* he thought, and took a deep breath. God, was Tuni *ever* going to call? *Why did she go back to Kenya? She just handed me off to Dad at this place and hopped on a plane. Guess she really got into the whole "excavating old stuff" thing. What was I thinking?* They had known each other for, what, a week? She hadn't even led him on.

"Hello, Matthew," said a blend of South African and English accents.

He looked up and saw her standing in the doorway, a brown box in her hands. He tried to speak, then focused his strength on not bursting into tears. *Damn it, now I'm all raw! Horrible timing!*

"Hey," he finally managed to say.

Tuni smiled as if holding back tears of her own. She stepped in and set the box down on a chair before walking to his bedside, where she rummaged in her purse for a moment.

"Sorry . . . hang on, " she said as she searched. "Ah-hah . . ."

He smiled and opened his mouth, and she popped the piece of gum in.

"I figured after two months you probably needed it pretty badly. Now, I've a couple of other things for you."

She watched him and dabbed her eyes with a tissue. They stared at each other in silence until she finally stuck her cupped hand out in front of his mouth. He crossed his eyes, looking down at her hand.

"What?" he said.

"Spit it out, dear."

He did, and she rolled the gum in a tissue, setting it aside, and leaned close to him. He felt her breath on his lips and looked at her eyes. He'd never really seen them so close. She put her hand behind his head, closed her eyes, and kissed him passionately. Putting his arms around her, he pulled her closer, and she climbed onto the bed with him.

A woman's voice from the doorway said, "Oh . . . ," but they ignored her and she must have left.

A few minutes later, an older nurse poked her head in and asked Tuni to move off the bed if they must carry on so in this facility. They laughed, and Tuni slid off. After wiping her lipstick from Matt's face with a tissue, she grabbed the chair from the corner, pulled it close to his bed, and plopped down on it.

"Sooo . . ." Matt said. "When did we start, um . . . maybe my memory is a little rough . . ."

"Hush. Don't ruin it." She reached into the box. ". . . and the final thing I've brought you . . ."

"Wait—was the gum the first thing?" he asked, grinning.

"Yes," she replied with an eyebrow flick.

"When can I have more of the second thing?"

"Plenty of time for that, dear. But I only have four and a half more hours with this one before it has to go back."

He tried to lean forward to see, but his abdominal muscles were still weak and unresponsive. Her hands reappeared, holding the shoulders of a full k'yot middle minus the holdstrip. He looked at the center of it and saw that it was fully intact.

Definitely not mine—er, Irin's, that is.

"They dug that up at the site?" he asked, reaching out for it.

"Whoa, crazy man! Are you trying to *touch* it?"

"Oh, God, what am I thinking? I . . . I guess I'm so used to touching them—can you grab some gloves from that box there?"

Tuni found the box of latex gloves and pulled out a pair. He slid them on and ran his fingers down the threads.

"No," she answered. "This was not at the site you knew. This is from a different place. I take it you haven't been watching the news." She smiled cunningly.

"No. They just have basic cable, so I've been watching the Discovery Channel and National Geographic since they moved me in here yesterday. What's happened? I don't know *anything*. My dad tried to tell me some stuff about Rheese and Hank, but I pretended I wasn't interested, and he stopped trying. So they found Hank? And did they ever catch Rheese? You know he did this to me, right?"

"Well, everyone figured as much after he fled, but no one knew exactly how he did it. Specialists wanted to run CT scans of your body—apparently, it's standard practice with comas—but your father wouldn't allow it. He said that *you* wouldn't have wanted it."

"That's true," Matt agreed. "You know a CT scan is like two thousand X-rays all done at once? And it's not like it was a normal coma. He knew they wouldn't find some brain anomaly keeping me knocked out. Although I'm still not sure what he stuck to me—do you know anything?"

Tuni blushed and looked away. "Actually . . . er, Pete and I sort of gave you a once-over to look for something on your body, but we couldn't find anything."

"You *what*? Did you, like, fully strip me down? What did you see?"

"Well, Pete did, actually. I was sort of *there*—anyway, it's not important. There's so much more to talk about. Your father's theory was that Rheese must have ground up a piece of the k'yot and injected the metal powder into a muscle or something. He said the tiniest little bit would still have an imprint. Seems to be a bit of an expert on you, actually."

"Yeah, I was his guinea pig for a long time."

"So anyway, in the end, he said to leave you alone and let you ride out the imprint. That he 'guaranteed' you'd awaken on your own. I said I'd stay with you and wait, and I did for a few days here, but then Dr. Meier called and told me what Pete had found. I decided I needed to be there for both of us."

"You mean the k'yot there?"

"No, Matthew, I mean the metal dome this k'yot was excavated from."

FORTY-FIVE

Matt leaned over to Tuni and pointed to his ears, mouthing, *Thanks for thinking of the earplugs.* She smiled and gazed out the window. Lulled by the muffled beat of the helicopter, he clasped his hands together and squeezed. He felt stronger than he had before any of this; the physical therapy had improved his physique while retraining his body for normal use. Breeze had told him he had progressed faster than most but that he was also fortunate in having only a couple of months of inactivity to work through. That had been four months ago, and he had bought a home gym to try to keep it up.

Tuni slapped his sleeve, and he turned to see her bouncing in her seat. He leaned over and peered out her window. *Oh, my God,* he thought, *it's huge!* Even though he had seen news video from helicopters over the sites, they looked so much bigger in person. In the distance he could see a massive clearing with vehicles and equipment everywhere. Tuni pointed farther to the left, and Matt could see another clearing, separated from the larger one by a half mile of forest. Both clearings were dotted with tree stumps.

The helicopter banked left and descended onto a white landing pad with a red circle, some distance from the field.

As they got out of the chopper, Matt saw Peter and Hank and several others running toward them from the lone baobab in the clearing. They all shook hands and hugged, then carried their bags from the helicopter.

"Look at this place!" Matt exclaimed. "How many RV's do you have here?"

"These eight and then three more at B site," Peter replied with a grin. "I tried to get a brand-new one for the two of you but couldn't get it approved for just a two-day stay—sorry. I think you'll find your accommodations acceptable, though."

Peter gestured at a pile consisting of a huge, brand-new tent, sleeping bags, plastic-sealed pillows, sheets and blankets, and a king-size air mattress.

"Where are the rest of the tents?" Matt asked.

"Oh, no one sleeps in tents here now—the RVs sleep eight each." He winked at Matt.

"Okay, so, Peter," Tuni began, "before you say anything, I haven't told Matt what you've got."

Matt rolled his eyes and sighed. "Yeah, she prefers to torture me and remind me every day. What is it?"

Peter and Hank merely smiled.

"Well, then, let's go to the office," Peter said with an air of mystery. "Could you all excuse us?" This to the rest of the group besides Hank.

As they walked, Matt surveyed the area around him, envisioning what it might have looked like with the tree cover it would have boasted in the recent past. Near the helicopter landing pad stood an area full of denuded tree trunks.

After meeting dozens of people, all of whom shook Matt's gloved hand, they finally reached the area with the motor homes, all parked in a row with little canopied spaces in between. Peter's, the closest to the tree in the middle, served as the office.

Matt looked around as he entered. The RV was a lot more spacious than Rheese's, but more cluttered as well. Stacks of plastic storage boxes rose to the ceiling, and various precision instruments and electronics were strewn on most of the available surfaces. What looked like a large laptop computer lay split in two pieces on the main table, with screws and other small parts scattered all about.

"Excuse the mess," Peter said. "As you know, we've got a hundred things going on at once. And I apologize in advance if I have to step away for an interview." He smiled and did his best conceited-celebrity pose. "Have you had to do any?"

Matt frowned, "Heck, no. Hopefully, my name's not being thrown around, so how would anyone track me down? Nah, all my information is from the TV news and my conference calls with you guys. Some of their mistakes are annoying; others are hilarious—it's really just crazy how big it's all gotten. Have you heard about the religious stuff?"

"Heard about it!" Peter exclaimed. "I'm talking to different groups every single day! And it's funny how quickly the believers' sentiments turned from 'It's blasphemy!' to 'It confirms everything we always believed!' They say it proves creationism, man's destiny to inherit the earth, and all the rest. Then there's the extraterrestrial-colonization ideas, the Maya calendar system experts who refer to the ages that existed before this one . . . It's actually all very interesting. I've had representatives from every major religion except the Vatican—who have requested that *I* go to *them*—all asking me these questions and telling me their thoughts. In the end, it's always the same. I'm telling you, one day there are death threats on my voice mail, and the next, I'm receiving flowers and notes of blessing."

"So . . . ," Matt began, "anything new happen with Rheese or Enzi? Has anyone checked it out?"

"Well," Hank began, "Enzi has a free pass out of jail if they ever catch Dr. Rheese. He's agreed to testify about everything, but without someone to testify against, he's stuck there for a while."

"And what about the whole diamond thing?" Matt asked as Peter put glasses of iced soda in front of him and Tuni.

"Yeah," Peter replied. "Hank put that whole thing together with the detective in charge of the case."

Hank leaned forward. "I'd already noticed that Rheese had identified impact signatures on all his maps—and that he was only excavating at those spots. I realized it after the detective told me who the kidnapper guys worked for—some mob-type guy who deals in blood diamonds from war-torn countries. See, when asteroids hit in certain areas where the right minerals are beneath the surface, bam!—instant diamond mine. It's not that common, though. The major operations look along tectonic and volcanic areas. With impacts, you'd have to spend a lot of time digging for nothing, and that gets pretty expensive."

"Unless you have a museum paying for it all," Peter added.

"So you actually found the Pwin-T impact site, right?"

They nodded.

"So has anyone checked it out to see if there's anything there?"

Peter laughed. "Yeah, you kidding? The Kenyan government owns the land where the impact took place. They didn't waste a second getting some contractors over there to survey the site. Sure enough, there's about two tons of diamonds beneath the surface. They've given us a lot of help"—he rubbed his fingers together to signify money—"and a lot of leeway after we showed them what was out there. Aside from the donations from all the religious organizations—which we're more than happy to accept in the interest of our research—the Kenyans are promising us a tiny chunk of the proceeds from mining it."

Matt smiled with them but started to feel a little sick. That same cache of diamonds that was making everyone so happy was created when thousands of people were vaporized and a city destroyed. People he had more or less met. He had to remind himself that it happened 150 million years ago, but it still seemed like yesterday.

"Did you find anything else there?" Matt asked. "On our last conference call, Collette said something about taking your ground-penetrating radar things over there."

"Like what?" Peter replied. "Signs of a city? Nope. But we did detect a significant level of aluminum-magnesium alloy below the surface and all around the area. Basically, the same alloy as the k'yots. Which leads me to . . ."

Peter opened a cabinet and then another door inside it. He pulled out his hands, and down dropped the two legs and two sleeves of a full k'yot. He reached behind the back and pulled up the top, which had been hanging back like a hooded sweatshirt. He walked it over to Matt and laid it on the table in front of him.

"Wow!" he breathed. "You got a *full* one?" He ran his gloved fingers over the rough surface. It was gray and colorless, much like the middle Tuni had shown him months ago. There was no shine to it, and the fibers were crimped all over and frayed at the edges.

"It's not just *any* full one," Hank corrected. "Keep looking . . ."

Matt frowned and looked it up and down. He turned it over and saw the holdstrip hanging from the top two loops but not the bottom ones. And then he saw it: the middle was missing a section—missing *the* section.

"This . . . ," Matt gasped. "This was . . . *Irin*'s. Where did you . . . how did you . . . ?"

"B site is a graveyard, all spoking outward from a single, smaller dome in the middle. This was embedded in the rock beneath the house."

"Yeah, I heard about the graveyard thing on the news specials," Matt replied. "They said there were no numbers yet, though. How many are there?"

"Well, no actual biological remains would have lasted in this type of matter, of course, and we haven't announced any figures to the media, but we'll take you over there later. Around the center dome, we found they had buried who knows how many people, but at some point they started embedding them in metal coffins, apparently pouring their molten alloy directly on the bodies—we're guessing, to preserve them. Now that type of containment—well, we're pretty excited to find out what's inside. At the very least, we'll have DNA. All in all, bouncing our ground-penetrating radar, we've mapped out about fourteen thousand of them so far."

"Fourteen *thousand*?" Matt swallowed. He felt dizzy. They actually made it—a new city. There had been only three thousand escapees, yet this was almost twice the premigration population of Pwin-T! But what about Irin? Did he really die? Did they do it without him? What about his child? How many generations lived after him? Questions raced through his mind. He looked back down at the k'yot, the one that he felt as though he himself had worn for those two months. He ran his glove over it while the others looked on in silence. Tuni stroked his back and stared at him with wide eyes.

"I've been wanting to tell you this *whole* time!" she blurted out. "But I knew you needed to see it in person and be able to read it—if you were comfortable with that, of course." She turned to the others. "Matt hasn't read any imprints since coming out of his coma."

"Yeah, about that," Hank began. "What did it end up being? They ever find a piece of the k'yot on you?"

Matt reached up and scratched the back of his head. "Yeah. I was half asleep at one point and dropped into an imprint. Figured out I could still access the whole story, so it was obviously still on me somewhere. A little ways into physical therapy, I was scratching my head and I felt something weird in the back. Like a little wormy bump. I had to get some shots—*ugh*—and they pulled out . . . this." He pulled out a small transparent capsule, like a perfume sampler vial, and laid it on the table. They all leaned in and saw the tiny thread inside. "I guess, with the laws and everything, I actually *smuggled* this piece out of the country. Well, here it is—if you get the original section out, the whole k'yot will be complete."

"So," Peter began again, "you want to . . . um, *check out* the k'yot?"

Matt looked down at it again and took a deep breath.

"I do, yes," he finally said. "Just not right at the moment. Can we maybe tour the grounds first?"

"Absolutely, though we only have a couple things excavated in B site, and nothing at all here in A site."

They all went outside into the damp equatorial heat.

As they passed the huge old baobab, Peter mentioned that the tree was thought to be over four hundred years old and that its preservation had been a condition of the museum's license to excavate. Matt looked up at the spindly branches sprouting from the impossibly enormous trunk some thirty feet thick. Four hundred years seemed such a short time. Then again, he would turn twenty-six in a couple of months. The thought made him feel suddenly small and brief.

They crossed a line of rope suspended six inches above the ground and extending in both directions to form a circle around the area. Every ten meters, foot-high stakes stuck out of the ground, connected by a grid of twine, just as the team had done at the old site. Each post had a tag hanging from it, bearing a code. They stepped carefully over all the lines until they had gone about four hundred yards.

At the center, they reached a large section that had been excavated. Matt stepped to the edge and looked down in the square-sided hole about five feet deep. A shovel stood stuck in the dirt in the middle, and two ladders leaned against the smooth dirt walls.

"What was in here?" Matt asked. Peter and Hank smiled but didn't answer.

"How much deeper is it?" Tuni asked.

"Less than a foot," Hank answered.

"Another secret," Matt said in a tone of mild annoyance.

"Not secret, dear," Tuni corrected. "'*Surprise*' is the word."

"We haven't pulled anything out of here, Matt," Peter admitted. "We'd like to offer you the honor of exposing the first house. We've got radar-grams of the whole area, and this one is the closest to the surface. There'll be press here tomorrow to capture the moment. You game?"

"Sure . . . I mean, why not?" Matt said. "That's cool of you guys to wait for me. How long's it been?"

"Well," Peter said, "we've known everything was out here for a while, but we just removed the overburden a couple of days ago. We've only held up the project for two days, really, but we've always wanted you to be a part of it. You sort of deserve it, you know?"

"Yeah. I really appreciate it—thanks. So this one is the closest one to the surface?"

"Oh, yeah," said Hank, "about a good twenty feet above the next highest roofs. We're estimating this one at about . . . well, you should just see it." He turned to Peter. "Can we show him the render?"

"Of course," Peter said. "Let's go!"

They followed Hank and Peter across the field to a small, black two-wheeled trailer, its hitch resting on a steel equipment crate. Peter opened a panel on the side and turned a knob. A motor whirred, and the back of the trailer slowly extended downward. After it touched ground, they stepped inside a cramped space lined with racks of computer equipment. Hank sat down in a rolling chair at a station with a keyboard, jiggled the mouse, and brought a large monitor to life. Clicking around, he found the file he needed, and up popped a map showing locations of trees and with silver circles representing the dome houses. Matt and Tuni leaned close and watched as he changed some parameters and the map switched to 3-D, displaying the area at an angle from above. Matt was impressed; it looked like the view from the old tree Peter had pointed out.

"Where'd the silver stuff go?" he asked.

"Hang on a sec," Hank replied. "Let's go in the order we discovered stuff. I still have the ground opaque—oh, and I apologize for the crude surfaces. There'll be textures and shading before we release it to the media."

"I think you're forgiven, Hank," Tuni laughed. "But what did you mean about the opaque ground?"

"It means," Peter cut in, "that this three-D site plotter takes all the data from the GPR and builds a map of what's underground. He can make the brown surface you see there disappear so you can see what we've found underneath. But just watch . . ."

Hank slid the mouse, and they flew up past the trees dividing the sites, to hover about twenty to thirty feet above the surface of B site. Hank clicked a bar on the side of the screen, and the ground became mostly transparent, revealing a warped dome shape perhaps ten feet below the surface. He slid another virtual dial, and the house turned transparent as well. Off to one side of the interior was a gray scribble, and another scribble lay a bit deeper, below the dome.

"What are those?" Matt asked.

"I can answer this one!" Tuni blurted. Peter and Hank looked back at her, amused. "What?" she said. "I was here when we excavated it! I'm not going to be able to tell him *anything* but this." She turned to Matt. "So, that one over there on the side is the full k'yot we found first. It was all covered in rock that had to be pulverized and removed from every little thread. Peter shipped the middle section to Jon, and you got to see that part when I brought it to you. The top and bottom are still here."

Matt nodded, fascinated that all this detail could be gathered without even lifting a shovel.

"Now, that one down below, we found it later, and that one is Irin's k'yot, which you just saw. Correct me if I'm wrong here, gents, but it was buried *under* the surface in *their* time. Then, sometime later, they apparently built the dome over the ground. They're guessing that—"

"Postulating!" Hank interrupted.

"Sorry! Gosh . . . they are *pasteurizing*"—she winked at Matt—"that it was put inside the house later and that it might have been a son of Irin and Orin. *You,* my dear, should be able to answer that question at some point."

Matt imagined it. The possibilities staggered the mind: getting to know a son of Irin and all that he might have experienced.

"So, moving on," Hank said, clicking another icon on the screen.

Now thousands of little silver capsules appeared under the surface. They looked like slightly elongated medicine capsules, all lying at slightly different angles around Irin's middle dome.

"And now," Hank began, "Pete, do I just roll over now or do I show them the render?"

"Do the animation—it's much more dramatic."

Hank closed the window and clicked a new icon, and a big window opened and filled the screen. He clicked the PLAY button, and the black dissolved to a simple computer-generated image of a tree. The view lifted up and moved forward, as if a bird had taken off from the tree. It flew higher, and they could see a panorama of small domes. The camera swooped low and passed between a couple of houses, almost running into one at the end of a path before zooming upward. Beyond the house, the vastness of the city became very apparent. There were thousands of domes, with several larger ones, the size of Pwin-T's Center House. In the very center, the "bird" circled an enormous new Center House, nearly twice the size of the others. It zoomed higher and made a wide circle of the entire area, giving a better view of the city's scale. Matt and Tuni watched, agape, as the camera turned upward to a starry night sky, rising higher and higher before turning back downward and stopping over a view of both sites: the city and the graveyard. The city appeared to occupy ten times more area than the graveyard.

"Amazing," Matt breathed. "That is just *huge,* and it really lets you see it as it was. I don't know if you realize this, but seeing it from that one angle, it was like the first time I saw Pwin-T from the mountain pass, though it looks probably three times the size that Pwin-T was. Crazy, guys, seriously."

"You did this, Hank?" Tuni asked.

He shrugged modestly. "Well, the program does all the heavy lifting, but I did give it the flight path."

They all looked at the still shot of the two sites.

"Now, hold on," Tuni said. "The A site looks far bigger than the clearing out here. Did you take a little creative license there, gents? For the sake of theatric effect?"

"Not at all," Peter said. "We've found houses another half mile into the woods! We just haven't gotten clearance to log over there. We're also not sure if we should, you know? Do we really need to dig up *everything*? We've got a good ten-year project ahead of us as it is, just for what you see gridded out there. At some point tourists are going to be walking the land here, like the pyramids in Egypt. I think it'll be fine to let some of the city remain hidden, but I don't know. It'll be someone else's decision down the road."

Matt wondered what else they would find in and around the houses. Surely only the metal items would have lasted this long.

"Okay," Matt said, "so what we saw in the video there—is that what the area will look like after you've excavated everything?"

"Not exactly," Hank replied as he cleaned his glasses on his T-shirt. "We can tell from the radar data that most of the domes are either crushed, warped, split into pieces, or otherwise damaged. A good number of them are pretty well intact, though. Also, the plain they're on is not flat like you see in here—erosion and continental plate shifting has it all a bit jumbled. But Pete has a plan for leveling it all out and arranging a whole side of A site that will be a representation of what it really looked like. I presume he'll be calling you to help reproduce some of the common items and other things one might have seen back then."

"Yep," Peter added, "it's going to be brilliant when we get there."

Matt sighed, realizing that he would have to return to Africa again despite his promise to himself before this journey.

"So . . ." He cleared his throat. "Can we see it again?"

Later, during dinner, Matt asked what time the news crews would arrive the next day.

Collette put down her chicken fajita, wiped her mouth daintily, and said, "Well, I've got the whole schedule in the office, but I do know that your unveiling ceremony will be at eleven."

Matt nodded. "Okay, and who exactly are you all saying that I am? Not to seem ungrateful for the opportunity, but I really don't want any attention on me personally."

"Simple," Peter interjected. "You were one of our key researchers in the initial phase at the old site. Also, you were the creative one who came up with all the interesting names for things like *k'yot* and *Pwin-T* and all that. Though, the government is insisting on calling them 'Kawai People' after the nearest town."

"Okay, that sounds cool. Can we use a fake name for me, too?"

Peter and Hank exchanged a glance.

"Er . . . ," Peter stammered, "we sort of already told them the name of the person uncovering the structure. Sorry—didn't know you wanted that level of anonymity."

Matt shrugged it off. "It's cool, I guess. I mean, it's not like I have the most unique name. There's probably thousands of me in the U.S."

"So, Matthew," Hank cut in, "what are you going to do after this? You leave tomorrow afternoon, right?"

"Yeah, actually, Tuni and I are going to Tahiti."

Oohs and aahs spread around the table. Peter gave Matt a knowing wink.

Tuni saw him and said, "Oh, grow up, Peter." And holding back her grin, she poked Matt in the side.

"Yeah, I've been trying to go for a while and lost out on the room I had reserved before, but it turns out there was another resort just as good that had the kind of conditions I was looking for. It took a little convincing before Tuni agreed to come with me."

"So, you two are seeing a lot of each other, then?" Peter pried.

"Matthew is very comfortable in his house—four bloody states away," Tuni replied loftily. "And I'm quite comfortable in New York. Let's just say that Skype is a godsend."

"She doesn't know it yet, but she'll be moving in within a year."

"Shut it," Tuni replied, giving him a little sideways kick.

At eleven the next morning, Matt stood in the middle of the square excavation, shovel in hand. Photographers and video camera crews crowded
the ledge above him, and the documentary filmmakers stood in front of
him with all their equipment. Peter stood on his right, Hank and Tuni on
his left. Three news helicopters circled above.

In the pit, the National Geographic channel's director gave Matt the sig-
nal, and after thanking everyone for coming, Matt pushed the shovel into
the dirt. He tossed a spadeful aside, then another, and on the third thrust,
there was an audible chink of metal on metal. Cameras snapped, film rolled,
and Matt kept digging. Four more shovelfuls revealed a dull, pitted metal
surface. At this point, all four of them—Matt, Tuni, Hank, and Peter—got
down on their knees and brushed the remaining dirt away. Matt ran his
work gloves over the surface and smiled for the pictures. Then, looking
down at the small section of exposed metal, he knew that he was ready to
do another session. He couldn't wait for the media business to be over so
he could read from Irin's recovered k'yot.

Walking back to Peter's RV, he refused a dozen interviews, then hid
inside with a can of mixed nuts. He wondered how weird he looked in a
hooded sweatshirt, jeans, and gloves while the other three wore shorts and
short-sleeved shirts.

An hour later, the helicopters were long gone and most of the news vans
had rumbled back up the highway toward Nairobi. Tuni had joined Matt in
the RV, then Hank, and finally Peter.

When Peter took the whole k'yot from the cupboard and spread it out on
the table, Tuni took a deep breath and massaged Matt's shoulders. "You
sure you're ready for this now?" she whispered in his ear.

"You don't think I should?" he replied. Then he quickly added, "You're
right, let's just forget the whole thing. I don't know what I was thinking."
She flicked his ear.

"This'll be like the good old days, huh, Matt?" Peter said, sliding in next to Hank.

Matt pulled off his gloves and gave them to Tuni, then looked in awe at the garment that lay before him. "Wait," he said. "Who has my timer?"

It appeared in front of him before he could finish asking the question.

"Sorry, pal," said Peter. "I thought of it right when you did. I've had it in my pocket since this morning—meant to give it to you a couple of times. It's all charged up."

Matt rolled up his left sleeve and set the timer for three minutes. They all watched his hand hover over the k'yot. He took a deep breath and dropped his hand.

I am Orin. I am from Pwin-T. I kneel over my man's lifeless body. Wil helps me to remove Irin's k'yot. I try not to look at the red around his head and on the rocks beneath him. I try to walk. It's a challenge. The edge of the waterfall is a swirling cloud of mist. I walk into it, hold the k'yot under the falling shower to cleanse blood from it once again. Everyone is looking at me and crying. They don't know what to do; they suppose we're lost. We're not lost, though. I realize this, and feel deep in my throat that I know what we must do. They just don't realize that we've nearly arrived. My man got us this far; he did his job. A thought strikes me—perhaps a crazy thought, but I reject my doubts and step into the k'yot bottom, pulling the torn middle over my arms. Wil hands me the top and tells me as I pull it over my head that I must lead our people now. We will build our new city, he says, and call it Irin-T. I hear my name pass quietly through the onlookers.

Orin.

* * *

Michael Siemsen

EPILOGUE

The sky seemed to bleed upward from the horizon, dripping the last of the sunlight across long, wispy clouds. On the deck of their suite, Tuni looked admiringly over at Matt. Here he was, wearing swim shorts— and *only* shorts—reclining on a deckchair in this beautiful, tropical setting. He sipped soda directly from the brand-new glass, held in his ungloved hand. She climbed on top of him. He looked her over in her bikini and grinned.

"How daft is all this?" She said, beaming a huge smile.

He gazed up at her eyes. "Which part, what do you mean?"

"Which part? Look at you! Bloody shorts? Not even a t-shirt!"

He smirked and stroked her arms. "Get what you pay for, right?"

She gave him a peck on the mouth and stood back up, peering out at the watercolor sky.

He said, "You are so fricken beautiful, it's disgusting."

"Odd compliment, dear. Let's stow that one away, shall we?"

"Sorry. Oh shit, what time is it?"

She glanced at the wall clock back inside the room. "Half-past six, why?"

He started to get up in a panic, "We have dinner at that place on the water!"

"Relax, they're not going to give our table away if we're five minutes late. I'm still all sandy anyway; gonna take a quick shower. Enjoy the view for a few before you get dressed, okay?"

He stroked her leg and smiled up at her lovingly.

She grabbed her robe and walked inside the sliding glass door. The air-conditioned room felt a bit cold, so she flicked the thermostat off on her way into the giant bathroom. The wall jets sprayed from all sides, and she tossed her bikini top and bottom in the hamper and stepped in.

Matt closed his eyes and leaned his head back on the deck chair cushion. Everything new, he thought. They had really done it: kept their promise, right down to the carpet and even the card key for the door. For four thousand a night, they'd better.

"Hello, Mr. Turner," an English-accented man's voice said from above his head.

Snapping his head back quickly, Matt saw Garrett Rheese looking down on him. Two tall men with buzz cuts stood on either side of him. Rheese was holding out a giant book.

"I'm going to need your help tracking down a little something. Thank you in advance." The book dropped onto Matt's stomach.

I'm Heinrich Strauss. I am thirty-four years old. I live in a mansion in Salzburg, Austria. The year is 1917. I'm crying, curled up in my bed. My wife has left me for a poor dancing man from Vienna. I pray on this Bible that I can find the strength to go on.

ACKNOWLEDGEMENTS

I would like to thank my wife, Ana, for her support throughout the writing of this book. The questions she posed as she read each chapter forced me to go back and answer them, resulting in the (hopefully) fully-described worlds of Matt and I-Rin.

Likewise, I send my gratitude to Vicky, to whom this book is dedicated, who read each chapter as it was drafted, and whose daily demand for the next pages lit the appropriate fire under me to stave off the writer's block/ laziness.

-MS

Fantome Publishing, LLC
www.michaelsiemsen.com
facebook.com/mcsiemsen
facebook/com/thedigbook
facebook.com/theopalbook
twitter: @michaelsiemsen
mail@michaelsiemsen.com

CPSIA information can be obtained at www.ICGtesting.com
Printed in the USA
LVOW05s0905281213

367216LV00002B/78/P